"I THOUGHT HANGING WAS FOR JUDGES AND JURIES TO DECIDE ON."

He answered like he didn't hear me. "The fellow we want still lives close to the old family homestead, I'll wager—Mr. Jesse James." He turned to me, his face as flat as Iowa. "You've heard of Jesse James, I trust."

I swallowed and it felt like about a handful of carpet tacks was caught in my throat. "You'd think a man would tell you, wouldn't you, before he got you all the way up here from Texas, that who he wanted you to go after was the James gang?" I spoke as even as I could. "And why's your pa so mad at them?"

"Why, you're not afraid, are you, Willie?" Mr. William Pinkerton asked, smiling and ignoring *my* question again. He looked down at me like he was enjoying himself real good.

"Why, yes I am," I answered. "The man who wouldn't be afraid to run counter to the Jameses has got horseshit between his ears."

Books by Charles Hackenberry

Friends
I Rode with Jesse James

Published by HarperPaperbacks

ATTENTION: ORGANIZATIONS AND CORPORATIONS

Most HarperPaperbacks are available at special quantity discounts for bulk purchases for sales promotions, premiums, or fund-raising. For information, please call or write:
**Special Markets Department, HarperCollins Publishers,
10 East 53rd Street, New York, N.Y. 10022.
Telephone: (212) 207-7528. Fax: (212) 207-7222.**

I RODE WITH JESSE JAMES

CHARLES HACKENBERRY

HarperPaperbacks
A Division of HarperCollinsPublishers

HarperPaperbacks
A Division of HarperCollinsPublishers
10 East 53rd Street, New York, N.Y. 10022-5299

If you purchased this book without a cover, you should be aware that this book is stolen property. It was reported as "unsold and destroyed" to the publisher and neither the author nor the publisher has received any payment for this "stripped book."

This is a work of fiction. The characters, incidents, and dialogues are products of the author's imagination and are not to be construed as real. Any resemblance to actual events or persons, living or dead, is entirely coincidental.

Copyright © 1996 by Charles Hackenberry
All rights reserved. No part of this book may be used or reproduced in any manner whatsoever without written permission of the publisher, except in the case of brief quotations embodied in critical articles and reviews. For information address HarperCollins*Publishers*, 10 East 53rd Street, New York, N.Y. 10022-5299.

ISBN 0-06-101049-9

HarperCollins®, ®, and HarperPaperbacks™ are trademarks of HarperCollins*Publishers* Inc.

Cover illustration by Tony Gabrielle

First HarperPaperbacks printing: September 1996

Printed in the United States of America

Visit HarperPaperbacks on the World Wide Web at
http://www.harpercollins.com/paperbacks

For Joan and Emily. Daughters dear.

ACKNOWLEDGMENTS

My deepest gratitude to Kjell Meling of the Penn State Altoona Campus for his support and encouragement; Professor Dinty Moore for his thoughtful suggestions on the story; Stephanie Gates of Pattee Library for her excellent research; Ray Matthews, my former collaborator, for his patience in teaching me about horses; Dr. Frederick J. Stefon for his information on the United States government's policies and practices concerning the education of Native Americans; Carole Bookhammer, for her tireless assistance; Gene Shelton, for knowing Texas so well; Pat Lo Brutto, who steered me toward this story in the first place; Professor Robert Hatten, for sharing his love of Chopin; Professor Marc Harris for his broad knowledge of American history; my agent Barbara Peuchner for her many kindnesses and considerable expertise; my daughter Emily Spencer for her research on the history of Grand Prairie, Texas; my daughter Joan Hackenberry, for getting me to look more deeply into Sarah's heart; Peter D. Barton and the staff of the Railroaders' Memorial Museum of Altoona, Pennsylvania, for helping me make sense of America's rail system and train technology of the 1870s; Director John Hartman and Angela Cooper of the Jesse James Farm and Museum of Kearney, Missouri, for allowing me to use their extensive collection and holdings, especially the research notes of their former curator, Milton Perry, the excellent historian of the James and Younger families; and finally my wife Barbara, whose patience and love make all things possible.

1

THE OLD PLOW

Now you might think an old busted-down saddle tramp that looks like I do probly never done nothing worth talking about or knowed nobody worth hearing about. But the truth is, I knowed Jesse James. Yes I did.

The day I got the letter from Billy Pinkerton, I was out plowin with a mule that didn't want to be and an old rusty prairie buster held together by stove bolts and baling wire. This was down in Dechman, Texas, and it wasn't even spring yet—eighteen and seventy-three. November, as I recall. Plowin to break in a field my pa had never got to very often so's it could be planted once warm weather showed up. Ground wasn't half bad on that farm—the Black Prairie they call it around there, from the color of the soil, only they call the town Grand Prairie now instead of Dechman. I can't tell you why they changed it, though, it was always Dechman when I lived around there.

It was getting so dark plowin I couldn't see what the hell I was doing—if my furrow was straight or not. I'd already worked twelve hours at Eli Walter's dry goods store in Dechman and was almost as sick of stumbling over that cold dusty ground as the mule was, I guess.

Ma's voice was welcome when she called me in for supper. I unhitched Charlie and left the plow right in the furrow, which anyone who knows anything at all about plowin will tell you is all wrong, but as rusty as it was, I didn't see it could hurt it that much. I'd be starting right there again tomorrow after work anyway, and that damned old plow would be my marker in the field, like my pa used to leave a stove match to mark his spot in a book.

That mule Charlie smelled the barn and it was hell to hold him back. I thought for a minute of just letting him run, but knowing him, he might of ended up in Chalk Hill or Mineral Wells or even all the way to Possum Kingdom and I knew who in the holy hell would be the one to have to go fetch him if he did.

Now, you might think I was a young fellow at the time I'm talking of here, living at home, but the truth is I wasn't. Matter of fact, I was pretty well along into my forties already and my ma was about at her three score and ten mark, as they say, but she had no plans to lay down and quit.

The reason I was back with Ma was, my pa had died not too long before and she didn't have no one else. And if truth be told, I didn't either, since I'd just finished up all eleven years of an eleven-year sentence in Huntsville a little while earlier. Eleven years for stealing a horse I never even saw, but that's another story.

After I washed up on the porch at the basin, I went in and saw a letter with my name on it propped up against the lamp on the front hall table, and damned if Ma hadn't went and opened it already—like she did all my mail.

She come in from the kitchen carrying a plate of fried meat and set it on the table.

"Ma, you opened my mail again!"

"Well, if I hadn't of brought it up from the post office you wouldn't even have it till tomorrow, would you?" As if that was an answer. "Besides, you're going to have to let

Mr. Jacobi down at the bank read it anyway, so I don't see why I can't read it too. After all, what secrets have you got from me?"

"That's not the point," I told her. "A grown man gets a letter addressed to him, he should get to read it first—and *then* let others read it if he's a mind to. Besides, what's this letter got to do with Jacobi?"

She shook her head, acting like I was crazy, and went back out to the kitchen.

The letter had the words *The Pinkerton Agency* printed large across the top. And then the date—October 19, 1873. It had only took that letter a little more than two weeks to get from Chicago to Texas. I get surprised, sometimes, how things keep getting faster and faster.

> Dear Mr. Goodwin:
>
> Our mutual acquaintance, Warden Thomas Shelton of Huntsville Prison, has suggested that you are well qualified for a position that our Agency has been trying to fill for some time. Warden Shelton informs us that you have been well trained in the art of tracking, both humans and animals, over varied terrain and in all weathers.
>
> While the Pinkerton Agency has always maintained a strict policy of forbidding the employment of former convicts as agents, we would be willing to make an exception in your case. Warden Shelton believes there was some doubt about your guilt in the matter for which you were sentenced. He also told us you were a model prisoner, on one occasion using your newly-learned tracking skills to recover stolen horses, and, on another, in finding his young daughter Alice after she had been lost for several hours.
>
> Your local banker, Mr. Norman Jacobi, is holding a draft in your name in the amount of $200.00. If you will kindly present him with this letter, he will issue you gold and currency to cover your expenses

to Chicago, where I will inform you further of your duties and see that you receive our standard training. By accepting our money, it is understood that you have also accepted our offer of employment, on terms we shall discuss fully when you arrive in Chicago. Should you not accept the money and our offer, I am prepared to inform Sheriff Vinton of your town that you have refused an offer of employment from a reputable firm with whom you could have made moral restitution for your criminal offenses. I remain,

    Cordially yours,
    Mr. William Pinkerton

I couldn't believe it right off. The Pinkertons offering *me* a job! Yeah, I could track all right, liked doin it too. But being a Pinkerton man, I didn't know about that. They had spied for the Yankees during the war, and I sure as *hell* did not want to belly up to the bar with any outfit that'd also bellied up with Abe Lincoln. They was a bunch of strike-breakers and arm-twisters who'd take anybody's side for the money. On top of that, I didn't like the way Pinkerton had put it there at the end of his letter, that he would tell Sheriff Vinton on me if I decided not to work for them. After he so much as said there was nothing to the horse thieving charges that'd got me locked up in the first place!

"You're going to take it, aren't you?" Ma asked at supper, straight out of the blue like she does.

I swallowed my bite of biscuit and shook my head. "I don't think so. I don't like them damn Pinkertons, and Lord knows where they'd have me working—not around here, that's for sure." Truth was, I was ready to go almost anywheres else, work for almost anybody, but it didn't seem right saying that to her, not when she needed me so bad.

"I'd count it a blessing if you'd go," she said, knocking the stuffing right out of me. "You haven't been happy a day since you moved back here, and much as I'd miss you, I think you ought to take it."

My fork was froze halfway to my mouth.

"It'd be nice if you'd send me some money sometimes, Willie, but I'd prefer you go." She went back to spooning up her applesauce.

I studied her a minute. "Now, Ma, that's awful nice of you, pretending you want me to go, giving me my freedom and all—when what you really want is for me to stay here and work the place. But I know where my duty belongs. I'll stay and let somebody else track for the Pinkertons." I went back to my biscuit, thinking that would be the end of it.

She stood up. "Well, you'll be a fool if you do!" she said, picking up the meat plate and going toward the kitchen.

I was about to take another piece of that pork, and it was thinking about that for half a minute that threw me off.

"A fool?" I said. "How do you figger that?"

She turned around to face me in the doorway. "Just how many chances do you think a man that's been in prison is going to get, anyway? A chance to make something of hisself?"

I was going to give her an answer of some kind, but she barged ahead and gave me no chance. "I did all right before you got out of jail, after your daddy died, and I can do it again. Bill Hudspeth can do the plowing and the heavy chores."

She went into the kitchen leaving me there sitting at the table, scratching my jaw and trying to figure out what in the *hell* was going on. I was still chewing on it when she put a big wedge of milk pie down in front of me. I didn't even know she'd baked it. Still warm from the oven and me not even smelled it when I come in from the field.

Milk pie, my favorite. She must of stirred it up right after she read my Pinkerton letter. But I still wasn't sure she really wanted me to go or if she just wanted me to be free to better myself if I wanted to.

"You really want me to leave, Ma?" I asked her, looking up into her face, more lined and tired than I always remembered her in prison.

She'd had the nicest blue eyes you ever saw when she was younger, when I was a kid, but of course they'd faded some by then. She brushed back a tired wisp of gray hair and then put her hand on my shoulder. "Well, when you put it that way, no. I don't feature you leaving, Willie. But I do want you to go, yes I do. It's best for you, and in the long run it'll be best for the both of us, mark my words." She leaned over and give me a kiss on the cheek, and it'd been some time since she'd did that, since the day I got out of prison, I believe.

"What about all the bad things they do?" I asked her. "Beat up miners, strike-breaking. You think I should do all them things?"

She gathered up some dishes. "Of course not. If they ask you to do something that isn't right, just don't do it. Worst comes to worst, you can always quit if you have to. Besides, they want you for tracking. It says so right there in the letter. I don't see how you can do much wrong just showing them where somebody went, do you?"

I hadn't looked at it just that way, but I could see what she was getting at. She carried a load of things out to the kitchen and I gathered up the rest and followed her, filling my coffee cup at the stove, finally. "But they was Yankees, the Pinkertons. What about that?"

"Well, so was a lot of your family, too," Ma said. "I know you don't remember them, you were so young when we come west, but my folks was from Pennsylvania, some of your pa's too. I don't see how that makes any difference now, though. That war's over, and it's time people forgot about it and went on with their life, though they don't seem inclined to much around here."

I seen then that she'd thought this over pretty thorough. She was a smart old bird, my ma was. Cocked her eye and looked at things from all angles. Maybe I got a little of that from her, I don't know. I like to think so.

We talked about it some more before bedtime, I still

wasn't sure. But Ma was, she was set on me going. I laid awake part of the night wondering what was the right thing to do.

Come morning, I saw it her way.

"I'm not going up there by stage and then the train, I'll tell you that, winter comin or not," I said at breakfast. "I'm going to take my horse, travel some and see things. Been a long time since I been up that way. Besides, I can go cheaper by horse, too. Leave you a little of this money they mention."

She surprised me. "Well, I don't need the money, but if you want to take your time going up there, that's your business. I didn't see any time mentioned for you to be up there by in the letter. And if you ain't learned to stay warm by now..."

I went to the bank that morning, and sure enough old Jacobi had the bank draft with my name on it right there. Didn't even ask to see my letter. He counted it out right in front of me and I signed for it. A hundred in gold, twenty in silver, and the rest in greenbacks and banknotes—drawn on his bank, I noticed.

With some of the banknotes, I bought Ma a new pair of shoes in town before I went back home. Hers was getting pretty shabby and busted over at the heel. She said she didn't need them when I showed them to her, but I seen the smile on her face when she tried them on. They fit her good.

I had bought myself a few things for the trip, too—a heavy wool coat, a new slicker and a pack of maps of all the places I would be going through. On adding it up, I discovered it was farther from Texas to Chicago than I had thought at first, and it would take me some time to get there, even if I didn't dawdle. I wrote Mr. Pinkerton a letter telling him I accepted his offer, but added that I needed to do some things before I got there. Which was the truth, even if it was just seeing the countryside that I had to do.

When I told him I was quitting, Eli gave me a little

mare he said was eating him out of house and home, one I could use for a packhorse. Next morning Ma had a lot of food fixed and wrapped for me to take along to eat on the way.

Shortly after sunup I made Ma take about half of what I got from the Pinkertons, though she kept saying she wouldn't need all that. I kissed her good-bye and mounted up.

"You write every so often, Willie!" she called.

I said I would and she was to take care of herself.

She waved from the dooryard, a hanky to her nose, and I was on my way north with the sun slanting through the trees sharp on my right. At the edge of our property I looked back, but I couldn't see Ma or the house from there. The last thing of home I saw was that damned old plow I had left in the last furrow I ever plowed.

2

THE UNLUCKY CLOVERLEAF

I headed north and just kept goin'.

I hope the folks back home don't ever hear this, but riding through north Texas kept remindin me of how overrated the whole damn state is, at least by Texans. It's windy in winter, blue northers stinging your face with sand and blown ice splinters. In summer it's twice as hot as it needs to be, chickens laying eggs already poached, my pa used to say. All that scrub and rough dead grass was awful dull to look at. Dry and worthless for nearly everything except raising cattle, and that never interested me much—maybe that means I ain't a real Texan, I don't know. Sure, whenever I leave Texas I brag it up one side and down the other just like all the old boys from back there does, but down home it's way too easy to see its backside to be crowing of it much.

The pack mare Eli gave me worked out better than I thought she was going to. I named her Maggie—for an old lady friend of mine from a long time back. She didn't look like no packhorse, that's for sure (the *horse* Maggie I mean, not the lady—who never looked like a horse of no kind at all). Maggie, the horse, was too long in the

pasterns and a little flat in the back to be built right for
packing. But boy was she smart. It would of been nice to
have took a few days to train her for the trail and get her
used to my old cross buck packsaddle, but there was no
time. So I just strapped her in, loaded her up and off we'd
went. She was settled in by the second day on the trail.
By the end of the first week, it was like she'd been packing all her life. Horses are like people, I think. Most are
dumb as watermelons, but thank god for the tart apple in
the barrel. I took to singing "When You and Me Was
Young, Maggie" to her, but I don't think she cared for it
all that much.

I struck the Chisolm Trail and traveled along it two or
three days, passing herd after herd going north, even that
time of year, which surprised me. I ate breakfast with one
outfit, supper with another—friendly fellows, all of them,
but then I took a trail heading more east. I swung away
from that damn Chisolm, a quarter-mile wide of loose steer
leavings where it wasn't trampled down hard dirt, or muck,
depending on the weather and the wetness, which was
slight just then. I crossed the Red somewheres downstream of Spanish Ford.

The Indian Nation wasn't no better for looks.
Halfway through it, about the time I started getting saddle
sore and the weather chilly, I begun to wonder why on
Earth I ever decided to go north on horseback, anyway.

But then I bought me a nice thick sheepskin from a
poor, young Cherokee sheep rancher I stayed with one
night, him and his almost brand-new wife, near as I
could follow—we signed about as much as we talked
American.

They was trying their damndest to live white-man
style, one young couple way out by theirselves on their
own ranch, a lot of miles from nowhere, but in their hearts
they was wantin to live like Indians again, camping along a
tumbling stream somewheres with their brothers and sisters and cousins and grandmas and the like, eating breakfast—supper and dinner too—with a whole herd of folks

they was related to three ways from Sunday. Don't know why they didn't just go back to their people and do it that way, they didn't say and me not thinking it was my place to ask.

After I waved good-bye to them, I put that soft pelt double between me and my old saddle and just settled into going mostly north by a little east across all that dead grass. Sure, I felt a touch hollow from time to time, but mostly I was glad to be traveling again. Getting up with the weak sun, riding all day, talking to myself or singing to my packhorse, and taking whatever weather and trails come along.

Somewhere down there where the bottom corners of Kansas and Missouri come close together, I hit another cow trail. A gal in a bar in Sedalia told me later it was the middle fork of the old Shawnee Trail, the one the drives from Texas took before the railroad got built further on. I rested a few days there in Sedalia, ate my Christmas dinner in a restaurant waiting out the tail end of a storm, if memory serves me right. When I left there I followed the railroad tracks a stretch out of town, but split off from them when they crossed back over on the south side of the Missouri River again. I cut more north.

Gad's Hill, Missouri
A Station on the Iron Mountain Railroad
January 31, 1874, 3:20 PM

Five men in long coats climbed off their horses in front of Pauling's Inn, their saddles creaking in the near freezing weather. Instead of tying up and going inside to sample William Pauling's fine, bitter ale and warm their hands at his stone fireplace, they walked toward the railway platform two hundred yards up the muddy road with GAD'S HILL painted neatly on the sign swaying in the wind. Two going together first, slowly and easily, followed by another two at about ten yards looking things over carefully on both sides, and one man hanging back leading all five horses after the others. Off on a low cutover rise about a quarter mile away, a sixth man sat his buckskin and peered through a brass spyglass he had pried out of a dead Yankee officer's hand after Chicamauga—watching the little parade of his friends go up the road toward the railway station. When they were halfway there, he called softly to another man, who started to shinny up a telegraph pole toward the crossbar, wire cutters stuck under his belt.

When the ticket agent heard the door, he called over his shoulder, "Just a minute, please, there's a telegram coming—" but the key suddenly died. After a second he turned around, a quizzical expression on his round red face, and saw two men with dark bandannas pulled up, black hats set low over deep-set, cold blue eyes, and large pistols—already cocked—pointed right at his heart.

"Oh . . . oh . . ." was all he managed to say as he put up his hands.

The taller of the two men who looked to be brothers motioned to two other men out on the platform with his gun and then the other brother came around the counter and pushed the ticket agent to the floor.

"Is this a—a robbery?" the ticket man asked, lying on his side and looking up with eyes as round as silver dollars.

Bob Younger, one of the bandits on the platform, went up the tracks a distance and turned the semaphore signal to STOP. *As he was walking back to the platform, he saw his older brother herding the people from the inn into the ticket agent's tiny office and getting them all down on the floor. That crazy Art McCoy was already going through the drawers of the office desk. McCoy, who had served under Quantrille with Jesse, always reminded Bob of a damn kid, even though he was older than any of the rest of them.*

"Lookit this!" McCoy yelled, holding up a handful of loot when he stepped inside. "Seventy-seven dollars, three pair of handcuffs, and a itty-bitty little magnifying glass! Cute, ain't it?"

At five after six they heard the train toot its whistle twice up the tracks and then the screeching, scraping sound of its brakes. The American 4-4-0 locomotive, which had recently been converted from wood to coal, nudged its oversized cowcatcher around a gentle bend and approached the station like a gradually-slowing, cautious cyclops with an enormous nose and a funny hat. Its noxious smoke and fumes shrouded the two passenger cars, the baggage and express cars, and even the small tender.

When Conductor Alford swung gracefully off the southbound from St. Louis onto the platform while the train was still moving slowly and took two steps with the motion—looking like he'd done it that way all his life, which, in fact, he nearly had—he expected to see the ticket agent and whatever passengers were to board at this jerkwater stop. Instead, he was met by three men with bandannas pulled up over their faces and revolvers in their gloved hands.

"How-dee-do, Mr. Conductor," the one said in a high, backwoods voice. "Jest turn back around, now, and climb back up. We got a little bidness with your passengers, and you're a-goin to hep see no one gets testy or kilt."

Further down the tracks a masked man sprang quickly up into the engine cab, startling the engineer and the fireman.

His brother stood on the ground below and pointed a double-barreled shotgun up at the cab window. "How-do, gentlemen," he said in a loud, broad voice, touching his hat brim after the engineer noticed him. The engine chuffed slowly. "Do as that fellow there says and no one will be hurt, I promise you." Engineer Sheehan thought for a minute the man on the ground sounded like a stage actor of some kind or a hellfire, orating preacher he had heard once in St. Louis, but then the other man was poking him in the ribs with his revolver and for a while he thought about little else than staying alive.

In a calm, even voice the outlaw in the cab told them to climb down and go along back to the express car. There, *they'd have to convince the express agent to open the door and the safe or he'd be forced to blow it open with dynamite, with which he was well provided, he assured them. He'd prefer no one "got themselves dead over this thing," (the fireman later remembered his wording) but he'd blow the car with the man inside if he had to. Engineer Sheehan believed him, yes indeed he did.*

"Open up, Henry," Sheehan called from the platform. "We need in there!"

After a moment the car door rumbled open and an express agent with a snowy white goatee looked out sheepishly. "I's afraid this's what it was," *he said.*

The leader of the outlaws jumped up into the express car. He spun the agent around, yanked his chin whiskers, and shoved the barrel of his .44 into the man's mouth. "Now you be a smart man and open that safe, you hear? Cause if you don't, I'm going to blow your brains all over your friends there."

The engineer and the fireman below winced and tried to avert their faces.

"Stand fast, if you please, gentlemen," *the brother with the shotgun said politely beside them.*

Inside the first coach (while two masked men stood guard with Winchesters in the second), three men with revolvers had the passengers on their feet. Some ladies were too overcome with fright to remain standing long, but all the male passengers had their hands out in front of them, palms up.

"Are you a workin man?" *the largest of the bandits asked a stocky fellow with calluses on his hands.*

"Yes, I am." *He looked around and sensed more was expected of him.* "I'm a plate-roller at the Cuyahoga Boiler Works, up in Cleveland, Ohio. Me'n the wife here are going down to Arkansas to see my brother that I ain't seen in—" *He looked around again, ashamed of his volubility and what it said of his courage.* "At least we was . . ."

"Well, you'll get there, I suppose," *the big bandit said.* "An don't you worry, Mam," *he said to the woman wearing a funny-looking ruffled bonnet.* "We ain't going to hurt you or your husband. Matter-of-fact, we don't want your money, neither, mister," *he said, handing back the surprised man's billfold. He turned to the next person in line and immediately slapped off his high hat, making the man cringe.* "What we want is the money and valuables of these here plug hat gentlemen!" *He nodded at the plate-roller's wife.* "And you can keep that pretty gold wedding ring you got on, too."

The woman tried to smile, but it didn't feel entirely right, what with her hands up in the air that way. My, but they'd have a story to tell her sister-in-law and her man, though, wouldn't they!

The leader jumped down from the express car with a little more than $17,000 in the belly of his gunnysack. "What's taking those boys so long back there?" *he asked the man with the shotgun, who shook his head and looked theatrically toward the sky. The bandits ushered the fireman and the engineer into the express car, then tied it shut with a short length of rope, and walked toward the passenger cars.*

"Any you men fight for the South?" *the big bandit yelled when he entered the second coach.*

"I did," *a lean man from the middle of the car said,* "G. R. Crump of Memphis, Tennessee."

"Me too!" *another called.* "Third Mississip. Say, you boys ain't who I think you air, air ya?"

"Don't say no names, please, friend," *the big bandit said softly after he'd strolled down the aisle and put his hand on the man's shoulder, grasping it a little tighter than friendship would suggest. The passengers watched this transaction closely.* "Whyn't you and yer friend down there step outside for a smoke?" *The Mississippian and his comrade-in-arms got themselves the hell out of there, though in a way they'd rather have been helping instead.*

"Hey, this'ns got a gold watch from the railroad and it's mine," *McCoy announced, pocketing the timepiece.*

"Let me see it," *the leader said, stepping into the coach. After McCoy handed it over grudgingly and the man in charge had read its inscription, he quickly went up to its owner. "You're John Morley? Chief engineer of the Iron Mountain Railroad?"*

The balding man in the green wool suit looked away and then nodded.

Without warning the leader of the thieves slapped him across the mouth with his heavy leather gloves, using all the strength he commanded. The balding man's face hit the window hard. Silently, after a moment, he spat a front tooth into his hand and looked at it. Then his nose began to drip blood.

"That's for all the land your railroad took from folks I know," the man in charge yelled. "Some of em my own family." He handed the watch back to McCoy, who grinned under his bandanna.

The man in charge turned slowly to the well-dressed man sitting in the aisle seat beside the chief engineer. "And who might you be, mister?"

A deep stare but no answer from the man in the derby.

"Which billfold was his," the leader asked. When he had examined it and found no identification, he had the man pulled into the aisle and searched well, which turned up a small-frame four-shot 41 calibre Colt Cloverleaf revolver in his boot with the letters P. N. G. engraved on the narrow backstrap of the grip.

"I thought so. A Pinkerton man," the leader said, coals smoldering in his deep-set blue eyes. Everyone knew that the organization had been called the Pinkerton National Guard during the War, when it had spied for the Yankees. "Take him back to the express car and search him all the way down to his skin. Let's see what else we can find."

In the express car, despite the cold, they forced the Pinkerton man to remove his clothing. When he refused to take off his underwear they beat him, tore it off of him, and tied him naked over a large, domed trunk.

"Which one a them Pinkertons gave you this hideout

gun, Mr. William in Chicago or that old Yankee Allen himself?" the leader asked.

No answer.

The chief of the bandits took a stove-length of firewood intended for the now-cold little potbelly and whacked the Pinkerton man hard on the buttocks. He grunted and squirmed.

"Come again?" the masked leader asked, drawing a laugh from McCoy.

"Stick it up your ass!" the Pinkerton man yelled over his shoulder.

The leader nodded and thought that over a minute. "Sounds like half a good idea, anyway." He tossed the small revolver to McCoy. "Here, you do it. And I want it all the way up there, too. Not just the barrel, you understand?"

"Yes sir, I do!"

The conductor shook his head and left the express car as quickly as he could. The passengers heard the Pinkerton man's screams clearly in both coaches, and you would have been surprised how quickly it quieted their grumbling.

When all the rest of the outlaws were mounted and ready to go, the leader handed an envelope to Mr. Alford, the conductor. "You've done you job well, sir. Thanks in part to you, no one was hurt. That's important to us."

The conductor thought about the Pinkerton man— still tied over the trunk in the express car, he believed—but decided to say nothing about that. Instead, he nodded as politely as his years of service had taught him to do.

The leader climbed up on his handsome gray horse. "In that envelope there you'll find an exact account of this robbery, the first train robbery in Missouri, sir, if you'll permit me to be so boastful. We'd prefer this be published instead of one of those exaggerated accounts that usually appear after reprisals of this kind. You'll find a blank space to write in the amount of the loss to the railroad. I'm afraid I don't have the time to count it accurately just now." He smiled at his little joke and then wheeled his handsome horse smartly, lifting his hat to the conductor. Then he and his band took off yip-yipping and yelling like boys going home a little drunk from a country agricultural fair.

When they were nearly out of sight in the gathering dusk, one of them turned back and gave the rebel yell—tearing the silence of the hamlet to shreds. The astonished conductor opened the envelope and quickly scanned the message.

The most daring robbery on record—the southbound train on the Iron Mountain Railroad was robbed here this evening by seven heavily armed men, and robbed of _____ dollars. The robbers arrived some time before the arrival of the train, and arrested the station agent and put him under guard, then threw the train on the switch. The robbers were all large men, none of them under six feet tall. They were all masked and started in a southerly direction after they had robbed the train. They were all mounted on fine-blooded horses. There is a hell of an excitement in this part of the country.

Other than omitting what they had done to the Pinkerton man and exaggerating the height of the outlaws, the account struck Mr. Alford as surprisingly accurate. After folding the note and putting it carefully into his vest pocket, he hurried back to see what he could do for that poor detective.

3

BUYING THE SAME HORSE TWICE

I took my time and looked the scenery over good. Some of it was even kind of pretty. Sure, I'd a rather been traveling through mountains, but there wasn't any. So I just kept moving north and taking what come along. I got rained or sleeted on very little, no snakes bit me, and once I got used to sleeping on the ground again, I slept good at night. I guess a man can't expect much more than that in this life. Not and figure on getting it.

Once I hit Illinois, it snowed hard and after a few days I was happy to see Chicago in the distance just to get out of it. I got to the city shortly after noon, I think. It'd growed a lot from when I was there before the War, mostly around the stockyards. I found a livery for my horses and a hotel for me, where I took a good hot sits bath. Then I found a tailor's place where I bought a ready-made dark suit and even one of them derby hats Pinkerton men wear. They finished off the bottoms of the pants legs for me while I waited.

After I bought my supper I walked around and took a good look at things in town, seeing what kind of fancy folks was sucking up whiskey in the bars close to where I was stayin, mostly. I slept in a good warm bed that night, by myself, damnit, and was up early the next morning. I felt more than a little oddish when I put on a boiled shirt, that dark suit, and my brand new derby hat instead of my dusty, nearly wore-out trail clothes.

At the cafe where I ate my eggs and sausage they told me where the Pinkerton office was. I took my time walking over there, seeing the sights of Chicago city in the pale morning sunshine. You could still see lots of buildings that'd been burned in the big fire Mrs. O'Leary's cow started. And lots of new ones, of course.

It was queer seeing so many people all at the same time that way, walking the streets, talking to one another, their breaths little white clouds in front of them. All close together, on top of one another and getting in one another's way, even bumping elbows on the sidewalks in places, if you can believe that.

At eight o'clock I knocked on the gold-lettered door of the Pinkerton National Detective Agency. A lot of half-grown willowy-looking trees lined the street, not a leaf on them yet, though, the carriages coming and going. Nobody answered the door. When I looked closer, I saw they was still closed, nobody at all inside. At eight o'clock in the morning. After a minute I went across the street and set on a bench at the edge of a little park they had there and tried to think what day of the week it was. Maybe it had got to be Sunday and me not knowing it. About that time a young fellow starts unlocking the place, so I walked over and spoke to him.

"Somebody die or something?" I asked him.

He turned around on their little stone stoop affair and looked down at me, serious as anything. "Not to my knowledge," he said, real polite and polished.

"I was told to speak to Mr. William Pinkerton when I got here. Do you suppose he'll bother coming around today?"

The young fellow laughed. "Yes, he'll be in at nine. Sharp, too, mark my words!" He went on in and I followed him and found a padded chair in the hallway to my liking and leafed through a *Police Gazette* that was just laying there. He opened some windows a crack at the top, dusted off some desks, gathered up a dozen or so spittoons, and then sharpened a lot of pencils and put them into a tinned box just so. I was glad I didn't have a job like that. Wearing a suit coat and a tie strangling away at you, and then only sharpening pencils with a little toy knife.

After a while some other people come in, a man who was pale and coughed a lot, a gal in a fresh white dress and smelling a little of lilac water, a red-haired man hot as hell about something, and a lot of fellows in dark suits you couldn't tell one from the other.

The big floor clock by the front door finally struck nine. The red-haired man was shaking his cane in the air, yelling something about a railroad something-or-other to a couple of those men in dark suits nodding their heads real stiff and frowning—and whatever it was he was complaining about seemed to make him even madder than before.

"Mr. Pinkerton will see you now," the young fellow said real soft, but surprising me a little anyway.

I followed him back between a lot of empty desks and then through a big oak sliding door. Behind a desk the size of an outhouse laid over on its side, and puffing on his cigar while reading a report or something he had there, was the man I guessed was William Pinkerton, the head of the Chicago branch of this outfit, whose daddy Allen had started it. Mr. William was younger than I thought he'd be, probly not quite out of his twenties yet—and a big fellow I noticed when he stood up. Well over six foot and girth to match. I'd not a wanted to get into a rough-and-tumble with him, by the size of his shoulders and hands.

When he looked at you, his stare went right into your brain. No wonder they called him the Big Eye around Chicago, not that I knowed that then, but it fit him all right.

His hair was already thin on top and he combed it straight back, not hiding the bald patches up front like some men will try and do. He was tugging at a corner of his big mustachio with one big paw and he waved the report at me with the other. "Let me finish this, please. Sit down."

The young fellow went out, I sat, and Pinkerton did the same, paying me no mind whatsomever. It was quiet in there while he caught up on his reading, the folks out in the big room going about their business but not much else to ruffle up the air. Out the window behind him you could see some trees, the buds swelled up big as walnuts, I thought was maybe horse chestnuts, though I wasn't sure, the time of year didn't seem quite right. "Thank you," Pinkerton said after a time, putting down his papers. "Sorry to keep you waiting. What was it you wanted to see me about, mister . . . ?"

It didn't strike me till then that he didn't know who the hell I was or what I was doing there. "Goodwin," I told him. "Willie Goodwin, and I thought it was you who wanted to talk to me, Mr. Pinkerton, not the reverse."

It took him a few seconds. "Oh! Of course. Mr. Goodwin. The tracker from Texas, right?"

"That's right," I told him, letting him straighten out the rest of it for himself. Maybe I already didn't like that fellow much when I walked in there, I don't know for sure. But Big Bill Pinkerton was not a man you took to right off, maybe never.

"What kept you?" he asked—not mad, but wanting an answer, that was plain.

I sat back in the chair and crossed my legs. Lemme say right now I just hate someone badgering me. And even if he was going to be my boss, I wasn't going to let him treat me like his huntin dog. "Well, like my letter explained, I had some things to do before I come up here."

"That's right, I telegraphed you to go to Missouri instead of coming up here after the Gad's Hill robbery. Why didn't you go there, or else telegraph me back?" he asked.

I shrugged. "Never got your telegram. I must of left by then."

"And no one there in Texas knew where to reach you? Where did you go?" Like before, he wasn't snappish or nothing, he just acted like he could ask you anything he pleased and you had no choice but to tell him. Sort of like he owned you.

"That's my business," I told him. "Now if that don't suit you, I'll give you back what's left of your money and get the hell out of here. Save us both the time and aggravation."

He seemed to think that over for a minute. "Well, that's all right, I suppose." He leaned over and snuffed out his cigar. "But you must agree to keep us posted of your whereabouts out in the field—regularly. That's the essence of our method, Goodwin. Communication. With it, we can catch any criminal, uncover any secret." He looked solemn as an owl over this communication business, whatever it was he meant, I wasn't sure.

I just nodded, not knowing what else to do.

"If you can agree to that, reporting religiously, then I can respect your wishes regarding secrecy about your own affairs, though, frankly, my agents have always been completely forthcoming with me, trust me implicitly." He laid them big words all out in a row like that, and started giving me that deep stare of his again.

"It's not like I got a lot of secrets to hide, Mr. Pinkerton," I told him. "Hell, you already know the worst about me, prison and all."

He looked at me with his head cocked for a minute—then nodded, came around that big desk and leaned back against it, half sitting on the front. "All right," he said slow and deliberate. "Just so you do as you're told." He offered me his hand.

I know he didn't notice, but something made me hold back just a hair's width of a second, but then I shook his big mitt and threw in a nod by way of agreeing to the deal.

"Good," he said. "Now let's get to work, shall we?"

He walked over to a big map on the wall, the state of Missouri, I saw, that little boot heel down there at the right corner givin it away, though I always thought it looked more like a pig's hind foot than a boot heel, which everbody else always says it is. He rapped the far side of it, the west edge, with his knuckles. "This is where you're going to do your tracking, Mr. Goodwin. Kearney, Missouri. Do you know who lives in Western Missouri, Clay County, sir?"

I hoped it wasn't who I thought it was.

He smiled sort of sneaky, nodded, waved me over, and then turned back to his map. "Kearney, Missouri. Not very big, just a flyspeck on the map," he said kind of quiet, pointing it out to me. "But somebody big lives there, Goodwin, somebody my father is very angry at. Someone he wants hung."

Kearney was small, all right. After a minute I said, "I thought hanging was for judges and juries to decide on."

He answered like he didn't hear me. "The fellow we want still lives close to the old family homestead, I'll wager—Mr. Jesse James." He turned to me, his face now flat as Iowa. "You've heard of Jesse James, I trust."

I swallowed and it felt like about a handful of carpet tacks was caught in my throat. "You'd think a man would tell you, wouldn't you, before he got you all the way up here from Texas, that who he wanted you to go after was the James gang?" I spoke as even as I could. "And why's your pa so mad at them?"

"Why, you're not afraid, are you, Willie?" Mr. William Pinkerton asked, smiling and ignoring *my* question again. He looked down at me like he was enjoying himself real good.

"Why, yes I am," I answered. "The man who wouldn't be afraid to run counter to the Jameses has got horseshit between his ears."

He went back to studying the map. "Don't be vulgar, Goodwin. That's one of the reasons we don't like to hire convicts. Pinkerton agents are gentlemen, as you will come to see and, I hope, emulate. Being a gentleman's something you'll have to learn."

I thought of three or four things I'd like to have said right then, but I kept them to myself. *The least said, the sooner mended* my ma always said. And after all, I did want the job. Not the money so much as what my ma had spoke of, the chance to pull myself up out of the mud.

Sure, I felt scared, just like I'd told Pinkerton, but I wanted to do it all the same, track that James bunch. Mostly, it felt like being asked to sit in on a high-stakes poker game, and I'd done that a time or two, betting money you'd be hurting for if you lost it, but doing it anyway because, by God, you only come down this old road once, and why the hell not? Yeah, I'd do it—even if it did mean coming within range of Jesse James's revolver.

William Pinkerton smacked the button on a little bell he had on his desk and the young man came back in on the rush. Pinkerton told him to go get someone, who banged into the office only a few seconds later and it turned out to be that loud, red-haired man. "When the hell am I leaving, anyway?" he asked Pinkerton, charging across the room.

His boss held up a big paw and pointed to a chair with the other. "Sit down and cool off, Whicher," he said. "We've got this mess almost straightened out now, and you should be able to go soon. This is our other operative, Mr. Willie Goodwin."

Instead of taking the chair he was offered, the red-haired man strode right up to me. I thought about shaking his hand but he didn't appear to have hand shaking on his mind, so I didn't offer.

He looked me over good from close up, hands on his hips, while I got the benefit of his hair tonic and the onions on his breath. "So, you're supposed to be my backup down there, huh? A Texas horse thief and Apache lover?" Don't know why I took no offense. Thinking back, you'd think I would have. Maybe I was too surprised.

"This is John Whicher, Mr. Goodwin," Pinkerton

said. "Though you'll be working with him, try to pay as little attention as you can to his crudeness."

The red-headed man turned toward Pinkerton. "Yeah, well, I bring the shitters in, though, don't I?"

"This one of them gentleman I'm supposed to act like?" I asked. They both looked at me, but only Pinkerton caught my drift.

The big man looked back at his map. "Yes, you do catch them, John, but your loose talk will get you in trouble some day, believe me. 'A good agent—'"

"'—shows discretion and moderation.' Yeah, I know what your daddy's rules say, but if I'd a been in Missouri when that son-of-a-bitchin Jesse James handed that note to that damn coward on the train I'd a shown him what-for, all right."

"I'm sure you would have, Whicher..." Pinkerton said, but he was only feeding out line to the red-headed fellow while he stared at me. "Goodwin, I know this will come as something of a surprise to you, but I'd like you to ride down to Missouri on horseback." He stuck up his hand quick like he thought I was going to argue with him. "I know, I know. It'll take you a lot longer to get there that way, and it's more uncomfortable than the train, that's true, especially this time of year, but the long ride there will get you looking like some kind of wandering vagrant or vagabond. And that'll be your disguise. Throw that derby away and get some old clothes somewhere. Get them dirty on the way down there so no one will guess you're a Pinkerton. Think you can manage that?"

"Vagabond..." I said, mostly to myself. I fumbled with my brand-new derby hat and took a minute before I answered, "I suppose I might be able to do that." I was going to tell him right then and there that was how I come *up* to Chicago. Get it off my chest and make good for it by doing what he wanted, going to Missouri by horse, which'd be the way I'd want to go anyway. But he jumped in with both feet before I could start.

"Good! Good to see you agree so readily, speaks very well of your enthusiasm about joining our organization."

"Well..." I begun. I like to think I was going to straighten him out about that too, but, as usual, he took it his own way.

"Yes, of course," Billy Pinkerton said, though I didn't know what he was 'of course'ing right away. "You'll need some extra expense money for trail clothes, a horse, and other . . . things." He dug a wood box out of his desk, slid open a little felt-lined drawer, and started counting out gold pieces. I saw then he thought I was stalling just to get money out of him.

"Well, sir . . ." I begun again.

"No, now you've already agreed, Goodwin. No backing out now." He said it like it was half a joke, but it rubbed me entirely the wrong way, like he really *was* partly expecting me to try and weasel out if he didn't pay me enough. Damn that Big Bill Pinkerton, anyway.

"Don't forget about money for a packhorse," I said when it appeared he was done adding coins to his pile.

"Excellent touch!" Pinkerton hollered. "Very authentic touch, I like that!" He clunked out another double eagle, then looked up at me, winked, and added an extra one—for good measure, I guessed.

"One more," I said.

With no more thinking about it than you might give to scratchin your ear he dropped another twenty-dollar gold piece onto the heap on that big oak desk.

4

A MOONLIT FERRYBOAT RIDE

Pinkerton said what he'd pay me each month, right there in front of Whicher, all the folks in the big room, and God and everbody, while he showed us the front door—like we was some kind of salesmen who'd already took up too much of his time. "Whicher here will fill you in on the rest. Be sure to explain to him about the reward money, John."

"Yeah, sure. C'mon Goodman, let's go," the red-haired man said, as much in a hurry to get out of there as Pinkerton was to get us out.

I wanted to ask Pinkerton if the talk we just had was the "standard training" he'd spoke of in his letter, but I let it slide. "Name's Good*win*," I told Whicher on the street. "Not Goodman."

"What? Oh yeah, sure. Say, where're you staying?"

I told him and we started walking in that direction. "What'd he mean about the reward money?" I asked.

Whicher had a long-legged, shanky stride and I had to walk faster than I'm used to to keep up. "It's what you don't get anymore," he said. "A few years back, some of the agents was cutting their own deals on the rewards.

With sheriffs, marshalls, and the like. Once, even with the men the reward was on themselves, right before we was about to shoot it out with 'em, trying to get them to surrender. Promised 'em they'd get half the reward money that was put up for them, save it for 'em till they got out of prison, if they was to surrender instead of holding out and maybe shooting some of us. Damned if they didn't go for it."

"Don't that beat all," I said. "Getting half the reward for your own capture when you get out of jail."

He pulled up and looked at me like I had just growed horns. "What the hell's wrong with you? They'll never see a *dime* of it. But the papers got hold of it, see? When Allen read that, well . . ."

He turned back to get a good look at the round rump of a real shameless black-haired gal who'd winked awful pretty when she'd passed us—I couldn't figger out whether it was her trade or her pleasure. After a minute Whicher remembered what he was talking about. "And then the boss's politician friend, Senator Parker, he made fun of us on the floor of the U.S. Senate. Halloo! Didn't we catch it that time . . . We get good expense money now, though, better than before, because Pinkerton charges the damn clients 'Whatever the traffic will bear,' is the way he puts it. But agents getting even a whiff of the reward money, hell, that's done with. The Agency collects that now. In my case it comes to about the same, though the paper out on these James boys, dead or alive—now *that* would add up to something, let me tell you." He did a smart step of some kind, like a little dance sort of thing, and tapped his cane on the brick walkway.

I noticed then it had a fancy gold handle in the shape of an eagle's head. Nice, if you liked fancy.

We walked by nearly a whole block of stores that'd burned up inside and hadn't been fixed. "Don't know how I'd feel about sleeping in a town that burns down around you every so often." I said.

"Ah, that'll never happen again," Whicher said. "They've changed the building codes, and lots of places are brick now." He hitched his thumb over his shoulder. "I saw you caught on to the expenses game pretty quick back there." And then looked at me a with the edge of a sharp smile on his face, thinking I was a big bug for skinning William Pinkerton out of a few dollars.

When we got to my hotel he told me who he'd be seeing down in Kearney and who else to find down there if I couldn't find him. "An if you *really* get lost, dig up Louie Lull or Buck Boyle. Both of 'em are with the Agency and'r down there somewhere, or will be before you get there, riding your damn horse, you poor son-of-a-bitch." He had a good laugh at my expense.

I was going to write it all down, the names and everything, but he said to memorize it instead, and made me say it back to him a couple of times before he left. I didn't see the need of that, but it was the way he wanted it, and after all, he'd did this kind of work before and I didn't. This wasn't gonna be the kind of tracking I *thought* I was gonna do, I'll say that.

"S'long, Goodman," he called back over his shoulder. "See you down in the bank-robber state." He walked off twirling his gold-headed cane, tipping his derby hat to all the ladies walking down the street, all the good-looking young ones, anyway, and whistling a cheery tune the while.

The next morning I threw away my derby hat. Right before I left I give my brand-new suit to a fellow standing outside my hotel who looked like he could use it and seemed happy to get it.

I took less time going south and west than I did coming north and east. Staying at inns and bars with rooms upstairs instead of sleeping out, even though in general it was getting a little warmer. I traveled pretty fast, though I admit I did burn more time than I should have by going back by way of Sedalia instead of cutting straighter down across Missouri. But that gal in that house there? The one who'd told me about the old Shawnee Trail? Well, she'd pulled up stakes and'd moved on.

Took off up behind a cowboy with bad teeth heading down to Mexico to find a man who owed him a deal of money, so a piano player there said, a beanpole of a man with skin the color of molasses.

"*Yes*sir, she took outa here *early* this mawnin faster'n you could button up yo shoes," he said, slapping at the keys of that old piano with his long brown fingers. He was playing a jumping-around kind of music I never heard the like of before. I asked him what it was.

"This? This ol stuff? Why, this's ragtime, son. Rag, we calls it, down to New Orleans." Only from the way he said it I couldn't figger out where he meant for a minute. 'Nawlins,' like it was all one word, run together like molasses and Mississippi river water, till all the sharp edges got washed and wore away. It made you want to march and dance around at the same time, that music, strange as that sounds.

I asked him if he knew any songs about Texas, but he just give me a long serious look that showed a lot of the whites of his eyes, then he stayed with his ragtime music. I stayed too—and listened a while, drinking rye and moonin over that gal who had took off, till I remembered I had better get on over to Clay County and see what needed doing over there.

I caught a look at myself in the foggy mirror behind the bar on my way out. I looked enough like a saddle tramp by that time to satisfy even the most persnickety of them Pinkerton folks. Another couple of weeks drinkin and living that way, I guess I wouldn't even reconize myself.

Liberty, Missouri
March 10, 1874

Valise in hand, John Whicher stepped off the train behind a stout woman with three children. She seemed more like their grandmother than their mother, but he looked her over anyway, more out of habit than anything else.

When they were gone he glanced at the few people standing around the station or sitting on green benches. Whicher stood there a minute and had almost given up on whoever had been going to meet him when he noticed a man sitting at a window table in a restaurant across the street looking at him.

The man raised his coffee cup slightly in a kind of toast. Discretion. Caution. Whicher liked that. He had little of those qualities himself, but he valued them in others.

Inside, he walked up to the table of the plain-looking man who'd signaled him—in his thirties, big-boned and muscular. "Hello, my name's John—"

"Yeah, I know who you are," the man replied, putting down his coffee cup. "Have a seat while I finish this, if you don't mind. Name's Moss, O. P. Moss." He didn't offer his hand.

"Don't mind if I do. I could use a cup myself." Whicher caught the eye of the waitress and ordered a ham sandwich with his coffee. "Moss, is it? You're the sheriff here, right?"

"Former sheriff," Moss said flatly. "Lost the last election by thirty-one votes. They forget pretty quick who cleans up their messes for them."

Whicher just nodded. He finished his sandwich in silence.

Moss paid the bill and they walked a few blocks down a quiet street, Whicher's valise getting heavier by the minute. But the late afternoon sun felt warm and you could smell spring in the air.

Moss left him at a small cheap hotel, where Whicher read the paper, went to bed early and spent a miserable night tossing and turning on a lumpy mattress.

The next morning in a foul mood he went to the meeting Moss had informed him of. The Commercial Bank squatted on the busiest corner Whicher had seen so far in Liberty, which wasn't much. In a small back room paneled in dark wood, he nodded at O. P. Moss and shook hands with the president, D. J. Adkins. Was it only the outlaws down here in Missouri who used their Christian names?

Adkins, a hefty older man wearing thick spectacles, got right down to business. "We're glad you're here, Whicher. Now tell us, how are you going to catch these Jameses and Youngers?" *He gave the red-haired man an even, glassy stare.*

John Whicher had expected a little more time—in fact, a lot more time. Look the place over a few days, lay it on thick for the local businessmen, play some poker, chalk up some expense money at a good hotel if Liberty had one. Spend a little more on some talented local whores, two of which a fellow agent had given him the names of and told him to be sure and try them when he got down here. Whicher had no idea at all that morning about how to go about capturing or killing the James boys or the Younger clan, but it was clear Adkins was expecting him to take things in hand right away. He'd catch hell from The Big Eye if the banker complained, which he surely would if he wasn't satisfied. And from the looks on these men's faces, he knew a stall just wouldn't work.

"Why, I'm going out there tomorrow and get a job at the James's farm," *Whicher said, looking from one to the other to judge the effect of his words. Actually, he had thought that he might get Goodman to try this once he got down here, but since it was clear Adkins insisted on action right now—*

Moss shook his head sharply. "That's the dumbest goddamn idea I've ever heard. They'll kill you on sight."

Adkins stood up from behind his desk. "Now, I think you ought to—"

"Gentlemen, please," *Whicher exclaimed, trying to get the upper hand again.* "The Pinkerton National Detective Agency has had years of experience in matters like this."

"They'll spot you right away," *Moss said.* "Hell, if I could pick you out getting off the train, they'll be able to in a minute."

Whicher stood and hiked up his pants. This damn sheriff was starting to get under his skin. "Well, you didn't see me in my disguise yet, did you?" he asked Moss, making it like a joke. "I'll get some gum boots and a pair of canvas pants—"

"And the Jameses will see through you easier than a pane of glass," Moss said. "Hell, their mother would smell Pinkerton all over you. The old woman would kill you herself if the boys didn't."

Adkins face was getting red and he liked to shake his finger. "We paid you Pinkertons a lot of money to do this work, and—"

"And we'll do it, too, by damn!" Whicher shouted.

"All you'll do is get yourself killed and us looking like fools," Moss said hotly.

"I'd say any man in office who lets somebody he ain't exactly sure of count the ballots is a fool already," Whicher said, smirking from ear to ear.

Moss got up and walked toward the door.

"Where're you going?" Adkins asked him.

"I was against this from the start, hiring these Pinkertons," Moss said. "This man doesn't know what the hell he's doing or what he's up against. I want no part of this. I'm finished doing this your way." He went out the door and closed it solidly behind him.

"You'll not be paid, Moss," Adkins called after him through the door. "You'll not be paid!"

"Let the son-of-a-bitch go," Whicher said. "'A faint heart never filled a flush.'"

John Whicher rented the best room at the best hotel in Liberty and told the desk clerk to send someone right away for his things at the other place. He said he would be gone for maybe a week—but to hold on to his room anyway. Then he bought a pair of canvas pants, a work shirt, a brown cap, and a tan jacket, changing into them in his new room. He decided his high-button shoes would be all right. Before he stowed his valise under the bed, he transferred his money and the new little double-action pocket pistol he had bought in Chicago to the inside pocket of his jacket.

He had to hurry to catch the 3:15 train to Kearney, a short ride, which was fortunate since he had to sit in the caboose with a brakeman who kept looking at him strangely. So too did the ticket agent in Kearney, whom Whicher asked to draw a map of how to get out to the James farm—which the agent kept calling the Samuel farm, Mrs. James having remarried after her first husband's death, the man said. Two other men were watching him when he turned from the window.

Whicher suspected he was drawing all this unwanted attention because of his new clothes, which still showed the folds and creases, and on the walk out to the James farm, he got down and rolled in the dust of the road to make them look "better." Instead, they looked like new, cheap clothes that somebody had intentionally gotten dirty. After another mile, he decided they'd look all right if he got them wet and let them dry on him. He was just leaving the road to take a dunk in a stream when a man on a handsome gray horse rode up behind Whicher quietly, surprising him. The mounted man told him to walk further up the road or he'd be shot where he stood, though he seemed to carry no gun.

"What's the trouble, friend?" Whicher asked, fighting to keep his composure, his hands high above his head. The sun had set by then and, with the rider's dark hat pulled low, he couldn't see his face very clearly.

"No trouble at all, 'friend,'" the mounted man said.

A man stepped out of the brush, pointing a lever-action rifle at Whicher. "Why, looky what we got here, a brand-spanking new Pinkerton man come to take in the whole dang James gang single-handet!" McCoy shrieked and laughed. He became so overcome with mirth that he fell to his knees. "Lordy-lordy!" he exclaimed.

"Me a Pinkerton agent? That's a good one," Whicher said, trying to laugh too. "Hey, I just came out here looking for farm work, that's all. Who are you boys, anyway?"

God, he hoped they believed him. But no one answered. "I suspect you fellows made a mistake, got the wrong fellow." Whicher realized he was talking too much and gave them his brightest smile.

"Not likely," a third man said, stepping out of the cut-over woods on the other side of the road. Long wavy brown hair hung below his Confederate cavalry hat with the brim pinned up to the side. His converted .44 Remington cap-and-ball revolver pushed hard into the red-haired man's middle while he searched him. He held up the small double-action revolver he took from Whicher's pocket.

The one up on the horse nodded, then strained in the dim light to read the words penciled on a piece of paper he had taken from his vest pocket. "No, not very likely we made a mistake about you, sir. You're Mr. John W. Whicher, from the Chicago office. One of old Yankee Allen Pinkerton's favorites, I believe."

"No," Whicher said, hanging his head and shaking it. "That's not me." McCoy took a quick step forward and smacked him just over the ear with the butt of his rifle—so hard you could hear the crack many yards away. The red-haired man went down so fast it looked like his legs had turned to gumbo.

"Not quite so rough, Art," the man on the horse said with a chuckle. "We don't want him dead yet. Not here in Clay County."

Art McCoy looked down tenderly at the crumpled man in the new store clothes who was now bleeding from a nasty wound just behind his temple. "Ah shit, don't worry bout it, boys. These Pinkertons got heads like iron."

Jesse James and Jim Anderson laughed at McCoy's joke despite themselves.

At three o'clock in the morning, while a good-sized slice of moon was still floating high in the hazy night sky, the ferryman at Blue Mills was awakened by someone pounding on his door. *"Go way!"* he yelled from his warm bed. *"Come back later!"*

"Git yer ass out here now and take us acrost," Art McCoy called through the barred door. *"If you don't we'll take yer boat ourselves—and then burn it!"*

On the trip across the Missouri, muddy and somewhat swollen with spring rains somewhere far upriver, the ferrymen looked his passengers over as best he could in the pale moonlight. Three of them had horses, but a fourth man was afoot, bound and gagged. At first the ferryman was unwilling to risk asking, but eventually his curiosity got the best of him. *"What's he all tied up for?"*

The one in charge kept looking across the river and said nothing.

"Horse thief," Anderson said after a minute. *"We're officers from Jefferson County, taking him back there."*

"Yeah, an I'm the depitty," McCoy added. *"Whatcha think a that?"*

The ferrymen bobbed his head and made for the landing on the far shore.

When the sun came up, Doc Swayles was driving his buggy slowly northward through Jefferson County toward the flats of the Missouri and Blue Mills Ferry. Mariah Jones's baby, a little girl as it turned out, had been one of the most difficult births he'd ever assisted. And the new little lady had caused everyone to lose a night's sleep. These country women almost never sent for the doctor when they had their children, but someone had done the right thing by getting him out there in time. Nearly thirty hours in labor, my, my. She'd be all right, though, Mariah Jones would. All right.

Swayles napped as much as he was awake, but his old mare was used to finding her own way home, for she knew the roads of Western Missouri far better than her owner. Swayles was jerked out of a dream about heavy ropes when the mare stopped short, backed up a few quick steps, and shook her head. Why, a man lying in the road, of *all things! Flat on his back and arms out wide—like the crucified Jesus, only naked as a jaybird. Swayles thought him merely drunk when he first woke up.*

But he was dead. Swayles saw that even before he climbed down from the buggy. It didn't take a doctor to know you couldn't live with half your head blown away. From the powder burns, it was clear he was murdered from up close. Small hole on the powder burn side, a big piece of the skull gone on the other. Orange hair glinting in the orange sunlight and blowing slightly in the dawn breeze.

What surprised Doc Swayles, though, was the wound of a bullet going out the hollow of the man's left, no, right shoulder. It had bled down over his chest quite a bit, so it probably wasn't the wound that had killed him. But where had the bullet entered?

Swayles knew immediately when he rolled the red-haired man over on his face and saw the walnut grip of a small revolver protruding from his rectum.

5

CHEAP WHISKEY AND DEAR SLEEP

I got to Kearney one afternoon toward the end of March. When I was signing for a room at the hotel, I ask if a Mr. Whicher was staying there. The clerk dropped his jaw and looked at me like he'd saw a ghost. After a second he shook his head hard. He handed me my key and hurried into a back room. Not exactly what you'd call a friendly place, I remember saying to myself.

When I come back downstairs to go see one of the men Whicher had made me memorize, I heard the clerk talking low to a woman in that back room and then saw him looking out the crack of the door at me whilst I was going out.

I had been in some pretty backwards places, but this one took the prize, I thought, walking down the street. A new face, mine, made just about everbody stop and stare, sometimes right in the middle of the street. I thought for a minute I might have got dirt smeared on my chin. But I looked at myself in a store window and I looked all right—for me, anyways. Sure I was a little dusty, and my trail clothes showed their wear, like Mr. Pinkerton wanted, but there was no call that I could see for folks to steer clear of me like they did.

Walking up and down the main street looking for the lawyering office of Samuel Hardwicke, Attorney-at-Law, got me nowhere but thirsty. A place named the Horse Head or the Horseshoe or something like that was a lot easier to find, and that's where I had a rye and asked the barkeep for directions. It turned out the lawyer I was looking for was over in the town next door called Liberty, not here in Kearney at all. I was tired from the long ride, and I decided tomorrow was plenty soon enough to talk to Lawyer Hardwicke about whatever the hell it was I should be doing down here.

After another two or three I left to head back to my room for a little nap before seeing about my supper. Maybe it was more, I'm not sure.

Stepping outside, I run right into a short fellow who tugged at the brim of his high black hat and give me a big friendly nod. "Could you do me a favor, sir?" he asked, polite and earnest.

He was a young man and looked about half Indian, maybe more. Though his skin was pretty light, his eyes had that dark walnut color and that half-wild look, the way Indian's eyes sometimes are. But smart, though, too. You could just see his mind workin away a mile a minute at something if you watched his eyes close enough—though you couldn't tell *what* he was thinking.

His face had that kind of Indian look that reminds you something of a wildcat—heavy bones in his brow and high cheekbones, his eyes just a touch slanty, and a broad nose like a cat's. Full lips, especially for an Indian, another thing that made me think there must be some white blood in him. Straight black hair hung long, a high-crowned black hat with just a little dent toward the top. And something in his eye, some spark or other, that said there was maybe more to this fellow than maybe you'd saw right off, even if you'd looked close, like I did that day.

Since he was shorter than me, I was more on a level with his hat than I was his face, and I guess I took a minute or more trying to decide whether he had put that little dent in the crown of his hat apurpose or if it was just accidental. I *was* drinking, you recall.

"Is something the matter?" he asked after a minute and me not answering him.

I don't know why, but the idea of that dent in his hat just wouldn't stop pestering me.

"Yes, I'm an Indian," he says. "And I suppose you've got something against Indians too, right?" His eyes flashed fire, but it was smouldering and smoky instead of the punch-you-in-the-face kind. He might of been a short man, but he was broad as a oak door and built about as solid.

"No," I told him. "I was just . . . What was it you wanted to ask me?" A drink or two less and I probly would have paid more attention to him than to the dent in his hat, and I felt a little stupid for not doing so.

After I stood there a while longer, rockin on my boot heels while looking him in the eyes, he must of seen I didn't mean nothing by not answering him right away. Maybe he even seen it was the rye as much as anything, I don't know.

He reached into his pocket, past a big holstered Colt I didn't notice before, and pulled out a half eagle. "Could you go back in there and get me a bottle, please?" he asked. "Any kind of whiskey will do, preferably cheap stuff." He looked up and down the street after he handed me the gold coin and then back at me, direct as anything. "Nobody around here wants to sell me whiskey, not that I blame them much, since it seems to go right to the heads of most . . ." Here he give the sign for *Indian*, rubbing the back of his left hand with the fingers of the other a time or two.

I nodded. "Yeah, and if there's anyone who holds their liquor even worse than an Indian, it's . . ." Here I give him the sign for *one-half* and then the sign for *Indian* right on top of it. Stalking Bear in Huntsville had taught me a lot of the sign talk whilst he was mainly teaching me to track, so we could both say better what we meant. I thought for sure this young half-breed'd be surprised I knowed it, maybe even a little sore, since I was about half insulting him with that half-breed stuff. You know how it is when you're drinkin.

He chuckled and nodded instead. Even half drunk I seen there was more to this fellow than met the eye. "Yes, I thought you might know that old hand pourparler." He had one of them smiles that changes a fellow's whole face, lights it right up from the inside out, and a whole mouthful of white teeth, big and even and straight as anything. You almost never see that, white man or Indian. "If you can get two bottles for that money, please do so," he said.

I went back in and told the barkeep what I wanted, laying the half eagle on the bar.

"Is that that Blackfoot Bill again?" he asked.

I didn't know what to say right off, so I didn't say nothing. He took the money, though, and put it in his gold box.

"Would it matter?" I asked him when he set the two bottles down and a stack of silver beside them.

"No, not really," he said. "I don't mind *selling* it to him so long as I don't have to sell it to *him*, if you see what I mean," he said.

Well, I didn't, exactly, but I nodded like I did and went out the door again. "With two bottles of this, you ought to be able to spare a man a drink," I said, handing Blackfoot Bill his whiskey and then his change.

He looked at me kind of surprised. "Well, yes, if you like. Come along back to my wagon and you can have *two* drinks—if you want them, not that it looks like you need anymore."

We walked down the street, him carrying a bottle in each hand and me carrying more of a load than I probly ought to have been, I suppose. I don't know why I went along, exactly. He was right—I didn't need no more whiskey, that was certain, but maybe it was because I didn't talk to almost nobody since Sedalia and mighty few before it.

Maybe because the way folks there in Kearney was so standoffish. And maybe too because this Blackfoot Bill was a friendly sort of fellow in his own peculiar kind of way—after he saw I was all right about Indians, that is. We got out of town a little ways and come to his wagon, staked and with a big white tarp throwed over. Parked beside a stream, a neat little camp all set up alongside.

He pointed and I sat on a camp stool. He soon had the fire stirred up and a coffee pot shoved into the coals, after which he squatted on a big stone, uncorked one of the bottles and handed it to me.

"Ker-raw!" I yelled after the whiskey cleared my throat. It was about like swallowing a nervous cat backwards. My eyes watered, my tongue felt like a length of dead water snake in my mouth, and my ears rung like Sunday morning in Central City. "What the hell is *that*?" I asked at last, hawking and spitting out whatever would go.

"That's the local product, sir. Your recent purchase," he said laughing at me and holding the other quart up to check the color. "A libation prepared especially for nearly-broke cowpokes and run-down redskins. Ready for your second drink now or will you care to wait for your stomach to try and grow a new lining?"

I handed the bottle back to him. "After you, brother," I said.

He slipped the cork back in and slapped her home. "No thanks. I never touch the stuff." He set the bottle down in the dirt beside the other one.

I just looked at him for a minute. "Then what'd you get me to buy it for, then?" I asked. "This ain't enough to run and sell to your tribe, not even by the shot."

"No," he said kind of slow, drawing it out. "But it's enough to give a little kick to my Heap-Big Medicine."

"Your *what*?"

He pointed at the tarp on his wagon:

44 / CHARLES HACKENBERRY

GENUINE AUTHENTIC
CHIEF BUFFALO SLAYER'S
HEAP-BIG INDIAN
MEDICINE CURE AND
SOPORIFIC

Big red letters shaded in blue. Beside them a red Indian chief painted with his arms folded in front of him, wearing a big blue war bonnet. He resembled Blackfoot Bill a little bit if you squinted your eyes nearly shut and had a real good imagination. And a big pile of dead buffalo laying all which way, also in red and blue, the only colors the painter fellow either liked or had left in his box by the time he come to do this, I couldn't decide which. "I'm surprised I didn't notice that when I walked up," I said.

"I'm not," Blackfoot Bill said, giving me a sideways smile. "Here, have a little coffee for your second drink." He poured me some and then got some for himself.

"Thanks," I told him after sipping hot coffee a while. "So you're Chief Buffalo Slayer, I take it," I said when the quiet got a little thick.

"No, that's just a name to sell the snake oil with," he said, looking for faces in the flames it looked like.

"A secret of the Blackfoot tribe, is it?"

"No," he said again. "Whiskey with a little dribble of iodine to make it taste terrible, and a good deal of swamp water when I can get it, for the color—creek water when I can't. And some other ingredients I probably shouldn't even mention. Incidentally, I'm not a Blackfeet. I've never even been to that part of the country, up north there where those people live. I wouldn't go to that wild, uncivilized region if someone paid me to, which no one ever will, I'm sure. Why would they?"

With his chin propped in his hand he watched the flames and listened to the creek run and so did I for a minute.

"What's it cure, then?" I asked.

"Gullibility," he said. I never heard of that particalar disease, I suspect he just made it up.

"Well, what's it got to do with slaying buffalo?" I asked after a time, all this stretching the truth so bad out of shape was starting to rub me the wrong way a little.

He drew himself up as tall as he could—for a short fellow sitting on a stone. "Absolutely nothing," he said, sounding a little disappointed and exasperated with me.

"But you *are* Blackfoot Bill, though, right?" I had him on that one, I believed.

He shook his head. "Actually, I'm not. My tribal affiliation, as you might imagine, is pretty murky, but there's certainly no Blackfoot, as I've already said. As a matter of fact, that tribe calls itself Black*feet*, no singular to it—a single Indian is, to them, a Black*feet*. But Black*feet* Bill just doesn't sound right to you white folks, so ... And my Christian name is Oliver, not that I believe any of that Eastern Mediterranean mumbo-jumbo they taught me any more."

I just looked at him.

He stood up and dusted off the seat of his pants. "Well, you wouldn't buy a magic elixir from somebody named Mostly Osage Ollie, now would you?"

I saw what he meant. "So I suppose that last part, that sop—whatever-it-is, that's just a lie too?"

"Well, no, that part is accurate. It's a first-rate soporific. Calms you down and knocks you right out. That in itself, I feel, makes it well worth the dollar I get for it—fifty cents if it's not moving well. Ever had a new puppy or a yammering baby keep you awake all night? One tablespoon and the baby's out cold, another and the dog's pacified, a third and you're out too, and everyone gets a good night's sleep. It's a reaction between the iodine and the alcohol, I believe. A doctor once told me it seems to cut off some of the blood supply to the brain." He reached toward the sky, giving himself a good stretch.

I thought it over a minute and saw how some things work out right even if they start out wrong, but then something else struck me. "Say," I asked him, "isn't iodine a poison of some kind? Don't it kill you if you drink enough?"

"Well, I've had no complaints thus far," Blackfoot Bill said, giving me his sideways smile again. "Naturally, I try not to stay too long in one place."

About then I got a fit of the yawns, like I do sometimes, and Bill throwed a tarp down from his wagon and then a quilt on top of it and said as how it'd be all right for me to take a nap there at his place. I said, no, thanks all the same, but I *would* lay down and rest my eyes a minute if he didn't mind.

Two hours later he pushed a plate of beans cooked with ham and onions under my nose. A couple more cups of his good strong coffee and I felt like a new man. He was stirring together a batch of his medicine, it looked like, and because I thought he might be a little jealous of the recipe, I wandered over and give the red and blue buffalo on his wagon cover a better look. They didn't improve any up close, though.

When he was done he come over beside me and we looked at the buffalo together.

"People fall for this stuff, huh?" I asked.

"Oh yes, sales are generally brisk," he answered. "At least they were. Since that murder the other week, after which my former associate decided to move to safer climes, things have been a little slow. You wouldn't be interested in a job, would you?"

"Doin what?" I asked.

"Being the barker for the medicine show," he said. "The customers prefer to think that a white man's in charge, so I generally work with an assistant who gives them that impression. He makes the pitch, I come out and do a dance, he extolls the virtues of the potion and makes the offer. I, then, in effect, perform the close—by running it out to the yahoos a bottle at a time and collecting the money."

"You mean you'd want me to make a spiel to the folks that are suppose to buy it?"

He nodded. "Yes, that's it—as well as wearing a big top hat and a red vest. And driving the wagon when we move on. I'll give you fifteen percent of the gross or eleven percent of the net, take your pick," he said. "My profit margin is the best in the industry. The most expensive part of the product is the bottle."

I shook my head. "No, I don't think I'd be any good at that kind of thing. I never did no public speaking to speak of, and I wouldn't feel exactly right selling folks something that could eventually kill 'em, even if it did make 'em sleep sound in the mean time. No offense meant, now."

He smiled and bobbed his head. "I understand, none taken. Not everyone has the stomach for business. If you hear of anyone who might be interested—"

"I'll be sure and tell them," I said. I thanked him for my dinner and the nap and the drink, even if the last wasn't exactly to my liking.

He invited me to one of his medicine shows, though he said it'd be sad that I'd miss the full effect, him having to do both jobs and all. Its always nice to meet a man who takes pride in his work.

Then he waved good-bye and called after me that I was welcome to come back any old time, though that's not just the way he put it, of course.

The next morning I went over to Liberty to look for Lawyer Hardwicke's place. It was a lot easier to find it over there in Liberty than it'd been in Kearney. They kept me waiting in an outside office nearly an hour, and I was about ready to go find a bar when they finally decided to let me in, no one come out at all.

"Why wouldn't you state your name or your business?" Samuel Hardwicke said even before he told me to sit. He was about my age and sort of like me, I guess you could say, only a little shorter and a lot fatter, with less hair, too, almost completely bald on top and in front.

And the framed piece of paper on the side wall said he'd went to college somewhere, if it wasn't a fake. Meeting Blackfoot Bill had left its mark on me already, you see. Also, Hardwicke had them quick jerky movements some portly men have that don't fit in with the way they're built. Put you in mind of a nervous beaver almost ready for winter. And he had learned, somewhere up the road, to frown better than almost any man I'd ever saw before, and he'd got so good at it that the deep lines on his face took on the set permanent. Me, I never saw no future in working your face that hard. And, come to think of it, I doubt he drank much.

Except for our ages, maybe we wasn't all that much alike.

"I thought that saying who I was maybe ought to be a secret between just you and me," I told him. "I'm Willie Goodwin, and I was sent down here—"

"Oh my God, don't say it. Not here!" He turned around quick as a groundhog and closed the drapes behind him, which made the room pretty dim, there being no other window in there.

Even in what little light was left I saw he'd turned about three shades whiter, not that it looked like he ever got out in the sunlight anyway. "Yes, I was advised of your coming, Mr. Goodwin, but what are you doing *here*? In my *office*?!"

"Is there something wrong?" I asked. "John Whicher of, well, you know who, gave me your name to look you up down here, and I couldn't find him."

"But you should *never*—" Lawyer Samuel Hardwicke stopped and stared at me a minute, then thumped heavy as a horse into his leather chair. "Oh my God, you haven't heard, have you?"

"Heard what?"

"John Whicher is dead. Killed by the Youngers and the Jameses."

I sat down. "No, I . . . "

"Well, it's true," he begun. He give me the details,

and even though I never thought of Whicher as a friend of mine, exactly, the more I heard the madder I got that somebody could a done that to him. And then I felt kind of sad he was gone, not that the world was going to be that much worse off for him not being in it no more, I'll admit. Still . . .

It wasn't till right then, sitting there in that dim lawyer's office, him scared over people even knowing I was in there, that I realized the dangerous corner I had gone and wedged myself into. It could be your life if these Jameses wanted you dead, I realized. Dead. I could get dead doing what I was doing. *Real* dead, not just talking-about-it dead. And here I'd gone and stumbled all over Kearney yesterday, half drunk and asking around about a Pinkerton agent the Jameses had took out and shot dead, probly in cold blood. No wonder them folks at the hotel—

"What are you going to do?" Hardwicke asked.

I shrugged. "I don't know. That's why I come to see you."

"Me? *I* don't know what you're to do! I've received no instructions whatsoever concerning what you're to do here."

"Then I guess I'll have to talk to the other men Whicher told me about. You know where could I find Louie Lull or Buck Boyle?"

"Oh my God," Hardwicke said, and if I thought he appeared white in the face before, it was nothing to what he looked then. "Lull and Boyle were in a scrape with the Youngers just the other day!"

"They were shot too?"

Hardwicke stood up quick and peeked out from behind his heavy drapes. "Well, Lull was. He's alive, but he's probably not going to live long. They've carried him to Roscoe. Imagine, a young man like that, married just a few months, I've heard."

"What about the other one, Buck Boyle?"

The lawyer shook his head. "Apparently he ran away.

No one has seen him since. The man with them, Ed Daniel, was shot in the neck."

"Well, that's who I was going to ask about next, Edwin B. Daniel. He's dead?"

Hardwicke nodded.

"Who have they arrested so far?" I asked.

"Arrested? In Clay County? I don't think any warrants have even been sworn out. This is not Chicago, Mr. Goodwin." Hardwicke sat back down at his desk. "This is the native soil of a lot of Confederates who have decided the War between the States is not yet over, not for them. All these men rode with Quantrill, or some other border ruffian, killing and robbing in the name of God, motherhood, Dixie, and the Stars and Bars. And the ones who weren't very good at it were shot or hung some time ago. So the ones left now are the very best of their breed—which is to say, the very *worst* of their breed—a dangerous, murderous bunch who are looked upon as heroes by most of the citizens around here, heroes who can do no wrong, no matter how much wrong they do." He stopped talking and sat looking off into the shadows.

I had the feeling he pictured himself in front of a jury giving that speech, that he'd had it all worked out and ready for some time—and'd had no one else to say it to so far but me. "Well, that leaves me just one more name on my list," I said. "A deputy sheriff named Fern or Moss or Weed or something like that."

"That would be O. P. Moss," Hardwicke said. "Not a deputy. The sheriff here, at least he was before the last election. A self-serving vigilante, some say—a good man, a *very* good man according to others, but he'll be no good to you, I'm afraid."

"Why's that? Somebody shoot him too?"

"No, but he had a falling out with your man Whicher and has severed his connection with ... your company, some say. Mr. William feels that a little more money ..."

"Uh-huh," I said. "That don't leave me very much to go on, does it?" I thought things over a minute. "Are you in contact with my company? The Chicago branch?" I asked him.

He looked right at me. "I am not prepared to say."

"Well, you better *get* prepared," I told him. "Hell, you so much as said so a minute ago!"

"That may be," Hardwicke said, cool as anything. "But I did not say so *directly*, did I?"

I took in a big breath and let it out slow. "Well, if you are, then you better tell them about all this confusion—and find out what I'm supposed to do down here."

"I understand," Lawyer Hardwicke said, but I couldn't tell whether he intended to do it or not.

"When I finally do talk to my boss up there, I'll be sure and let him know you ain't certain whether you're with the company or not. Maybe they won't be exactly sure whether you're on their payroll, either."

"Threats will have no effect on me, sir, I assure you," Hardwicke said, not at all hot under the collar. "What will you do in the mean time? Until you hear from ... your employer?"

I sat and thought for a minute. "I guess I'll go back to Kearney and try and get a job on a farm or a ranch or something. Maybe out at the Jameses' farm."

"Oh my God," he said, shaking his head. "That's surely the one think you should *not* do, Mr. Goodwin. That's precisely what John Whicher was trying to do when they caught him and killed him so barbarously. They'll do the same to you. They surely will."

"Well, I'll think of something else then," I said, though I didn't know what in the world it would be.

He told me *never* to come back there again. Then he give me a sheet of paper with some kind of code on it and said I should use that if I was ever to send him a telegram, but I couldn't see how it was supposed to work. I didn't tell him that, though. He said I should check the telegraph office in Kearney every so often. Maybe he'd send me a telegram signed Mr. McCandlass—instead of Hardwicke. I was to be Mr. Baldwin in our telegrams, supposing we should send any. It all seemed like boys playing at some kind of a game to me.

He tried to get me to wait in his woodshed till dark, so no one would see me leave his place, but it wasn't much past noon, and I couldn't see sitting out there half the day. I did say I'd go *out* the back way, *through* his wood shed. And that's what I did.

Stepping outside on a nice spring day, a warm breeze blowing up from the Gulf of Mexico, I thought of just packing up and heading back to Texas, but that didn't seem right either. Instead, I walked down an alley toward what I guessed was the main part of Liberty and what I hoped would be a nice quiet bar where I could think things through. Frankly, though, I didn't have a single idea in my head about what to do next.

6

PICNIC BY THE RIVER

I guess I shouldn't have drunk so much that next week. No, that ain't right. I *know* I shouldn't have. But the thing was, I didn't know what to do. Lawyer Hardwicke was not going to be no help, that was clear. Everyone else I had memorized the names of was either dead, shot-up, run-off, or as disgusted with the Pinkertons as I was.

Another thing that would get you to drinking was you didn't know *who* you could trust, who might be reporting back to the Jameses—even the law. One man in a saloon in Liberty said Sheriff Patton was as fine a man as walked upright in Missouri. And then a fellow I was drinking beer with in Kearney laughed and said, sure, go ask Patton about the Jameses and you wouldn't have to go riding around trying to get a look at them, they'd find *you*.

I went into Saint Joe on the train the day after I talked to Hardwicke and sent William Pinkerton a telegram saying I was going to be Mr. Baldwin in Liberty and that's who he should send back to, telling me what I was to do. But thinking on it the next day, while I was having my first one in the Silver Dollar in Kearney, I wasn't even sure

Pinkerton'd know who that telegram was from, since I only hinted around at who I really was, not wanting to give my right name to the young man who took the telegram and kept looking at me strange, or so I thought. Even over there in Saint Joe. You know how everbody in small towns knows everbody else's business. And if they didn't yet, about mine, they soon would. But what else was I to *do?*

I guess that was what got me drinking at first, not knowing who knowed your business and who was against you. After them first couple days, it got easier to just drink and forget about it, like it always does. Easier, but you needed to drink a little more every day to drown remembering what you didn't do the day before—and who might be watching you. More the day after, and so on. You know how that goes.

I left my horses in Kearney, but I'd go over to Liberty one day on the train, back to Kearney the next, and into Saint Joe once in a while in between. And the only thing I knew to do in each place was go into the saloons and drink their rye whiskey, check the telegraph offices for anything sent to Mr. Baldwin, and then get back on the train the next day and go somewheres else. One thing all that drinking did do, though, especially in Liberty, was make the folks in the saloons there a little less cautious of me, the steady customers, I guess you'd say. Hell, after less than a week they thought I was just another one of your regular knocking-around kind of drunks. What you might almost call a vagabond.

> *Just south of Kansas City, in the small town of Harlem, Missouri, Jesse James rode his brother Frank's beautiful bay mare slowly down the main street in the late morning sun. Frank had an eye for the lookers, all right, but even with her arched neck she wasn't the horse his Roman-nosed gray was. One advantage she did have over the gray, though: she was so new that no one in Harlem identified her with the Jameses.*

Nor, he hoped, would they recognize him either—wearing a silly pair of loudly-striped trousers and a wide-brimmed floppy hat. It should keep Zee's sister happy for a while, at least—that the neighbors would have no new cause to remark that an infamous bandit was once again courting someone on their street.

These Mimms people struck him as a little too reserved and just a little odd. Methodists through and through. He couldn't imagine his short little aunt ever marrying that gawky old uncle of his. And the idea of them in bed together—but you could never tell which way love would have you jump in the underbrush, could you? Look at Zee and him, for instance. Who'd have thought that?

For that matter, he wouldn't have guessed that his Aunt Mimms and his mother could have been full sisters either, but they were. His aunt as docile as a well-behaved setter by the fireplace, his mother scrappy as an British bulldog. Now which, he wondered, would have been the pick of that litter at the age of eighteen or so?

When he turned the corner onto Water Street he saw Zee sitting on the porch swing. Waiting for him in a bright blue dress and bonnet to match. She hadn't seen him yet, though she was looking down the street one way and then the other. The strange horse, perhaps? Or the trousers? A little nearsighted, Jesse realized after a second. Well, she'd have to be to love him.

He dismounted and tied his horse in the side yard several houses down the street and stole toward her porch staying close to the buildings, hoping she wouldn't see him. In her next-door neighbor's yard he quickly picked a few blue and white flowers and a long stem of grass to tie them with. Looking around the corner of her house, he tossed the bouquet. When he was sure it would land in her lap, he ducked back around the side of the house and waited. He heard the swing chain clatter, her light footsteps bounding down the hollow porch stairs and running across the lawn. He timed his capture perfectly—stepping forward and catching her suddenly at the corner of the house, kissing her hard—all the while pulling her slowly but insistently back between the houses, under the shade of the tall, dark pines. For a moment she struggled and then yielded softly.

After a while she pulled away breathless. "Why, shame on you, Jesse Woodson James! Scaring a girl so . . ."

Jesse released her and took a step backward and bowed low, removing his hat. "I apologize from the bottom of my heart, Miss Mimims. I shall never again do that, or anything like it."

Again he had surprised her. So earnest did he sound that she half believed him for a second. She could never predict him. She rushed laughing into his arms. "Well, you'd better never stop doin' things like that if you know what's good for you, Jesse James!" She loved saying his name aloud. It was wicked as red, it had the burnt sulphur smell of Satan to it, and she loved the very sound of every syllable. Zee gave him a sudden deep kiss, a quick peck on the cheek and another on his mouth.

He waited until she'd finished kissing him. "Is that all I get?" he asked. "For doing exactly what you asked?"

"That's all you get here, Mr. James, sir!" she cooed. "After all, you must let a young woman preserve at least a shred of her maidenly modesty."

"Why, I'm surprised you have any little scrap left at all, after the last time I was here, the way you—"

She feigned an exaggerated expression of shocked surprise, slapped him softly with just her fingertips, and then turned and ran back around the front of the house. "Sissy! He's here!"

Jesse James, the deadliest man in all the United States of America, the most dangerous country in all the world, walked after her, a lover's smile brightening his handsome features—until he realized he'd probably have to face her sister again.

Later, as they strolled arm in arm along the river with Zee carrying the picnic lunch she had packed in the large basket, Jesse felt comfortable again. He had slung his jacket over his shoulder, the sun warm on his face and arms, the bright green grass blowing in the spring breeze.

They stopped on a low, flat promontory and together spread their blanket. Zee arranged the lunch while Jesse sat and looked across the river, then turned and watched her graceful, lovely hands at their work. She looked up and caught him admiring her. "You were very patient with my sister," she said, smiling at him.

Jesse shook his head. "I still don't understand why she doesn't like me," he muttered. "What she said about supporting a family—Why, I could provide for you very well, much better than her husband does for their family."

"Well, it's not just that," Zee said, handing him a cold fried chicken leg. "There's our bein' cousins, of course. Cousins never married on Momma's side of the family, which Sissy has always favored. It's as common as dirt on our Daddy's side, though, as you well know."

"That's just being pigheaded," Jesse said hotly. "Don't she know there's ways other than her own? Perfectly good ways?"

Zee stiffened and looked across the river to where she supposed Jesse was looking, straining to see what he saw. "Yes, she knows there are other ways, just like you do. But, also like you, she believes her own ways are better just the same. And what she said about supporting a family? She meant supporting it without robbing and stealing."

They ate silently. "That again," he grumbled, tossing the chicken bone into the basket and wiping his mouth and hands on his checkered napkin.

"Yes, Jesse, that again. And you must remember, it's not just Sissy who's against outlawry. It's me too."

"But it's not—"

"Call it what you will, it don't make it right," Zee insisted. "Even more important, at least as far as I'm concerned, it means someday you'll be shot and—"

"Ha!" he yelled. "Some damn sheriff or detective shoot me?!" He reclined on his elbow, smiling at her.

"Well, you have been shot, sir. You might remember that it was I—"

"'Who nursed you back to health,'" he said along with her, mimicking her. They both laughed. "Those were the best days of my life, Zee, us being together like that day after day. It's why I'm so sure you've got to marry me."

She took a sharp breath. He could say things that pierced to her very heart. "Oh, dear, I do love you so, Jesse," she said, tears welling in her soft blue eyes.

He moved closer, catching her rich warm scent. He untied the strings of her bonnet and removed it. She shook out her lustrous deep blond hair in the sunshine, then lay back on the blanket and welcomed him into her arms.

I was coming out of the Silver Dollar late one afternoon when who should I run into, with a five-dollar gold piece in his hand, but Blackfoot Bill.

"Willie?" he asked. "Is that you?"

"Well of course it's me," I told him. "Who else would walk around looking like this if he could help it?"

I went back in and bought him his whiskey. Like before, the barkeep ask if it was for Blackfoot Bill. Like before, I didn't exactly answer him.

When we was walking to his camp, I fell down and he helped me back up and sort of dusted me off. After the second time, he latched onto my arm and wouldn't let go till after we got to his wagon.

He didn't give me a drink this time, and I didn't mind that much. He throwed his quilt and tarp out right away and wouldn't hear of nothing but that I stretch out and sleep it off. Hell, it was the next day till I woke up that time.

"I thought perhaps you'd died," he said when I went over to the fire that morning. "At least I had my hopes up after listening to you snore for a while. I thought, at one point, that you might run off the stock." He poured some coffee and we got started on a pile of biscuits he'd made.

They'd of been better with some butter or sorghum syrup, but there wasn't none.

I didn't bother to argue with him about my snoring. I'd heard talk of that before. Besides, my head wasn't in no condition for any serious arguing. What it was mostly fit for that morning was pounding and ringing and aching. That much it could do just fine.

"You seem to be making a profession of this whiskey drinking business," he said after I'd washed up and was drying in the sunlight. "I don't see the profit in it, myself."

"No, I can't neither," I admitted. "Not this morning I can't. Seemed to make sense yesterday, though." Them biscuits in my stomach was starting to feel like a big tub of dirty wash water sloshing around in the back of a wagon going down a steep stony road.

"What are you doing here, anyway? You're not from around here, are you?"

"No," I said. "I ain't from here, and at this point I don't know what I'm doing here. I wish the hell I did."

He laughed. "Well, it's your business, certainly. But mine's the medicine show trade, and you could work at that until you had a better idea of what you ought to be doing. Like I said before, I could use the help."

He talked about it some more, saying how it was easy as pie to do, and all the while my head was hurting like blazes. He went over the money part again, how much I could make, and I acted like that was a big selling point with me, though I don't know why, I still had a lot of the money the Pinkertons give me. After a while I could see he really did need some help, wasn't just trying to reform what he thought was a mostly worthless drunk. To tell it short, what with my headache and his line of talk, which didn't seem like it was ever gone to stop, he wore me down.

"All right, all right!" I said. "Just stop talking. I'll do it."

He looked a little surprised. "You will?"

"Yes, I will," I told him. "Just be quiet for a while, can't you?"

He shut his mouth right up.

"Good," I said. "Just keep on like that. Only before you do, answer me one question honest. Then I'll wear your damn red vest, your stupid-looking top hat, and I'll memorize your spiel and yell it out loud enough to be heard in three counties." I said this last waving my arms around sort of like a short, fat politician I'd listened to once down in Texas, and loud enough to scare his mules and to get my head pounding even worse than before.

He smiled. "Say, I think you just might be good at this. What's your question?"

"Did you put that crease in your hat apurpose, or did you just bump into something?"

Blackfoot Bill started to laugh out loud. "Well, you'll just have to figure that one out for yourself!"

Like usual, he was in a good humor—joking and talking and before long it was dark. I went back to my hotel then, but the next morning I paid my bill there and at the livery and took all my truck out to Bill's wagon, it wasn't much. That was part of the deal—I was to stay there with him and learn my part of the show. Now I know Indians has got the reputation of being moody and sulky, and maybe some are, I don't know. But Stalking Bear back in Huntsville never was. And neither was Bill.

Sure, it took me a while to get used to someone else's ways and someone being around a lot of the time, but Bill had as much of that to get used to as me. And he was as even tempered and agreeable a man as you ever saw, and when someone's like that, it generally rubs off on you, don't it? I don't know where folks get their ideas about Indians and a bunch of other things, I truly don't. If people operated on even half the truth, it would be a whole differnt world.

Anyway, Blackfoot Bill started teaching me the "medicine show business," as he liked to call it. It was a little bit of common sense, a little bit of putting on a show, and a whole lot of the idea of money being more important than anything else. The first sat well even if the last didn't always.

I memorized the spiel pretty quick, Bill got out his needle and thread and tailored up the red vest to fit me, and the high hat was just a little snug, not bad. When I was starting to shave one morning, my new partner said I might want to leave the whiskers on my chin and my mustache, so I did. It felt oddish at first, but he said it looked good—good for the show was what he meant, good for making money. Like Buffalo Bill gone to seed is how it looked to me, but I didn't care.

We had a practice show there by the stream next day, Bill running out of the trees in his buckskin Chief Buffalo Slayer's getup, surprising me a little that first time, what with his war paint and whooping and feathers and running around like a crazy man. But that's what they liked, he said. I got through the spiel without a stumble and Bill said we were ready for the yahoos, that's what he called the folks that gathered wherever we set up, the yahoos. I don't know where he ever got that name for them.

The next morning early we went over to a little town close by in the wagon, Mosby it was called, and after Bill put up our posters and then run screaming down the main street, we did the show. More'n a hundred people turned out. I was kind of nervous at first, standing up on the back of the wagon and all those folks looking at me. But I got through it to the end and damned if we didn't sell the Heap Big to about eighty of them yahoos—at an even dollar a bottle. That was my start in the medicine show business.

We was going to stay that night there in Mosby, so toward afternoon I went out and had a dust cutter or three, but I come back to our camp early and sober. Bill was gone, though.

7

SLINGING THE LINGO

Monegaw Springs
Jackson County, Missouri

Just before sundown, the people of the settlement stood outside in their packed-dirt dooryards and silently watched the five riders go by. The first two they all knew, of course. That was Jesse James himself on the gray and his older brother Frank on that good-looking mare.

The two riding behind were something of a puzzle, one with long hair falling over his shoulders and the other one dark and not looking to either side.

The man riding out to the left of Jesse grinned and tipped his hat to everyone along the way, and they all smiled and nodded back, proud to be noticed by anyone in this band of raiders that was getting writ up in every paper in the country these days. McCoy, wan't that his name?

And what did it matter, anyway, after the riders were out of sight, if some of their daughters snuck off and followed after, brightly-colored hair ribbons flying? Scootin up the holler toward the Youngers' place, which everybody knew was where they were headed. Well, hell, that was only natural, wan't it? Maybe they'd do all right for theirselves. It never hurt to try.

At the Younger cabin, Cole stood out by the road watching the riders approach, his new lever-action across his arms, his brothers with their revolvers strapped on and tied down, flat-faced behind him. Women on the broad veranda, cooking at an open fire in the yard. Dirty-faced children leaning against trees, boys and girls watching to see what would happen next. But quiet and still, even the youngest of the brood. And if they did speak, they spoke in whispers.

Jesse nodded after his horse stopped. "Evening, cousin," he said. "Someone down the road said we might get a good meal up here."

Cole Younger stood mute and rooted, not responding.

"What happened? Did we come on the wrong day?" Jesse asked.

Frank chuckled and so did one of the men behind him.

None of the Younger men moved. A moment passed.

"We were all sorry to hear about John," Jesse said, turning in his saddle toward James Younger, who leaned against a wagon. "I'm sorry you lost your brother, Jim, but I know he'd be proud of how you took care of them damn Pinkertons."

Another moment slid by, but everyone sensed the change in the air.

"Step down if you've a mind to," Cole said, then turned and walked toward the house.

Later, after everyone had finished eating, the men sat or stood outside, around the fire, some smoking their pipes in the deepening twilight, the women having already gathered up the smaller children and making sure the older ones were elsewhere. Someone started a jug around.

When it got to Jesse, he stood and held the whiskey high. "Gentlemen, I drink to the South." He swallowed twice and passed it on. "The South," each man said quietly in turn before he drank.

"What'd you bring that damn Pinkerton man over here to Jackson County to kill him for?" Bob Younger said suddenly and angrily, asking the question that had rankled their clan for more than a week. "Now everbody thinks it was us, and we got law troubles enough without you makin it worse."

Men of both factions turned expectant faces toward Jesse, who nodded and cleared his throat before speaking. "I apologize for that," he said softly and with obvious difficulty. "I am truly sorry. It was a mistake, not something we meant to do, put more of a burden on our kin. Truth is, one of us went further than he should have when we stopped to eat some breakfast. We were going to kill him, true, but not up there close to Blue Springs Ferry."

"Well, whyn't you jist carry him off, then? Or bury him?" Bob Younger asked, half a chip still on his shoulder.

"Moss and some men came along and we had to git," Jesse said. "There was only three of us and more than twice that of them."

The fire cracked and sent up a shower of sparks. "Who done it?" Cole asked. "Who killed him?"

Jesse looked at the ground and shook his head. No one had to explain to Cole Younger that Jesse James didn't intend to say who in his gang had killed Whicher so inopportunely. It was Jesse's business, and he'd already taken responsibility for it. He certainly would not allow anyone else to lay the blame on one of his men—least of all, to decide what was to be done.

"I'll say this," Cole muttered, understanding the situation completely and immediately. "If it was one of mine, he'd be out." That was all he said, all he could say.

Jesse looked Cole squarely in the eyes. "I'm sorry, cousin. Nothing like this ever came between us before—and it won't happen again, you've got my word on it. Last thing we need is to have these Pinkertons come between us."

Cole thought about it, grunted, and nodded once. Some of the other Youngers nodded too. That was the end of it.

After a moment Frank stood up. "If I could have your attention for a moment, gentlemen, I have an announcement to make. As you all know, Jesse has been courting Zee Mimms for some time, as everyone in Missouri knows—hell, as everyone in America knows, thanks to all these newspapers!" He laughed and so did the others. Even in the firelight everyone could see that Jesse's face had reddened.

Frank took off his hat and held it over his heart. "I thought she had better sense, I truly did, but Zerelda Mimms has consented to marry my brother Jesse, God protect her!" Everyone cheered, women coming out of the cabin and joining the men. Two or three youngsters had an impromptu whistling contest, and Art McCoy gave a bloody rebel yell, though Frank turned and shot him a dark look.

"The important thing," Jesse said, bashful as a boy, "is that you're all invited to the wedding. It'll be mostly family, and I want you all there, your wives and children and grandmas and—everybody!" They all cheered again.

"One other thing before we settle down to some more of that good corn liquor," Jesse said after the noise subsided, standing beside Frank. "I brought someone here you all should meet. He doesn't ride with us, understand, but I'd trust him with my life—have done so already. Now some of you may have seen him before this, but not looking like he is tonight. I doubt any of you knew just what you was looking at behind all that war paint and feathers. But he's the one told us those Pinkerton men were coming, the ones you took care of proper, and the one we gave a Missouri welcome to—even if we did leave him laying in the wrong place. This is the man who warned us about the Pinkertons who came looking for you folks, Cole. The ones we told you about. Wasn't for him, you might have lost more than poor John. Stand up here, Bill. Let the folks have a good look at you without your getup."

Blackfoot Bill stood up, nodded and smiled at everyone, but few of the Youngers smiled back.

Bob Younger walked up behind him and knocked off his tall hat. "Hell, you're a goddamn Injun, ain't you?"

Blackfoot Bill turned and gave him a look. "Actually, half of my ancestors painted themselves blue and threw rocks at the Romans who were raping their women."

Bob gave him a quick shove that staggered him backwards. "Now what the hell's that suppose to mean?" Bob asked, a lot louder than he had to.

"Cole!" Jesse yelled.

Cole Younger nodded. "All right now, Bob. Let him alone. Didn't you hear what Jesse said? He's on our side."

"Yeah, I heard him," Bob said, "but he's still a damn half-breed, ain't he."

"Yes, and he's still working for us, Bob, whether you like it or not," Jesse said, coming up close to the shorter man, but keeping his hands at his side. "He's not going to start riding with us, but he can go places and see things that you can't and neither can I—because more and more people are starting to know what we look like. We need what this man can do. And your people should recognize him so he can send word back to you as well as us."

Cole Younger leaned back and glared up at the standing half-breed. "What's this I hear about another Pinkerton in town? Askin around about us?"

Blackfoot Bill sat back down. "There's nothing to it. Just a drunk drifting through, more curious about the notorious Youngers and Jameses from these parts than he is smart enough not to ask. He's all right, and it'll be easy enough to keep an eye on him now, just in case I'm wrong—I hired him to give the spiel in my medicine show. I work for you and he works for me."

A few saw the humor in it.

Cole nodded, but Bob Younger shook his head. "What the hell's the world coming to when you need half-breeds and snake oil salesmen to look out for ya?" He walked away from the bright circle of faces. In a moment they heard a horse running at breakneck speed into the night.

"Better party without that damn hothead, anyway,"

Frank James commented, and even Cole chuckled. "Now where the hell's that jug?"

Jim Younger's wife's uncle got out his banjo and his father's friend found his fiddle. An even bigger jug started going around after the first, and before long people were singing the old songs and then dancing to the faster ones in the firelight.

A girl so blond her hair looked nearly white sat across the circle from Jesse and stared at him till she caught his eye. After he recognized her, he didn't look back her way again. The girls from the settlement paired off with boys they knew or men they wanted to know, and after a while the moon came up.

Somewhere around midnight Jesse declared it was time to leave.

"Go if ye must, mon frere," Frank said, sitting across the fire, a woman in each arm and a bottle of blackberry wine between his knees. "I am too besotted to travel on tonight." He dropped his head and those around him laughed.

"So too am I," Blackfoot Bill yelled a little drunkenly beyond the edge of the firelight.

"He sure is!" a girl's voice added, bringing hoots and shouts from the younger men.

"If it's jist the same, I'll stay a while longer too, Jesse," Art McCoy said, his arm around a dark-haired Younger girl.

"No, you'll go back with Anderson and me now," Jesse told him. McCoy glanced at the girl and then went to get their horses.

They yelled good-byes to the three departing horsemen, then quickly lost them in the tangled, twanging rhythm of the music, the circling of the jugs—and out beyond the rim of the firelight, the heady, intoxicating musk of human copulation.

Bill was cooking breakfast next morning when I crawled out of my blankets. We ate pretty quick, got packed up and headed back to Kearney. I drove and he napped back in the wagon for a while. He didn't sleep long, though, and come up and sat beside me while I mushed the hardtails.

"Busy night?" I asked him.

He smiled and nodded, looking over the countryside.

"Well, since you wouldn't answer me straight about your hat, I think I ought to get to ask you something different."

"I certainly can't tell you the lady's name, if that's what you're wondering about."

"No, that's your affair, not mine. What got me speckerlating is something I wanted to ask you about that first time I bought whiskey for you. I's afraid you'd take offense then, though."

He was right away on his guard. "What is it?"

"Well, how come you talk the way you do?"

Blackfoot Bill laughed and then gave me one of his sideways smiles again. "Is there something wrong with the way I speak?" he asked.

"No, there ain't a damn thing wrong with it, and that's what's wrong with it," I told him. "I never heard nobody talk so straight up and down like you do, especially no Indian or half-breed—no offense meant, now."

He laughed good. "Am I too grammatical for your tastes, Willie? Does my verbal primping and parsing grate on your ears?"

"Well, I wouldn't say it just that way, if I understand you right," I said. "Then again, I wouldn't say nothing just the way you do. Where'd you ever learn to sling the lingo like that?"

He nodded, took the reins, and clucked at his mules. "Back East. The Quakers were in charge of the reservation where I grew up, and they decided that another fellow and I would benefit from a first-rate education. So they sent me to a preparatory school in New Hampshire and then to Bowdoin College. I lived in the same room Hawthorne had lived in earlier. God knows why they picked that school, it certainly had nothing to do with the Quakers. And God also knows, I presume, what happened to him—a Shoshone, I believe."

"Good lord," I said, surprised as a skunk tasting turpentine. "You mean to say you been to college and here you are running a medicine show instead of doctoring or lawyering—like old half-assed Harwicke is over in Liberty? How come *you* ain't doing something like that?"

"Getting a degree in a college that accepts Indians is one thing, Mr. Goodwin, but it's quite another to be allowed to become established in a profession." He liked to call me Mr. Goodwin like that ever once in a while, specially when he was explaining something. "And I'm sure I make more with the Heap-Big than most lawyers do anyway—with their scrimping little practices. Yes, I suppose I could read the law and then open an office on a reservation somewhere, but frankly, I couldn't afford it. Indians have no money, you see."

Well, I'd never thought it through that way. "And that Shoshone fellow, Hawthorne I think you said his name was, didn't you ever hear what become of him afterwards?"

Bill blinked, looked at me strange, and then shook his head fast like he was trying to clear his brain or something. Finally he and shook his head normal. "No, I never did," he said, a nice smile on his face. We rode on quiet for a while, but I guess he kept thinking in the same direction as before, for when he spoke up some minutes later he was still chewing on the same idea. "But a bigger influence on my language, my spoken language at any rate, were the two years I spent in England."

"What was you doing over there?"

"Ostensibly, absorbing the culture. Studying music when I found the time for it. Mostly, though, I peregrinated over the countryside and dallied with the damosels. Oh, I was quite the proper-looking English gentleman, Willie—bowler and all. Those lily-white, upper-crust English ladies *do* have a taste for aboriginal males though they absolutely insist their dusky swains know when to say *who* and when to prefer *whom*."

"Well I'll be dogged," I said, meaning as much the *way* he talked as what he'd just said.

And it wasn't just how he talked and chased after them English ladies that surprised me about Bill, either. We was hawking the Heap-Big a few days later, packing up our gear to leave, when Bill asked me if I wanted to go along with him to a bar, there was one there that would let him in, he said. Lone Jack, it was called—the town, not the bar. I don't recall just what the bar was called.

I said sure, I would go along, though I thought it was kind of funny he would want to go to a bar, since first off we didn't need no whiskey for the medicine right then and second him not being a drinking man, you'll recall, despite he was half Indian.

We walked in and there was only two men at a table and only a few at the bar. I walked right up and ordered a shot of rye, but Bill nodded to the barman, who nodded back, and then went off somewheres behind me.

When I picked up my second shot and went back to where Blackfoot Bill was, I seen he'd lifted the dusty canvas cover off some odd sort of a piano they had there, one that looked like a heavy wood coffin set up on thick, tapered legs. He sat right down to it, on one of the long sides where you played it, like he knowed what he was doing.

Well he run up and down those keys like water tumblin over stones in a brook, stretched his arms over his head, wiggling his fingers, and then took a deep breath. Wellsir, he started to play this music I never heard the like of. It was awful pretty, you understand, but I couldn't imagine nobody singing to it, on account of it being so unregular, despite it was so nice—sort of dreamy, you could say. It went good with sipping rye, I'll tell you that.

Blackfoot Bill glanced over at me whilst he was playing. "What do you think?" he said. I seen then we'd come here apurpose for him to play this here piano. He sure liked playing it, the look on his face said, and I liked that—the playing and him liking to do it both.

"That ain't ragtime, is it?" I asked him.

He started laughing a little to himself and then out

loud and then after a while he was laughing so hard he couldn't play and laugh at the same time, so he stopped playing and just laughed.

"Well, don't just quit like that!" I told him. "I was just starting to feel at home in there. I want to hear how that damn fool thing comes out. What do you call that stuff, anyway."

"It's Chopin, he said, like he thought I'd of knowed that, at least, but then he told me how it was spelled, you wouldn't believe it. It was the fellow's name who'd *wrote* it, Chopin. A Frenchman, I think he said. This fellow was all the rage when Bill was over there studying his music, I took it. "A nocturne, which means night music, Willie. Opus twenty-seven, number two." Can you believe a name like that? For a *song*?

He started playing it again, from the beginning again, and talking about it at the same time. "The piece starts out with an overtone series ..." he said, not that I knowed what he meant by that, but it went up and then come back down, maybe that was it. "There's this sense of magical at-oneness, rather like a trance state," he told me next, closing his eyes and playing a little more. "And sort of an hypnotic accompaniment..." he said, touching some notes real soft, pushing pedals, saying a lot more things like that, still playing, but that's about all I can remember of what he said, if I remember even *that* much of it even half right. He talked a while more, trying to explain it all to me, but I got kind of lost, not knowing a lot of the words he used, and after a while I seen it didn't matter that much—not if you just sort of let it take you along where *it* wanted to go and just forgit the explaining, it was so pretty.

Sort of like riding a raft down a long, broad river—like the Missouri or the Mississippi—in the moonlight is the best I can say it. After a bit more he give up on the explaining and just played. You didn't need to know nearly so much about it if you had somebody else to play it for you, I figgered that much out. And so I just drifted along on that raft, sittin quiet beside Blackfoot Bill, floating farther down that silvery river—that's how I remembered to say about that trance stuff he'd said, because listening to it was like what I guess that must be like, floating off somewheres into a trance—on a raft, sort of, on a nice warm night in June, the smell of night flowers blooming off somewheres and the mud of the river bank. I don't know.

Matter of fact, I didn't even notice the two men who'd come over behind us, I was lost so in that feathery, sleepy music. I'd pulled a chair over beside the bench Bill was sitting on, facing the same way as him. All of a damn sudden this big fist come down hard on a bunch of the low notes, right between Bill and me, right while he was playing, the banging loud as hell. Bill jumped and I jumped and them two men started roaring, they thought it was just funny as all *hell* they had done that and we jumped.

Bill started saying something to the one who'd banged down his fist on the keys, but I didn't see no sense in talking. Standing up quick I brung one up from the floor hard under his chin, hard enough to snap his head back to last Thursday and send his hat flying after.

Wellsir, the other fellow fumbled for his iron. What I done to his pardner took him about as much by surprise as his pardner's banging took us.

But Bill was ready for him. "Stop or you're a dead man!" Bill shouted, and right quick the second fellow *did* stop, his revolver still in his holster, worked around sort of behind him like it was. I followed the man's wide-open eyes back to a little nickel-plated hideout piece Bill had pointed right at him and full cocked. Bill'd turned about half around on his piano bench and held his little shooter right by his vest pocket, where it must of come out of, I figgered. From about four feet he would of blowed a hole in that scared man big enough to stick your thumb in, should you want to.

The one I punched was out cold as a week-dead mullet on the floor and the one still on his feet started backing real slow toward the bar with his hands high, his eyes still wide. The barman pointed to the door, meaning us.

We didn't see no reason to argue, since the other fellows in there was looking at us like they were thinking of having us for tomorrow's breakfast—with a couple eggs on the side. We stepped outside polite and gentle as anything, Bill tipping his hat just before he stepped out after me.

"Let me see that!" I said to him once we was up the street a little ways, nobody following us and him starting to put that peashooter away in his vest pocket again. "I didn't know you carried that," I said, looking it over.

"And I didn't know you carried a punch like that, either," he said. "That man will be lucky if he wakes up any more this week, and he'll be paying someone else to chew his beef for him after he does." We both had a chuckle at that. And maybe also at getting out of there without no holes shot through us or not getting our noses broke in the bargain.

"I guess we both have a few things the other don't know about, don't we?" I said, thinking of me and the Pinkertons but not saying so to him.

"I guess we do," Blackfoot Bill said, a funny look in his eye just then.

While we walked up the street I looked over his little nickel-plated revolver some more. It had his initials on the bottom of the grip strap—and something else engraved there— "From a Friend." Tiny, but that's what it said. That and his two initials, B. B. All real fancy engraving. Some of that flowery, leafy stuff engraved up on the barrel at the same time, it looked like.

"Who give you this?" I asked, handing it back to him.

He took it and stuck it back in his vest pocket. "A friend," Bill said, that funny smile still on his face. And that's all he said.

8

THE SPRING FAIR IN DOGTOWN

Working for Blackfoot Bill worked out better than I thought it would. I made more money than I could spend, doing the shows was easy once I got on to it, and I had plenty of time to myself—time to trail them damn Jameses if I ever figured out how to do it or if anybody ever said just what it was I should be doing.

And I laid off the drinking, not that I worked at it all that hard. Having something to do, even if it was only once in a while, like the shows was, kept me out of the bars and that was all it took. On top of that, I met a gal who bought a bottle of medicine from me at the show we give over in Gladstone. Only she was from a little place near there called Dogtown.

"Dogtown?" I said to her while Bill was getting back into his regular clothes. "Where the devil's that?"

"Yonder, over that way," she said, pointing with her chin, squinting the sunlight out of her pretty green eyes. "Two or three miles—maybe more." She was some younger than me, I saw, but not too much.

"Sounds like a real fancy place, Dogtown," I kidded her.

"Oh, you'd be surprised how nice it is over there,"

she said. "You ought to come over and see for yourself some time."

"Lots to do over in Dogtown, is there?" I teased.

"Well, no, there isn't," she admitted, smiling and looking bashful up from the ground. "That's why we came over here to your show, to go some place of a Saturday." She looked away, over under the trees nearby, at a blond gal and a good-looking young fellow who'd bought the Heap-Big too.

"My name's Willie Goodwin, and I'm glad you come, Miss . . ."

It took her a few seconds to figger out I was fishing for her name. "Sarah," she said, all of a sudden when she realized it. "Nice to meet you. Sarah Parsons. Parsons was my husband's name before he died, and I'm glad I came too. My maiden name was Cole?" She looked at me like I might reconize it.

I just nodded.

Sarah rolled her eyes and took a deep breath. "You know, there *is* something to do over in Dogtown *next* week. The big Spring Fair is next week," she said, brushing a curly strand of hair out of her eyes.

"Is that so?" I asked. "Why, I'll just have to write that down on my calendar now, won't I?" It sounds kind of smart-alecky, I know, but that wasn't the way I said it to her. She was a pretty little thing with her curly dark brown hair streaming out of her bonnet all around her face and blowing in the breeze.

She laughed. "Yes, sir, you just come on over next week. I'll be there both nights, at the dance pavilion, in case you were wondering." She blushed and couldn't hide it. I had the feeling she had half surprised herself, being so bold with me.

We sort of run out of things to say after a bit. She fingered her bottle of the Heap-Big, then nodded and turned to go.

"Well, say, don't I owe you some change for that medicine?" I asked her.

"I don't think so," she said, looking back, a hint of a smile in her wide green eyes but still a little cautious.

I handed her back two of her quarters. "I can let you have that for the special interductory price, four bits," I said. "Here, take it."

She give me an even sweeter smile, and then leaned close and let my fingers holding the coins stay in her hand a little longer than they needed to. "It doesn't really do all the things you said, does it Mr. Goodwin?" she asked. "You don't have to say if you don't want to."

It was my turn to blush then. "Well, maybe not *all* of that." I was at a loss for words for just a second. "But it is a mighty good soporific, though."

She blinked her big eyes a few times and I knew right away she didn't know what that meant. "Is it really?"

"Yes, it is," I told her. "But you got to be careful how often you use it. Don't you ever buy a second bottle, now, for it may be habit-forming," I warned her.

"Habit-forming?" she asked, a sly sort of look on her face then. "Isn't that the way of most things that make you feel good, though?" She give me a quick sharp look and then turned away fast, flouncing over to join her friends under the trees. Just the way she said it, you knowed it was a joke of some sort.

I didn't catch on till I remembered she'd said she was a widow woman. "Well, I'll be dogged," I said, looking after her while they all walked away.

We hit a little dry spell with the shows then, didn't do none for three or four days—I don't know why. Bill was gone more than he was around, I didn't know where he went most of the time. I thought maybe he had a gal somewheres, but I never saw her.

Bill's general plan with the Heap-Big was to go to a good size town, like Kansas City, and then run a circle around it. That's what he told me, anyway. I couldn't see the sense of spending so much time on the little burgs near Liberty, but it was his business and him doing it that way would work out all right for me if I ever got a chance to trail them Jameses. So I didn't say nothing about it.

Come the next Saturday—it was into April a day or two by then, I think—I saddled my horse and rode over to Dogtown. The afternoon had pretty much wore away by the time I got close. From quite a distance you could see the maypoles they had set up on a hill, streamers and ropes hanging down with little flag things of all colors flapping—and it wasn't even May yet.

You could hear the music from town, too. None of that ragtime music like over in Sedalia. No, these folks liked their waltzes and polkas. Nothin fancy or up to date for them, thank you. There's something about music you hear from far off. It's always sweeter than up close, especially the fiddles and horns, but folks always goes up close to where its being played for some reason.

I put my horse in a rope corral they had made for the purpose—and walked over to where the band was and the dancing was going on. Sarah had said about a pavilion, but it really wasn't one. Just a low platform of rough planks with high posts on the corners and sides for putting lanterns on, though they wasn't lit yet. And them little flags here too, strung around the top. But roof, it didn't have none. So you had to stretch the meaning of pavilion out of shape some to call what they had a pavilion. It was fine for the purpose, though, I don't mean to make fun of it. It wasn't going to rain anyhow, and the boards was stout and strong, so that the folks dancing didn't bounce too much or have to fear for broken legs should they go through.

A woman put a cup of juice stuff into my hand while I watched them dance, and I thanked her. Punch, they call it. It was all right, awful sugary though. An equal amount of good corn whiskey mixed in would have made it more tolerable.

I seen Sarah before she seen me. She had on a dress and matching bonnet of shiny green stuff that made you notice the green of her eyes more. White ruffles, too. You could hear her laughing while she danced, and once in a tight corner when she and her partner banged into some other dancers, she whooped and hollered. That's when I caught a glimpse of her well-turned ankles in thin white stockings. She was dancing a polka with another gal I thought at first was old, though so spry it didn't make sense. When they whirled past, I seen her partner had hair so fair it just looked white.

Sarah no more than went by than she spied me and stopped in her tracks and then dragged her friend with her over in front of where I was standing down off the platform.

"Mr. Goodwin! I was hoping you would come, but I had just about given up on you."

"I don't see how I could miss the big doings at Dogtown. Why, then I'd have to wait a whole year for them to come round again, wouldn't I?" I said, giving her my hand, and then her partner too, for they was stepping down off the platform to join me.

"See," she said to her friend, "what did I tell you?" Sarah told her friend my name and then told me hers—June. The white-haired gal looked a little bit worried about something, but I couldn't see what.

"Don't you ladies want to finish your dance?" I asked.

"No, that's all right," the white-haired girl said, pulling away from Sarah. "I'll see y'all later. Nice to meet you, Mr. Goodwin." And then she left before I could answer.

"Darn it," Sarah said, watching her go. "I wonder what's wrong with her?"

"I'm sorry to break up your dance there."

"Come on, then," she said taking my hand, happy again already. "Prove it. Come finish it with me."

Well, I tried to say no, but she wouldn't let me. It'd been a long time since I'd tried to polka, but I did manage to stumble through it without actually knocking no one down.

When it was over, we stepped down off but she kept hold of my hand. We went over to a big pit fire and ate some roast pig they'd cooked the whole thing over the flames, its half done head—looking at me like it was bawling, only making no sound—cut off and put up on a stick stuck into the ground. Made me lose my appetite, I'll tell you, but it didn't seem to bother Sarah's none.

It was just turning evening by then, a nice sunset blazing away for us to enjoy while we walked. "So this here's Dogtown, is it?" I asked her. "Kind of pretty."

"Yes, this is it. It isn't much, I suppose." She had took my arm and there was other couples out strolling too, all of them younger than us, I noticed.

"No, it looks like a nice place to live," I said. "But how'd it ever get such a dumb ... How'd it ever come to be called Dogtown, anyway?

She laughed. "Yes, if you're not from here, it must sound queer." We turned left at what was only the second cross street in the whole town. "... so these folks from Pennsylvania moved out here all together," she said.

"Pennsylvania? Why, I have family back there."

"Are they Quakers?" she ask real bright, setting me back a step.

"No *mam*, not that I knowed of," I told her.

"Well, the ones who came here were," she said. "Called the town they started, this one, Foxdale—after the man who had started the Quakers over in England. Not that we knew George Fox from a fox terrier when I was a little girl."

"Uh-huh," I said. I couldn't see where this story was going.

"Well, this man who was the last of those Quaker folks from Pennsylvania, before he died, he asked my grandma if she would look after this old dog he had."

"And *that's* why it's called Dogtown!" I said.

Sarah squealed. "No, silly. Just listen! Every Sunday after that, that old dog would scratch to go out and then go down the road."

We was away from the buildings of town by now, but there was still a good bit of pretty orange light in the sky.

"One day grandma decided to follow that old dog. Right down here is where he went," Sarah said. I looked, and down by a little stream, behind a bunch of overgrown bushes, stood a plain white clapboard building, pretty low.

Sarah walked down, pulled open the door. "Here's where he pawed at it till he got it open," she said, showing me the heavy scratches on the pine wood. "Every Sunday old George, that's what grandma called that dog, would come in here, lie right over there by the fireplace for about an hour, and then start home."

Sarah lit a lamp and then we went over and sat on a bench.

"Where's the pulpit, where the preacher stands?" I asked, kind of quiet.

"No preachers," Sarah said. "Friends don't have them."

I looked around good and it appeared there was nothing else in the place but the benches.

"Quiet, isn't it," Sarah whispered.

You could hear the stream out back trickle a little if you listened real hard, and a few birds singing their good night songs. But that was all.

She kept talking in a whisper. "Grandma got so she liked coming along with him, sitting here, waiting for old George. Said the quiet gave her room to think. She told ma and my aunt how nice it was just sitting here, and they came along to see. The next week, my aunt brought her husband, and after that, more and more people came to see the dog that went to Quaker meeting by himself. Before long nearly half the town was coming down here, sitting here quiet. He's buried down by the stream, a nice stone with his name on it, flowers planted and everthing."

I didn't know for sure whether it was the dog or that last Quaker man that was planted down beside the flowers, and it didn't seem like it would be such a good idea to ask.

"Anyhow, *that's* how the town came to be called Dogtown, after old George," Sarah said. "It's nice, the quiet of this old meeting house, of a First Day morning." She give my hand a squeeze. "You should come back and see *that* some time too."

Sarah stood and went over to the lamp, and I did too. She blew it out. And then—it was nearly dark in that old Quaker meetinghouse—she leaned up and kissed me. Nothing real big, you understand, but it *was* a kiss, mind you.

I didn't know just what to say.

We walked back over to the pavilion and danced a few more, waltzes mostly. We drank some more fruit punch, though it was no better than before, and then she walked me down to where my horse was. A man there was saddling them for everybody, since some were in their good clothes.

"Shouldn't I walk *you* home?" I asked.

"No, I'll have to tell momma and daddy about you first. I'll find June and go home with her." She looked up at me a minute, the band still playing down the street, the hanging lanterns lit now. "And I'll have to say something to my boy, too. I didn't say so before, but I have a boy who'll be eleven come September."

I nodded. "Well, I knowed you was married, so I'm not so surprised you have a boy. I'd like to meet him some time, if you think it'd be all right."

She give me a serious, quizzical look there, standing by my horse. "You're not married, are you Willie?"

I shook my head. "No, mam, never was." And never will be, we used to say back home, but it didn't seem polite to say that now.

"Yes, that would be nice if you met Billy," she said, smiling up at me. "You'll like him. He's a good boy."

I give her another kiss. It was a shorter and even more polite one than she'd gave me before—there was a few folks standing around—but I could feel the heat of her body through my shirt. I mounted my horse and waved.

She waved back. "Now you be careful riding home in the dark, Willie Goodwin, you hear me?" She made a joke of it, not the bossy way it sounds now.

"Yes *mam*! I'll be extra careful just because you say so."

God, that gal had the prettiest laugh.

I stopped in the telegraph office in Saint Joe the next day and asked if there was anything for Mr. Baldwin, and the operator surprised me and said there was two telegrams. This is what the first one said.

> Mr. Baldwin
> You are hereby apprised to remain in the vicinity and conduct business as usual. Stay in contact with the customer I told you about. I shall send you another telegram in about two weeks regarding my visit to your place of business.
> WP

That was all it said. I figgered out what the message meant right off, but how to do it—stay in contact with our customer—that was more than I knowed how to do. I didn't like the idea of William Pinkerton using his initials like that, for if I could figger out who it was from, so could a lot of other folks I'd just as soon not know I was getting such telegrams. You know how small-town folks like to know everbody's business. I thought about sending one back, but what could I say that wouldn't give me away?

The second telegram was just a mush of letters and numbers, no spaces between them, and I asked the operator if there wasn't some mistake in it. He said no, he'd had it checked twice and that's the way it was sent, how it was supposed to be. He give me a funny look, and I remembered then about Hardwicke and his code, but I had throwed away that damn code paper he'd gave me a long time since.

I tore them both up in little pieces and put them in a trash can they had there.

> *The farm of Dr. Reuben Samuel and his wife,*
> *Zerelda Cole James Samuel,*
> *the mother of Frank and Jesse James.*
> *A few miles from Kearney, Missouri*
> *April 1874*
>
> Blackfoot Bill sat his horse nervously outside the low log farmhouse waiting to talk to Jesse, who sat in a pool of lamplight inside drinking a cup of coffee and talking earnestly with his mother. Bill could see them through the window, and Jesse knew he was there, waiting.
>
> Nearly an hour ago Bill and a man he knew only as Anderson approached the house on horseback and were looked over by a young man with a Winchester who told Bill to stay on his horse. Anderson had gone inside then and told Jesse that he was here. Bill had seen Jesse look out the window at him. Why was he being made to wait like this?
>
> Anderson sat quietly on the ground now, leaning against a tree, and held the reins of both horses. Did they think he was going to try to ride away without their permission? Did they think he was that stupid?
>
> Finally, Jesse's mother rose and went into another room and Jesse came out and looked up at the stars for a minute, stretched, and then walked slowly out to where Bill sat his horse.
>
> "May I have your leave to step down now?" Blackfoot Bill asked in something less than an entirely friendly tone of voice. "It's mighty uncomfortable just sitting here in the saddle like this."
>
> "I'm sorry," Jesse James said. "I had forgotten you were out here. Please step down."
>
> Bill assumed they would be going inside, but Jesse continued to stand there, looking down at him between the horses and making him feel even more uncomfortable.

"Did you get my message?" Jesse asked quietly.

"Yes, of course. Didn't you get mine?" Bill asked back, a little too quickly perhaps.

"Oh ... yes, yes I did. There's been so much to do lately, so many details to...."

Blackfoot Bill waited for Jesse to finish, but when he kept looking up at the stars, Bill grew impatient. *"Then you know I said it would be all right."*

"Yes, that was ... what your message ..." Jesse said absently. *"I just wanted to see you and make sure."*

"Well," Bill replied, trying to sound casual and at ease, *"I guess you can never be one hundred percent sure of anything, can you?"*

"Oh?" Jesse said, turning his gaze sharply on the half-breed. *"Then you're not completely sure he's all right, are you?"*

What was that in his voice? Bill asked himself. Fear? Anger? *"There were rumors about him when he first came here, of course, but he's done nothing suspicious at all. And I don't think the Pinkertons would hire anyone who drinks as much as he does."*

"Of course, of course," Jesse said, sounding distant and detached again.

"If you're still concerned about it, the safest thing would just be not to invite him to the wedding," Blackfoot Bill suggested.

Jesse James chuckled to himself. *"Oh no it wouldn't, not if you knew Zee Mimms as well as I do, sir, it wouldn't do at all. No, not the way she is about her family. If Zee says her cousin Sarah must be there, and Sarah says she won't come unless this Willie whatever-his-name-is brings her, then that's the way it's got to be."*

Blackfoot Bill nodded. He was glad it was so dark that Jesse couldn't see the expression on his face. *"I beg your pardon, but if that's the way it's got to be, then what are we doing standing here talking about it?"*

Jesse laughed softly. *"Yes, yes indeed. Why are we indeed? I was just worried, is, I suppose, the best answer.*

Certainly you don't mind humoring me, do you? As much money as we pay you?" He started walking toward the house.

"No, I don't mind," Bill said as he climbed back on his horse and turned the roan's head.

"Bill!" Jesse called after him insistently—yet quietly at the same time.

Blackfoot Bill stopped his horse and looked back. He could see little of the man's face, only a smear of lighter stuff in the darkness.

"Invite him yourself, why don't you? But if it turns out he is a Pinkerton agent, I'll kill him."

"Of course," Bill answered.

"And Bill?"

"Yes?"

"Then I'll kill you too, you know. Or else I'll let Bob Younger do it. He'd like that."

"I'd expect nothing less of you," Blackfoot Bill said, turning his horse again, glad of the enveloping gloom.

One night at dinner, not too long after I got them two telegrams, Bill being in camp all day for a change and made a son-of-a-bitch stew, we was sitting by the wagon eating and out of nowhere he asks me, "Willie, did you ever see Jesse James?"

"Jesse James? Why, no, I never did. I was trying to for a while there, when I first come up here. Somebody'd told me this was where he'd grew up, but when I started asking around, it was like everbody was afraid to talk about it so I give it up."

"Yes, there were rumors of your being a Pinkerton man when you arrived."

"Me? Now that beats all, don't it? Me, a Pinkerton!" I don't know why I didn't go ahead and tell him the truth, but it just didn't feel right to for some reason.

He nodded, took a spoonful of stew, and looked real thoughtful. After he had swallowed it he says, "There *were* several detectives nosing around here just before you came..."

Whatever else he was going to say he let slide, but then after a minute he says, "Well, would you *like* to meet Jesse James? If you had the opportunity, I mean?"

I didn't know whether he was only talking or whether this was goin somewheres, so I just played it out. "Why, I surely would! He's one of the most famous men in the country, you know. Maybe the whole world. I guess you also know by now that I'm a Texan, and he did fight with Quantrill, didn't he?"

Bill took a minute. He seemed like he wished he hadn't of started on this. "Yes, he was one of Quantrill's men, I believe."

"That's what I thought too," I said.

Bill didn't say nothing for the longest time, just kept eating his stew and sopping up the gravy with a hunk of bread, like I was doing. I wanted to ask him how I could do it, see Jesse James. But the way he was acting, I said to myself, Willie, you got to let him make the next move. You *got* to.

When he was done eating and had tossed his plate on the ground he says, "You've seen him already, you know."

I shook my head. "No, I'd remember that, even as drunk as I get sometimes, I'd remember if I ever saw Jesse James."

"Well, I'm sure you've seen him," Bill said, pouring himself some coffee. "As a matter-of-fact, you sold him and his fiancee a bottle of the Heap-Big at the show we did over there in Gladstone the other Saturday. Shortly before you sold one to Sarah Cole."

Then I remembered that young fellow and the gal I thought was Sarah's friends, the ones over under the trees. She had looked at them when I was talking to her, and then walked off with them. That fellow, the one with the short beard, *that* was Jesse James?

9

UNDER THE ROSE ARBOR

In a flash I seen how close I'd just come to getting myself killed. If I'd a told Bill about the Pinkertons like I was thinking of doing there for a minute...

"How'd you know that, about them Jameses being over there in Gladstone and buying the Heap-Big from me?" I asked him. "And how'd you know about Sarah? I never told you nothing about Sarah."

He eyed me square, a dark look on his face I never saw the like of before. You could just see the wildness of the Indian side of him rising up to the surface and shoving the smooth talking, easy-going fellow underneath. At least he *looked* more Indian than I'd ever saw him look.

And it was clear he wasn't enjoying me poking around in his affairs, but he'd started this and now he didn't have no back door to slip out of. "You're in with these Jameses and Youngers, ain't you? That's who told you, wasn't it? It wasn't that you just saw them over there in Gladstone, no, you'd have said so then—pointed them out."

He still didn't say nothing, just continued to stare at me.

"That's where you go when you go off like you do," I said. "Either you go out where they are or you head off looking into things they want looked into, spying for them, ain't you?"

He let out a whoop. "Well, that's a little grandiose, isn't it? Calling what I do *spying*? I think of myself as Jesse James' scout, that's all. Colonel Chivington had his scouts—and so did Major Anthony. Certainly Jesse James deserves a scout as much as either of those two 'worthies.'" He got up and poured himself some more coffee and some for me as well. I was still too surprised at all of this to know what to say back to him.

"Yes, I am in the employ of the James brothers, if you want to know," Bill said after he handed me my coffee and had settled back into his place. He sipped from his tin cup a time or two before he went on. "And the Younger clan as well, though the latter only pays me for information because the Jameses tell them to. But what's it to you? What do you care?"

It felt like when your foot goes down a gopher hole when you ain't expecting it, like you never are. "Well, I don't, rightly, I suppose," I said. "Except that's why you give me my job, wasn't it? The Jameses said to—so's you could keep an eye on me to see if I was a Pinkerton man or not. That was it, wasn't it?"

He just looked at me some more.

"Well, that smarts some, I'll tell you. But I been fooled worse than that before." I ate stew a while, thinking things over. "What's this got to do with Sarah, anyways?"

Bill shook his head. "As well as you've pieced everything else together, I'm surprised you don't know already." He looked me over good again. "But you don't, do you?"

"Well, I ain't in the habit of asking to be told something I already know," I said. "Now are you going to tell me or do I ride over to Dogtown and ask *her*?"

He looked a little surprised that I was as hot about this as I was, and in a way, I was half surprised myself, too.

Even though I could of set my foot down into a dozen differnt kind of snares and springs that would of got me caught at this Pinkerton business, I still felt kind of tricked and took advantage of by Bill holding out on me about the Jameses, like he done. Even though I would of done the same if it was me, can you believe it?

Stranger still, any way you sliced it, I was being at least as crooked with him as he'd been with me, for I kept quiet about working for the Pinkertons even after he had come out and told me he worked for the Jameses—even though he didn't come *right* out and say so. *Still*, what he'd did, seeming to be my friend while really keeping an eye on me for the Jameses, that stung like a fresh wasp sting.

"She's a *Cole*, Willie," he said. "Sarah's a Cole. Didn't she tell you?"

"Yeah, so? That's her name. So what?"

"So *what*!? I guess you don't know who the Coles are around here, do you?"

I thought it over a minute. "No, I guess I don't. Who are they, then?"

Bill nodded. "I suppose the most important thing to know is that Jesse James' mother was a Cole before she married Mr. James."

"I'll be dogged," I said. "You mean I went and got myself mixed up with a gal from Jesse James' mamma's clan?"

Blackfoot Bill smiled. "Which means Jesse James' clan too when you come right down to it," he said, sort of correcting me. "You white people are every bit as clannish as the Indians, only you won't admit it." He stirred up the fire. "The rest of it is that the Coles and the Youngers are kinfolk of some sort too—through Mrs. James' side—Mrs. Samuel her name is now. They were Kentucky people before they came here, and Virginia before that, most likely, the old ones. That's why they sided with the Confederacy. The James boys and the Younger boys call each other cousin, though it's a little more distant than that. You knew that the oldest of the Younger brothers—that his first name's Cole, didn't you?"

"Uh-oh," I said.

Bill laughed at me. "Yeah, but it still wouldn't matter all that much if Sarah wasn't so set on your taking her to the wedding."

I heard him wrong there for a second and it tripped me up and threw me off. I thought he was saying somebody thought I ought to *marry* Sarah, though we hadn't so much as—and then it struck me he said *taking* her to a wedding, meaning somebody *elses's* wedding. "Who's getting married?"

Bill laughed again and shook his head. "I don't see how they ever figured you for a Pinkerton, Willie. You're probably the only man in Missouri who doesn't know that Mr. Jesse James is going to marry his cousin Zerelda Mimms in a few weeks. A cousin on his mother's side, by the way, a good looking young woman with the same first name as Jesse's mother—probably named for her aunt, come to think of it."

I listened to the wind in the trees for a minute. "So that was Jesse James over there in Gladstone, the straight one with the short brown beard and the real blue eyes," I said.

Bill nodded. "The same."

"And that was his cousin, the lady he's going to marry, the pretty one with the light hair—standing over there with him?"

He nodded again.

"And Sarah's good friends with the both of them, I suppose. And she told the lady Jesse James is going to marry that I was supposed to take her to their wedding. That just sounds like her."

Again Bill nodded. "Friendlier with Zee than with Jesse, I'm sure, but fundamentally that's how it is."

I shook my head. "They cut it pretty thin with all this cousin marrying cousin business, don't they? Isn't that how idiots get born?" I asked him.

He smiled. "Not if the blood's strong and healthy to begin with. Inbreeding is how the Europeans have been improving their stock for nearly a thousand years—as well as establishing some rather exotic diseases among their royalty. Come to think of it, inbreeding might account for a certain propensity for viciousness becoming the dominant genetic trait of this particular backwoods Missouri strain."

"Come again?" I asked him.

"It doesn't matter," Bill said, waving it away. "What does matter is that you're invited to the wedding. Jesse himself told me to invite you. And if you know what's good for you, you'll go."

I thought it over for a minute. "Well, it don't seem like I could miss it, then, could I?"

A day or so later I got a note from Sarah, Bill give it to me. She said as how she'd take it as a kindness if I'd accompany her to her cousin Zee's wedding, that it wasn't just right she should ask me but since I couldn't ask her, because only family and special friends was invited, she hoped I wouldn't think it too unladylike that the invite come from her. Usually she wouldn't be so bold, she said in this note, and I should forgive her if I could, but even if I couldn't she still hoped I'd take her, because there was nobody else she'd rather go with, but then she shouldn't say that to me neither, and she hoped I wouldn't think her unladylike for doing so.

My word, all the work and bother of this *ladylike* business. It seemed even worse than having to show everyone you were a *man* all the time. You'd think there'd be an easier way, wouldn't you?. And all this being real ladylike, mind you, after *she* had been the one to bring up how sleeping with someone gets to be pleasurable, and also after she had so much as said I was to go over to the country fair in Dogtown and dance with her, and then she was the one who'd kissed *me* in that Quaker church over there, don't forget.

Anyway, I wrote her a note back saying I would go. And while I had my pencil out and a spare sheet of paper laying in front of me, I decided I would write my ma a letter too.

>April 1874
>
>Dear Mother,
>
>I take my pen in hand, even if it's only a pencil, to let you know I am well and hope you are the same. The work here is going fine, just like you said it would go. I am getting on well and have even found a second job, so please take the money I send here in good conscience, for I can surely spare it.
>
>And do not worry about me drinking too much again either. I did have a little spell of that a few weeks ago, but am over it now. I have met a nice ladylike woman here, though we are not serious or nothing. We are to go to a good Christian wedding of some important folks she is related to next week, so you can rest easy that she's a nice gal, not another of them whores you're always afraid I'll marry some day.
>
>Love from
>Your son,
>
>Willie

Come the day of the wedding, the 24th of April I believe it was, a Friday, Bill and me had a lazy morning around camp, for the big doings wasn't till afternoon. Toward midday I put on the new suit I had bought special in Kansas City, blackened my boots, and brushed my hair, my chin whiskers and then my hat—in that order. I thought of that other new suit I had give that door-holding fellow in Chicago, and I wished I had that one back again, for it was more comfortable than the one I wore out to the farm of Zee Mimms's sister, a Mrs. Browder who lived a ways out from Kearney with her husband and children—I don't think I ever did hear what her first name was.

Bill had stripped the painted tarp off our wagon, lifted the stakes out and tied the tarp upside down over all our trap in order to make the rig look more presentable than the Heap-Big Traveling Medicine Show usually looks— like a big sore blue thumb going somewhere to fester.

Along the way, there was men sitting their horses, their rifles out and laid across the saddle horn, eyeing everone going by. Lookouts, Bill said. Riding out there to the farm beside Bill, it struck me as odd that I had come to Missouri to trail Jesse James, to help catch him for the Pinkertons, and here I was all dressed up and going to his wedding in the company of a half-breed instead. Somehow, it didn't seem right.

I don't know why Bill wasn't content just to ride the horses out there, that's what I wanted to do, but he said it was more proper to go to a wedding in a wagon—I don't know where he ever got his ideas on such things. As bad as they treated him out there, he was about as welcome as a striped snake in Sunday school, it's a wonder he would want to go at all, let alone worry over what folks thought was proper and what wasn't. If it was me and they treated me like that, I'd of left half an hour before I got there.

But people treated *me* nice, though. I guess that was because nearly everbody knowed I was with Sarah and everbody who didn't learned it shortly after I got there, I suspect. That and not being an Indian, of course.

Sarah was standing where the farm lane come up upon the large stone and white frame house, under the tallest willow tree I ever saw, a little bouquet of posies in her hand, lilacs if I remember right. I saw her at a distance before she saw me, there was some buggies and traps in the lane ahead of us taking their time, and she was looking everone over and waiting for me.

I don't know why it feels so good to remember her the way she looked that day, standing there pretty as a patch of spring sunshine in her pale yeller dress and bonnet, and looking over everone coming to the wedding to see if they was me or not. I thought at the time maybe she needed spectacles—either that or it was my suit that throwed her off so long.

"Willie!" she called when finally she reconized me, waving her lilac flowers back and forth over her head. "Willie, over here!" As if I could have missed *her*.

I jumped down and left Bill to take the horse and wagon back behind the barn.

Sarah give me a big hug right there in front of God and everone. "Why, don't *you* look mighty handsome today, Mr. Goodwin, in your new suit and all?" she said, smiling to beat anything.

She put her arm in mine and we walked over to where folks was dipping pink drinks out of a big crystal bowl with a crystal ladle and drinking them out of little crystal cups. All laid out together on a table set up on the grass under some trees. I swear it was the same punch I had drunk over in Dogtown, but somebody had put some liquor in it this time. And I was right, it *did* make it a whole lot better.

Sarah pointed out who the folks was—Mrs. Samuel, a stern looking lady, Jesse James momma, and her husband Dr. Reuben Samuel, who looked a little feebleminded to me. They was up on the porch on a swing. Sarah explained the Doctor was that way from what some Yankee soldiers did to him during the war, hanging him by the neck till he passed out, letting him down and throwing water on him, and then stringing him up again when he come to. He was never quite right after that, Sarah said, and it wasn't even his own boy he wouldn't tell them where he was—but his wife's boy by her first marriage, Frank James, his stepson. As cross as Jesse's mamma looked, something terrible like that must of happened to her, too.

That friend of Sarah's from the Dogtown dance, that white-haired young gal, she was there in a deep blue dress and bonnet to match, looking awful pretty. But she was acting sulky and didn't seem to have nothing to say to nobody, including me. Frank James was standing over under another tree, leaning against the trunk, drinking punch and talking to a gal Sarah thought was too young for him, so she didn't want to interduce me, not that I was all that eager for her to. Some of the Younger boys was there too, but not all of them, Sarah said, and it looked like they didn't take no pains to slick themselves up much. One person there I did know already, and I was surprised to see him—the sheriff of Kearney, Sam Gilpin, and there was even a reward out on both the James boys at the time! And there stood old Sam sucking up Jesse's wedding punch with the rest of us.

Matter-of-fact, there was more punch drinking going on around there than anything else for quite a while, though nobody actually got what you might call falling down drunk. Blackfoot Bill come over and I interduced him to Sarah. I was surprised at how quiet and tight-lipped he was out there, compared to how he always had something to say and make fun about at the medicine show and back in camp. Or make one of his college educated statements about things you couldn't tell what the hell it meant. But it was like he was a differnt person that day, half shy and awkward as anything.

Sarah, she was real nice to him, though, asking him questions he could easy drag out the answer to. A lot nicer than those women under the willow tree I saw turn away earlier so they wouldn't have to talk to him when he walked by. After a while Sarah went off to see what was holding up the wedding, and Bill and me went out to the barn, where the more serious drinkers was sharing a jug.

Among just the men, who were joking and telling lies, Bill seemed a little more at ease—and them with him, too. We got in the circle the jug was making, and a couple of good pulls put us both in a more celebrating frame of mind.

After a while I went back over to the house, and Sarah said the wedding was being held up because Jesse was late. Sheriff Gilpin was standing nearby and said that it was only natural that Jesse should hold up his wedding, for, hell, he had held up nearly every other damn thing in the country, including trains and even a county fair, so he might as well hold up a wedding too.

Nobody but him laughed, though, and Jesse's momma kept glaring at him after he said that. Her eyes was like those of a big hawk I had once watched catch a snake and start to eat it while it was still squirming. A minute later Gilpin headed out toward the barn.

A man Sarah said was Dr. Doolin, or something like that, stood up on the seat of a chair and called for everbody to listen to him. "The bridegroom, Mr. James, has been somewhat delayed, unfortunately, but will be here as soon as he can. Rather than take our supper after the wedding, as had been planned, Mrs. Browder suggests that the company have our repast now, since it is ready, and, if you are at all like me, we're ready enough for it, too! So if you would just go back to the tables set up outside the kitchen . . ."

So that's what we done, stood in line with the other folks there and then they gave us cold-sliced ham and hot fried chicken, beans, greens, mashed potatoes, fried okra, biscuits, red-eye gravy, applesauce, butter, pickles, fresh bread, biscuits, and all the fixings. Lemonade for those that wanted it. There was a few other tables set up, but not enough for everone to sit down together, so Sarah and me went out alone under a rose arbor in the backyard with a white-painted wood bench underneath, holding our plates on our laps.

She told me some more of who everyone was and how she was related to them, if she was. And what the men did for a living, except if they was Youngers or rode with the Youngers or the James, or so I suspected. Them she just said who they was and maybe where they was from.

"How come you didn't say what your cousin Bob Younger does for a living?" I asked when she stopped explaining.

She shot me a quick little look. "Well, I figured you

knew already," she said, somewhere between sheepish and peeved.

"Sort of the way you figgered I'd know what it meant, I suppose, when you said about you being a Cole and all?"

She had made a little sandwich of her ham slice and biscuit, and she took a bite of that and chewed it a good while before answering, glancing up at the climbing rose bushes that was leafed out but not in bud yet and then looking down at the grass at her feet. "Everyone around here knows the Coles and the Jameses and the Youngers," she said, putting her tiny sandwich with one little bite taken out back on her plate and keeping her gaze on the grass in front of her.

"Yeah, only I ain't from around here, and I believe you know that," I said.

"I know," she said. "Only it *seemed* like maybe you knew about the Coles, or maybe I just wanted to think you did and it would be all right, I don't know. That maybe it wouldn't matter to you."

"Only I *didn't* know, and it might have got me shot being friendly with you, because some folks around here believed for a while that I was another one of those Pinkerton men, like them that got theirselves killed a short while ago. Maybe thinking I was trying to get in good with you to get at the Jameses."

She had started giggling before I'd even stopped talking. "Isn't that funny?" she said, laughing at the same time. "Folks thinking you were one of those damn Yankee Pinkertons?! Why, even cousin Jesse thought so for a while."

I almost told her right there. I know I *wanted* to tell her, it didn't seem fair not to. Maybe if I had *felt* more like a Pinkerton I would have, but the truth was, it didn't seem like I was a Pinkerton even to myself.

"But I understand," she said. "And I won't pester you to take me anywhere after this. You won't have to see me any more at-tall after today if you don't want to."

"Well, I didn't mean *that*," I said, kind of surprised she had mistook what I said. "And your being a Cole don't really *matter*, don't enter into the way I feel about you, Sarah."

It was her turn to show surprise then. "It doesn't?" she asked.

"No, not at all," I told her.

She scratched at the grass with the toe of her pretty little white shoe. "Well, how *do* you feel about me, Mr. Willie Goodwin?" she asked, looking up at me sudden with her green eyes flashing, a hint of a smile curling up the corners of her pretty little mouth.

I didn't know what to say. "Well, mostly—right now, that is—I feel like I wish you wouldn't get me into no more spots where I might get shot," I told her. "And I feel like it wouldn't be exactly ladylike of you to push me into saying just how I feel towards you at this particalar minute, because, well, just because it wouldn't." I knew that wasn't much of an answer, but it was all the answer I could muster up that minute. I think she read the look on my face more than anything.

She laughed, my word did she ever laugh. "Oh all right! All right!" she said through her laughing. "I guess I understand anyway," she said. She leaned over and give me a quick peck on the cheek, then blushed for all she was worth. My, it's so pretty when a woman blushes like that.

10

THIS GROUNDED WEDDING

Sarah and me had finished our "repast," as Dr. Whatsisname had called it, and was walking our plates back to the tables by the kitchen. I was asking her about there not being no berry pie and she was saying as how we'd likely get some wedding cake later on.

All of a sudden two horses come busting out of the trees behind us all hell-bent-for-leather at full gallop, both riders skidding them to a stop as soon as they hit the slippery short grass of the yard. They both swung out of their saddles together before you could turn around twice. Looked almost like they'd practiced it.

The younger one grabbed the reins of both horses and just stood there holding them like a statue. The other one right away begun walking straight, tall, and not hurrying at all though the crowd of people—toward the house, saying hello to everone as he went along. He took time for a word or two to a bent-over old man about the age his great grandpa would of been, but I couldn't make out what was said. His brown hair I remembered from over in Dogtown, but he had shaved off his short brown beard and mustache. About thirty years old, I judged. Of course it was Jesse James.

When he was going by us he nodded and smiled at Sarah.

"Why, good evening, Cousin Jesse," Sarah said, kind of teasing. "Fancy meetin' you here!" He nodded and smiled some more, till a quick dark cloud come over his face and he turned his head sudden and laid them eyes on me.

If you'd ever saw Jesse James' eyes you'd remember the look of them till the day you died. They was just a icy kind of blue, nothing special about the color, a little darker toward the center than around the edge, maybe, but lots of folks have eyes like that. No, what you noticed about Jesse James' eyes was how *clear* they were. That rounded, glassy part covering the blue looked a good inch thick, but of course it couldn't have been. That—and how big and dark the pupils was. Deep as a pair of wells at midnight on a moonless night. It was like he could see things other folks couldn't. Like he *knowed* things, just by looking, that other men would never see, and if they did, never figger out.

What he was staring at with them awful eyes just then was me. "And this is Mr. . . . " he said, speaking to Sarah, but still looking at me.

"Goodwin," Sarah said, almost whispering. "Willie Goodwin."

"Goodwin . . . " Jesse James repeated, but then didn't say another word after that or offer to shake my hand, didn't even nod, just looked. Then he turned slow and walked on, the smile gone from his face. Right then I remembered his mamma's hawkish eyes when she was glaring at Sheriff Patton.

With the rest of the crowd, Sarah and me followed Jesse James around to the front of the house and up to the steps. When he went on up, a young woman come out of the house and onto the veranda to meet him, a young woman who looked something like Sarah only younger, lighter of hair and a little fairer of skin, and dressed in her white wedding dress and veil—her eyes filled with love of the man standing before her there, meeting him just before he got to the top of the stairs.

He took her hand and kissed it right there in front of everbody, everbody hushing up. Except three young gals down in front of us who pretty much sighed all together, you could hear them plain, and folks chuckled a little at that, but sort of quiet and respectful, I guess you would say, like they had almost done the same theirselves.

"Zerelda, come back in here!" some deep-voice man called from inside the house, plenty loud enough to be heard all the way to the back of the crowd and maybe even out to the barn. "Come back in, I say!"

Well, everbody was soon buzzing over this! Sarah whispered as how it might be because Zerelda was supposed to greet her husband for the first time today at the altar and not before then, but it sounded a whole lot more serious than that to me. An older man in a black suit stepped out and took the young lady's arm and Jesse went on up. I couldn't hear just what he said to the older man, it come out in such a raspy snarl. All I caught was the "By God!" Jesse James tacked onto the end of whatever else he said. I *did* see the face of the older gent go pale, though, since he was facing me. He cringed backward toward the door after Jesse spoke, more or less pulling the bride along with him, who looked for help from Jesse. The older gent appeared like he'd had the steam pretty much let right out of him, his face froze like he'd saw a ghost after hearing whatever it was that Jesse James had said to him.

"Frank!" Jesse's mamma called, standing up sudden from where she was sitting on the swing. In a second Frank James sprung up on the veranda and got Jesse and the bride and the older gent all inside, and then turned back and spoke to us. "Just a little delay, folks, that's all. Just a little misunderstanding, I assure you. Please have some more punch, or the gentlemen may want to retire to the barn for a while." He took off his hat and put it over his heart, and then looked from face to face before he spoke again. "There are bound to be a few rough spots in even the best regulated families, you know," he said with a smile, meaning it for a joke people saw after a second. "Shoo, now!" he said, waving us away with his hat, "Shoo!

While I repair the rent in this bouquet,
And get this grounded wedding underway!"

And that's what folks did, sort of drifted away from the house, at least from right there in front, so that the family could plug up the holes, patch things up and put them back together—if they could.

Now, I didn't know nothing of what was going on inside at the time. I just went and had another glass of punch with Sarah and then went and had another couple of pulls from the jug after some woman come and took Sarah inside. But from what she told me later, I was able to piece most of it together.

The older gent, he was the uncle of both Jesse and his bride, Zerelda Mimms. His name was William James, and he was the Methodist minister that was supposed to marry the pair! Only after he got there, he kept hearing more and more about what Jesse was supposed to have did—the price on his head and all.

Well, *Reverend* James, he decided his niece Zerelda hadn't ought to marry his outlaw nephew Jesse, and he decided he *wouldn't* marry them, no matter what. Maybe he also found out Jesse really wanted the minister at the *Baptist* church in Kearney to marry them, but that preacher had read Jesse out of the church some weeks before, maybe that had something to do with it too. I ain't sure. All this before Jesse got there, mind you.

After that business on the veranda, Sarah told me, the bride kept after Uncle William about how bad the newspapers had it out for Jesse, that he didn't do even half the things they'd printed about him, and she could prove it. That's why Sarah was needed.

Sarah had some of the worst of them lying articles

clipped out of differnt papers from all across the state of Missouri and even from across the country. Collecting differnt articles about her famous cousin was something of a hobby with her. Had them all in a big green velvet scrapbook, I saw them later. Sarah'd showed her cousin Zerelda some of those articles that very morning, just as a kind of a curiosity, you might say.

Sarah said that after Uncle William saw some of them articles saying Jesse was one place and other articles saying Jesse was somewheres else—on the same day and hundreds of miles apart—he changed his mind and guessed he would marry them after all. But the way I see it, the look on Jesse's face, and whatever it was he'd said to the Reverend there, that may of had just a little bit to do with it too.

All of this took a long time to straighten out, you understand. Things almost always take longer than you think they should. It started getting dark and some of the men was getting flat-out drunk, some of them Younger boys especially. They started making the kinds of dirty remarks that always goes along with weddings, I suppose, though not always so loud and most often they put that stuff off till after the bride and groom leaves. While we was all waiting to see what would happen next, there was a fist-fight broke out between a Younger and the gentlemen friend of some gal the Younger fellow wanted to smooch with, but that was the only one. Nobody got shot or cut up, and there was very little eye-gouging to speak of, so it was just a mostly good-natured fistfight sprung up from high spirits and alcohol spirits.

It wasn't till after eight o'clock that Frank James called out that everthing was finally set up for the wedding, and *this* for a hitching that was supposed to start a little after noon. It was decided to hold it inside the house, it being too dark for it to be outside by this point. So I didn't exactly get to see the couple joined together as man and wife. I heard it all, though, for I had a good seat on the veranda. Matter-of-fact, on the very place on the swing where Jesse's mamma had sat before, for she was one of the ones who was allowed inside then, she being who she was and all.

Sarah was inside too, but I didn't mind. It was nice outside, a little breeze blowing after a warm spring day, everthing smelling of cut grass and flowers both from all the bouquets that was being carried and the flowers and bushes and trees that was planted and blooming all around that handsome farm. A mock orange somewhere, my gramma's favorite. Yes, and horse shit too, you never get completely away from the smell of that on a farm. It don't smell near as bad as most folks let on, though, especially if it has had the chance to rot some. And it *does* make the flowers smell sweet later on. You have to say that for it.

Anyway, halfway through the wedding ceremony a night bird off somewheres started doing his lonesome call. And I'll take that over parlor organ hymns any time.

Reverend James' deep, rumbly voice was easy to hear, even if you did have to strain a little to catch Jesse and Zerelda saying their "I do's."

But say them they did, finally, and soon people was wishing them well going down the front steps, a lot of lanterns lit, and all the men shaking Jesse's hand, though I didn't. I didn't wish him no harm, you understand, but it didn't seem entirely right going up and shaking his hand, either. After all, the Pinkertons was still paying me to try and catch him, you recall. Didn't seem seemly. That's a word Bill taught me, *seemly*.

The couple left a short while later in a fancy open phaeton someone had loaned them. Everone was yelling "Good-bye, good-bye!" to them as their carriage flew down the stony lane in the light of a nearly full moon, the steel rims striking sparks from time to time.

"I hear they're going to Texas for their honeymoon," I said to Sarah while we watched them leave from down in the yard. Right away I wished I hadn't of said that, for it was spying on my part that made me say it, I know it was. I knowed it even then. I didn't really hear no such thing as them going to Texas.

"No, silly," Sarah said. "They only spread rumors like that so they can be alone for a time, with no one trying to find Jesse where they're *really* going, which is down to Uncle Albert's log cabin there close to the Elk River, all the way down in the southwest corner of the state. Way off in the woods."

I saw right away how important a thing she had told me while we was standing there in the moonlight, me holding her pretty little hand. Everone else was going back for more punch or getting ready to go home, or off somewheres else by then. Yes, I had said that about Texas apurpose so she might tell me where Jesse was going if she knowed it, but I never for the life of me figgered she really would.

"You're off all by yourself on a honeymoon, ain't you?" I asked her. "Specially if you're going off in the woods in a log cabin."

In the light of the lamp she was holding I could see her blush a little. I was just kind of thinking out loud, not remembering that she must of went on a honeymoon once upon a time herself, and I was not trying to remind her she knew what the real business of honeymoons was, neither, even though that's how it must of sounded. After a minute I figgered out she wasn't going to answer me. Maybe she thought it wouldn't be ladylike to. Not *seemly*.

"Well, what do I know?" I asked her. "I've never been on no honeymoon," I said. It was a lame thing to say, sure it was, but it was the best I could come up with right then.

"But maybe you will some time," she said, looking up at me, not bashful at all now.

I put my arm around her and we started up to the house. "Maybe I will some time," I repeated, for want of something better to say. "Maybe I will at that."

I don't know what ever possessed me to say that.

* * *

106 / CHARLES HACKENBERRY

The next morning Bill wasn't around, and I went in to the telegraph office. I wasn't sure if I was going to send one to William Pinkerton or not, saying where Mr. Jesse James was spending his honeymoon. But if I decided I *was* going to send one, I'd be in the right place to do it. You might think that because I went in there I'd made up my mind for sure, but that wasn't the way it was. It was just like I said.

"Mr. Baldwin!" the young fellow behind the counter said as soon as I walked in, the same one as before with the slicked-down hair, surprising me because he remembered my name. "I've been trying to reach you. I have two telegrams for you." He fussed around in a pigeonhole affair he had there and then handed them to me.

"How'd you remember me?" I asked him. "With all the folks that come in here to get telegrams and this is only my second or third time?"

He grinned pretty big. "Oh, that jumbled one," he said. "We always have to check those two or three times, the one from Lawyer Hardwicke over in Liberty? The one in code? We have to keep a list of who gets those, write down the names and everything."

To tell you the truth, I wasn't that surprised. Neither of the ones he gave me this time was in that mush of letters and numbers like before, though. This is what the first one said:

Mr. Baldwin

You are hereby appraised that I will be in Kansas City within the week. It is very important that I talk to you concerning your principal customer there in Missouri as soon as I arrive. Telegraph me immediately confirming these arrangements.

WP

And this was the second one, dated two weeks later.

I RODE WITH JESSE JAMES / 107

Mr. Baldwin

Your refusal to answer my telegrams violates our agreement concerning communication. I have not yet heard anything from you concerning your principal customer or our meeting concerning same. You must come to my new Kansas City office on 41 Locke Street by noon on the 27th of April, or I will have to assume you are no longer connected with the company and will inform Mr. Vinton of your town of same.

WP

"Think you'll lose your job," the young fellow asked, looking worried some over me, while I was standing there reading it a second time.

I shook my head. "I don't know," I told him. "I don't know."

That was Saturday, the day after the wedding, which would make it the 25th of April. The 27th was Monday.

11

DAMN YOU, WILLIE GOODWIN!

"But why the hell didn't you answer my telegrams!" William Pinkerton yelled, jumping up from his chair behind the desk and poking a hole in his cigar smoke with his finger.

I put out the fat cigar he had gave me in the ashtray on his desk, taking my time before I answered, waiting for him to calm down some. "Because I was afraid it would get back to Jesse James who I was if I'd a done that, like I told you, and it would have, too. You got no idea how people look out for him over there in Clay County—lawmen on the take, others paid to act as spies and such."

"Horseshit!" Pinkerton yelled.

I took some more time. "Well, that's about what I'm getting in here, all right. If you don't want to hear what happened and find out what I know, I'll just leave now. After you pay me what you owe me for my time, that is. I haven't had no pay from you folks since I left Chicago, you might recall."

"And not likely you'll get any, either, since you haven't been in *contact* with us since Chicago!" Pinkerton yelled. That man *was* fond of rattling the windowpanes.

"Suit yourself, then," I told him quiet and peaceable, getting up and going toward his door. "If you don't want to know what I found out at his wedding, then that's—"

"Wedding?" William Pinkerton said. "We'd heard that he was planning on getting married, but—you were *there*!"

"Yes I was," I told him. "Day before yesterday. Shame you wasn't. The punch was *real* good." I went out his office door, closed it quiet after me, and walked toward the front door with him yelling his head off in his office all the while behind me. I'd a been surprised if he hadn't of followed, but I was ready to just keep going if he didn't, that man could anger me so. I saw him come into the outer room just as I was closing the outside door.

"Hold on there, Goodwin!"

But I didn't. I closed the outside door the rest of the way, went down the stairs, and started walking up the street. The hell with him, I said to myself. I got about two dozen steps.

A man named Tom Farnum grabbed my left arm and a big fellow with a beefy face took my right while Pinkerton got around in front. "Now look here, Goodwin. You're being too hasty about this."

"Me? You're the one just jumped up and said you wasn't going to pay me for the work I already done." I yanked my arm away from Tom, but the other one grabbed on even tighter. I looked him mean in the face, and he looked at Pinkerton, who nodded at him. The two fellows let go and then left us alone there on the brick sidewalk when they walked back down the street.

Pinkerton stood up close and spoke low. "This might be very important information you've collected, Willie," he said. "How in the world did you ever get yourself invited to his wedding?" He glanced up and down the street to see if anybody was listening to us, I guess, and then back at me. He'd changed a lot in five minutes, from the dark-faced look he'd gave me in his office to wanting something from me now.

I didn't rightly know how to answer him at first. "Well, how I got in on that wedding's going to have to be my secret. I have ways of doing things you have no idea of. And I don't want them spread around." Which was *sort* of true, being invited by Sarah Cole and all, but I let him take it howsomever he pleased.

"He married a cousin of his, on his mother's side, didn't he?" Pinkerton asked, getting so close I could smell the stale coffee on his breath.

I put a hand on his chest and pushed him back. "I'm not saying nothing till I'm paid for my time. And I want an extra two hundred dollars, too. It was more dangerous work than you let on." I don't know where that idea ever come from, about the extra two hundred dollars. It just flew in there. I didn't have no need of extra money. Hell, I was living rich as a hog on just what I was getting from Bill.

He looked mad for a minute, but then a slow smile spread over his face. "Damn you, Willie Goodwin, you do know how to work this system, don't you?" How a man could admire you for being good at blackmailing him was more than I could reason out.

We went back down the street, into the building, and back into his office—where he called in a fellow who paid me in full for my time and then gave me that extra two hundred just like I had asked for, no questions asked. It come to more money than I ever had my hands on before—all at one time, that is. Pinkerton *did* ask me a hundred or more questions about the Jameses, or so it seemed, and I answered best as I could, except for two of them.

"I told you outside I don't want to say nothing about how I got invited to the wedding, and I don't," I told him. "It won't help you catch him, however it was I done it." Looking back, I'm kind of surprised he sat still for me talking to him like that, but then I *did* have the goods and he was itching to buy them.

"Where is he *now*?" Pinkerton asked at last, like I knew he would and was wishing he wouldn't. That was the second thing I didn't want to say nothing about. "That's the important question. Where did he go on his honeymoon?"

I shook my head, not knowing what to do or what to say. Then I remembered a thing that Lawyer Hardwicke had said to me. "Well, I'm working on it, but right now I'm not prepared to say."

He blinked at me a couple of times, and put me in mind of Sarah when I had told her about the Heap-Big being a good soporific.

"Well, all right, but you telegraph me *every day* until you find out, you hear me?"

I said I did hear him, plain enough, and I would telegraph him oftener than before, as often as I could. But it wasn't going to be no every damn day, it wasn't. And we made different arrangements about our telegrams, the new place where I'd get mine from him, who I'd be and how he'd sign his, mostly.

I walked out of there, down the street about fifteen rods till I come to a bank, where I went in, opened me an account, and put in most of the money WP had just gave me. It didn't feel safe carrying all that around, especially in a big place like Kansas City. I had a couple of ryes in a quiet bar there in town and then went and caught the train.

On the way back out to Kearney I worried some about whether I was doing the right thing or not, trying to see how my ma would see it. It didn't seem right using what Sarah had told me, only because she trusted me, to nail her cousin Jesse James down there where he was learning the pleasures of married life, maybe even while I was sitting there looking out the coach window watching the countryside go by, I thought to myself. Besides, Sarah'd never talk to me again if I did that.

On the other hand, it didn't seem entirely right, either, that I should be working for the Pinkertons and not do what they had already paid me to do—with a good-sized stack of Yankee greenbacks. I got off in Kearney still not knowing what I was going to do next.

* * *

The next evening, though, I went over to Dogtown. I wasn't sure just where Sarah lived, I knowed it was with her folks, so I had to stop and ask for directions, which I hate to do. But finally, a little before sundown, I found it.

A big old farm almost the twin of the one where Jesse James' wedding was a few days before, only this one looked like they kept more dairy cows than the other place.

I tied my horse at the iron ring pinned into a big upright stone under a tall shade maple. By the side of the road stood a slate watering trough for my horse—seemed a friendly thing, water trickling out of a pipe and tumbling into it. I had a drink myself out of a dipper hanging there. Nice cool, sweet water. Up at the house you could hear someone playing a piano, a song I'd heard before but couldn't remember the name of. I hoped it was Sarah playing, that would be nice if she could play.

I was surprised no dogs come to sniff at me and bark out a warning, but they didn't.

Through the window I saw a young sandy-haired fellow sitting at a piano. While I was going up to knock on the door, he finished his song, laughed a good one and held up a wine glass, talking to someone else in the room, making a joke it sounded like. I wondered who he was, Sarah didn't say nothing about having a brother or anything.

An old Negro woman with her head tied up in a bandanna answered my knock and looked at me pretty suspicious through her screen door, even after I had told her my name and who I wanted.

"Did she know you was comin?" she asked, eyeing me a little sideways.

"No, she didn't, but she knows me all right," I told her. "I ain't no salesman, if that's what you're thinking. Well, I guess I *am* a salesman, you could say, but—"

A boy about ten looked around her shoulder and give me the once-over. "I'll go get her," he said and then went as quick as he'd come.

The Negro lady shook her head and walked away slow, shuffling her feet. She left the door open a crack, and I just stood there. Whatever they'd had for supper smelled awful good, goose or maybe a guinea hen. I had forgot to eat any supper.

"Why, Willie Goodwin!" Sarah said from inside as soon as she saw me, and then come out on the porch and closed the door behind her. "What on earth are you doin' here?" She smiled at me, sweet as milk pie, but there was something else in her face too, only I couldn't quite see what it was. I was surprised she was as dressed up as she was, but maybe that was how she always dressed at home, I didn't know.

"Sarah, I have got to talk to you, because—" I had took both her hands and was standing close to her by then. That's when I seen what looked like worry on her face. "What's wrong?" I asked her.

"Nothing, I declare!" she said, brightening up some, but you could see there was. We stood there a minute, neither of us saying nothing.

Finally, I decided I would just go ahead and tell her what it was I had come to tell her. Maybe she was just surprised to see me was all. "Sarah, I have got to—"

"Sarah?" a man's voice called from inside, "Your dessert's . . ." That tall, good-looking younger fellow in a long striped coat stepped though the doorway and out onto the porch with us, the fellow who was playing the piano before. "What's the matter?" He looked at me and then at Sarah and then back at me again, with none too friendly a look on his face, I'll tell you. Like he might just have to take care of me.

"This is Willie Goodwin," Sarah said. "The man I was telling you about earlier," she said, her eyes on the porch floor.

Now I have seen smart-ass looks on fellows' faces before, lots of times, but if there's ever a contest for it, this fellow ought to get in on it, for he'd win the prize hands down. "Oh yes! The white medicine man! How do you do, Mr. Goldfine, how *do* you do?"

I did shake with him when he offered his hand. But it felt like a dead creek chub.

"This is my cousin Thomas, visiting from Nashville, Tennessee," Sarah said, looking like she wished she didn't have to do this. "We were just finishing dessert, Willie . . . "

"Oh, I'm sorry," I said. "Most folks . . . but that's fine, I'll—"

"Won't you come in and join us for coffee?" she said. "You could meet mamma and daddy now. I've had time to—"

"No, I'll just come back another time," I said.

Cousin Thomas clapped me on the shoulder. "Yes, you do that, Mr. Goldfine!" he said, starting back inside.

You could tell he'd messed it up apurpose, just the way he said it. "The name's Goodwin, sir. Not Goodfart or Goldfine or Gold-anything."

"Willie!" Sarah said before I could say more.

He looked surprised I'd called him on it. "Of course, of course! Sorry! Another time, Mr. . . . Willie!" He quick ducked back inside, the smirk back on his face again.

"Why, I'm ashamed of you!" Sarah said. "Cousin Thomas meant nothing by—"

"It sure as hell is thick as fleas with cousins up here in Missouri, ain't it?" I said, hating myself for it before the words was even out of my mouth.

Sarah looked like I'd slapped her. After a minute she said, "Why, whatever do you mean?"

"Why didn't you just get Cousin Thomas to take you to Jesse's wedding," I asked her. "Seems friendly enough. Seems like he would of enjoyed it, too, you two being kissing cousins and all."

"Because I wanted *you* to take me," she said, jutting her chin out towards me and putting a hand on her cocked-out hip. "It seemed like a good idea then, but I'm none too sure now!" Her green eyes flashed fire.

"Well, neither am I," I told her. "And if you ever get the idea to ask me anywheres again, Miss Cole, like you shouldn't ought to have done in the first place, let me tell you right now—the answer is no." I turned and went down the steps.

"Damn you, Willie Goodwin!" she called after me, the second time someone'd said that to me in as many days. Damn I was mad. I kept going down the yard.

"Willie!" she called while I was untying my horse. I half turned to sneak a look. She had both hands up to her face, tears streaming down. I almost went back, her crying like that. But then I thought of her liking that damn Cousin Thomas better than me, the smart-ass way he was.

"Willie!" she called again as I was going down the road, but I didn't look back that time.

The next morning I telegraphed William Pinkerton.

12

THE JOLLY BARGEMAN

29 April 1874

Mr. Greenbough

I have located our customer. Get together four good men and meet me at the railroad station in Anderson, down in McDonald County, about forty miles south of Joplin. Get there on the closest train to noon on Friday, May 1. Don't be late. Our customer will not stay there long, I don't believe. I will arrange for horses, but you must bring anything else you'll need to make the deal with our customer. Do like I say here and don't be too early neither.

Mr. Bradley

That was the telegram I sent William Pinkerton. I told Blackfoot Bill I couldn't do no shows for the next couple of days, he said that was all right. I left Kearney early that afternoon, Wednesday, going by train—down there to Anderson in the lower corner of the state, the bottom *left* corner, where that pig's foot would get to if it ever traveled the whole bottom width of Missouri. From there I figgered we'd travel by horse on down to that Elk River country, which had almost no people to speak of living around there, if the new telegraph man was right.

The train didn't pull into Anderson till late Wednesday night, there being some track repairs or something that made the ride even longer than normal, which would of been long enough anyway since that damn train stopped at every little burg along the way. What my pa would have called a milk run. It was too late to find a place to stay in Anderson, so I slept on a bench out on the platform, out in the open but under a sort of roof affair there at the station, with my trap piled up and my slicker throwed over me. My old revolver in its holster and rolled up in its belt for a pillow. Slept better than I expected to.

Come sunup I went and found a livery, the only one in town. The man there had only two saddle horses he could let me have for Friday, but he said if I was to come back at ten o'clock he could tell me then if he'd be able to round up a couple more. *Six* was what I needed, I told him, but he didn't know about getting all that many, he said, scratching his head under his hat. I said he would be well paid for them, he could charge more than regular, that would be all right. He said he would do the best he could, but couldn't promise nothing.

I went and ordered my breakfast in a cafe. While I was waiting for my food to be cooked, I used the basin and bucket around back to wash my face, wet and combed my hair. While I was at it I changed my shirt. After my eggs and sausage I had a drink at one of the better looking class of saloons on the main street with the early crowd—a hard-looking younger gal who was up all night, just like every night she said with half a laugh lighting her cigarito, and two old beer-sucking drunks who'd lived in that town all their lives and'd knowed each other ever since God had invented dirt, so they said. From the way they talked, it sounded like they spent more time in that saloon recalling the wild and wooly days around there than they did at their homes, supposing they had some.

Come ten o'clock I was back at the livery, and the man there said the best he could do for me was five horses for the next day and one mule, but it was a good riding mule, he had it there now if I wanted to see it. And yes, he had saddles and bits and everthing needed for the lot. I told him that would have to do, then, and I'd take the mule and try him out today. I paid him for everthing for four days, starting right then, just so's he wouldn't let nobody else have them before tomorrow. It cost a piece of change so I had him write me out a receipt so Pinkerton would pay me back later.

I saddled the mule myself, Buster his name was, one of them tall rusty black ones, more to get to know him than anything else, a sorrier-looking saddle on a young mule you never did see. I put my gear in an old pair of canvas saddlebags the livery man let me use for a quarter, slung them up behind, damn he was a long-legged mule, and headed toward where the Elk River curls around down there. Anyone looking at me up on Buster and thinking Pinkerton would of been out of his mind.

At the tavern where the road crossed the river, the Jolly Bargeman I think it was called, I was working on my second rye when I asked the barman the way to a Mr. Cole's cabin somewhere around there and the place got quiet. I quick made up a story.

"The reason I want to find it is, a couple years ago Mr. Cole lent me ten dollars when I really needed it one time," I said. I didn't mention what it was I needed the money for, just didn't say nothing a while and let whoever was listening besides the barman make up his own reasons why I probly needed that ten dollars. People will do that if you let them. "He said if I was ever up by Kansas City or down this way I could pay him back, but a course he never expected it back, you could tell it. He's a fine man, is Mr. Cole," I said.

The barman nodded a little, still suspicious, though,

but the man next to me wearing a wore-out straw hat nodded a good one. "Yes he is," he sort of mumbled to himself. People like to think the worst of their neighbors, what they do in private and all, but they also like to hear them praised to high heaven, too, especially by strangers. I never did figger out why they like both, thinking the worst and hearing the best, since the two *do* sort of conterdict each other. Just the way people are, I guess.

Anyway, that was the story I told.

"Well, I have thought of how nice that fellow was to me a hundred times," I said, slapping the bar with the flat of my hand. "And I said to myself if I ever got a little ahead I'd come down here apurpose and pay him back. Well, my grampappy died the other month, left me a little money. Not a whole lot, y'understand, and here I am. But I need someone to tell me where his place is, Mr. Cole's, if you gentlemen don't know." I looked around the room, pretending I was looking for someone who might know, but I suspected all the time these gents knowed, all right.

The barman rubbed his chin and still wasn't certain about me, but the other fellow was took in. "Why, that's the old Musser cabin, isn't it George? The one that fellow Cole bought?" he asked the man behind the bar, who nodded just the least little bit and then frowned at him.

"Well, you go out this way about three mile," the fellow wearing the worn-out straw hat begun, pointing south by east, and told me what to look for, which way to turn when I saw this, that, and the other. Of course he finished up by saying, "You can't miss it," though I had proved dozens of folks wrong who'd said that to me before.

The man behind the bar nodded right along with all the directions, even correcting them once, and when the other man was finished the barman finally spoke up, though it was mostly to put me off again. "But he's not likely there now. He don't really live there. It's just a log cabin. He don't come down much any more. Just to hunt in the fall."

"Well, thass true enough," said an old fellow with no

teeth sitting down on the other side of me. He must have been listening to all this. "But I was by there yesserday or the day before and there was shmoke coming out the chimbley. Hoss tracks going up too, I blieve. I din stop, though, I'us in a hurry to git somewheres, I fergit where."

I had the fellow with the wore-out hat go back over the directions again, thanked him for his time, bought him and the bartender and the fellow with no teeth each a shot of whiskey, along with another for myself, and when they was drunk up I headed out the way the man'd said.

Well of course I got lost twice and the sun was nearly set by the time I got to where the cabin was. I smelled the wood smoke first, then saw it curling blue over the trees a couple hundred yards up off the pike into the woods. I tied the mule on the opposite side of the road, a distance off into some pines so no one could spot him should they go by.

Moving up toward the house, I heard someone chopping wood and, keeping low, got up close enough to see the whole clearing from behind a big rooty stump overturned.

Jesse James was working with his shirt off, sweating in the slanty sunlight, splitting firewood with a double-bitted axe from lengths of limb wood sawed to stove length, a big pile of each on either side of him. After a time he turned and called something I couldn't understand to someone inside the cabin, the door was standing open, and she laughed and called something back. He laughed too, a good long one from his belly, and then, leaving the axe stuck in his chopping block, gathered up an armload of split wood, a damn big one, and carried it inside, staggering a little at the door sill, which he had to step up over, being a little higher than it should of been and no step.

Somebody shut the door behind him, and I heard the load crash to the floor inside and both of them laugh again. Then everthing got quiet, some spring peepers down by a tiny run, the mosquitoes humming away and getting at me. I thought of creeping up close and looking into the window, but I just couldn't get myself to do that.

The cabin was a little affair, only about a rod wide and not much more than that long, the logs more like bigger saplings than real logs. Wasn't much, a low roof, a shed on the back for the horses, a door on each end and a small window on each long side, but it was all they needed, I guess. I looked at his red and black checkered shirt hanging there on a limb, swaying a little in the breeze, and guessed what they was probly doing inside, it being so quiet now. Damn it felt odd as the devil being there spying on them. So this's what the Pinkertons call tracking, huh, I says to myself.

I *was* kind of proud I'd found him and all, y'understand, but it was uncomfortable as a brand-new pair of boots to be hiding behind a rooty upturned stump, slapping at mosquitoes, knowing what the two of them was there for, what they was probly doing in there right *then*, starting out their new married life together—and also knowing it was going to be me to be the one to put an end to it all, permanent, in a day or so.

I left after another couple of minutes and went back to town quick as that mule Buster would trot, got a room and a meal, and put back a number or whiskeys that night in the same saloon in Anderson I was in that morning. That hard-looking gal didn't show up all night, though.

"Bleedin' at the crack!" one of the old timers said when I finally got lubricated enough and asked after her, how come she wasn't there.

The other one sniffed the air, nodded big, and then laughed and hooted like a woodpecker. The first joined in.

The next morning I went out to the little house out back, threw up, did my business, and then threw up a second time. Fine way to start the morning. I swore off whiskey again, but of course I knowed it wouldn't stick.

I drank some coffee and ate some bread, but couldn't see keeping nothing else down but that. Since I'd slept late, it wasn't no time at all till the 10:30 train come in, but there weren't no Pinkertons on it. I was starting to wonder if they'd even got my telegram, but then I realized I'd just have to wait, since I couldn't do nothing else at that point. The station master said there'd be another one in from Kansas City at 3:00 p.m., so I had some time to kill, supposing they were even on that. I had a rye to settle my stomach. It was peaceful in that dusty saloon in the morning, the only other people there were the two old-timers from before. I read a newspaper from somewheres down in Arkansas, that damned old drunkard Grant was in trouble again, and took a nap sitting in a chair with my feet up on the table and my hat down over my eyes. I felt better on waking up and had a beer with an egg in it and ate some cold sliced beef from a plate on the bar.

The three o'clock train was nearly an hour late, and you could spot the Pinkertons the minute they stepped off. I didn't even want to go up to them, people there'd know I was with them then, but I saw no way out of it.

William Pinkerton and another man, his assistant he called him, was both in suits like it was Chicago they was going to instead of backwoods Missouri. The other three wasn't much better dressed for the job. Tom Farnum and the big fellow who'd stopped me on the street in Kansas City was two of them, and they both said hello. The other man I didn't know.

"Well, where is he?" Pinkerton asked right off.

"About twenty miles south of here. By himself, except for his new wife, staying in a log cabin in the woods."

"Excellent! Excellent!" Pinkerton said, but then his face clouded up. "How come you didn't meet us closer to where he is?"

"Well, we needed horses, him not being the least bit considerate about sending us way the hell out in the country in order to catch him." *Considerate*, that's another word I got used to hearing being around Blackfoot Bill so much. "And we can't *get* horses down there because, hell, there

I RODE WITH JESSE JAMES / 123

ain't even any *towns* down there. And he *is* Jesse James, you might recall."

Pinkerton frowned at me. "What the hell are you trying to say, Goodwin?"

"I'm trying to say that the men you brought don't look like they're ready for much rough work, and you and that fellow you call your assistant ain't going to be a lot of help either, by the look of your shoes. This ain't going to be no turkey shoot, even if he ain't with his gang."

"Horseshit!" Pinkerton yelled, standing right there on the train platform in front of everone. "You're starting to believe all that crap they print about him in the newspapers. He's no giant, you know—just a man. Now let's go get him before he escapes!" Pinkerton started walking away.

"All right, if you want to spend the night in the woods," I said, traipsing after him. "Which you and your fellows don't look too prepared for. There ain't no inns or farmhouses to stay at between here and there, in case you didn't know. And if you go tromping this bunch you brought along down there tonight, even saying we could get there, Jesse James will be long gone by sunup. These country people *tell* him when the law shows up. They warn him, but you don't seem to understand that or be willing to work around it, I don't know which."

He stopped and faced me. He wasn't too happy about it, but he did see what I was telling him was true, I believe.

"What *do* we do, then?" he asked, cocking his head.

"Why, we take what little gear you brought along over to the hotel—where I took us some rooms. Then we look over the horses I got us, decide who rides what, and then make some plans—after I show you a map I drew up, showing the way the cabin sits and the lay of the land down there. After that we could get some supper and ask around at the cafe if there's any hogs or cattle people wants to sell, on the off chance somebody just might believe that's what we was doing around here. Then we go to bed early and get a good night's sleep. Get on him in the morning before sunup, ride there straight and hard before anyone has a chance to tell him about us coming. And have as much of the day as we need to do the job right. That's what I say we do."

He turned right around and told his men just what I'd told him—only making it sound like it was all his idea. And that's what we done, just the way I laid it out. We didn't get started next morning as early as I'd a liked, but we was close to the cabin not too many hours after sunup.

"Now what?" Pinkerton asked when I stopped my mule.

I didn't see any smoke above the trees, so I was hoping they might still be in bed. "We're there. I'll go on up and see what I can see," I told him. "You get your men ready. Get one of them, probly that assistant fellow of yours would do best, get him to hold our mounts here close to the road. The rest of you men make sure your guns are loaded and then come on up, being quiet, now, in about fifteen minutes. We'll surround the place then and call out for him to surrender. For God's sake make sure nobody's gun goes off down here, or you'll spook him sure."

"Wouldn't it be better to charge in on horseback?" Pinkerton asked, checking the cartridges in a pocket revolver her carried inside his coat. I had to look to see if he might be making a joke. He wasn't.

"No, this ain't going to work like no cavalry charge, too many chances for him to get away," I said. "If we're lucky, he'll give up without a fight because his wife is inside there with him, and she might get shot if we was to fire into the cabin, which we'd have call to do if he was to shoot out at us. But you can't tell what will happen, though."

"All right," Pinkerton said, looking at his big round pocket watch. "We'll wait here a quarter of an hour and then sneak up there. That's the way to do it, is it?"

"Yes," I told him. "You catch on pretty quick."

I left him to chew on that while I worked my way up

to the cabin, stopping to listen every three rods or so till I got to that upturned stump. Nobody out chopping, no smoke coming from the chimney, no noises at all. There were horses in the shed like before, though, so they was still there all right. Much as I didn't want to, I sneaked up to the cabin and looked in one of the little windows.

Jesse James and his woman was in bed doing what men and women have been doing ever since time started. I looked away as soon as I saw what it was they was doing—thinking I shouldn't be seeing what I'm seeing, but then it struck me they weren't paying the least attention to what was going on out that window—and I'd already seen what I seen.

I looked again. He was on top of her, holding her knees up high, and she was thrashing around to beat anything and making groaning noises I was surprised I didn't hear before.

Something come over me standing there watching them, I don't know what it was. For a minute I felt like just running away, let the Pinkertons find them this way, take care of all this theirselves, let Jesse James and his wife get caught while they was at it. But I couldn't run off, and I couldn't just let the Pinkertons take them like that neither.

I run to the door and busted in before I even knowed what I was doing for sure. "Mr. James, you got to get out of here right away! There's Pinkertons down by the road and—"

That quick he turned and had his gun cocked and pointed at me, though he was still in bed, her legs still around his middle. His clear blue eyes quick with fear. "What the devil—Goodwin? Is that you!?"

I put my hands up. "Yes it is," I said. "I'm sorry as hell to bust in here like this, but you—you got to get out right now. There's Pinkertons down by the road getting ready to come up here even while I'm talking to you. You and your wife—"

He sprung out of that bed like he was made of spring

steel. Stepped into his pants and went to the window all in one motion. "I don't see anyone," he said.

I put my hands back down, since he wasn't pointing at me no more. "I know, but they're coming, I swear to God they are!"

He come over and looked me in the eye, the gun still in his hand, but down at his side now. "How did you know—"

"I was—Blackfoot Bill sent me to warn you, and I saw them coming up the road behind—"

"Are you sure about this? I mean *sure*?"

"Yes sir, sure as I ever was of anything, and you got to leave right *now*, or you and your wife will be caught and you will be sent to prison or hung, for they—"

Jesse James looked me square in the face, up close now, and I could tell he believed me, finally.

"You're mistaken about one thing, though, Willie," the lady said from over in the bed, slow and easy. She was still laying on her back, hadn't even raised up from where she was laying when she and Jesse was— But she did now, and looked me in the eye bold as anything. Only she wasn't the lady I had saw Jesse James marry the week before.

13

NO COLD-BLOODED SNAKE, NEITHER

"Well I'll be damned," I said before I even thought.

She was that good-looking white-haired friend of Sarah's.

Jesse James turned from the window and looked at me direct with them clear blue eyes, smiled just the least bit, and I couldn't help thinking of the devil right then. After a second he looked back out. "I need you to take her to my mother's, Goodwin. Can you do it?" I could see how men would follow him, do what he asked them to.

"Yes, I suppose I can."

"I'll pay you, of course. Pay you well."

The woman—June—I remembered her name whilst I watched her stand up buck naked and then step into a pair of man's pants without putting nothing on underneath. June seemed about as bashful at being bare in front of me as my mule did. "I don't need a nursemaid, thank you," she said, looking around for whatever she had wore over her chest, but not seeming in no hurry to find it.

I couldn't tell whether she was speaking to me or to him. Oh, she *meant* me clear enough, I just didn't know if I was to answer her or not. She finally put on one of his shirts, the red and black checked one I had saw him leave out by the woodpile yesterday, and knotted it at her waist instead of letting it hang down so far as it did. Was that June or his wife I had heard laughing in here then? She buttoned it up over her loose breasts. Then strapped on a pistol.

Jesse took her arm and looked down at her. "Let's do this my way, June. I know what I'm about here and you don't."

She pulled away, but she wasn't going to argue any more with him, you could tell. She put a man's hat on, pushing her snowy hair up underneath, and then pulled it low. "All right," she said, but so quiet you could barely hear her.

"We got to go *now*," I told them.

"Yes, I understand," he said, gathering up some of his things, a leather bag with a strap, another pistol, a lever-action rifle, a big box of cartridges, but leaving other things behind, the three of us going out the door pretty much in a rush. "Where's your horse?" he asked me when we was outside.

"Down the hill," I said.

"Then how can you take her if that's the way the Pinkertons are coming? You can't ride double on hers. It won't last."

"I can work around behind and get mine." June was tightening her cinch by then. I said to her, "How about you go off a ways and I'll meet you somewheres soon, after I get my mule?"

"All right," she said, finishing up her saddling. "There's a cave about three miles south and east of here—up from a creek. Go down the river till you come to the bluffs, then go up the creek that comes in there. Over on the right bluff. At the only place you can see the rimrock on both sides, go up the side on the right and there's a cave. Think you can remember all that?"

Jesse nodded and smiled but didn't say nothing so I didn't neither.

"I'll wait for you there two hours, but no longer," she said, climbing up and then looking at him. "I don't see why I should wait for someone who's supposed to be wet-nursing *me*. What are you going to do, Jess?"

"Lead them off, right Goodwin?" Jesse James was grinning at me, acting half like he was enjoying this. Best I could figger, it reminded him of his days dodging Yankees.

"Yes, that would make sense," I said. "Make a clear track diagonal down to the road, so they can follow easy, and then go like hell. The horses they're on, you'll be shut of them soon." By then he'd mounted—one of the best looking horses I ever saw, a fine big dappled gray in top fiddle. It struck me then that I'd been the one who'd planned out how the Pinkertons could best catch Jesse James, and now here I was telling him how best to get away.

June went off at a good canter with no fare-thee-well at all, and Jesse started the other way at a fast walk, but then stopped and looked back at me over his shoulder. "I owe you for this, Goodwin, if you've told the truth here. But I'm going to stop along the road in an hour or so and see if anybody's coming after me. I'll make sure you get what you deserve if no one is."

"Just so's you make sure I get what I deserve if they *are* coming—and you better make that half an hour," I called out after him as he was boot-heeling that gray sharp in the ribs and moving off at a good clip. Mostly to myself I said, "Cause in a whole hour they'll have give up and quit." Jesse James was a man who knew when he'd heard enough.

I stood there listening to the sounds their horses' hooves was making for a minute, shoes cracking against rocks once in a while, going different directions. Then all I was listening to was the quiet of the woods—feeling how odd this was, too, me doing what I'd just did, and wondering how it'd all come out. Then I turned and run down toward where I'd left William Pinkerton and his men. I didn't have to go far, for they was three-quarters of the way up to the cabin, nearly out of breath.

"He's getting away!" I called when I was sure they saw me good, waving both my arms like a crazy man. "He must of heard us, for he rode down that way," I said, pointing, just the way his tracks went.

"See!" Pinkerton yelled, "I *knew* we should have been—on our horses! God damn you, Goodwin!" He sent one of the men back for them. "What about his wife," Pinkerton asked, still panting like a dog in dog days. "Was she with him?" My, was he ever mad at me. But not half as mad as he would of been had he knowed twice as much.

"No, I saw nothing of her today," I said—which was true.

He looked at the cabin. "Come on, Tom. My bet is the dirty, cowardly son-of-a-bitch has run off and left his new bride behind—and she's still in there. *You* stay here, Goodwin, and help bring the horses along when they get up here. I knew I should never have listened to you. This is all your fault." He led the way up toward the cabin and I watched them go. Well, he was right, there, at least. It *was* all my fault, more than he knowed.

It took that man quite a time to bring the animals up. When he finally did come, I walked my mule over to the cabin, that was all the "help" I give. Pinkerton and the one called Tom was standing outside talking.

"Did you catch her?" I asked.

He looked at me cross. "No, we didn't, no thanks to you. You must have missed her when she left." He turned to go back inside. "You were right about their being here, though. At least *some* man and woman were here until just a few minutes ago." Well, no shit, I says to myself. That was about as hard to figger out as the tits on a cow.

Pinkerton decided to chase them, of course. But it took him and his men so long to get packed up again, fix their saddles just so, decide what order to go in, and what they'd do once they caught him, that Jesse James had a good twenty minute lead by the time they got going. Twenty minutes with him on that sleek horse of his was as good as twenty days.

And, hell, they didn't even *notice* the track of the girl's horse going the other way. Naturally I didn't see it was my place to point it out to them. Even though I was hired on as the tracker of this outfit, I was told to bring up the rear, so that's what I done—till we got down to the road.

"Hold up!" I called.

Pinkerton stopped and so did the rest. "What's wrong now?" he yelled back.

"This damn mule of mine's going lame," I said, stepping down off him, a long ways down. "Feels like he bruised his frog or something. He won't carry me no further." I picked up a front hoof and looked, but of course there wan't nothing to see—nothing wrong, I mean.

"Too bad," Pinkerton hollered back, but he *sounded* happier'n a pig wallering in shit. "You'll have to look out for yourself. We can't stop and wait for you, and carrying double would slow us down too much."

Sure, like that would matter now.

"What'll I do?!" I yelled, trying to sound real worried. "How'll I get back?"

"Beats me, Goodwin," he called. "My guess is you'll just have to walk. Good luck! Send me a telegram if you ever get back to Kearney." All his men laughed at the boss making me look the fool.

"Good luck yourselfs," I said after them—after they'd moved on down the road a piece and couldn't hear me, that is. "You'll need a good *deal* of good luck to catch that old boy, the start he's got and the rate you're going."

Jesse James sat quietly on Stonewall and watched the road below, checking his backtrail. A short time earlier he'd found what he'd been looking for, a stream that crossed the narrow dirt pike—with a shallow ford instead of a bridge. About three hundred yards from where he sat he'd urged his horse into the current and then headed him upstream, moving slowly through the rushing water that sparkled in the midmorning sunshine. He came out on the same side of the stream that he'd entered, at the foot of the low hill on whose crest he now waited. From where he sat, looking though a stand of young pines and chewing a corn dodger from his war bag, he could see the road below perfectly.

After deciding on his escape route, in the unlikely event that he'd need one, Jesse James let his mind slide out of focus, as he often did when he was alone and safe. Let his thoughts spin to their own rhythm and depth, their own sense of time. He found it strangely refreshing to let his attention slide inward toward what he thought of as his private grove of oaks, slip into an open clearing of quiet and solitude, domed high overhead with large gnarled branches and quietly rustling leaves, a dim place where he half-grudgingly let a warm happiness steal over him, his body put aside for a while, though any sudden noise or strange movement could awaken him instantly from his musings. His mother's farm, where he grew up, always his mother's farm. Cousin Lucy's beautiful farm, too, the wedding and the trouble with Uncle William drifted by in seconds. Zee's lovely face.

He heard them before he saw them, about half a dozen riders trotting unevenly on the hard-packed dirt of the road below. He drew his Winchester from its scabbard and levered a cartridge into the chamber, sighted down its glistening length. But when they came into view he nearly laughed. In the lead, two men in dark suits and derby hats sweating and red-faced, obviously poor riders. The two who followed weren't much better in the saddle, big fellows who were far too much for their light horses to carry very far, one of which was staggering already and the other was trying valiantly to keep up, wheezing badly. Another man, riding last, who kept looking back over his shoulder as if he feared a hundred cavalrymen with drawn sabres were overtaking them. Jesse remembered the feeling from the War, riding with Quantrill and Bloody Bill Anderson. Of course, he had been only sixteen then.

The leader yelled something Jesse couldn't make out to the rest just as they were crossing the little stream, none of *them even looking down for tracks. They turned the bend beyond the ford and were gone. Jesse James waited a moment, picked his way slowly down through the young pines, turned the gray toward the right, and went back up the pike in the same direction from which both he and the riders had come, not once looking back.*

I did like the girl said, went down to the river, turned downstream and found the creek coming in by the bluffs. I went up it a mile or so to where I could see rock up on both sides through the trees, up a nearly flat valley not a hundred rods wide, then went across the stream and headed up toward the right. Didn't even get my feet wet.

A sharp whistle up above, one that could of been some strange kind of a bird they had around there, but was more likely a person, a young woman kind of a person. I kept heading up till it got too steep for the mule and then got off and led him on up.

"Over here!" June called from over on the right some more and a little higher still. In a minute I could see her standing there on what looked like a nice broad ledge, her hands on her hips and looking down at me. Sort of striking a pose for me to look at, or so it seemed. Good looking women will do that from time to time is my experience of the matter. "I'd about given up on you," she said when I got there. "Did Jess get away?"

"Well, I didn't see it myself, but I'm sure he did," I told her, starting to tie my mule to a tree.

"No, bring him in here where he can't be seen," she said. We went back under the overhang and into a hole the size of a big lopsided barn door. Inside the cool, damp cave was a nice size room, where she'd fed her horse some grain. You didn't notice how warm the day had got till you went in there, the sweat sticking my shirt to my shoulders and back. She got some grain for the mule, too.

"Are we staying here a while?" I asked her. "Seemed

like you were in an all-fired hurry to get somewheres when we were back there." I was enjoying the cool and looking up at them big icicle things stuck to the ceiling. I like me a good cave from time to time.

"I'd just as soon we wait, now, until those damn Pinkertons are out of the territory, since it took you so long to get here," she said, straightening up and standing a little too close, facing me full. "You have anything to say against that?" she asked, her hands on her hips again.

"Well, no, not really," I told her. "But them Pinkertons ain't that hard to stay away from, if you know what I mean. There ain't no danger now, really. We could start up to Kearney today if you was of a mind to. Make a few miles by nightfall."

She shook her head. "I think it'd be better to stay here tonight and start out fresh in the morning," she said, uncinching the mule's girth. "Unless you want me to tell Jesse James that you risked my life after he so much as told you to look after me, that is."

"Whoa!" I said, and it echoed in there a few times. "Just a damn minute, girl! I said I'd take you up there to his momma's and I will—if you can manage to keep a civil tongue in your head. But I ain't being shoved into doing it your way by having you say you'll sic Jesse James on me. No *mam*!"

"You never saw what he can do to a man, did you," she asked, pulling the saddle down off my mule, though it was a reach for her. She threw it on a heap beside hers and then smiled a crookedy, dirty grin at me.

"No, I ain't, but I've heard tell," I said. "But I *could* just ride out of here. I ain't *in* the damn James gang, you might remember—just doing him a favor is all, though right now I can't rightly say why."

Well, she laughed at me good and walked through the hole to the outside, talking as she walked away, swinging her shapely backside so's I'd be sure to notice. "Yes, sure, you go ahead and do that. Just ride off and leave me behin' after you told Jesse James you'd look after po' l'il-ol' me.

I'll just *bet* you got the balls to do *that*." She must of turned around when she got outside.

What she saw, I guess, was me throwing the saddle blanket and then the saddle back up on that tall mule. She come in again. "You're going? Even if I stay!"

"Yes, I am," I told her. "Tell Mr. Jesse James whatever you like about me not nursemaiding you up to his momma's, but tell him this, too, while you're at it. Tell him if he ever needs someone to kick your ass up between your shoulder blades, he can come'n get me for the job, cause I'd much prefer that job to the one he already give me. An then tell him the woman he prefers to stick his pecker into, instead of his brand-new wife, ain't half the looker she thinks she is, even if she *is* more'n twice the pain in the ass of anybody I ever run into before. And then tell him . . ." I said a few more things like that I wisht now I wouldn't have, it's hard to stop once you get going. But, god, I hate to be treated like that, especially by a woman who trades on how she looks. Like being pretty means you *are* something other people ain't.

She stood there and took all them "Tell him's" chin up, without so much as a no-sir back or a blink of the eye. And when I had let all the fire out of my belly and had that mule all ready to go, she walked back outside ahead of me. I was surprised she didn't give me a load of hot tongue right back on the way out, but she didn't.

I walked past her and over to the edge and was just about to start down when she spoke. "Don't go, Willie. Don't, please. I shouldn't have said that. I—I'm . . . I'm sorry." She looked away, across the valley.

I just stood and looked at her for a long minute. I was wrong about *one* thing I'd said to her. She really *was* a looker, not that that had anything to do with anything, mind you. "Heck, I don't mind staying here a while, if that's what you want. It's nice and cool inside there, and I was wondering what the rest of it looks like. Going wasn't the—"

"I know," she said, looking at me direct now, her

milky blue eyes leaking big tears. "I don't—I'm sorry, what I said." She looked away again. She went back inside, got her horse and carried her saddle out and started getting ready to ride.

I climbed down off. "Shoot, I don't care if we stay, now," I told her. "Fact is, I'd sort of like to see more of what this old cave is like inside, and I ain't really in no hurry to get nowheres."

She turned and give me a look I didn't know what it meant, shook her head, and wiped a last tear away. She smiled a little to herself while she undid what she'd done on her horse. I had the feeling these animals were probly about as confused as I was at this point. Saddles on, saddles off. What was it gonna be, stay or go?

"All right, enough said about all that," I told her, and took my mule back in and unsaddled him myself this time. She come back in with her horse and saddle, sat down and watched me, but didn't say nothing.

Later on she showed me a whole big stash of food and things there—candles, lanterns, things put up in jars, soup and stew, mostly. Tins of peaches and biscuit things like hardtack. Pounds and pounds of coffee. Dried fruit and peanuts and dried beans in jars and I don't know what all. Good water running back in the cave, you could hear it. And cartridges, my God, cases and cases of all calibres.

I started looking further back in, but she said the other side was better, not so wet and muddy and why didn't we go over there? But I *could* go back in on this side if I wanted to, she didn't care, she just *thought* ... I followed her out the front and into another way inside the cave, pretty much hid by bushes.

On this second side it was cool, like the other side, but not nearly so damp. We walked back into it a little ways, a tall echoy hallway sort of affair, and it was almost dark as night till we got to a room with a small fire she must have built earlier, a round room it was—round flat floor the size of a maypole circle or so, and a rounded, domed ceiling with a hole going up to let the smoke out—

looked like swirling water had maybe washed it out round and smooth like that, and cozy and bright as anything once the fire was stirred up and fed. A big pile of dry wood there beside. She made us dinner from the stored food, it being about noon by then. Beans, bacon and biscuits, I recall.

I crawled around some of the cave with a couple of torches after that, while June went for a bath in the stream down below. She said there was a pond inside the cave, and I seen it later, but she spoke about how the water was so cold, and she was more afraid of snakes bathing in there—her, that is, not the snakes taking a bath.

Later on I went out and sat on one of the ledges higher up, watched some hawks doing their slow circles in the sky and tried to figger out why the *hell* we was waiting here. She didn't seem scared or nothing, before or now. Down in the room with the horses was a pile of newspapers and a stack of books I went through, hoping to kill some time.

The newspapers was nearly a year old and most of the books was about crops and farming. One, though, with Frank James name writ inside the front, was by William Shakespeare. Well, I decided that'd be the day I found out what the fuss everbody makes over him was all about.

It was the damndest stuff. This old fellow, best I could make of it, was getting on some, and he thought as how he'd divvy up his herd and whatever else he had among his daughters while he was still full of piss and vinegar instead of leaving it to them after he was stiff and gone—and the courts screwing it up, probly, like they do down in Texas.

But no sooner did this old king give two of his growed daughters big chunks of the ranch than they begun to do him dirt, though they was sweet as berry pie with milk and sugar on before. The other daughter, a younger one, I think, the one that he thought had went to whoring and he had cut out of his will? It turned out she was the only one that looked after him after he went blind, which seemed to come on all of a sudden like. And she wan't really whoring either, finally, the young one, at least that's my guess. Just being a little free with it, probly. A son or two and it might of been a whole differnt story.

It turned out all right in the end, though. They got everthing all straightened out—like books most always do on the last few pages—but such damn talk you never did hear the like of. I had to read some parts two, three times just to make sense of it and even then the spelling was all wrong, even I could see that.

That's how I spent my afternoon and evening, watching hawks and reading about an old man who seemed to know even less about women than I did.

June come back right after I finished reading about the old blind man, and I told her the story while she was making us some supper. She didn't see much sense in it either. Didn't he know he should of made them wait for the place till after he was dead? What did he expect, anyway?

"Was the young one pretty?" June wanted to know.

"It didn't say," I told her. "It wasn't writ like the other books I read before, it only told what they said and when they left—I think that's what that funny word meant."

She shook her head. "You spent all that time reading that story and they didn't even tell you what the people *looked* like?" she said, handing me a bowl of soup she had put together from food from the cache.

She told me how nice her bath down in the stream was, and she'd show me where if I wanted one. She asked me about Sarah then, and I said we was all through with each other. Yeah, that was what she had heard, but she just wanted to be sure that's how I saw it too. She said as how we should get an early start in the morning and it'd be good to turn in soon cause of that.

There was some straw there for bedding, and it was a damn good thing since that floor was solid rock. I can sleep on nearly anything if I have a blanket—desert sand or mucky bottom it don't make much diffrence to me, but I'd never tried sleeping on solid rock before and was glad not to have to that night. She spread her blankets on one side of the fire, so I spread mine on the other. We talked a little, falling asleep, but I was soon dreaming about them hawks circling, only that old king and his daughters was flying up there with them, goin round and round and round, only that king was also Jesse James sometimes, I think.

Next thing I knowed, I woke up feeling something crawl into the covers with me, bare skin against my shirt and the back of my arm, and it weren't no cold-blooded snake, neither.

14

LIKE A YOUNG COWBOY'S WEDDING NIGHT

"Are you asleep?" June whispered right in my ear from behind me, not a stitch on.

"I *was*," I said, then didn't say nothing further. The fire had burned down some, but it looked like she had throwed a few sticks of wood on before she had crawled in with me. It got a little higher and hotter—the fire, I mean.

"I was cold and afraid," she said, kind of pouting in my ear like a schoolgirl. "Over there all by myself."

I looked across to where her blankets was, her clothes in a heap where she'd just stepped out of them. "Yes, I can see as how it'd be a lot safer over here naked behind me."

She giggled. "You aren't going to throw me out of bed, now, are you, Willie?" It sounded like she didn't expect no answer so I didn't feel the need to give one. She'd put her arm around in front of me, and after a minute she had my shirt half unbuttoned before I even noticed. Maybe I had started to fall back asleep. Maybe.

"What're you doing there?" I asked her.

"You know what I'm doing," she said soft in my ear.

Damn I was surprised and didn't know what to do. "Will you tell Jesse James on me if I don't do this?" I asked her after a while, making a joke of it.

She laughed. "Why, yes I will! And then I'll tell Aunt Zerelda, and just everybody! So you better give me what I came over here for, or I'll run off and tell the whole James gang, the Youngers, all the aunts and uncles and cousins and everybody else that you wouldn't oblige me, sir! That you are not a true Southern gentleman!"

I sat up and looked down at her. She had rolled over partway onto her back, her hips still sideways. June was looking right back up at me, smiling sweet and dirty at the same time, brazen as a ferret—her large, smooth breasts uncovered, her hands moving slow over my arms.

The firelight got brighter with the pine she'd throwed on, and it crackled and lit up that whole cave room the color of sundown, the shadows deep and dark, water dripping far off, further into the cave. I never felt more *with* another person and so *away* from everbody else as I did right then.

She was beautiful. Her hair glowed like spun snow and the sea smell of her body was arguing me into doing what she wanted, even when I knowed at the same time I shouldn't.

"Wouldn't Jesse be kind of mad if he was to see you here like this with me?" I asked, still looking down at her. I didn't really care what he'd have thought by that point, you understand. I thought of Sarah then, though, what she might say about all this if she was to find out, but she was probly doing even worse with one or another of them damn cousins of hers, maybe at this very minute, too. And her and me was all done with now, anyway. Time to face it. I promised myself I'd try not to think of her so much, though I didn't know just how to do that.

June shook her head, rolling it back and forth slow, her fine white hair falling loose around her lovely face. "Would Jesse James care if I was in bed with you? No, sir, he wouldn't think nothing of it. We have no claims on each other, especially now that he's married to Cousin Zee." She rolled her head over far, stuck out her tongue and licked my arm like a puppy, just there above the wrist where it's so tender, her eyes on mine the whole evil time. I felt my willpower turning to mush and wet sawdust. "You've heard of kissin' cousins?" she asked. "Well, Jesse and me are sort of like that—only . . . Just something our families have always done, I guess."

I looked away from her beautiful face and shook my head. It was like I was still in a dream, like with them hawks and those daughters flying around, and trying to wake up. "June, I ain't never met no lady who acts like you do."

She just laughed and stroked the hair on my chest beneath where she had opened my shirt. "All right, Willie. I guess I can be ladylike for you tonight, at least *talk* ladylike if you want, if that's what you *really* want." She sat up slow and kissed me, a nice gentle one on the lips. "But don't expect me to make love ladylike, I warn you. I ain't no lady, and I couldn't pretend to be, not when it comes to that."

"I ain't decided yet if I'm going to do that with you, June," I said.

"Yes you have," she said and put her arms around me strong, kissing me so hard I felt her teeth paining against my lips, bringing the salty, metal taste of blood, hers or mine I couldn't tell which, and didn't care. Her breasts tight and hot against my chest. And something told me she was right, yes she was, oh my, yes she was. She knew what I was going to do, all right—right or wrong—and then, finally, so did I.

I just can't bring myself to tell what-all that girl and me done that night. I thought it'd be good to be as plain and open about them things as she was, but when push comes to shove, I'm sorry, I just cain't do it.

Some I can tell, all right.

Now I have known women who was fast at it and others who was so strong of muscle and grip they surprised you, but she was both. Moving strong and fast as a brook trout's fins in a high mountain freshet, faster than the trill of a prairie lark's song, a prairie lark's tongue, and then she screamed and I screamed and right away heard the echo of both our screams come back to us in that hollow old black cave, the cave room nearly dark by then, the fire burned down to red embers and me not even noticed.

After a time I got my breath back and then a little strength into my shoulders and legs so I could first sit up again and then stand. I'd stagger around some, and then, finally, I fed the fire, for I was feeling cold—underground and wet with my sweat and hers. She laid there without moving, staring upward into the dark without stirring for so long I feared she had maybe died.

"Are you all right?" I asked her.

"Oh yes, I'm all right," she said, but still not moving any. Sounding a little mournful, if I wasn't wrong, kind of far off somewheres.

"You don't *seem* all right," I said, sitting down beside her again.

"Oh, I always get a little, I don't know, like this, right afterward." She turned to face me and I seen that she was crying a little. "It's all right." she said quiet. "It doesn't mean anything. *Nothing* really *means* anything, I guess, does it, Willie?"

I nodded, not knowing what in the world she was talking about or what to say.

But I could see on her face there was something she wanted to say or ask of me, so I just waited till she got it out, which after a time she did. "Willie, you've been around some, traveled pretty far I guess, not just Missouri and all. How do ... I mean, what are women ... like? Other women, in bed, I mean?" She looked a little worried, like this was important to her and she'd had nobody to ask it of before.

I thought it over a minute, her question, tried to see what she was getting at here, what troubled her. "I got to say they ain't many as good at it as you are, I *got* to say that.

Nor none I ever met so honest about what they liked and wanted, though most women like it more than they let on when they ain't doing it. Is that what you mean?"

She smiled. "No. I pretty much knew that—from what other men have said. What I mean is—aww, you know, don't you?" She was looking at me square by this point, still on her back, but more uneasy than before.

"No, I really don't." I looked at her and waited, and after a minute she looked away. If that wasn't something like bashful I read on her pretty young face right before she turned her head, then I never saw it before.

And her not wanting to say something after what we done! What in heaven's name could *this* girl be shy about? I could not figger it out. "I'd be happy to tell you whatever I can, June, but I don't know . . . "

She looked back sudden and there was anger and big tears in her eyes and she was shaking hard as she cried. "I know it, you don't have to say it! I smell bad, don't I? Go on and say it! I can't help it! I already took two baths today and I *still* smell bad!" She rolled up in a little ball, turned away from me as much as she could. She cried harder than I ever heard anybody do before.

I could not believe it. She was worried over how she *smelled*?

I put my hand on her shoulder, but she yanked away. "I don't know where you ever got that idea, honey, but they ain't a damn thing wrong with the way you smell. Did Jesse or someone say there was?"

"No . . ." she whimpered, turned away from me still and her hands covering over her face. "Not since . . . they called me—'stinky,' my brothers and cousins did, when I—"

"Ha!" I hollered. "*That* old thing! Don't tell me you fell for *that*!"

She turned and looked up, kind of startled, the tears stopping already. "What? What are you talking about?"

I laughed a big one. "My goodness, didn't anyone ever tell you about calling pretty girls 'Stinky?!'"

She sat up and pulled my blanket up over her breasts, looking pretty suspicious. "No, and I—"

"Well, it's a thing boys do, don't you know that? Didn't you ever notice how weak in the knees a *real* pretty gal makes a young fellow? Surely you've noticed *that*." I waited for her, didn't hurry her none.

"Well, yes I have. And I developed early, too, and the boys . . . well."

"See what I mean?" I said, like it was already explained. "To keep a young gal from getting too much of the upper hand over you, some boy figgered out if you called them 'stinky' now and again it gave them something to think about, something to worry over instead of figgering out how to use being pretty against you. And then maybe they wouldn't be so damn sure about theirselfs, their looks and all. Wouldn't make you feel so much like a ball of horse shit if they worried a little over how they smelled. Nobody ever told you that, huh?"

The doubt was a little thinner, and she sure wanted to believe me all right. "I always thought when it got to—that I smelled, I don't know, too strong? But it *was* a boy that wanted me to do it with him who said that the first time. We were so young, though, we never—"

"See? What did I tell you? Why, they pulled that on my very own sister, a beautiful little gal with hair only a shade or two darker than yours. She was crying and crying one day, and like you, she didn't want to say what it was about, but after she told me and I straightened her out, why, shoot—"

"But I *do* smell when I get . . . I can even smell it myself then, a little."

I put my arm around her shoulder. "Well, yes, of course you do. You start to smell the way a woman does when she gets—well, like you said. But that don't smell *bad*, for heaven's sake, no it don't, not a bit of it." I shook my head.

"It doesn't?"

"No, mam. It's as much of what gets a man raring to

go as the look of her body or the look in her eye. Yes, there is a smell, sort of like the sea at low tide, like down on the Gulf Coast, but it's mixed in with a spicy smell too, and something that smells like flowers or honey or sweet-smelling roots, as well. And all of it together, my word. Didn't you ever smell that?"

She thought about it. "Well, maybe..."

The fire caught up then, but an even brighter glow was coming from her, the way her face shined when she believed that her womanly parts did not give nobody cause to think poorly of her. My, the odd things folks believe about themselfs and the heartaches it brings them sometimes.

She kissed me then. A sweeter kiss no woman ever give me. She pulled me down on them blankets again and showed me what it meant to her—what I'd said.

It was like she knew, in a partly sort of way, that I'd been just trying to make her feel all right about herself, whether she smelled bad or no—but she didn't, mind. In another part of herself, she believed me the whole way, that her smell was maybe good instead of stinky, like they'd called her. And it was them two parts of herself meeting up together for the first time and shaking hands with each other that she made love with that second time there in that firelit cave as old as those hills. It was something like I would guess a young cowboy's wedding night would be, supposing he'd never laid with a woman before, and supposing also that his bride'd been the pride of a fancy whorehouse somewhere like San Francisco, but despite all her tricks and such had him believing it was her first time too, and all as brand spanking new to her as it was to him. It marveled me she could do that after we'd finished and I'd sat up and had a minute to think about it.

"Very pretty," a man's voice said of a sudden over toward the way in, but deep in the shadows.

15

A NEW NAME

Whoever he was, he wasn't in no hurry, the way he spoke, though *I* was sure scrambling around for my clothes and my revolver.

"Don't shoot, Goodwin," he said, standing up and walking slow toward us. "It's me."

"God damn you, Jess!" June screamed, throwing one of her boots but missing him. "How long have you been over there watching us?"

"Let me see," he said, bending down at the fire and shoving the coffeepot into the coals. "I heard how you don't smell so bad, though I don't agree." He gave her a odd smile then. "And after that I saw you lazier in bed than I'd ever allow."

He sat down on June's bedroll and looked across the fire at me. "Why don't you get dressed and go outside for about an hour, Goodwin? June and I have some unfinished business to attend to, don't we, cousin?"

She looked at him straight for a minute, but then she smiled just the least little bit.

I buttoned up my shirt the rest of the way and pulled on my boots. "Why should I?" I asked him, not very happy about him busting in there and ordering me around, not to mention him butting in on the business June and *me* was taking care of.

He chuckled and shook his head. "Because if you don't go, I'll blow your fool brains out," he said, cool as water from a deep well. Still smiling, too, but you could tell he meant it.

"Go on," June said quiet, talking to me but staring at him, letting the blanket fall down off her breasts.

Well, it didn't seem right to me, to get told to clear out of there like that, but since June had said to go too, I didn't see how I could rightly argue to stay. Going out I looked back and they was still sitting there eyeing each other across the flames.

I went on out, sat on the big ledge, dangling my feet over, and watched the full moon hanging just above the ridge opposite, wondering what in the *world* I was going to do now that I'd done what I done. Was I still working for the Pinkertons or not? I was working for Jesse James now is how it *seemed*, but he didn't sign me on or nothing. What would the Pinks do if they found out? Try and send me back to Huntsville, most likely. More important, what would Jesse James do to me if he found out about them? No need to guess about that.

June screamed and I jumped up to go in and see what was wrong when I remembered that was just how she'd screamed with me only a little while before, that first time. I sat back down and looked at the moon again. Sometimes that damned old man in the moon looks just like he's snickering at you, like he knows he's put a good one over on you, did you ever notice that?

Anyway, after a time Jesse come out, come over and sat down beside me in the moonlight, and then handed me a cup of hot coffee.

Neither of us said nothing.

But after a while he did. "It . . . must seem a little odd to you, June and me. The way the cousins in my family . . ." He didn't finish it, just let it hang there. "Zee knows about June being here, in case you were wondering. You don't have to worry about whether or not you should tell her, Goodwin."

"She knows?" I asked, kind of surprised, looking at him good in the moonlight for the first time.

He was smiling up at that full, yeller moon, calm and easy now. And you knowed he was telling the truth about his wife knowing. He cleared his throat. "Yes, but I'd rather no one else knows, if you see what I mean. Not everybody has our... ways—nor understands them."

I nodded and I guess he saw me, but he didn't say nothing again for a while. We sat and watched the moon and I sipped my coffee.

"Oh yes, she knows all right," he repeated after a time. "She's a cousin too, you see, Zee is. June and her brother came down to tell us Zee's sister had taken a turn for the worse. You may have noticed she wasn't at the wedding, Zee's older sister, the one she calls Sissy? Most folks probably thought it was because she doesn't approve of me, which she doesn't, despite she was—" He dropped whatever he was going to say there, and then took a look at the moon and a drink of his coffee before talking again. "But the truth of it is that she's been sick, very sick. And it was Zee's idea that June stay down here while she went back and attended to things, not mine. I was surprised she knew June would want to, though. Zee's full of surprises."

He looked at me quick, sort of like he wished he wouldn't of said that last is how I took it. I had my own surprise, I'll tell you—that he was telling *me* all this—even without that last, about his new wife being full of surprises. He cleared his throat again. "She'd planned to come back soon as she could, but now with these damned Yankee Pinkertons spooking around down here—"

He turned and looked at me sharp, and for just a sliver of a second I thought for sure he knowed about me. I kept looking at the moon and sipping my coffee.

"Come on," he said, finally, slapping me on the knee

and then standing up, offering his hand to help me up. "We could all use a good night's sleep."

Damn, I wish I had knowed I would soon be going to bed instead of having my brains shot out of my head. I wouldn't have drunk that damn coffee, for it kept me tossing and turning most of the night.

Come morning June shook me awake and shoved a cup of coffee into my hand, but she didn't say nothing to me. We ate some biscuits with jam on them, I forget what kind, and was outside and nearly ready to go before the sun come up.

"I suppose you'll be taking June up to your momma's yourself now, right?" I asked him.

"No, I still want you to do that," he said, yanking the front cinch of his double rigger tight. "I'm heading east to look over a business opportunity me and my partners have heard about, a Yankee bank in West Virginy that needs a little work done on the safe door." He give me a grin, sort of like he was half proud and half ashamed of himself, I reckon, his line of work and all. Then he fished in his pocket, pulled out a leather drawstring pouch stuffed full of gold coins. "Here, take this," he said, tossing it to me. I didn't count them at the time, but it come to between four and five hundred dollars.

"I didn't warn you for this," I said, pocketing the man's gold anyway after feeling the heft of it in the pouch. Heavy as it was, you didn't have to open it or ask if it was gold.

"I know," he said, stepping up on his horse. "That's why it's as much as it is. And before I forget it, thank you, Goodwin. They'd have had me back there if it wasn't for you. I couldn't have killed all five of them, not with June in the cabin. I waited and saw them ride by on down the trail. A sorry lot, but with that many . . . Thank you again, Mr. Goodwin, sir." He touched brim of his brown fedora and nodded for a bow.

"Do you suppose you could call me Willie like everone else does?" I asked him.

He looked me over real curious then. "Yes, I suppose I could," he said leaning down, pulling off his glove, and offering his hand. "Lord knows you deserve it after what you did, Willie."

I shook it, but I didn't know just what it was I deserved or what exactly I was shaking on. I didn't realize it at the time, but I had just asked Jesse James to trust me, to treat me like family. And he had just decided that he would. It wasn't till weeks later I found out that he called everone he trusted by their first names and them he wasn't sure of by their last. It was one of his ways of being square with people is what I was told. And everbody that knowed him knowed that, of course. Everbody but me, naturally. I was just wanting to be called by my name is all.

Our shaking hands sealed some kind of a bargain, I saw that later, but I didn't know it at the time. The next couple of months I found out what-all it would mean, though, but I'm getting ahead of myself here.

"I'd like you to work at my neighbor's farm after you get back up to Clay County, Willie. Look out for us from there instead of working with Blackfoot Bill, who'll be leaving in a few weeks or so anyway. I'll pay you twice what you were making with him. Will you do it?"

I thought it over a minute and then told him that I would, after Bill left and he didn't need me no more for the medicine show. He nodded and said his neighbor's name was Dan Askew, but that he kept a right neat, straightened up little farm anyway. It took me a second to catch on, I never thought Jesse James would make jokes, be foolish once in a while, but he was a good-natured sort of a fellow when he wasn't half crazy, and with a fine developed sense of humor—when he wasn't thinking about killing you, that is.

I was to go by the name of Jack Ladd now, he never told me why, I certainly wan't no lad no more. Another one of his jokes, maybe, I figgered. I was to tell Askew we'd talked about it. It'd be all right, Jesse was sure, and he'd square it off with old Dan Askew when next he got up that way. I wouldn't have to do much real work on Askew's place, he said, just as much as I wanted while watching for detectives, sheriffs, and the like. Somebody would come to the Askew place from time to time to find out if I'd saw anything, but if it looked like something big was happening, a raid by the law or something like that, I was to run to the Samuel farm and tell somebody there, Jesse's mamma or even Dr. Samuel would do. Also, would I let the rest of my beard grow, please, and get a pair of spectacles and a straw hat the next time I was in Liberty? And let my mustache grow longer, while I was at it.

All right, I told him, I would. That's how I got took into the James gang, just like that.

Jesse James turned that good-looking gray horse around and called back over his shoulder. "So long, Willie! Be sure and tell Zee what happened, June. And you two have yourselves a good time going back, now, y'hear?" He laughed as he rode off and I just shook my head.

Truth is, June and me didn't hit it off so good going back up to Kearney. We slept separate, neither of us even once speaking of what'd happened in the cave. And not much talk of anything else, either. I guess it was mostly my fault it was like that between us. But it was plain, after I'd thought it through good, that June kind of liked me all right so long as Jesse wasn't around, but as soon as he was, I could go sort the fly shit out of the pepper so far as she was concerned. And that sort of puts a crimp on things between a man and a woman, even in bed, knowing you are only second or maybe even third fiddle—at least with me it does.

When we went up through Anderson I bought the mule and saddle from the man there who'd rented it to me. Pinkerton'd turned in the horses by then, the man there told me while June was off somewheres.

It took us a good while to get up to Kearney, since June all of a sudden wanted to stop overnight at Monegaw

Springs along the way, and visit some with her relatives there. The Youngers, which I suppose everbody in the country has heard of by now, so that took some time. I drank whiskey with some of them Younger boys while she did God-knows-what with some of the others, she didn't say and I didn't ask. And believe me, they wasn't virgins in the whiskey drinking department, either.

So finally, after the better part of two weeks, I got her up there to the Samuel farm, and explained to Jesse's momma what had went on down there in the Elk River country, about the Pinkertons and all if not between me and June and her boy Jesse, who she thought was the greatest fellow to wear britches since Jesus Christ—and Frank was third. I said where Jesse told me to work, the Askew place, and what he had told me to do over there, watching and the lot. Said that I might come hurrying over here to warn them some time or other, so she was not to shoot me if she saw me come running, not to mistake me for a Pinkerton. I meant it more as a kind of a joke, but she just nodded her gray head serious as a judge and paid careful attention to everthing I said, sitting on her ladderback rocker there in her front room, stabbing me with that hawkish look of hers all the way through while I stood talking with my hat in my hands.

I was about to leave, June had wandered off someplace, but Mrs. Samuel wouldn't hear of me going without she'd fed me, and she wouldn't take no for an answer no better than her boy Jesse wouldn't, I guess that's where he'd got it. She called a Negro woman in from another room, Charlotta her name was, I believe, and they sat me down all by myself at a table outside there in the shade. Jesse and Frank's little half-brothers and sisters, the Samuel kids, was playing croquet in the side yard, squabbling over whose turn it was. It was getting warm that day, and the women kept bringing me cold chicken, snap beans cooked with ham, fresh baked bread, lemonade, cups and cups of coffee, shortcake and raspberries and cream, and then Jesse's momma and that

Negro lady, they both acted about half put out when I couldn't eat no more than two pieces of rhubarb pie after all that. I never liked rhubarb pie all that much anyway, it never seems sweet enough to me.

I was still uncomfortable full when I rode my mule up to Blackfoot Bill's camp alongside the creek outside of Kearney. He was stirring up another batch of the Heap-Big, or so it looked like, and didn't notice anyone coming up on him right away.

When he did, he jerked around quick and was going for his nickel-plated pistol till he saw who it was.

"Whoa! Hold on there, young son!" I yelled at him. "It's just me."

He grinned kind of sheepish. "Sorry, mate. I'm a little jumpy these days."

"How come?"

"Step down here and I'll tell you," he said, looking things over out beyond me and then bending down at the fire again. "I was thinking of stirring up an omelette for supper. Will you join me?"

I told him, no, I'd already ate out at Momma James place. He raised his eyebrows and asked what I was doing out *there*. That got me onto telling him about June, bringing her up here and all. Well, not quite *all*. And that got me telling about Jesse James, but not all of that either.

"By the way, I told something of a lie down there, I'm shamed to admit," I said. "To the effect of you sending me to warn Jesse of the Pinkertons. Can you see your way clear to back me up on that, if it comes up? Without me going into it any deeper?" I hated to ask him.

He squinted at me and took a deep breath, letting it out slow. "I suppose I can, just so long as it doesn't get me breaded and fried in the same pan with you," he said. "I can't help but be curious, but if you don't feel you can tell me what this is all about . . ."

"Thank you," I said, then said nothing more. Part of it was I didn't want nothing to happen to him because of something he knowed about me, for I'd of had to tell him about the Pinkertons to put any sense to it, you'll recall he didn't know nothing about me being a Pink. And part of it was I felt stupid as a calf for changing sides all of a sudden like I done—no figgering things out first or nothing. Damned if it wasn't about as complicated working for Jesse James as it was working for Billy Pinkerton, only it did feel more like I was doing more the right thing now, though. A little bit, anyway. On the right side, at least.

He shook his head. "You'd be wise to ride clear of this Missouri horse shit," he said, looking up at me with them deep dark eyes—seeing more than I wanted him to, I thought. "That's what I'm doing. Heading east. I'm going to try some of those Pennsylvania towns you mentioned."

"Yeah, I'd heard you was pulling up stakes," I said, sitting cross-legged and taking the cup of coffee he handed me.

That made him shoot his eyebrows up again. "Really? You do seem to hear a lot of things these days, don't you? Why, I wouldn't be surprised if you inherited my old job eventually." He'd meant it in fun, but then looked at me square.

I didn't see the need to conterdict him, and that was all the answer he needed. I never met nobody quicker on the uptake than Blackfoot Bill.

He nodded. "It seems as though you're pretty close to the horse's mouth these days. Just be careful that other end doesn't swing around and begin talking to you."

"What do you mean?"

He shook his head. "Nothing, really. Except for you to be careful, Willie. These Jameses are a whole other breed of cat. That's why I'm getting out now, it isn't safe anymore. And while I liked the money, I do value my life. You'll live longer too if you look at things the same way, my friend."

I thought over what he'd said and sipped my coffee. "I'm surprised he'd let you just up and quit on him."

He laughed, stood up, and went over to the wagon. "I'm smarter than to try *that*. No, the truth is I priced myself out of the market. Kept telling him I needed more and more money until he finally fired me. I was surprised just how much he *was* willing to spend for good information, though I never did tell him my suspicions about you."

He give me a funny look from over at the back of the wagon, but when I didn't say nothing he went quiet till he come back. "Raising your price is a trick you might want to remember when the time comes to pull out, though I think the time's right now, with the new reward Governor Woodson's put on Jesse's hide, dead or alive. Don't you think it might be time to move on too?" He put down the armload of stuff he'd brought, and then started breaking about half a dozen eggs one after another into a heavy little bowl. He crumbled up some dried up leaves of one sort or another that he had in a jar and throwed that in there with them. Other stuff too.

I just shook my head. "You was going to tell me why you was so jumpy. Ain't been no posses or Pinkertons spooking around here, has there?" I thought maybe Billy Pinkerton and that dumb bunch he was captain of had managed to get up here.

"No, nothing like that," Blackfoot Bill said, taking a fork and whipping up his eggs fast in his bowl and then sliding them into the smoking, butter-greased pan he'd already set in the coals. They sizzled like a rattlesnake gone crazy. Smelled good, too—a little strange, but good-strange, if you know what I mean. "I'm afraid it might occur to Mr. Jesse James, sooner or later, that when I leave here, there'll be someone on the loose who could point him out to the authorities very easily—and could also testify to quite a few things he'd rather not have come out. Before a jury, if it came to that."

"You think he'd do that to you?" I asked.

"You think there's anyone he wouldn't kill if it meant his own safety or freedom?" Bill asked for an answer.

I thought it over. "His wife, maybe. And a cousin or two."

Bill looked up at me from his fry pan with half a grin on his face. "Maybe . . ."

It turned out I wasn't as full as I thought, and Bill ended up giving me about half them eggs he'd cooked with onions and some cheese, they smelled so good. I think it was being on the trail with June all those days and things gone sour between us that'd give me such an appetite once we'd split up. Lord knows I had ate little enough while I was with her.

While I was finishing them eggs and some biscuits, I told Bill what all I had already eat out at Jesse's momma's and that I couldn't figger being so hungry as I was.

He laughed and said as how I ought to weight two hundred pounds, the way I ate. I offered to work the shows till he left, but he said, no, that'd be all right. He was leaving day after next and wouldn't be hawking the Heap-Big before then. The batch he'd just finished was for the next place down the road. I spent the night there with him, talking and laughing and drinking a little whiskey. And then eat a big breakfast too the next morning before I was to go.

We stood and shook hands, the sun up little more than half an hour.

"Good-bye, Willie. You're a good fellow. Look out for yourself."

"You ain't half bad yourself, pardner," I told him. "And you look out for them Philadelphia gals in there. I ain't been there since I was a kid, but my daddy always said Philadelphia gals could rope and hog-tie you before you could count to three, and once one wanted you bad enough, there was no getting away. That's where my momma was from, I think. From near there, anyway."

He laughed. "I'll be careful," he said, a big smile on that face that looked more like a big mountain cat's than anything else. A face I'd got used to—and then started to like the look of after a while. Maybe because I got to like the man standing behind it as much as I did. "Are you sure you won't change your mind and come along?" he asked me, standing there.

"No. My doin's is here for right now. Some day I'm going back in there to see where the hell the Goodwins hailed from, maybe I'll bump into you again. But for right now, this here's it for me."

I mounted up and rode a little ways out, turned back to wave, and saw he was standing there beside his smoky breakfast fire watching me ride off. We both waved. A good old boy was Blackfoot Bill. The next couple of months, I often wondered what become of him. Sad part was, I later found out.

16

ANOTHER THING ABOUT THE OUTLAW TRADE

I had only got about halfway up the Askew lane before I saw him leaning on a dung fork beside the barn door, watching me ride up. A skinny old farmer with a long red nose who should of been thinking about turning this big place over to a younger man and moving into town. He looked like he was afraid I was going to try and sell him something, once he noticed my packhorse and the mule trailing behind. He didn't ask me to step down.

I told him what I was there for, what Jesse James had said, and that Jesse would be around to talk to him before long.

He shook his head and said he didn't know nothing about it. How was he to know I weren't no Pinkerton man, anyway? Maybe after he talked to Jesse. What if I was just seeing if he was in with the Jameses? A dozen other damn questions I had no patience or answers for.

I swung down without being invited, finally, he went on so long, and I walked up close to him. "Jesse James told me to come here to work and that's what I'm doing," I told him.

You could just smell the scared coming off of him. He

didn't know what the hell to say, didn't like having me there, that was plain, but didn't see nothing he could do about it. Knowed he couldn't get away with ordering me off the place, even though he owned it outright on paper. I stepped in even closer.

And he took half a step back. "Well, all right, you can make it look like you work here, I guess, but I'm not paying you, you understand. Come ahead, I'll show you where to put your things."

It struck me then, walking toward the buildings behind the barn, watching how he limped as we went and leading my horses and mule, what it was going to be like being in with the Jameses. Part of it, anyway. People paid attention to you, what you said and what you wanted. Most often they *did* what you wanted, too. That was some of it. You didn't have to really do nothing to them, neither. I guess I got used to that over the next couple months, stopped noticing it, I suppose—like you do with something that's there all the time. But that day it was plain as the nose on Dan Askew's face that folks would give you what you wanted when you was one of the Jameses. How they looked at you differnt.

He took me to what he called the hired man's house, a bare board shed only a little bigger than the fancy three-hole outhouse too close by. There was a saggy white iron bed in the middle and a dresser with two drawers missing, a pitcher and bowl on top with big chunks knocked out of both. And that was all there was room for in there. Nails in the wall to hang things on. A packed dirt floor somebody had throwed an old musty braided rug down on before they drug the bed in, one window with no glass. Cheesecloth tacked over it and shutters outside. Dark as a cave, almost, in there. Bugs crawling over everthing, more bugs inside than out, it seemed like. A tin roof. And hotter than a cookstove in the summer kitchens of hell.

I was thinking of telling him, no, this wouldn't do, he'd have to put me up at his house, but then I changed my mind. At least I'd be off by myself here, away from the likes of him and whatever nagging, godawful wife he probly had.

That was another thing about the outlaw trade I noticed. People did what you said and give you what you asked for, but even so you lived hard and poor as dirt most of the time. On account of doing what had to be done to stay clear of the law—or not drawing attention to yourself, fitting in with folks who have to scratch for a living, who there's a hell of a lot more of to fit in with than them with money. Out in the country, anyway. And rich folks don't want you fitting in with them, either, is another part of it, while poor folks don't seem to care so much if you're on the outs with the law, because a lot of them are too, some way or another—or has kin that is.

They sure liked the Jameses, though, most poor folks, Missouri poor folks in particalar. Them that wasn't their neighbors, anyway. Why, they'd give you whatever it was you needed with a smile and a nod—share what little miserable food they had, a place to sleep or to hide. Rich folks and well-off farmers, that was a differnt story. "All right," I told Askew, and he went somewheres else.

I unloaded my packhorse and unsaddled them both and found places for them and the mule in the barn, turning an old nanny goat and her kid out into the barnyard to make room. Fed my animals some grain and looked the place over.

A nice old farm, a lot nicer than our spread in Texas, I have to give it that. More damn water on the place than you knew what to do with. Jesse said I didn't have to do no real work there, but I couldn't see just sitting on my ass day in and day out, not doing nothing. So instead I took to draining one of Askew's fields that was swampy as molasses. With ditches and pipe from town laid underneath the ground, which meant a lot of soggy digging, of course.

Frank came around the third or fourth week and asked if I'd saw anything, but didn't even get down off his horse after I told him no, I hadn't. Frank was always stand-offish with me, though he was more sociable than Jesse to most others. I was hoping to see Jesse again, talk to him and show him the field I'd two-thirds finished draining by then, but I guessed he was still East looking into that work they had planned to do on the door of that bank safe.

Draining that field give me an excuse to see better what was going on, too, it being close to the road and on the corner toward the Samuel farm both. After a while I kind of liked the work, despite I was muddy as a muskrat by nine o'clock in the morning, I got bit up by mosquitoes pretty bad every day and my feet was wet that whole first week. Along with a straw hat and a pair of reading spectacles, I bought a pair of gum boots in town and also a long-handled hoe that was just right for the work. I put that last on Dan Askew's tab at the hardware along with more pipe. My beard itched a little, the new part, but not for long. At first my long mustache was hard for my tongue to let alone but I got over that too. I've had it ever since, the mustache I mean, but it's shorter now.

Askew would come out and watch me from a distance once in a while, he didn't think I saw him but I did. He was surprised I was doing what I was doing, and said so one evening at supper, which I took with him and his wife, who turned out to be a nice old gal—played the spinet in her parlor better than most fellows doing it for money in the saloons around there, though mostly what she knowed was hymns. And a better cook you'll seldom find.

Askew said he'd always planned to drain that field himself one day, but had just never got around to it. The end of the first month he offered me a week's pay. Handed me two dollars and fifty cents come Saturday evening, forty-two goddamn cents a day for slogging and sweating in the summer sun of Missouri from the time it come up to the time it set—except for dinner, of course.

I laughed, handed it back and told him, no, thanks just the same. Jesse James was paying me *good* money, and Askew should maybe feed his stock a little better with that two-fifty, they looked like they could use it. His jaw dropped and he took offense at first, it seemed like, but then he clammed up, shook his head and walked away, having nothing more to say on the matter. Either that or he didn't want to say what it was he was thinking for some reason.

At the landing just below Saint Louis, Jesse James sat his horse in the shade of the river maples, waiting for the boatmen to finish unloading the ferry that would then take him back across the Mississippi River to Missouri, his beloved Missouri, dense with haze over there on the far tree-lined shore. He never felt quite right whenever he was away from her for very long.

A little drowsy with the midday heat, he watched the carts and wagons from the other side rolling off the boat one at a time. A showy green-painted rattan vis-a-vis got stuck and they had to lift it back on the tracks. When he suddenly recognized the red and blue buffalo painted on the cover of the next wagon, he quickly sat up straighter in the saddle and smiled. Choosing this route, the route he believed Blackfoot Bill would follow eastward with his wagon, Jesse had hoped for this very thing. A bursting-ripe plum that unexpectedly falls into your hand just as you reach for it.

Once again Providence had been kind to him, as it nearly always was—as, indeed, he had at last come to half-believe it always would be. All week he had fretted over letting this persnickety Indian get away. If anyone could point him out to the Yankees and show them how to lay a snare for him, Blackfoot Bill could. And now all Jesse had to do was reach out his hand.

Jesse James turned and backtracked to another grove of trees several hundred yards up the road, away from the river. There he turned his horse and rode far enough into the thick undergrowth so that he would not be noticed by travelers on the double-rutted dirt trail, but from where he could see everything and everyone who passed by. An easy rifle shot from the pike.

I had nearly finished one of my main cross ditches one morning toward the end of July, one that'd drain the upper part of my field into the culvert I had laid under the pike, when I noticed a fancy one-horse black phaeton sort of affair, a light carriage it was, pulled off the road with the bonnet up, despite it being so hot a day you'd want to have it down to get whatever little breeze there was stirring. The rig was up the pike a piece, a big black horse swishing its long black tail and stomping the flies off its flank every minute or so. I didn't think too much about it, but when I looked back some time later, wiping the sweat off my face and neck with my bandanna, it was still there. A woman by herself driving the thing, I thought, odd as that was. Looking back my way, too, it seemed like, though her white bonnet mostly hid her face.

I wonder if maybe something's the matter there? I remember saying to myself, but even before I said it I sort of half knowed who it was. I cleaned my shovel and started up that way. I had stepped in over top of my left boot and it sloshed inside as I walked.

"I see you're making good progress on this old worthless field," Sarah said when I walked up, looking off toward where I'd been working, no hello at all. She wrapped the reins around a brass knob put there for the purpose. "I didn't know you had such talents around a farm or I would have had Daddy offer you a job on ours."

"And it's nice to see you again too, Miss Cole," I said, lifting my hat. "But in answer to your question, it's just kind of a way to pass the time with me is all," I said. "I don't do this sort of work as a rule."

"Yes, I know," Sarah said, setting those bright green eyes on me for the first time, looking down her nose a little from up where she sat. "And so does everyone else in Clay County." My, she was a handsome woman was Sarah Cole.

Nobody'd ever accuse her of being a beauty, mind you, she was too sturdy and bright for that, but you could look her in the face all day long and still want more the next morning.

"What do you mean?" I asked her, though I had a good idea, all right.

"What I mean, Willie Goodwin, is that everyone around here knows you are working for my cousins the Jameses, living here at old Dan Askew's and seeing if anyone's spooking around after Frank and Jesse—like them Pinkertons were a few months back." I thought she meant me at first, but then I seen she didn't. I was thinking she'd smile if I just kept my mouth shut, but after a minute it was plain she wasn't going to.

"Well, I don't see how you can have no complaint of me doing that, trying to keep that outfit safe, them being family and all to you. Cousins, I believe you said, and their momma and stepdaddy. And I recall being at the wedding of one or the other of them boys with you, though I forget just which one it was right now."

She smiled then, but it wan't turned up very high. "Yes, Jesse and Frank and I *are* cousins, but my side of the family never robbed anyone, never stopped a train and took the money from ladies' handbags. True, we are all one blood, but there are some things the James boys and their *friends* are fond of doing that *my* branch of the family tree never would."

I took off my hat and scratched my head. "I sure hope you'll excuse me, but all this complicated cousin business has got me a little confused, seeing as how I ain't a James or a Mimms or a Cole, and—"

"Or a Woodson, either."

"No, no Woodson either," I said. "And nobody's fancy Nashville cousin or nothing like that, I was going to say before you cut me off."

She looked at me for a minute. "You're referring to my cousin Thomas, aren't you?"

It was my turn then to let the time pass without saying nothing.

"You were mistaken, you know, what you supposed about Thomas and me," she said, quieter this time and fussing with a handkerchief in her lap.

"Is that so?" I asked. "It sure looked pretty cozy, him and you."

"I don't care how it looked, but if you *knew* more and presumed less, you'd understand there couldn't be anything between Thomas and me, no matter that our kin have married together back four generations or more."

"Is that so?" I asked again, more sharp-tongued than I felt.

"Yes it is!" Sarah snapped. "Thomas is a nelly, an auntie, and he can't help it!" She was all upset over this, whatever it was she meant, big tears in her eyes and then rolling down her cheeks.

An *auntie?* I says to myself. An uncle, sure, I could see that, but ... it couldn't be *that*, could it? "You don't mean he ... ?"

"Yes, for God's sake," Sarah said, still crying, but laughing a little through it, relieved she had got it out, it seemed like. "He ... prefers men to women. He stays with us when he comes out here to visit his ... gentleman friend ... in Independence. He and I have been good friends since—" She stopped talking and just looked at me.

"Well then why the hell didn't you say so back there on your—?"

"Because you didn't give me a chance to!" she hollered. "I didn't want to say anything in front of him, I was afraid he'd be embarrassed in front of *you*, and then not knowing how you'd act. And *then* you went riding off like some—like some—"

"How does 'damn fool' sound?"

"Yes! Like some damn—" She shed a tear and then wiped it away. "No, Willie. No, more like ... you had started to care for me before you knew just what you were letting yourself in for—with my family and all."

Muddy as I was, I stepped up into that road cart sort

of carriage, the spring bouncing again when I sat beside her. There was only room for two on the seat, and barely that, we was so close. "And you come over here apurpose to tell me, didn't you? Even after I went and acted like a damn fool," I said, seeing for the first time that this was more than just puppying around, the way she was with me and the way I felt towards her. I took her hand and held it. She had nice hands.

She turned and smiled pretty then. "You can ask anyone about Thomas, anyone who knows him. Even Jesse, once he gets back."

"I haven't seen him since I started here. Where is he?"

"The rumor is that he and Zee have repaired to Texas and are going to raise breed horses there. But I'm surprised someone in so tight with Cousin Jesse doesn't know that."

I felt better then, her digging me a little that way.

I let it slide on past. "I don't need to ask him about your cousin Thomas, Sarah. It was just jealousy was what it was. Thinking you might prefer some other man over me. And he is awful good looking, your cousin Thomas."

She give me such a surprised look!

"No, no! I meant—"

She couldn't pretend it very long and laughed good. "I knew what you meant!" She was such a tease like that, quick and bright as a brand-new silver dollar. We both had to chuckle then.

"I'm sorry about that with Cousin Thomas, truly I am," she said. "Part of it was pridefulness on my part, I know, and he's very nice, really. I didn't like you talking sharp to him like that. I'm not ashamed of him, I want you to know, and I hope you won't hold his ... too much against him." She reached up then and touched the whiskers on my cheek, smoothed them down a little. They was an inch or so long at that point, my beard looking like one of them short ones, like in the pictures of President Grant during the War or General Sherman's, much as I hate to say it, only with a little more gray in it than theirs.

"I don't know about this, Willie," she said, meaning my full-face beard, a funny little frown mixed in with what was left of her smile, a trace of where a tear had rolled down her cheek you could still see.

"Well, I don't either, but it's what Jesse wanted," I told her.

She smoothed my mustache, petted it sort of, then looked at my lips and then into my eyes. Of course I kissed her, muddy as I was, what else was I to do?

It was some time till she pulled back and straightened her bonnet. "My, I—I haven't . . . felt like that since I was a married woman . . . Oh, I'm sorry, Willie. I guess I shouldn't be talking about when I was married. Men don't like it, Momma says."

"It don't bother me none," I said. "Not when you're talking about how you feel toward me and all. Lord, I missed you, Sarah. Thought about you every day, thought about coming out to your house again to ask you—I don't know what I was going to ask you, but I wanted to see you again so bad is all."

She kissed *me* that second time, and it was an even sweeter one than before.

17

THEM OLD TEXAS CEILING-GAZERS

The next couple of months I saw Sarah pretty regular, but she was a little diffrent, somehow. She'd send me a note over to Askew's every so often and I'd meet her someplace in Kearney. That kind of a thing the churchified folks of backwoods Missouri shook their fingers at, but since we was older it didn't seem to matter so much. Or I'd go over to the farm on Saturday night if that's what we'd said and then we'd go somewheres from there.

Oh, we got along good after that business with her cousin Thomas, laughing and having fun most of the time. Going to the stomps at all the little towns around there, for Sarah loved to dance, she surely did.

Picnics in the woods. Even an ice cream church social once. That time not speaking to each other I guess would be the real reason we liked each other's company even more than before. We saw what it would be like *not* seeing one another again, and that tended to rub off some of the burrs.

But even so, some things wasn't exactly perfect, you understand. For one, she stopped asking me if I wanted to meet her folks and her boy. When I went out there for her, we'd sit on the porch a while and then leave, or when we'd come back we'd sit on the porch till she went in.

I didn't notice at first, but it come clear after a while. My guess was it had to do with me being in with the Jameses. As I understand it, her folks didn't like that even less than she did. I couldn't figger about the boy, though. Maybe it was just easier if she throwed him in with her ma and pa, I don't know. She didn't say nothing about what it was, so I didn't see that I should. So there was that.

And then there was the other thing, of course. Which is always a piece of trouble between a man and a woman whether they're seventeen or seventy, I suppose—no matter what else it is. Never being seventy, I don't know firsthand, but I don't guess it's much differnt than when you're younger, at least it hasn't been as old as I am now. And I sure do remember trying to get them to say yes when I was seventeen, in the worst way.

What was so free and easy for June and any man between wearing diapers and his coffin suit seemed like it was always going to be a knotty tangle for Sarah and me. After we made up, we come close to sleeping together a couple of times, mostly through me wanting to. It was like she'd want to too at first, but then at the last minute, either at the hotel in Liberty once or once out at my place at Askew's, after I'd got Mrs. Askew's lady to clean it up good and got it fixed up a little, when we'd went there apurpose—apurpose to see what I'd done to the place is what we *said*, but apurpose for the other reason too, though we didn't say nothing about that.

She changed her mind at the last minute both times. Oh, and once out on a picnic, too. I couldn't see what the matter was and she didn't feel comfortable talking about it. So I didn't push her on it, not after that with her Cousin Thomas, you understand.

And then it got more tangled still, tangled up with the way I was starting to look at things. Once I was in with the Jameses and Youngers solid. That outlaw life *will* change you, you know, and them that think it wouldn't change *them* should go try it for a while and see. My pa used to say, some people should go to hell for a week or two, once they come back they'll know something.

I ain't at all proud of the way it changed *me* back then, riding with the Jameses, some things I done and the way I talked. Most of all, the way I was to people. Like I was some kind of a big bug or something, and I wasn't the only one seen it in me, neither.

Once I was down at Monegaw Springs with Jesse, Frank and a man named Art McCoy, a real hell-raiser of a fellow, seeing about getting back at some Kansas Jay-Hawkers by helping ourselves to a herd of their prize horses they had put together from all over, top blood all the way through was how Jesse put it. Down there where the Youngers lived I saw June, she was bringing a bowl of mashed potatoes out to the outdoors table where we was eating one evening, like the regular women was doing, her still dressed like a cowboy, though.

I tried getting her to notice me so's I could talk to her alone later, but it didn't seem like she could see me for looking. "June!" I finally called to her when she was across the table from me, "I want to—"

"Oh, I know what *you* want, Willie," she said real sassy for everone to hear, making it seem like—like, well, you understand what she made it seem like I wanted. So did everone else sitting there.

"No," I said. "I got to talk to you about some—"

"The answer's still *no!*" she said, and everbody laughed. "I took pity on old Willie down there where Jess was honeymooning, and he's ready for a second helping now," she said so everone would be sure to hear, slopping a big spoonful of mashed potatoes on Jim Younger's plate. That wasn't true, of course. She was just having fun I seen later, her kind of fun, but I got steamed up—like she sure as hell shouldn't ought to treat *me* that way! "He hasn't let me alone a minute ever since," she said real loud. Well, they all roared at that.

Made me mad, though, I'll tell you. And when you're mad you sometimes say things you wisht later you wouldn't of. I stopped eating and stood up. "No, what I wanted was to tell you was I think you give me a good dose of the clap down there in the Elk River country." It got awful quiet at that table all of a sudden, and I sat back down.

Toward fall I'd begun getting a terrible burning itch down there in the manly parts, and it'd got so sharp I went and saw a doctor in Kansas City. Of course I was pretty sure what it was before he told me, but I *was* worried about how serious it might be. Some of them damn things will kill you, I don't know whether you knowed that or not. But I was lucky there, the doctor said, for it wa'nt one of the worst ones. He give me some medicine to swallow every morning and some yeller ointment to rub on it twict a day, and told me to stay away from the ladies and the sheep if I didn't want them getting what I had.

The smile slipped right off June's face when I said about her having the clap, and I says to myself, *well, she asked for it, treating me like that*, kind of proud of myself, I hate to say it.

She come over beside where I was eating, her arms folded in front of her. "My guess is you should've stayed away from those old Texas ceiling-gazers you must have rented before you came up here," she said.

"Yeah, and my guess is three-fourths of the men sitting around this table probly has got a good dose of it from you themselves, and they'd be smart to get to town and see a doc—like I done. Before they goes blind and their whangers falls off." Of course some howled when I said that. Jesse too, sitting down from me still eating a chicken leg, but June didn't think it was funny. And neither did some of the Younger boys, them staring up at June like someone might've stomped on their toes but they was too proud to squeal.

June said humph, there was nothing wrong with *her* and went off in a huff. Right away a lot of them Younger boys asked me if I was sure it was June, and I told them, like I told her later, that I wasn't *with* no one else but her for several years, coming out of prison and all.

"Well, you got it from one of those Texas convicts, then," June said later after she'd cooled down some and we was talking alone. "I've heard what goes on in those prisons."

"I'll bet you have," I told her. "But the truth is— and you can believe this or not, I don't care—I never done nothing like that when I was in. It was you was the one who give it to me, all right. No doubt about it."

She shook her head. "No, I don't have . . . anything."

I just shrugged.

"I see you've changed some, Mr. Goodwin," she said.

"What do you mean?" I asked her.

"Oh, lots of things. Making that up about me—just to get even for me teasing you a little, for one."

I thought it over. "No, mam, I didn't make that up at all. And if that was teasing, I'd sure as hell like to hear you bad-mouth someone."

June shook her head and walked away.

Riding back from Kansas with all them horses, Jesse dropped back alongside when I was riding drag one afternoon.

"Was that right, what you said about June back at the Youngers on the way out?" he asked.

"Yes indeed it was," I told him.

"What?" he yelled. We both had bandannas pulled up over our mouth and nose to clear the dust, so it wasn't easy to hear what was said.

"Yes!" I hollered louder.

He nodded and we rode on silent a while together till he said something I couldn't hear and yelled for him to say it again.

"Then how come I didn't catch it?!" he hollered.

I just shrugged and then he done the same thing back. After a minute he rode back up to where Frank was in the lead.

It wasn't till right then, right that very minute, that I remembered that gal from Sedalia, the one I slept with on the way up from Texas. "Oh my God," I said out loud, but I never told nobody the mistake I made, blaming June. And so to keep from looking no worse a fool, I let everbody keep thinking it was her. I wish now I would have spoke up and straightened that out, but I never did. You can't go back and change nothin, though—nothin at all.

Of course after the doc told me that about staying away from women, that ruled out sleeping with Sarah, which is what I was talking about in the first place, in case you forgot. Sure, we kissed and I held her a lot, but nothing beyond that. She couldn't catch it from just that. Naturally, that's when she changed her mind again.

"Don't you want to anymore, Willie?" she asked me, snuggling close on her porch one night before she was to go in, her bonnet off and in her hand.

"Well, I do and I don't," I told her. "Why don't we just wait till you're sure this time?"

"I *am* sure, now."

I nodded. "I know you *think* you're sure, but you remember them other times you thought you was sure? That time we went over to my place?"

She sat up of a sudden and stuck her bonnet back on. "Of course I remember, but that was different."

"Yes, sure it was, only—"

"Only now you don't want me, isn't that it? Now you're thinking of one of those Younger girls, and—"

"No, I ain't wanting no one else. It's not like that, Sarah. It's just that—" And of course I had to make up a lie then, because I couldn't tell her the truth. I sure as hell hated to do that, lie to her. I didn't fall *that* low, that I would *enjoy* lying to someone.

And if we went over that subject once, we went over it half a dozen times. It struck me, somewheres around the third or fourth time we done it, that things had got turned around and screwed up pretty bad between men and women somehow, what was fair and all—and what wasn't.

And it didn't look like there was ever going to be much of a chance to set it right, either. What I mean is, if a man tells a woman he's interested in sleeping with her, or lets her know it more round about than that, there's lots of ways she can act that are supposed to be all right, all of them fair ways of doing that old, old man-and-woman dance.

For example, she can say she ain't that kind of a girl and go off in a huff, more often than not hoping he won't fully believe her and ask again. Imagine if a man was to do that when a woman lets him know she's interested in sleeping with *him*. If he was to say, like, "Gee, I'm sorry darlin, but I don't do that kind of a thing. I got my principles, you know. And if I broke down and did it with you, supposing you got me drunk enough to, you wouldn't think no more of me in the morning than a bucket of cow shit." Why, she'd have him dragged off kicking and screaming to the crazy place. And she'd have no trouble whatsomever convincing anyone that that's where he belonged, too, if he was to say that.

And a woman can milk a man for all he's worth, cooperating in the bedroom department only when she gets a new dress or some ruby jewelry or taken on a fancy trip to some big city like New Orleans for the week. Once, when Sarah was letting me know she wanted to, I had the idea of telling her how maybe I'd be more of a mind to do it with her if only she'd get me one of them new Winchester lever actions like all the other fellows who rode with Jesse James had, or maybe a pair of fancy Mexican spurs. Or maybe if she'd come around to my place first in a nice spiffy road cart, took me out to a fancy restaurant and then paid my way in to see the strip show in some smoky saloon, her having to act the whole time like watching some skinny lady taking her clothes off one at a time was one of the greatest pleasures on earth for her, mind you. Can you imagine a man getting away with something like that? Why, she'd have the sheriff on him.

And how about if a man tried holding out till they was

married and then she couldn't do nothing about how rotten he was between the sheets, not willing to try even half the things she wanted him to do in bed?

Of course those was just things I was thinking of, nothing I really done, you understand. It was just something to keep me from going loco when Sarah wanted to and I wanted to and the doc said no. Naturally I couldn't say nothing to Sarah about the real reason for not doing what she wanted—or at least what she *thought* she wanted just then, you never know.

Anyways, things went on like that well into the fall. Sarah and me taking in all the dances and fairs and not sleeping together, though my problem was clearing up a little more every week. I was helping out Jesse and the boys from time to time, like going after that horse herd over in Kansas—mostly when they needed an extra hand quick and had trouble rounding one up in a hurry, but nothing much. Nothing dangerous, you understand, nothing requiring no revolver work, because I warned them I couldn't hit nothing.

They laughed. McCoy thought I was yeller, I think, but didn't say so right out. The rest took me at face value. Most of the time, though, I was just living at the Askew's and working on draining my field while looking out for anything suspicious.

I was up along the road clearing leaves out of my culvert one morning, a nice sunny day toward the middle of October, dry and cool after a warm spell, when I noticed this horse I was pretty sure I'd saw before. It was tied up in the trees on the other side, up toward Samuel's. A light buckskin, he was. A gelding I saw when I got closer, a fine looking horse, good enough to be one of Jesse's though I knowed he wa'nt.

Jesse was over visiting at his momma's at the time or I wouldn't of been so much concerned about it as I was. The reason I knowed, Jesse had sent word over the night before that I was to come over to his momma's the next night for supper, tonight that'd be then.

Looking at that buckskin I remembered the rider then too. A fellow about my age, someone I didn't know his name right off but had saw around town a time or two, though I couldn't remember if it was Liberty or Kearney where I'd saw him. Wore a Montana, I remembered, but then couldn't recall much more about him than that except he looked like a tough customer. Not dirty and ragged, I don't mean that, no—but like you would *not* want to have to go up against him with either fists or a pistol.

I was still looking that buckskin over when he spoke up behind me. "Something the matter there?"

I turned around quick and he was leaning up against a tree watching me. Wearing that dark brown Montana like I remembered, a Colt's strapped to his hip. He was one of them fellows always looks like he just had a bath and a shave no matter how dusty it is, stood real upright, even when he was leaning against something, but not stiff— straight though, you'd say. I was surprised I didn't hear him come up. "No, nothing the matter except you're on Dan Askew's ground," I told him. "And he asked me to look out for anybody spooking around up here. Mind telling me your name?"

He chuckled under his breath and started coming over. "Sure he did . . . "

I couldn't see what he was tickled about nor what he was getting at, but I had the idea I ought to be careful with this Jasper. Wait and see the lay of the land.

He stopped with most of his grin still spread over his face, but it didn't look one hundred percent friendly. His voice was deep and it rumbled in his thick chest when he spoke. "And no, I don't mind saying who I am, not since you put it that way. You don't know me, huh, Goodwin? Name's Moss, O. P. Moss, and I'm working for the same outfit you're with, I believe." I wondered how he knowed my name.

I couldn't figger out whether he meant Jesse James or the Pinkertons—the outfit we both worked for. And I sure as hell didn't want to chance going the wrong way. "Is that so? Does old Dan Askew have another hand I don't know nothing about?" I asked him.

He looked at me hard. "You can cut the bullshit, mister," he said. "I think we both know what's what, don't we?"

"I'd know a hell of a lot more if you told me what the devil you're driving at," I said. "Otherwise, I'm going to have to ask you to move your ass off Dan Askew's land." I stood up to him, though he was a couple inches taller than me.

He tried to look me down for a minute, until he started to smile again. "All right, all right," he said, flicking his hand, a little less growl and with not quite so much edge to his voice. "Look, I know you're a Pinkerton man, sent here to spy on the Jameses. Fact is, I'm on a special assignment for William Pinkerton myself, though I ain't one of you Pinkertons, by *damned* I ain't. He told me himself you made it look like you worked here for Askew, William Pinkerton did. I was to 'let myself be known to you if the opportunity arose.' That's how he said it. And I guess this is it, isn't it? The opportunity, I mean."

I wondered how Billy Pinkerton learned about me working here.

I remembered who he was then, this fellow. He used to be the sheriff of Liberty and had been trying to nail the Jameses for quite a while, some said. The reason he lost the election, the way I heard it, he was trying to nail the Jameses a little harder than folks around there wanted him to. It made sense he'd throwed in with the Pinkertons now. "So you ain't *really* a Pinkerton, then?" I asked him.

"No, I'm just working for wages," he said.

"Well, that's what most of us are doing in this world, ain't it?" I let him take that howsomever he cared to. "But what are you doing *here*?"

His horse shied then, at the sound of my voice, I suspect, and he patted him and undid the reins, which was tied pretty close. "Here! Easy, easy." When the buckskin was calmed down he turned back to me. "Mostly, I'm here to find *you*, Goodwin. To tell you they want to see you in the Kansas City office. I was to tell you you have pay waiting. That's the message, 'There's pay waiting this time.'" He stopped to see what I was going to say.

"Uh-huh. I get it." I said it that way to make him think what he said might've meant something more than what it did, which it didn't, of course. I still wasn't sure what this old boy was up to, you understand, though I knew for certain by then he wasn't working for the Jameses, trying to check up on me. I knew *that*, anyway. "It would've been easier to just come up to the house. If that's *all* you was doing here, wanting to talk to me."

He mounted that buckskin and give me half a smile over his shoulder. I had the feeling he wasn't used to smiling this many times all in the same day, but he didn't quite know what else to do. "Well, no, I took the opportunity to walk up to the edge of the tree line and watch the Samuel place a while. I heard somebody shooting, target practice it sounded like, but I couldn't see anything. I wanted to check whether Frank or Jesse's horses were there—if they were maybe visiting their mamma, which they do from time to time. Pretty often, I hear."

"I wouldn't know nothing about that," I said.

"Yeah, I'll bet you wouldn't," he said, turning his horse. "I don't know why the hell you're being so goddamn skittish. We're both working the same side of the fence, you know."

If I listened close I could just hear the shots he'd talked of from the Samuel place. "Just my way," I told him.

"Well, take a good look at my face, Goodwin, because you'll be seeing it again soon, and I don't want to have to go through this bullshit with you a second time." He steadied his mount, which was prancing some there under the trees. "I don't know what the hell's wrong with him," he said, reining him in. "He's never like this."

"I'll remember you," I said. "Don't worry about that."

He started walking his horse away, but stopped and sat a little sideways in the saddle, looking back at me without turning that buckskin—which was more of a looker than well trained. I told myself to remember that, too. A man's horse says a lot about him.

"I gotta hand it to you, Goodwin. I'm surprised you pulled this off," he said. "Working for Askew and not have the Jameses shoot you up the ass like they did Whicher. I warned him, but no . . ."

"You knew him, huh? The one they say the James boys killed when he was down here?"

"*Say* they killed? Where the hell've *you* been, your goddamn right they killed him. And, yes, I met him. A real pain in the ass, but—" He caught himself then, heard what he'd just said, shook his head and started over. "A son-of-a-bitch, but he didn't deserve to be shot like that. I warned him."

I nodded. "Yes, but who gets what he by-God *deserves*, huh?"

He just looked at me, then turned to go.

"One more thing," I said, and then waited till he'd stopped and turned back. "Don't come up here again trying to get a second look at the Jameses, see whether they're around or not. If they are around, I'll be the one to do something about it, not you. Now *I'm* warning *you*."

He stared at me square a long time, hate or whatever-else in his eyes I couldn't tell. Finally he turned and looked into the trees, thinking over what I'd said, maybe, not very happy about whatever it was he was thinking. And *then* he reined his horse around and walked him down toward the road. He was about the only man I never liked right off.

18

A SHOOTING LESSON, OR STUCK WITH THE TRUTH

I walked down to where I could see which way Moss went at the road. He turned toward town. Then I right away scrambled up Shay Hill—where you can see the road farther in, and a little while later I saw him, nearly half a mile off and walking that good-looking skitterish buckskin toward Kearney.

I took down my bridle, grabbed two lumps of sugar and whistled my horse in from the jingle pasture, but didn't bother to saddle him. Five minutes later I was down at Samuel's.

"They're down by the creek," Jesse's wife Zee called from the porch when she heard me ride up. She dusted flour off her apron with both hands. Two of Jesse and Frank's little half-sisters was dressing up doll-babies under a lilac bush. Their brother Archie was sitting there beside the doorway whittling a stick to a point. He wasn't notice me till Zee called out, then he looked up, stood up, smiled, and waved to me to beat anything. He wasn't exactly right, Archie Samuel wasn't, but he was a rosy-cheeked child with a little angel's face and that sweet way to him a lot of folks have who ain't quite all there.

I waved back to him, thanked Zee, and went down the way she said.

"Willie! What the hell *you* doing here?!" McCoy said as I was sliding off. Frank was there too, his hat over his face, taking a nap on a blanket beside the embers of a dead fire—despite a shot fired every half minute or so—and a couple new fellows I'd saw before but didn't know their names. Something of a camp back there, a rope corral and all.

"Somebody's spooking around. I'm going up to tell Jesse," I said, heading that way. Now Jesse practiced his pistol shooting often, every day some said, even when he was visiting folks, like there at his momma's.

"Whoa! Hold on!" McCoy yelled before I got half a dozen steps. "He don't like no interruptions when he's workin on his shootin."

"Like it or not, I got to tell him now," I said, stepping around McCoy.

"Okay, it's your ass, not mine," he said behind me, and then giggled at his joke. "He sure as shit don't like people watching him when he targit shoots."

I got up into the trees another ten rods and saw him aiming. He spun quick as a bull whip when he heard me, had that gun leveled at my chest at two rods.

"It's just me!" I yelled, throwing my hands up.

"Ha!" he hollered, letting the gun down. "Willie, how are you doing? You're a little early for supper, aren't you? I nearly shot you, you know."

"McCoy tried to warn me, but I—I should have shouted. Next time I will. No harm done." My heart was still beating faster than a hummingbird's wings, though, and I was more out of breath than I let on. I stayed back, thinking he might want to shoot some more—and not have me looking over his shoulder.

"Come on over, that's all right," he said, drawing aim. "What brings you down here?" He fired. I saw a nut of some kind fly apart, a black walnut still in its hull—or was—though it might of been a butternut. There was a dozen or more of them still lined up, setting out on a board twenty or thirty yards off. Empty spaces and pieces of a dozen or so others that had already went to meet their maker, a big bag of whatever kind of nuts they was at his feet.

"I saw somebody spooking around and thought you'd want to know right away."

He glanced at me first and then aimed again. "Anybody we know?" He fired and another nut went to heaven.

It was a question I didn't think about him asking me. I reached back for a lie then, but none come to mind quick enough. I was stuck with the truth. There I was, about to tell the one man I didn't want to know it the name of the one man around there who knowed I worked for the Pinks. No way out of it.

"It was O. P. Moss," I said. "Used to be the sheriff around here before I come."

"Yes, I know," he said. "But I'm surprised you do." He cocked his revolver, aimed careful and fired again, another nut dead. That was when I first noticed he was left handed, it seemed so awkward, shooting with the wrong hand. He lowered his pistol, pushed out the empties one at a time with the ejector rod built in, and started loading cartridges from his pocket.

It was quiet for a minute, the sharp smell of burnt powder in the cool air. "I heard it around," I said.

"Was he riding by or was he watching from somewhere?" He cocked and aimed again.

"He was watching your momma's house from up there where you can see it above the road. He didn't see nothing, though. It was a good thing you hid the horses up here."

He lowered the revolver without shooting it and looked at me square. "Oh, you spoke to him then?"

Damn, I had backed into that one in the dark. "Yes I did. I had to chase him off. I saw his horse and he come up when I was looking it over. He said what he was doing right off, watching the house here, I didn't even have to ask him. Acted like I should be happy he was doing it. Nothing I could do at that point except ask him to leave, was there?"

"No, it's all right, Willie. That was all right," he said nodding at me. "Certainly, there was nothing else you could have done—except kill him, of course." I thought at first he was making a joke, but he wasn't.

He looked down for my shooting iron. I wasn't wearing one, like I almost never do. If you can't shoot any better than me, what's the use? is the way I see it. "What did you say to him?" he asked.

Much as I felt like shuffling my feet, I stood still. "Only that he was on Askew's land and the Askews didn't want no trouble with the Jameses or the Samuels, who was always good neighbors to them. So he would have to leave."

"*Did* you say that?" he asked, and then said, before I could answer, "That was a very intelligent lie, sir. Very intelligent. The heart of the idea is true, and that is the genius of it, but that you could . . ." He looked at me close. "And how did Mr. O. P. Moss take *that*, being asked to get off Askew's property?" A sly smile slid across his face as he aimed his revolver again, still cocked of course. I didn't know if he was doubting that I'd really told Moss what I just said or if he was laughing at Moss, and I couldn't ask. He fired again. He missed that time and looked at me to see if I saw, but I never let on.

"He sure as hell didn't like being told to clear out, but there was nothing he could do about it except shoot me, and he didn't seem interested in doing that just then."

Jesse turned and nodded again, a little amused, so it seemed. "Here, take this," he said, handing his revolver toward me. "This is the new model Colt's revolver I just . . . acquired. I'm trying to decide whether it's better than my Smith and Wesson. What do you think?"

I shook my head and didn't take the pistol. "I'm the wrong one to ask on that question. I couldn't hit a barn door if it was swinging open to hit me. Don't you remember me saying?"

Jesse James smiled. "Oh, that's right. I remember now." He held it out to me anyway. "Come on, Willie. Let's see how you shoot."

I shook my head.

He kept holding it there. "Come on, then," he said, kind of coaxing. "Don't be bashful, now. Let's just see what you can do with it."

I took the pistol. It was warm from his touch, from him holding it, despite he was wearing thin black leather gloves. It struck me then I could shoot him, shoot Jesse James dead, right through the heart, right then and there. He didn't have no revolver at all now. One laying at his feet in another holster, true, but he'd of never been able to get to that one in time. The reward was big, too. Not so big as later, you understand, but near ten thousand dollars, anyway—a lot of money. I was not a good shot, but not as bad as I'd let on. I could hit a man three feet off, hell anybody could do that. This's crazy, thinking this, I remember thinking to myself.

The look on his face right then, I'll never forget it. Like he could read my thoughts almost. And it was like he was more concerned with seeing what I was gonna do next than he was worried for his life, if you can believe that. "Go on, aim it," he said.

I cocked the thing with my thumb, bringing it up on one of the nuts out there, slid the blade of the sight down in the notch, and pulled the trigger. The hammer fell. Nothing happened.

That look of the devil on his face again. Did he do that apurpose? Hand me a gun I'd think was loaded to see if I'd try and shoot him? I don't know. I've thought it over, reasoned it out a hundred times since then, remembered everthing about that minute, including the odd look on his face, and I still don't know.

"Oh, I'm sorry," he said, taking the Colt's back from me. "I must not have loaded it full." He took cartridges from his pocket, loaded it up tight that time, I watched him do it, and then handed it back to me. "Did you notice how you flinched when it didn't go off?" he asked.

"Did I?" It didn't seem like I did.

"Yes you did," he said. "Pulled down on it. Most people who don't shoot much do that, try to anticipate the explosion and compensate for the recoil with the muscles of their arm and shoulder. That's probably the main reason you can't hit what you're shooting at."

What he said made sense. When I really thought about it, I could see I'd done that, jerked downward when it didn't go off like I thought it would. "Well, what'll I do about it?"

"Put it up and fire it, but don't aim. Concentrate on how it *feels* as it goes off. Out toward the direction I was shooting, only don't aim."

I cocked it. "Don't aim?" I asked. It felt wrong not to aim at something.

"Don't aim," he repeated. "Concentrate on how it *feels* in your hand—and in your arm too."

I shot it that way.

"Did it hurt?" Jesse James asked me.

"No," I said.

"Did it jump up and bite you? Do anything you didn't expect, anything you couldn't handle should it do it again?"

"Why, no. Of course not."

"Well then, remember *that* instead of all the stupid damn things you only *imagine* are going to happen when you pull the trigger. Because it's going to shoot like that *every time it ever shoots*. It's never going to change, Willie. It's *never* going to hurt you!" He reached out and took my shoulder in his strong, black-gloved hand, squeezed hard. Looked me in the eye close with those clear eyes of his, eyes that looked like you was looking down through fifty feet of spring water to the blue-gray pebbly bottom and not seeing so much as a drop of all that water in between, eyes that could see things you and me never could. "Pay attention to what's *real*, Willie, the way things *really* are," Jesse James said to me. "And forget most of that bullshit that's only in your head!"

I was surprised he took this all so serious, this target shooting business. Hell, this was only shooting at nuts, and I wasn't even one of his pistoleros anyway, he didn't depend on me to shoot straight for either his loot or his life. But then I realized shooting good was a big part of his *trade*, his profession, if you can call it that.

It was important to *him* because he wanted to be good at what he did, even if most folks thought it was wrong to be good at robbing trains and banks like he done. Probly he wanted to be the best there was, and probly he *was* the best, too. The best ever. I'd never thought it through before, the way he was about things. I guess he believed shooting straight should be something important to me, too.

I pulled up that Colt's 45 and shot again. Now it would make a better story, I know, to say I killed the nut that time, but the truth is I didn't. Because I still needed lessons then of how to aim—what to look at—and how to squeeze the trigger just so instead of jerking it, and half a dozen other damn things I was doing wrong. Toward the end, though, and he had me shooting back there for almost an hour, I was hitting a nut every so often, damned if I wasn't.

The funny thing, though, it didn't last. Oh, I could shoot pretty good whenever Jesse *James* was around, specially if he was watching me. We'd shoot targets together from time to time after that, and I got more lessons. But afterward, ever since them days? Hell, I'm as rotten at shooting a revolver now as I ever was, maybe even worse. And I don't even pretend to know why.

When we was done shooting nuts that first time, I handed him back his Colt's, but he shook his head.

"You keep it," he said. "I was just trying it out. I like my Smith and Wesson American better."

"Are you sure?" I asked him. It was brand-new, I

doubt it'd ever been shot before. And the action smooth as a baby's behind, too.

"Yes, I'm sure," he said. "It's a fine one, shoots very well, but for reloading on horseback I still like my break-open Smiths." He picked it up and showed me as he talked and while we walked down to where the other men was. "See, it ejects all the empties at the same time, and the whole cylinder is open in front of you, so you can load it easier—especially at a gallop. Whenever Sam Colt makes something better than this, I'll use it. Until then, I'll stick with my Smith's." He patted it in his holster. "No, you keep the Colt's, Willie. I want you to have it. Another way for me to say thank you for what you did down there along the Elk River. The Colt's might not be quite so good as this, but it's sure as hell better than that old thing of yours." He said this last kind of joking, teasing me about my old percussion revolver. I was surprised he knowed what it was, what I carried when I did carry a revolver. Remember, I wasn't wearing it. Wellsir, I prized that new Colt's something awful after that, I'll admit. It was a fine piece of work, but I don't have it no more. I'll get to how I come to get separated from it in a while.

That first week after I talked to O. P. Moss there at the Askew place, I decided I was just going to act like I never even heard of them damn Pinkertons, but then I seen that wouldn't work. If they'd sent Moss out to find me once, they'd send him again—or somebody worse who wouldn't be so careful about where he talked to me or maybe couldn't keep his lip buttoned up so good as Moss must of been doing. I knowed he was, or the Jameses would of been asking me questions, which they wasn't.

The next week or so I thought of coming clean with Jesse. Telling him what was what, what the truth of things was. Lay it all out in front of him, how from the start I was taking pay from the Pinkertons, but I never *wanted* to do what they wanted me to. Didn't me warning him down there on his honeymoon prove that? Didn't that show whose side I was *really* on? That's what I wanted to do, come clean and say them things to him, and there was only one thing wrong with doing it. He would of killed me. No doubt about it, he would of killed me.

Wouldn't a mattered a good goddamn if I *was* on his side now, even if I'd offer to tell the Pinkertons whatever he wanted me to. Or tell him whatever they told me they was going to do, no ... Nothing like that would of counted, for he would of figgered that if I was against him once I could go against him again. That's what he'd think was *real*, and hell maybe he was even right, I don't know. There was just no reason for him to take the chance.

Because they didn't *need* me on the robberies, that was plain. He could get almost anybody to do what I was doing at the Askew's. And damn I couldn't even shoot straight, didn't even *think* of killing Moss when I'd caught him spooking around. Now how good an outlaw did that make *me*?

About a month after I talked to Moss, toward the middle of November, I knowed I had to go in to Kansas City to the Pinkerton office. I didn't want to, but I knowed I had to—there was no telling *what* they'd do if I didn't. I don't think I slept a whole night through that whole month. Kept waking up before dawn with the sweats and couldn't get back to sleep.

But Mr. William wasn't in, he'd went back to Chicago more'n two weeks ago the young man in there told me. I felt good for a minute. But then they said to come back Friday, he'd be back in Kansas City on Friday. He'd left word there he needed to talk to me, and if they was to hear from me, they was supposed to tell me to be *sure* and come back Friday. Damn it.

Come that next Friday I went back in to Kansas City, and just like they said, William was there and was more or less waiting for me.

"Willie!" he said coming around his desk at me, hand stretched out and loud as anything. He give me a big fat cigar, lit it for me, sat me down, and praised me up one side and down the other over getting a job at Askew's where I could spy on the Jameses for him.

Then he paid me in full for all my time from the last pay and then even throwed in a two hundred dollar bonus. Lot of money.

"Even Whicher couldn't figure out how to get himself in down there, but you did—first time in the field, too." I thought at first he meant that field I was draining, but he didn't mean that. "By damn, I'm proud of you, Willie!" He come around and shook my hand again. I thought for a minute there must be something fishy going on. I'd never saw WP like this, all pleased and excited like he was, and I thought this might be some kind of a trap before they arrested me and throwed me in jail for working for the Jameses. All they was waiting for was for me to say the wrong thing, maybe.

After a time Pinkerton looked at me solemn and didn't say nothing for a minute, sucking on his big cigar. "Willie, all the pieces are in place to capture the Jameses, can you believe it?"

I just sat there.

"It's like a chessboard at a pregnant moment. The bishop and the queen are poised at both sides for long thrusts and the knight is in close for the kill. That's you, Willie, you're the knight! You're in a key position and will play one of the principal roles."

He looked at me like I ought to be happy as a pancake, but I just sat there. "I never played that game. I'm a pretty good checker player, but I never learned about pregnant queens and knight keys and such."

He looked worried then. "What do you mean to imply?" he asked after a time. "Do you mean to say you won't participate in the capture of the Jameses because I left you down there in McDonald County with a lame mule? Is that it?"

"No," I said. "All I meant was, I don't play chess."

He waited a minute to see what else I was going to

say and then waited another, looking at me the whole time, his chin resting on his fist. Finally, he let out a big howl and laughed and laughed till tears come to his eyes. "Oh, I see! I see! You were just talking about *chess!*"

Some times I couldn't figger out what the hell was wrong with that man's brain.

Then he "filled me in" on lots of things. That's what he said, "filled me in." I kept thinking of a tooth that'd started to go bad. According to him, the railroads had made it hot for Governor Woodson, and the governor was worried about the next election—both the money the railroads was supposed to give him to run it and the stories they promised to spread about him if he didn't catch Jesse James like they wanted. The railroads was mad as hell that the Jameses had got away with that robbery over there at Gad's Hill and nobody'd hung them for it yet. That note Jesse give the conductor, that was "the straw that broke the camel's back," so far as the railroads was concerned. He didn't say so right out—like he did about that poor camel—but it sounded like the railroads was promising the Pinkertons more greenbacks for taking Jesse and Frank than even the Pinks'd ever dreamed of asking for.

A whole lot of men was coming down to Kansas City to go out and capture the James gang, not that half-assed bunch that tried to catch Jesse down by the Elk River. No, real "hard-knuckled men." That's the way he put it, "hard-knuckled men." I almost reminded him that he was the one leading that "half-assed bunch" down there, but decided not to.

My part was to report to Moss twice a week on whether the Jameses was there at their momma's or not. That's where these hard-knuckled fellows was going to capture them.

"No, I won't do it," I told him.

"Why not?" Pinkerton asked, surprised at me.

I said twice a week was too often, the Jameses would catch me at it and I'd be dead before they could ride in there and get even one of that gang. I didn't really think that, it was just a way to get out of it. He said once a week would be often enough, then. Except if the Jameses showed up.

Then I said there wasn't no safe place to meet Moss, and he told me of a place on the road down to Excelsior Springs, not far from Askew's, where I could leave my weekly message in a bottle, under a fence post, and Moss would get it there and leave me one back. Perfectly safe, he said and then explained how it would work, over and over again, till I started getting sick to my stomach. Everything I brought up, he had an answer to, and after a while I just run out of reasons not to.

I told him, before I left, that I still wasn't decided on it. What I *said* was it didn't seem to me like it would work, capturing them there at their momma's. I'd think it over and let him know, but it didn't sound good to me. He talked, though, while he was showing me out his back door, like I was going along with the idea just the same. I reminded him of what I'd said. He nodded and then kept right on going down the same track. I couldn't seem to get it through to that man that I wasn't making no promises about this thing.

I took that big wad of money he'd gave me down to the same bank as before, intending to leave most of it there in my account. A slick-haired young man in the barred bank window cage acted surprised as hell a man my age, dressed like me and looking like I did, would push so much money across his marble slab at him to put in the bank. Didn't say so out loud, but that's what his look said plain enough.

Seemed to me he thought it'd be more likely that I'd be the kind to be pointing a revolver at him and making him give *me* that kind of money instead of me giving it to him. Well, I pulled my money back, the whole lot of it, stuffed it into my coat pocket, and told him he could just plain go to hell, thank you. How'd he like *them* apples, anyway? And then I walked out of there—with his jaw still dropped.

I thought about what it would feel like shoving a revolver at him and telling him to give me *all* the goddamn money, that sonofabitch. I kept thinking on that all the way back out to Kearney on the train.

19

A HUNDRED AND ELEVEN YEARS OLD

"I want to go along," I said to Frank and Jesse and two of the Youngers. It caught them all by surprise, near as much as it caught me the same. We was down at Monegaw Springs, the whiskey jug with just a slosh or two left in the bottom by then, sitting in front of the fireplace late one night, the weather turned cold and damp. A few days after I'd talked to William Pinkerton in Kansas City and decided I was never having nothing more to do with them rotten sons of bitches ever again.

I'd went along down there to the Younger's to tell about O. P. Moss watching the Samuel house. Jesse wanted to figger out a way to catch Moss sneaking around his mamma's farm and fix him so he wouldn't do it ever again. If Moss just didn't *say* nothing when they took him was all. Say nothing about *me*, that is. But after a while the talk that night turned to their next job, a fat train Frank'd had his eye on and knowed just how it should be done.

"Do what?" Cole Younger said about a minute after I spoke up. He was pretty drunk by then, keeled over at such a angle on the bench he'd pulled up to the fireplace, leaning on an elbow. If he'd a been a canal boat he'd of rolled on over.

"Just like I said, I want to go along." I told him, brazen as a jaybird. "Be in on it. I sat around Dan Askew's farm long enough now, damn it."

"No," Frank said, and that was all he said, though he looked dark at me.

"It's Frank's affair, Willie," Jesse said after a time. "If it was up to me, I'd be inclined to let you in at a quarter share, but—"

"No!" Frank said, louder than he needed to. "I've got this all worked out for five men, we've *got* five men and don't need a sixth!"

Frank wasn't himself lately. He never did like me too much anyway, truth be told, but he'd got himself married just a little after Jesse did, eloped with Annie something-or-other, I never met the lady, they teased him enough about it, though. The talk was she was at him all the time to quit riding the outlaw trail. These days he was crabby as a bear with a sore ass. This train robbery he had figgered out was a way to quit outlawing with a good stock of dollars in his pocket and buy a little farm back in Tennessee, that's what I heard later.

"It's true I don't shoot too good," I said, trying to sell myself into this job. "I *do* track good, though, and you might have need of a man with them talents along on this raid," I boasted. I had hit the jug pretty hard too, you understand, almost as much as Cole Younger, or I'd of just let 'er go.

"Yeah," Frank said, a sneer on his face you could slice bread with, "we sure as hell need a *tracker* along—like I need another asshole. Yes sir, we probably couldn't follow the goddamn *train* tracks to the station without *you*. Yes *sir*, you could go along and show us which way the goddamn trains go! Point 'em right out to us." He stood up, a little wobbly, knees bent, and shaded his eyes with one hand and pointed off into the distance with the lead finger of his other hand. "They went that-a way!" To top it off he started making farting noises with his mouth, looked over his shoulder real embarrassed, and then made more fart noises that same way.

Of course everbody laughed, and being drunk didn't hurt none. After a while I seen the fun of it too and, much as I hated to, couldn't help but laugh right along with them. That was the end of it, of course. I wasn't going.

Only that *wasn't* the end of it.

I was telling Sarah what I'd said down there at the Younger's, about going after the train with Jesse and the boys and all. I knew she wouldn't like it but I thought I had best tell her myself before she heard it elsewheres, and she didn't act surprised or mad at me at all.

"It would be all right with you, then, if I was to start with them?" I asked her.

She pushed harder with her pretty little foot, against the porch railing, and higher we went. Almost like kids will work a porch swing, that's how she liked to swing. And she *did* like to swing, because the leaves was all off the trees by then and it was chilly sitting out, the sun just down too. "Seems to me like you've 'started' already, Willie," she said, a little pouty. "And no, it's not all right. But if that's what you want to do, much as momma and daddy hate all that, I won't say anything against it."

"Why not?" I asked her.

"Because I heard Annie go on about Frank the other night, for about the tenth time. It's just plain selfishness on her part, that's all it is. All you have to do is listen to her. And it sounds terrible. He won't love her for long if she keeps that up, trying to change him," she said. "I'm never going to be like that with you, Willie. I don't think that's right, trying to change each other." She looked at me with them big green eyes. My, that woman could touch your heart in a minute.

"Then you're going to be like Zee about it, then?" I asked her.

"Oh Lord no," Sarah said, bringing her hands up to her face. "I couldn't be like *Zee*! Why, to her, having her husband wanted in six states is just as common as—him going out to mend fences. Can you believe it, they're even trying to start a family! Imagine, being shot at by the law with a couple of little children around your skirts? No, I couldn't be like Zee, Willie. But I'm not going to be like Annie, either."

I nodded a couple of times. "Well, that's good. But for right now, it don't make much diffrence, I guess, because Frank don't want me along anyway. I asked, but he said no."

She wanted to know why Frank didn't want me and I explained it best I could. She didn't seem very pleased Frank wouldn't have me, though, even if *she* didn't want me to go, if you can believe it. She said she'd see about that, but I didn't know what she meant.

"What does Jesse say?" she asked.

"He didn't say much, one way or the other. I have the idea it would be all right with him, though."

She pushed the swing hard and swung us a while. I heard an owl off somewheres. "And what does June say?"

I looked at her good, but she was looking out in the yard. "June? What's June got to do with me riding with Jesse?"

She look at me. "I know about you and June, Willie. Down there in the cave where Jesse was on his honeymoon. She told me. I also know why you didn't want to make love with me after you came back."

All you could hear for a minute was the squeak of the swing chain and that old owl. "My goodness," I said, planting my feet, stopping us, and standing up. "You know a awful lot, don't you?" I was surprised about all this, specially since she didn't seem mad about it. Truth is, I didn't know what else to say.

"I know enough not to get upset about something that can't be changed," she said, looking down the yard again.

I looked to see what she was looking at, but there was nothing I could see.

"Will you sit back down, please? Or get out of my way? I'd like to swing a little more before I go in."

I sat back down and she started up that swing again.

"And also, you believed that Cousin Thomas and I . . . so I don't blame you for what happened, Willie. After all, men are . . . the way they are. Just so it's not going to happen again—you and June."

I shook my head and looked at the toes of my boots. "No, it's not, Sarah. I ain't even sure why it happened in the first place. I didn't try to get her to—"

"Yes, I know," Sarah said. "She told me that, too. That's how June is, how a lot of the cousins are, I suppose." She drug her feet till we stopped, stood up, and so I did too. "I'm getting cold, I'm going in now." She went over and opened the big front door. "I'd like not to talk about this anymore, Willie. As far as I'm concerned, it's like it never happened. We both know it *did* happen, but . . . I don't want to talk about it again, if that's all right with you."

"Yes, mam, that suits me fine," I said, my hat still in my hands.

She kissed me good, pulling my face down to hers. Then studied me good and close. A piece of a smile brightened her looks. "You!" she said, pinching my chin through my beard like she liked to do. "Good night, Willie. In a way, I'm kind of relieved. I thought it was something about me you didn't like, didn't want to—" She give her head a little shake. "You tell me when the doctor says—" She give up on that idea too, blushed a little, I think, but it was sort of dark by that time. Then she said, "And I'll speak to Annie tomorrow."

She turned and went in of a sudden, leaving me standing there wondering what in the hell she was going to talk to *Annie* about, anyway. Not about me and June, was it? I remember shaking my head, much like she'd did a minute before, and then walking down the front steps thinking I would never understand women, not if I lived to be a hundred and eleven years old.

* * *

One night about a week later, I was asleep a good three or four hours at my little place there at Askew's, when I woke up hearing someone scratching around outside. I slipped that new Colt's revolver Jesse had give me out of the slick holster I'd got for it, cocked it, opened my door quiet, and stepped out into the bright moonlight in my long underwear and boots over my bare feet.

A little tick of a noise behind the outhouse, and when I looked that way, the shadow of a man's hat on the grass—the man wearing it still behind the outhouse, but his hat clear as anything, the shadow of it anyway.

I took a couple steps that way and leveled the Colt's. "I see you there," I said. "I'm pointing right at you, mister, so you better come out slow and easy with your hands grabbing for stars."

"Psst!" someone said *behind* me, around the corner of my shed. "Don't shoot, Willie! It's me."

I almost did shoot, though.

Of course it was Jesse James, and he come around the side of my place laughing to himself and chuckling like you wouldn't believe. "You've come a good ways with your shooting, Willie, but you're not an accomplished shootist just yet."

"You wouldn't of thought it was so funny if I'd of put a couple holes in you, mister," I told him, lowering the piece and uncocking it. I'd saw by then he was just having fun.

"I'd have been surprised if you could've hit me, even at this range," he said going over to get his hat from where he'd propped it on top of some firewood someone'd racked against the back of that old outhouse years ago for a windbreak.

"What're you doing here this time of night?" I asked him.

"Talking to you, *mister*," he said once he come back, quiet and low. "Though you ain't much to look at dressed in your Sunday best like that. How'd you like to go on that raid of Frank's?"

"Well, I'd like it just fine. That's was I was angling for down there at the Younger's, you recall, but as I understood it, there was enough men already."

"There were," Jesse said, hunkering down there in the moonlight, "until Miller shot his middle toe off right through his boot. Carrying one under the hammer, the damned fool. It's not too serious, but he won't be much good until it heals up. So there's an opening for you if you want it."

"You're damn right I want it!" I told him, hunkering down too. It *did* feel better being down closer to the ground like that, safer like, more by ourselfs also. It felt odd though, too, being outside talking to someone in my long johns—and carrying a pistol I had nowhere to put but keep it in my hand. "But I'm surprised Frank picked *me*. He don't seem to like me too much."

Jesse James giggled—yes he did. "No, Buck doesn't like you very much. But Annie had something to do with you being picked. And so did Sarah, I suspect, and Zee, of course. Sarah got Zee on your side somehow, you old Texican. And me too—I spoke up for you."

"*You* did?" I asked him.

"Yes, Frank said you weren't fit to sleep with the hogs and I said you were."

It was an old joke, even back then, but it took me a second or two to catch on, you'd never think Jesse James would fool like that, but he did once in a while. It was rare, yes it was, but he was more coltish that night than I ever saw him, before or after. I don't know what'd set him off, but it was like being a kid again with one of your friends showing up a little drunk in the middle of the night outside your window, back when you was still living at home.

"Well, good," he said, standing back up. "You'll get a quarter share of whatever we take, like I said before." He turned to go.

"No I won't," I said after him.

He stopped. "What do you mean? I thought you said you wanted to go."

"I'll get a *half* share or I ain't going. If I ain't worth a half share, it ain't worth my while going against the law—not for no quarter share it ain't. I don't know if you know this or not, but I got no paper out on me now. I'm clean as a newborn baby. Nobody's after me for nothing, I served my time. A half share or forget it." I was surprised at myself being so bold with him.

He only chuckled some more. "Well, you've got balls, Willie. I've got to say that for you. I'll see what Frank says." He clapped me on the shoulder then and walked back behind my shed without no other good-bye. I stood and waited for the sound of his horse. I stood there a good long time, but I never heard it.

"Whadda you mean he gets a half share?!" Art McCoy yelled, glaring at Jesse and then at me. "Hell, that's all *I* git, and I been riding with this outfit for more'n two years now!"

"Let it go," Frank grumbled, cleaning his rifle. We was getting ready to go after Frank's train.

"Like hell I'll let it—"

"He said to let it *go!*" Jesse yelled, his eyes flashing cold fire. I always had the feeling he held something against McCoy from a ways back. Some old sore that'd never healed entirely.

"It ain't—" And that's all McCoy got out.

Just that quick Jesse had drew his pistol and cracked McCoy hard across the forehead with it. Like a snake out of a hole. It was over before you could rightly say you saw it. McCoy on the ground thrashing around like a half-crushed copperhead and bleeding bad from double gashes above his left eyebrow, the hinge must of caught him somehow. Both his hands up covering it, blood streaming from between his fingers, moaning something over and over I couldn't hear right. Jesse went back to putting things in his canvas bag calm as anything, just like he was before, a look on his face like nothing at all'd happened.

Frank walked over and cogitated over McCoy, who was still squirming in the dirt something fierce. It must of hurt like hell, for whatever else you could say about Art McCoy, he wasn't no crybaby. It felt about half wrong I'd held out for that half share, for McCoy'd never of come to this if I'd settled for the quarter. I did pity that man, even if I didn't like him that much.

Looked like I was about the only one who did, though, because Jesse paid him no notice at all, and Frank looked down at McCoy like he was watching some odd kind of a bug he'd stepped on by accident, one that didn't have the common decency to up and die quite as quick as Frank'd like him to. "Oh, this is wonderful," he said, his voice loud and like a big sheet of tin in a high wind. He dropped his arms so his hands slapped against his legs. "Thank you, brother! Just when we're ready to leave you put our most experienced man out of commission." It didn't strike me till right then how cold they both was, McCoy squirming on the ground, hurting like he was there. Like something was missing in both them boys.

Jesse turned slow and looked hard at Frank. Instead of yelling, he spoke quiet. "Let it *go*, brother."

Frank stared him right back, but you knowed who was in charge here. "Where ignorance is bliss, 'tis folly to be wise," Frank James said—though I didn't know just what he meant by that. Something against Jesse, though, that much was plain.

I had the notion if Frank'd pushed it an inch farther he would have got just the same as McCoy. Or worse.

20

THE MILK OF HUMAN KINDNESS

Muncie, Kansas
A Station on the Kansas Pacific Railroad
December 8, 1874, 2:10 PM

A few miles west of Kansas City, five riders on sleek horses rode into the little town that perched upon the railroad tracks like a sleepy bird on a telegraph wire. At the station, four of the men dismounted and stood looking both ways up and down the dirt street, two going up on the wooden platform after a minute and the other two staying with the horses. There seemed to be no one else around.

The fifth man continued out along the tracks some distance to the semaphore signal, where he found he could not turn the device without a key of some kind—a new precaution the railroads had instituted since the last time they had been robbed.

The stationmaster spotted the man out by the signal through the soot- and-rain streaked panes of his office window and stepped hurriedly out onto the platform, closing the door behind him to preserve the potbelly warmth inside and excusing himself to Frank and Jesse James as he walked between them. "Hey, there! Stay away from that!" *he yelled at Bob Younger down the tracks.* "You don't—"

Frank James stepped forward and hit him on the back of the head with the steel-plated butt of the double-barreled shotgun he had concealed under his long coat. The station manager went down like a sledged steer. Frank and Jesse each took an arm and dragged the limp man back inside.

"You need a key or something for the goddamn signal now!" *Younger said as he came in. All three looked at the unconscious trainman stretched out on the floor.*

Jesse glanced down the tracks the other way and saw a gang of eight or ten men a few hundred yards away laying ties for a new spur. He told Frank to go down there and get those men to pile the ties across the main line. Bob drew his pistol and went along, pulling up his bandanna as he went, like the rest had already done.

"All right, gentlemen," *Frank James said to the surprised train crew, holding the butt of the shotgun on his hip and pointing the twin muzzles toward the low gray sky that threatened rain.* "Your assignment for this afternoon has been changed somewhat. Do what I tell you and no one will get shot, I assure you. Now stack these ties on the main line." *He pointed to where he wanted them. The workmen stood looking at each other. Frank James shoved the dark eyes of the cocked shotgun against the temple of the nearest man's head with a thunk.* "Now!" *he yelled. They scrambled to comply. Bob Younger chuckled to himself watching them scurry. He sat down on a switch box, his pistol still drawn.*

Jesse motioned to Goodwin, one of the new men, to come inside. "Look around for some kind of key that unlocks the semaphore signal," *Jesse told him.* "Start by searching him," *he said, pointing at the unconscious man lying on the floor by the stove.*

When they still hadn't found the key ten minutes later, Jesse walked out and shouted down to Frank to have the crew hurry up with that pile of ties and then to lock them in the tool shed behind the station, the train was due in five minutes.

Jesse then called to Bud McDaniel, the other new man. He should leave the horses now, they'd be all right, and walk up the tracks. When the train came into view he should wave a red flag at them and yell "Track torn up!" when they went by. That would stop them.

"Where'll I get a red flag?" McDaniel asked.

"Look around," Jesse said. "For Christ's sake, it's a railway station!" He shook his head as he watched McDaniel go.

As it turned out, the train was a little late, giving the crew plenty of time to finish piling ties across the tracks. Bob watched their worried, mute faces disappear from view as he pushed the door of the tool shed closed upon them—strange, they looked very pale for men who worked in the sun every day—and then snapped the padlock over the latch.

Jesse heard the train and then its brakes screeching, so he assumed McDaniel had done what he was told. The engine came into view around a long curve, wobbling heavily on the rails as it slowed. Jesse, Frank, and Goodwin ran up to the puffing engine when they saw it was going to stop short of the huge pile of ties.

Jesse, who got there first, climbed quickly up into the cab.

"What's wrong?" the engineer asked, half knowing by this time, seeing men with bandannas covering their faces.

"This is what's 'wrong,' sir," Jesse said, holding up his Smith and Wesson American after he'd looked around the compartment for weapons. He turned to the fireman. "Get down and uncouple the passenger cars—after the express car. And then you," he jabbed the engineer in the ribs with his revolver, "pull right up close to the ties. You understand me?"

"Yes, sir," the engineer said, removing his cap for some reason and wringing it in his hands. "Don't hurt the passengers, sir! Please, I beg you, don't hurt the passen-

gers." *The fireman scrambled down as quickly as he could. Goodwin went with him.*

Jesse smiled beneath his bandanna, nodded, and stuck his head out the cab window. "He doesn't want us to shoot the passengers," *he called down to his brother.*

"Tell him we'll consider it," *Frank said.*

Jesse looked at the engineer inquiringly, who nodded a grateful thank-you. "You see, my wife and children are riding back there today. This is the first time they've had the chance to ride with me . . ."

Jesse clapped him on the shoulder. "Just do as you're told, and you'll all have stories to tell your grandchildren some day."

"Yes, sir," *the engineer replied quickly, and then ventured half a smile.* "You're not . . . ?"

Jesse winked.

The engine, tender, and express car pulled forward without the passenger cars, which Younger guarded from the ground on one side and McDaniel on the other. Jesse had no trouble convincing the engineer to tell the man in the express car to unlock the car door and then the safe.

Jesse tossed the two canvas bags down to Frank without opening them. On one knee, he watched Frank's expression change when he looked inside—even with the bandanna he could see it clearly. Pleasure, pure pleasure. Frank held his arms out wide, a heavy bag in each hand and looked at the sky. "Yah-hoo! Thank you, Lord!"

Frank became gracious. He decided then and there not to rob the passengers, though McDaniel grumbled about it. He got Bob to unlock the tool shed and let the workmen out so they could remove the ties while he personally guided the grinning engineer's locomotive back to hook up with his passenger cars again. The train would proceed nearly on schedule, courtesy of Frank James.

After the track crew was locked safely back in the tool shed, Frank waved to the engineer to pull out. The engineer waved back. As the passenger cars pulled by the mounted robbers, Frank also waved to the folks inside, who called and waved back. Until Bob Younger sent two quick shots toward the heavens and everybody inside ducked. The train suddenly looked empty.

Frank laughed first and then Jesse joined him, and soon they were all laughing at the sight, McDaniel shaking so hard he fell off his horse.

When we was coming back into Missouri, it'd started to rain I recall, Frank said as how he'd like to go see an old friend he'd rode with under Quantrille—who lived near where we would cross the river. They'd be sure to offer us some supper, too, and we was hungry, wasn't we?

So we went off down this old corduroy road to a little road, following Frank now, to an even littler road after that and then up into some woods and through a kind of a rough place till we come to a log house wasn't much bigger than down there where Jesse had went on his honeymoon. This was it, Frank said, he was sure of it. There was the bullet holes in the windowsill some Yankee cavalrymen had embroidered the place with when they was chasing him and his friend Stan.

Nobody come out, even though we sat there a minute in the rain and watched the smoke go out the chimney, so after a time Frank went up and knocked on the door. After a longer time, a lady opened it, about Frank's age, and you could see she was crying before, her eyes all red and puffy. Worried, too, till she reconized Frank.

Frank's old friend from the war days had passed on last winter and she lived there alone now, she said. Frank asked if she would feed us, he called her Wilhelmina, Wilhelmina Gay her name was, and we'd be happy to pay her for it, pay her well.

She said she'd be proud to feed Stanhope's old friends, only she didn't have much in the house, could she run over to the Lorichs' across the way and get some slices of ham?

Frank give her some money to buy the meat, about

ten times what it would cost, I figgered, but that was all right, and she went off to get it, telling us to help ourselves to some coffee she'd just made, and there was fresh bread there too if we was hungry and couldn't wait for the ham and beans.

Jesse told McDaniel to water and feed the horses, and we went inside. Frank decided that'd be a good time to divvy up the money and he brought the bags in with us. After McDaniel come back, Frank dumped it all out on the table. I couldn't believe it was so much, he didn't say before how we done. I mean, I knowed it was good from the way he'd went on back at the train, but I didn't think it would be *this* good.

"Yee-haw!" McDaniel yelled when he seen it all.

"I told you it would be a good one, didn't I Bob?" Frank asked him, and Younger grinned and bobbed his head.

Jesse just smiled, looking more at us than at the loot, I noticed. Course, he'd did this dozens of times before. There was packs of U.S. notes in wrappers, all hundreds and fifties, loose greenbacks too, mostly twenties, piles of it, a heavy leather bag of new ten-dollar gold pieces and a box with ladies jewelry wrapped in velvet cloths inside—rings with big glittery stones, some of them real diamonds and rubies, pins the same, bracelets of all description, necklaces of pearls, other things I didn't rightly know what they was.

Frank asked Jesse to divide it the way we'd all agreed to, if that was all right with everyone, and of course we said it was.

First thing, Jesse counted out the whole amount of the money—nice and neat and in stacks of a thousand dollars each. It come to nearly thirty-two thousand dollars. An *awful* lot of money. Frank figgered it'd cost him about five thousand in expenses setting up the job, paying off someone who worked high up for the railroad and all, and he said as how he ought to be paid back for that first. I didn't see how it could ever cost that, but I didn't say nothing about it, there was still so much.

McDaniel's quarter share got him just a shade over thirteen hundred dollars, and he was happy as a pancake with that till he saw what Bob Younger and me got. Bob had signed on for three-fourths of a share, which give him thirty-nine hundred dollars, and I got my half, which amounted to twenty-six hundred and sixty dollars by Jesse's reckoning. I don't know how Jesse and Frank split up what was left. They didn't divide theirs there and I never asked.

McDaniel right away started grousing about him getting less than anybody. He'd did as much as anybody, he said—except Jesse and Frank, of course—but more than *some* he could mention. He looked at me and then at Bob and then back to me.

Jesse'd had about enough of Bud McDaniel and told him so, but Frank said maybe he could make things a little evener by how the jewelry was split up. Instead of sticking to our shares, each man could take a piece of jewelry to his liking and then the next and the next and so on, till it was all gone. And Bud could go first. Frank asked Jesse if that was all right with him. Jesse nodded, but got up and started outside, saying Frank should pick his jewelry for him. And that's how we done it.

About that time Mrs. Gay come back with three big slices of ham and a basket of eggs. Frank give her a little gold engraved child's ring and one pearl earring that was left over, and then we went out to the barn, where Jesse was already, and just laid dry and cozy in the sweet-smelling hay, listening to the rain on the tin roof till she called us in for supper at the table where we'd sat before. Ham and fried potatoes and eggs. I don't know what happened to them beans she'd mentioned before.

Mrs. Gay didn't sit down with us, but brought us coffee and bread and such, and from time to time she turned her back to us over by the stove and had herself a good little cry. Quiet, but you could see her shoulders shaking. Jesse said we wasn't going to hurt her, what was wrong, anyhow? Did she still miss her husband Stan that much? After all that time?

Well, yes... "But I thought you was someone else when you came up," she said. "That's why I'm so quivery inside, and why I didn't come out." She dabbed at her eyes with a handkerchief. She'd feared we was the banker she owed her mortgage to. He was supposed to come to collect the balance today, and if she didn't have it, which she didn't, he was going to turn her out. She'd asked him for more time, but he wouldn't hear of it.

"So the sonofabitch's going to foreclose on you?" Jesse asked her, steaming up around the edges you could tell.

She nodded yes, and that sent her into another crying fit.

Jesse asked her a lot more questions about this banker then. His name and what he looked like, and what kind of a rig would he be driving, the kind of horse, and where was he coming from, and what road would that be, and would he be going back the same way? I didn't see what he was getting at with all these questions, but of course I didn't say nothing.

"How much do you owe him?" he asked her last.

"Eight hundred dollars," she said through her hanky.

Jesse thought about it a minute, all the rest of us was watching him at this point. He turned to me. "Willie, give this woman eight hundred dollars from your share, will you, please?"

Well, I didn't want to do it because he didn't say nothing about paying me back. But I couldn't see no way out of it, and it seemed cheap to ask about how I was to get my money back. So I pulled out what Frank had give me and counted out sixteen fifty-dollar notes and shoved the pile across the table.

Jesse handed it to her—that was the first I ever noticed he was missing a joint on his left middle finger. Her face said she didn't know if she should take it. "Go on," he told her, kind of coaxing. "Just be sure to get him to sign the receipt my brother Frank will write out for you.

Be sure his signature is on the receipt before you give him the money. Do you understand?"

She nodded that she did, and then come over to take it. I saw how skinny her hand was when she reached for the bills, that little child's ring with the initials engraved on it fit her ring finger with room to spare, and her hand trembled so when she reached.

She fell to thanking Jesse, and then Frank, and then all the rest of us, and she went on and on about it, crying and laughing and praising the Good Lord and Jesus and then us again. I got squirmy sitting there hearing all that praise said about me and the others that'd just robbed a train, and so did the rest of the men, it seemed like, Jesse saying it was all right, finally, she was not to go on so about it.

Naturally, she said she would pay him back, though she didn't know just when she could. I wondered why she didn't say nothing about paying *me* back, but he was the one that'd handed the bills to her, I guess. She'd work and save it, but she didn't know when she'd have all *that* much money together. Jesse said that was fine, he'd stop by on his way through some day, and if she could pay him then, that would be all right. But if she couldn't, that would be all right too, because he'd just come by some time later then.

We left a short while after that, saying how good the food was—each of us giving her a ten-dollar gold piece for feeding us, except for Bud who give her a quarter, I think—and Jesse saying not to worry about the money, now, but just to remember to get that bastard's name on the receipt, not to forget it and not to take no for an answer, either.

She run out in the muddy road after us as we was riding off. "You're a wonderful man, Mr. James!" she called, meaning Jesse.

"Yes, and brimming over with the milk of human kindness, too," Frank said, so only we could hear it. Jesse laughed and the rest of us did too.

Instead of going back the way we'd come, we went

further on, though Jesse didn't say why. Some time about then the rain stopped. Three or four miles along we saw this democrat wagon coming towards us, same as the lady had described, and the man inside was just like she said too. A black suit tight across his little paunch and some kind of a fancy Eastern hat that he tipped when he got close to us, showing his bald head. Something the lady'd forgot, but then I thought maybe she'd never saw him with his hat off. I says to myself—all right, this is why we come this way. This man's in for it now.

But Jesse and Frank just smiled and tipped their hats back to the man, so the rest of us did too. I was surprised, though, they let him get away like that. A short while later, where the woods was thick and a road come in from the side, Jesse stopped but stayed on his horse, looking around for a minute.

"This is where we'll be saying good-bye to you, I guess, McDaniel," Jesse said.

"Naw, I'm going along to the Youngers," Bud said, not getting Jesse's meaning. "Wouldn't want to miss *them* doings!"

Jesse shook his head. "No, this is where we part company. Frank and Willie and I will be going along with Bob, but you're going somewhere else, because I've had more of you than I can stomach. You don't know what you're doing, you're stupid, and some day you'll get somebody killed. I wouldn't care if it was just you, but . . ."

Bud McDaniel finally caught on, his face twisting up mean. "Oh, you think I ain't *good* enough to ride with the James gang or the Youngers, huh?"

"That's right," Jesse said, like he was explaining something to a backwards child. "Now just ride on, McDaniel, because we're waiting here a while."

"You son of a—" Bud stopped right there, for I believe he got a good look at Jesse's eyes just then, and he knowed what was coming next if he went on so much as an inch more. I was a full rod away from Bud, all of us sitting there on our horses, and I could see him swaller dry and hard even from that distance. He didn't let out a peep more.

"Don't spend any of that money for at least a month," Jesse told him. "And that jewelry will get you caught if you're not careful with it. I'd head west and keep on going if I were you. They say California's nice."

McDaniel still didn't say nothing, just sat there and glared at Jesse a minute.

"Good-bye, McDaniel," Jesse said to him, and that was all there was to it. McDaniel turned his horse and walked it away. Didn't look back.

"Good riddance," Frank said after him, but more to Jesse and me and Bob than to McDaniel. "I never liked the man anyway. Always reminded me of Calaban." He looked at Jesse. "I suppose you want me on the back door. Right, Dingus?"

Jesse nodded. That was his nickname, Dingus, but Frank was the only one could call him that. McCoy tried it once and got a swelled lip for it.

"Come along, Bob," Frank said. "We'll be the slammer on this mousetrap today." They went back up the road the way we come—about fifty yards and then went off into the trees. I knowed then what was up.

Jesse climbed down and spread his bedroll out on a rubber sheet, it was still wet. "I'm a little drowsy after that heavy meal, Willie," he said. "And this may take a while. Do you mind keeping watch?" He didn't wait for me to answer, but stretched right out still wearing his duster. "There's a bottle of good whiskey in my saddlebag if you like," he said. I went and got it and offered him a drink, but he waved it away and put his hat over his eyes. In a minute he was breathing deep and regular.

I was only a little ways down into that bottle when I heard a wagon coming. I put down the whiskey and leaned over to wake Jesse, but he sat up before I touched him. "You stay on the ground," he said, standing up, stowing his gear quick, and then stepping up smart into the saddle.

When the democrat wagon was almost to the crossroads, Jesse moved out in front of it. "Evening, mister!" Jesse said, touching the brim of his brown fedora to the man like before.

The bank fellow stopped his cart, looked at me and then over his shoulder and there was Frank and Bob behind him, Frank up on his horse like his brother. The man tied the reins to the dashboard rail and sat real still. "This is a highway robbery, I presume," he said after a minute.

"Indeed it is," Jesse said. "So if you would just toss down your wallet and that satchel beside your seat there . . . " Jesse turned to me. "Get those, would you please?" I went and got them, the banker looking straight ahead, and took them to Jesse, who got a big wad of fifties out of the satchel first, all sixteen of the ones I'd give him before, it looked like, and then handed them to me. Then he opened the wallet, took out a lot more money, and handed me that, too.

"What's this?" I asked him.

"Why, that's what these *businessmen* call interest. Every investment should earn a generous amount of interest, shouldn't it, sir?" he asked the banker.

That banker didn't say nothing, just kept looking straight ahead.

"It appears Mr. St. John of the Groveland Bank has nothing to say on the matter," Jesse said. That was the name Mrs. Gay had said to us, and the name of the bank, too.

That got the man's attention, and he turned his head and stared at us. "I was curious about where Mrs. Gay suddenly got that kind of money," he said. "Now I know—the notorious outlaws Frank and Jesse James, with whom Mrs. Gay's husband rode during the recent war. In the service of Quantrille, I believe?"

"At your service, sir," Jesse said, lifting his hat and bowing a little in the saddle. Frank and Bob come up from behind.

"If you *are* at anyone's service, other than your own,

sir, which I doubt," Mr. St. John said, "then I'll ask you to return my money and let me be on my way. It was money honestly loaned—and at a very fair rate of interest, I might add."

"My ... he certainly has a lot to say for himself, doesn't he?" Frank said from behind. "If you're so damned fair, how come you didn't give Stan Gay's widow an extension on her mortgage, you damn gouger."

The banker went back to looking straight ahead. I had to kind of admire him, the way he stuck up for himself. Didn't show no fear, either, which he must of had, seeing as how he knew who he was talking to and what they could do to him if they was of a mind to.

Mr. St. John turned around again to look at Frank. "As a matter of fact, she's had two extensions already, and if she could have paid anything at all on the interest the last time, I'd have given her another. The truth is, in her reduced circumstances, since the unfortunate death of her husband, she couldn't afford the property she's living on. It doesn't look like much, I know, but it covers nearly three hundred acres, and she's not even having anyone farm the parts that could be farmed profitably." He sounded pretty satisfied with himself, like he was in court and had just made his case. "But of course that's all changed now, isn't it? Since you've decided to play Robin Hood once again?"

Jesse got down off his horse, pulled St. John down off that cart, and threw him hard into mud and stones of the road. "We don't *play* Robin Hood, sir. We help deserving people whom the banks and the railroads have robbed."

The man was slow getting up, the fall had hurt him more than he wanted to let on, you could tell. When he stood up you could see he was a lot shorter than Jesse. He put his hat back on and brushed himself off as best he could with his hands. He looked Jesse square in the eye, which meant he had to look up some.

And you could see by the red of his face that his blood was up, no matter he was in danger here. "No, you are certainly no Robin Hood, Mr. James. I was wrong about that. Robin Hood stole from the rich and gave to the poor. You rob from the railroads and the banks and give poor folks only enough to make the papers *call* you Robin Hood. So the common people *believe* you're like—"

Jesse's Smith and Wesson sprung out like a rattlesnake strike and caught that little banker under the chin, whipping his head back something awful and snapping his jaw shut—you could hear the teeth breaking in his mouth. He fell down on his ass, and when he stood back up his mouth was all blood. It was me, I would of stayed down. Not him, though. He wobbled for a minute, spit out some teeth and blood, and poked around in his mouth with his fingers to see what he'd lost in there. Blood run down his chin and dropped off. He got out his handkerchief and mopped at it.

And then damned if he didn't start to talk again. I was hoping he'd just shut up, but he wouldn't. "—no Robin Hood, no. What *you* are is a common criminal, and so is your brother. I fought for the South too, but the war is over. We *lost*, sir, in case no one has informed you yet!" He turned and looked at Frank. "And you will end up like common criminals, I assure you—strangling at the end of a rope or dead by a pistol ball." It was then he turned back to Jesse, his dark eyes wild, and started wagging his finger like a angry schoolmaster with a bad boy. "Your whole family will end in disgrace and in—"

Jesse shot him right in the heart. And while he was falling backwards, Jesse shot him again in almost the same spot. It surprised me so I jumped, even though I half expected it.

The man was flung backwards into a big puddle, his arms out wide and his blank eyes toward the heavens. Dead before he come to rest, probly. But Jesse was on him like a mountain cat, firing the rest of his three shots right down into the man's face, standing right over him. And even then he thumbed the hammer back and pulled the trigger twice more, it took him that long to come to his senses enough to know his Smith's was empty and that banker surely dead by then. Jesse stood there bent over the man, out of breath like he had run a mile full steam. He was panting so, muddy and wet with sweat, and then he half sat and half fell down in the mucky water beside St. John—working to get his breath back.

It got real quiet there in that little patch of woods. The birds had stopped singing or had flew off with the shots, and there wasn't no sound at all that I could hear but Jesse James breathing hard and raspy, struggling to get his breath back.

After a minute Frank asked Bob if he would drag the dead man off the road into the bushes, please. Then Frank come up and undid the reins from the banker's rig, slapped the carriage horse good on the flank with the broad side of his revolver. It took that cart off at a gallop and after a while you couldn't hear it no more.

Frank walked his horse forward, past where Jesse still sat in the road, his head bowed low. "Yes, simply *filled* with the milk of human kindness," he said, looking down at his little brother a second and then passing on. "Except when you piss him off."

21

EVER SINCE HE WAS A PUP

All the way down to Monegaw Springs I kept seeing Jesse bent over that little man, that banker, shooting him in the face over and over. I couldn't believe it. I only dreamed it, maybe, and then I'd look over at Jesse, and, yes, that was what'd happened.

He was quiet going down there. Oh, he'd answer if you spoke to him, but the talk fell off from there. That night when we stopped at a farmer's Bob Younger knowed, Frank pretty much left Jesse be and Bob done the same. Not ignoring him or nothing, but just letting things go howsomever they was going to.

We ate what the farmer's wife cooked us, I don't remember what it was, something plain. It had got dark before we'd tied up there, and as soon as we finished our food Jesse went upstairs to the room they got ready for him and Frank, not saying nothing. That night I dreamt like I was still awake and seeing him shoot that man. Over and over I dreamt that—only that little man kept changing, he was my packhorse once and Blackfoot Bill another time, and then that damned old rusty plow back home. They was so clear, those dreams, I would of swore I was back there in that wet patch of woods again, there at the crossroads where he'd did it. In the morning, sitting in the outhouse, I felt so tired it was like I didn't sleep at all, only I knowed I did.

When we got down closer to the Younger place, Frank started making his jokes again, and Bob was eager for his people to see how good we'd did with that train in Muncie, laughing and saying what he was going to give his lady friend of the jewelry he'd picked and what he was going to give his wife and his little girl. It was like Bob and Frank had left what Jesse done back there behind them, alongside the road with that man's body, and they could just go on their way like it'd never happened. Hell, maybe they didn't even remember it no more, I don't know. Maybe Jesse didn't either. But damned if I could just forget like that, much as it would of been a comfort to—instead of seeing Jesse bent over that man shooting him to death every hour or so.

Well of course I'd thought about the chance of people getting shot when you robbed them before I asked about going along. You have to take that sort of thing into account because it's going to happen from time to time. And also the chance *you* might get shot, too, no getting around it. But not straight-out murder like that, not just killing someone because you was so mad you couldn't stop yourself from shooting him in the face over and over. No, I never thought it would be anything at all like *that* riding with Jesse James. Once, walking the horses across a narrow bridge, when I chanced to look Jesse straight in them clear blue eyes of his, my heart jumped.

We come to the Younger's place a little past noon. Going up through the trees you could see they was all outside waiting for us, somebody must of told them we was coming. Zee was there, I saw, along with Frank's wife Annie, and dammed if Sarah wasn't right there with them too. I don't think I was ever happier to see anyone than I was her right then, it was like I was away a year instead of only a few days, for some reason. All three of them fine-looking women up on the veranda, leaning against the railing and waving to us as we come up.

I looked over and Jesse was looking at me just then, the first little hint of a smile since he'd shot that man. He touched his hat brim to me.

Both Frank and Jesse beat me up to where our women was waiting for us, and they had hold of theirs before I got to Sarah. I had the feeling I wasn't the only one felt he was gone longer than he really was. Where Bob and his woman had got to I couldn't tell, I didn't even know if the one he latched onto right off his horse was his wife or his lady friend. I was just going to give Sarah a little hug there when she grabbed me and give *me* a big hug and then a kiss for all the world to see. Well, at least all the Youngers, little ones included—who giggled at all this smooching going where they must of played every day.

We all went inside, it'd got cold the night before, and to warm ourself Sarah and me stood in front of the big open fireplace they'd built a roaring pine fire in, that big room smelling of a hundred years of chimney smoke—the ceiling black with it and so low Jesse's hat almost touched.

Frank and Jesse had dug out pieces of jewelry to give their wives, so I got into my bag and got out a nice pin for Sarah. A big green stone in the middle, more or less a color to match her eyes, though truth to tell it was a shade darker, and a oval of little pearls all the way around it. She caught her breath when she seen it, but held back a minute I noticed before she asked me to pin it on her dress.

They fed us smoked turkey and roast pork, dishes of mashed potatoes with fried onions stirred into them, pickled lima beans from a big jar and three kinds of pie for dessert. Frank started giving away smaller pieces of the jewelry we had took down there to the different Younger women while his wife showed off the big diamond ring he had just gave her, his first pick. Sarah ate her food slow, not saying much, squeezing my hand once when it happened to touch hers on the bench we was sitting on.

While he was eating, Jesse got out some money and started handing that out too, and more and more folks come into that big room and stood around the table, mostly men, waiting for theirs I finally figgered out. Some of them was Youngers, and then cousins of Youngers, and then some others that the Youngers had to tell Jesse and Frank who they was. At one point Jesse asked Cole Younger, who come in late but was done eating already, Cole always wolfed his food down faster'n a dog, he asked Cole to get out that box of things he'd left there, and Cole went outside and come back a short time later with a small wood crate under his arm.

Jesse started handing things out from that too, there where he sat down the table opposite me. A candlesnuffer, one made like a pair of scissors cut off that looked like it was made out of gold, a big gold pocket watch and chain. This was loot from other robberies, I thought to myself, that's where all this had come from. Each one there got something, a few bills, a necklace, or something, and then they more or less left us alone to finish our meal.

Jesse was setting the box down on the bench beside him and saw me watching him. I was just curious, you understand, I'd never saw nothing the equal of this before. Sort of like a king in a story I remembered from when I was a kid, giving out things to poor folks. "Here, Willie," he said, passing the box to one of the Youngers to give to me. "Help yourself."

"I don't need nothing," I said, not taking the box.

"Go on," Jesse said. "You did real well yesterday, especially for your first time— Didn't he Frank?"

"Hell of a lot better than that damned McDaniel," Frank said, shoveling a forkful of mashed potatoes and onions into his mouth right after. Folks laughed. That was as good a word as I ever got from Frank James.

I took the box and looked inside, letting Sarah see too, but she seemed embarrassed for some reason, almost right away standing up and carrying her plate out. That wood box was still about half full—strings of pearls, a lot of leather billfolds, some little hideout guns in the bottom, more watches and chains, and then I spotted something I had saw before. I pulled out the fancy gold handle of John Whicher's cane, the one in the shape of an eagle's head. The long wood part was gone, of course, but this gold handle was his a while back, I was sure of it.

I looked at it a minute, remembering the little dance sort of thing Whicher'd did walking down the sidewalk up there in Chicago that day. "What's this?" I asked Jesse down the table, holding it up. Of course I already knowed what it was.

"I think it's the head of a cane. See the hole underneath?" Jesse James asked me. "Looks like gold. Do you want it?" If he had any recollections about who it'd belonged to or how he'd got it, you couldn't read it in his face.

"No, I don't have much use for a cane," I said. It's hard to say how holding Whicher's gold cane handle in my hand made me feel. Mostly it was like I wasn't quite all there, that I was about a hundred miles off looking at all this—the things in the box and the people around me at the table there. Like it wasn't really me sitting there holding the heavy gold handle of John Whicher's cane, it getting warmer by the minute there in my hand, sucking the warmth right out of my fingers. The closest I can come to it, I looked through the wrong end of a spyglass one time when I was a kid, and it felt more like that than anything else.

When I was putting that gold cane handle back in the box, I saw something else that looked familiar. A small nickel-plated revolver just like the one Blackfoot Bill had. Since everone was saying as how I ought to take *some*thing, I figgered having a pistol like Blackfoot Bill's might be a good way to remember that old boy by.

I took it out of the box and for some reason turned it over—like I did Bill's that day after he'd pulled it in that bar—when he first showed it to me outside. And I'll be damned if his initials wasn't on the bottom of the grip strap of that pistol right there in my hands, a pair of fancy B's engraved side by side in the fanciest handwriting you ever saw, sort of overlapped, you might say, their loops linked and locked together. "From a Friend" it said there.

This wasn't like Bill's, it *was* Bill's! At least it used to be Bill's. I looked down the table and saw that Jesse seen me turn it over, seen that I knowed whose it was, too. And maybe he even knowed I knowed what that meant. Jesse James looked away. That's when it first struck me who that "friend" was that'd gave it to Blackfoot Bill. I reached down and touched the Colt's Jesse had gave me.

"I'll have this," I said, meaning Bill's little nickel-plated peashooter—not my Colt's. Not offering no thank-you after, either, like I noticed everone else had did.

"I don't know what's wrong, Sarah," I said to her. We was in bed together that night down there at the Youngers, they'd gone and figgered we'd want a room together, that we slept together all the time, I guess, even though we never did before. And to be nice that's how they put us up, though some Youngers or other was probly sleeping in barn straw that night so we could have that nice little room to ourselfs with the fireplace going.

Before I left with Jesse and the boys to go over to Muncie to rob that train, I'd told Sarah the doc said I was all right now, and I could "resume normal relations," that's how he said it. I didn't know if wanting to sleep with Sarah for so long and having things come in between all the time was exactly what you'd call "normal relations" or not, but at least I told her what the doc'd said, like I said I'd do.

She didn't say nothing at the time, back there before I left, just nodded as solemn as somebody as pretty as her can. But it was her one of the Younger women must of asked about us sharing a room, and Sarah didn't say nothing against it is my guess, for there we was in bed together, her earlier taking my hand and leading the way up the stairs and down the hall to it, her even carrying the key and me trailing along with an old candle lamp.

Only now this had to go and happen.

"It's all right," Sarah said, giving me a kiss on the forehead. "It was that way with my husband once. It went away after a while with him, and I suppose it'll do the same with you too."

"I sure as hell hope so," I said, sitting up. "It never happened to me before this, and I'd be just as happy if it never does again. I'm real sorry, Sarah," I said, turning and looking down at her pretty face, the covers pulled up under her chin. "I was—I don't know how to say this right—looking forward to this so, wanting it to be right for the both of us, and now . . ."

She smiled pretty there in the candlelight and held out her arms to me. "It's all right, really it is, Willie. Maybe it's even better this way, the first time, just being close like this."

I held her in my arms a long while, neither of us saying nothing, and after a time she started breathing slow and regular in that big soft feather bed. I blowed out the candle in the lamp and fell asleep marveling at how things turn out the way they do sometimes.

In the morning when I woke up, the sun coming through the window strong, she was gone from our bed. On the washstand, beside the pitcher and bowl, there was the pin I'd gave her and underneath it a note, and beside, the pencil she'd wrote it with.

Dear Willie—,

I'm sorry to leave like this, but I'm not happy here, always thinking about what these people do and all. They're nice to me, but it's just not right. I woke up early and couldn't get back to sleep so I'm going home now, don't come after me.

I'm awful sorry to have to give you your pin back. It's very beautiful, but I can't help thinking of how the lady who owned it before me came to lose it—and how she must feel this morning. You wanted me to have something beautiful, I know, but I just can't keep it.

I'm afraid you'll think I left this way because of last night, but I really didn't, for I do love you, Willie, and hope you will still want to see me again, even if I must go off like this, leaving behind

All My Love,

Sarah

I dressed quick and hurried downstairs, hoping she might not of went yet. But down in the big room there stood June beside the fireplace reading from a newspaper, Frank and Jesse sitting on a bench in front of the fire drinking coffee, and Cole on a chair—all of them turning and looking at me when I got down.

"You're too late," June said. "She borrowed my horse and left nearly an hour ago. She told me to tell you not to follow her, either, if you decided to."

"Why not?" I asked her, tucking in my shirt.

She didn't answer but went back to reading her newspaper out loud to them like she was doing before. It was the story of how we'd robbed both the Muncie train *and* some bank down in Corinth, Mississippi.

"How the devil could we have robbed *that* damn bank the day before we hit the train in Muncie?" Frank asked Jesse. "They're five hundred miles or more apart!"

Cole chuckled. "Hell, that's easy. Stash some horses down there ahead of time, then take the train both ways. Looks like they mistook Lehr and us for you boys," he said.

Frank and Jesse looked at each other and then laughed loud. June went back to her paper. "It says here you got better than eighty thousand from the Muncie train."

"Ah, those damn liars," Frank said, waving it away with his hand. "The railroads lie like hell and the newspapers swear to it."

"Oh, Christ," June said, still looking at the paper. "They've got Bud. They don't give his name, but it says here 'a drunken vagrant was arrested in possession of jewelry positively identified as having been stolen from the Muncie train. The culprit was unable to give a coherent account of how he acquired the booty.' They've got him in jail over in Lawrence."

They all sat there a minute quiet, till Jesse jumped up and flung his cup into the fireplace, shattering it into the stones in back and hissing the fire good. "I *knew* I should have—" He turned his head slow and looked at me. "*This* is what happens when you leave loose ends," he said, like Bud McDaniel getting caught was my fault.

I shook my head and walked out of there. I'd had enough of Mr. Jesse Woodson James and the way he done business to suit me, to *more* than suit me. I was in the barn putting the bit in my horse's mouth when he come up behind me. I knowed who it was before I turned around.

Jesse James looked like he was tasting something sour. "We're going to spring McDaniel, Goodwin, so you'd best stay—at least until we decide when we're going."

You know, I've often thought, if he'd a just called me Willie right then instead of Goodwin, everthing might of come out different. But he didn't, he called me Goodwin. It's funny how one little thing like that can matter so.

"No, I ain't getting into no jailbreak," I said. "I didn't hire on for no—" It was right then he must of hit me. The back of his hand, I think, though I was never sure. It was so fast I didn't even see it coming. One minute I was standing there talking and the next I was down on my ass on the barn floor, my hand up to my mouth feeling the blood run. Bill's little nickel five-shooter was loaded and tucked under my belt, and I still wore the Colt's then, too, but I didn't even think to go for either one. I don't know why.

When I looked up Jesse James was striding out the door like he had somewheres important to go right quick, and Frank was looking around the side of the door frame, eating an apple and chuckling at me sitting there bleeding like a stuck hog. He waited a while before he walked in and then spoke. "I think you'd best go back to Askew's and wait there," he said, biting off a big hunk of his apple and then taking his time chewing and swallowing it. "You don't seem to have caught on to how my little brother doesn't like anyone saying no to him. Never did," he said, turning and starting toward the door. "Ever since he was a pup."

Frank tossed the apple core over his shoulder on his way out into the bright morning sunlight, and it landed a foot or so in front of my boots, stretched out in front of me. I sat there in the deep shadows, on the floor of that dusty old barn, looking at that chewed-over apple core a long minute.

22

THREE NOTES, OR A LONG WAYS FROM NOWHERE

"What happened to your—? "Dan Askew asked before he caught himself and swallowed the rest of his question. But he did keep ahold of my arm a minute, looking at my split lower lip through the bottom of his bifocals, his head tipped up, like he was a doc who might decide to sell me some awful-smelling greasy stuff I'd have to rub on it if I wasn't careful.

I didn't go back to the Askew place because Frank James told me to, though I let *him* think I did. No, I went because I knowed it would be the best place to watch the Jameses from—so I could tell the Pinkertons when to make their raid. Right there on the barn floor, before I even stood up, I decided that. And I figgered even if Jesse was going to try and kill me because I knowed enough to get him hung, he probly wouldn't do it right away if it appeared I was still of some use to him—being a lookout like Blackfoot Bill was.

I think knowing they killed Bill was what really decided me to get out of the James gang and turn them in. Getting punched in the mouth just hurried it along. I could see why they would maybe have to kill Whicher, even if I couldn't go along with how they did it. And I suppose I could even get over Jesse shooting that banker, after a time I guess I could, though I didn't see how right then. But Blackfoot Bill, that was a whole nother deal altogether. For if I'd a been able to make *that* right with myself, it was like I would of been done being me, I knowed that. I might as well of shriveled up and blowed away right then if I could make Jesse shooting Bill seem right to myself. But the fact was, of course, I *couldn't* make it right, what they done to him, and didn't even want to try to any more by the time I got back to the Askews'.

What I couldn't figger out riding back to Clay County was how they'd come to *catch* Blackfoot Bill in order to kill him, because I knowed Bill must of rode off when nobody'd expected it—probly in the middle of the night—and probly while Jesse was off somewheres, too. He was smart and he was careful, Bill was, and *still* Jesse got him. It had to be Jesse by himself, I figgered. I couldn't see Frank doing it—couldn't see him even helping. Much as I didn't like him, Frank James was no killer like his little brother was.

It wasn't but about a day or two after I got back that I heard about Bud McDaniel busting out of jail, or somebody busting him out, and that someone'd shot him a short time later out in some farmer's field a long ways from nowhere. No, I wasn't surprised at all about that, and I was damn glad after I heard it that I done what I done, left from over there at the Younger's when they was talking about going off after Bud. It wasn't that I liked Bud McDaniel all that much, but to go and kill someone because they *might* say something that'd get you in trouble, the same as with Bill, that was just wrong as hell.

I have to say it, the idea of turning Jesse in to the Pinks rubbed me pretty raw at first, when I was coming up from the Younger's. I kept remembering the fooling-around way he was that night he come over to talk to me at the Askews' in the bright moonlight. And how he wanted to *help* that widow lady pay her mortgage off when she couldn't do it herself.

It got easier to talk myself into turning him in once I was back a while, though, and could think it over more careful. Even if you could see your way clear to say, well, Whicher *was* a Pinkerton man and he *was* trying help arrest them so the law could hang them—even if you *could* say that, how in the hell could you make right what Jesse done to Bud and Blackfoot Bill?

One evening about sundown I went down toward Excelsior Springs to see if I could find that post hole safe again. Well of course I could, I was just sort of hoping I couldn't. I'd wrote a note to put in it, had it in my shirt pocket, and this is what it said.

> I'm keeping good watch again for when they're back at their mamma's. The reason I didn't put nothing here as soon as I said, I was off tracking them when they done that train robbery over in Kansas. I believe they'll be here before long. Check this place regular from now on.

When I took the post out and opened the jar, I seen it already had a note inside. This is what it said.

> We are still waiting to hear from you. Our man Moss checks this every day. Do not fail to report any activity of either brother who might be in the area.

After I read that I almost didn't put mine in the jar, but after standing there thinking everything over again, the sun going down and a nice sunset blazing away—for December, anyway—I tore their note up and put the pieces back in the jar and put mine in with them. I set the post in careful and went back to the Askew place and went to bed, though I didn't sleep much that night.

Strange thing about that quiet little strip of time soon after I got back from Monegaw Springs, I didn't go visit

Sarah over in Dogtown right away. I *thought* about doing it lots of times, I do remember that, but I guess the truth is I was still a little mad that she'd left me like she did over at the Younger's. I got to thinking how, if she wouldn't of left like that, I wouldn't of got sideways with Jesse, either, and everthing would of been all right. More or less blaming her for things. But after a day or two I seen how wrong-headed that was, for Jesse still had shot Whicher and that banker and Bill, and *that* was the real reason it all come apart like it did. Not Sarah leaving while I was still asleep and me coming downstairs just then. And finally I seen that I loved her, that time with nothing special to do let me see that clear. That was brand new to me, old as I was, knowing I loved a woman and not wanting to be parted from her ever again.

After I had a few days to chew it up good there at Askews'—what it was I had to do about Jesse, I mean—it didn't line up no differnt from the way I was thinking it all the way up from Monegaw Springs. I couldn't keep in with a killer, couldn't and didn't want to both. Only I couldn't see ahead clear what would happen then with me and Sarah—once the Jameses was hung. There was no way my part in it would stay quiet. She might not even have nothing more to do with me, that's what I thought. And if I told her how it was *before* hand, right now, before I told the Pinkertons when and where the Jameses was, even if I was to go and explain it all to her, even though she was so set against robbing and killing, she was *still* their cousin. And if there's anywhere I ever been where blood it thicker than anything, it's Clay County, Missouri.

Which meant she might even tell them about me, no matter she had said in her note how she loved me. Try as I might, I couldn't see which road to take with her or where either one might end up, and I suppose that's the biggest reason why I didn't go see her after I got back.

I didn't do much more field draining work there at Askew's, either. It was well into December by then, you'll recall, and too raw and rainy out to take much pleasure in drainage work, though I did a little just to be outside, miserable as it was—and to see if I could see the Jameses coming to visit their mamma and step daddy. Mostly, though, I drank to pass the time.

I was just leaving Askew's to go to town one Saturday when a boy come along bareback on a big old work horse and pulled up at the gate. I seen then he was the boy I had saw over at the Cole farm that time I had run into Sarah's cousin Thomas—Sarah's boy, it hit me after a second.

He was one of them freckled, tousle-haired, red-headed boys. That dark, reddish brown kind of hair that shines so in the sunlight, even on a boy who don't wash it and brush it so often as his ma probly wants him to. *He ought to have a cap on*, I said to myself, *this time of year anyway*, and then I seen it shoved into his back pocket and sticking mostly out, about ready to fall out and get lost in the mud along the road somewheres. That's how I was when I was a kid, hated anything on my head. Even hats I liked the look of.

He kept sitting on his horse—it was a big old black devil and quiet as can be, which was probly why they let him ride it at his age. He'd reconized me right off, keeping his eyes on me till I started walking over to him. Then, like boys will do, he looked off like he was watching a bird or a cloud or something far off and up high.

"You're Sarah's boy, ain't you?" I asked him after I stood there a while and him not looking down.

Of course he acted like he didn't see me before I spoke to him. "What? Oh, yeah. Yes sir, I mean. Are you Mr. Goodwin?" He had got Sarah's big green eyes to go with what must of been his daddy's dark red hair. He made you remember how awkward it was being his age, which I took to be ten or eleven.

"Yes, I'm Willie Goodwin. And what's your name, young man."

"It's Billy. Billy Parsons. Billy Parsons, *Junior*." You could tell someone'd been after him to say the junior part at the end there when he said his name, much as he didn't like to. He went to touch his hat, found out it wasn't there, and patted his back pocket quick to be sure he still had it, then fished around in his shirt pocket, under his jacket. "I have a note for you ... " he said, finally finding it in his pants pocket and handing it to me, all this with the straightest face you ever saw. Not frowning or nothing, just being as serious as he knowed how to be and doing what he was told.

It was folded into quarters, the note he handed me, and kind of bent up some. I opened it and saw it was from Sarah, like I guessed it would be.

Dear Willie,

I've talked to my father about inviting you for Christmas dinner and he approves of the idea. If you're still angry with me, however, I'd rather not embarrass Daddy by having you refuse his invitation. You understand, I'm sure.

If he sends you an invitation, will you accept it? You needn't write out your answer. Just tell Billy if you will or won't, but I'm hoping you will

With all my heart,

Sarah

"Do you know what this is about?" I asked the boy.

"Yes, sir," he said, looking off.

"Well, what do you think I should do?" I said.

That got him looking at me. "I—I don't know," he said, kind of surprised at me asking him.

"Well, I don't know either," I said, crossing my arms. "I think I'll let you decide. I don't have no place else to eat Christmas dinner, it's true, and I'll bet it's good at your house, ain't it?"

"It sure is," he said. "My grandma's roasting a goose this year, and it's *all* dark meat!"

"I figgered it'd be something good like that," I told him. "But I'm going to let it up to you, like I said, whether

I'm to come or not. It's your house too, and I'll bet nobody even asked you if your mamma's friend should come for Christmas dinner, did they?"

"No . . ." he said, looking like he half expected some trick.

"I didn't think so. Well, should I come or not?"

He appeared like he didn't really believe me, but I just waited him out. "It's all right with me," he said at last, still looking at me suspicious I seen out of the corner of my eye.

"Well, good," I said. "I'd a hated to miss a good goose dinner like that, all dark meat and all, but I do want it to be all right with you." I looked him square in the face. "I guess you already know I'm sweet on your momma, don't you?"

He had one of them smiles that makes a young fellow look about a hundred times better. "Yes, I . . . Should I tell her you'll be coming, then?" He turned his horse—mostly with his knees, I noticed.

"Yes sir, you *do* that!" I called good and loud, slapping the big black draft horse at the same time, not so hard as to spook him but enough to get him going good.

Did he ever move that big old horse out of there at a good clip.

23

CHRISTMAS WITH THE COLES

"Will you have more roast goose, Mr. Goodwin?" Sarah's mother asked me.

I looked at Billy. He appeared even more stuffed than the goose'd been about an hour before. By this time we'd already ate our vegetable soup, fried fish of some kind—sucker or mullet, I guessed—and a rabbit dish with little onions stewed in wine with a crust sort of like biscuits. There was even a hole cut out of the middle of the crust in the shape of a rabbit hopping somewheres or other.

A bowl of string beans with tomatoes mashed up and spices, another of canned peas, another of carrots in brown sugar and butter, applesauce with lots of cinnamon, applesauce *without* cinnamon because that's how Mr. Cole liked it, pickles, celery, a basket of rolls wrapped in a linen napkin still hot from the oven, pear butter Sarah'd put up in September, and on and on like that all over that big table. A tall bouquet of dried flowers in the middle, candles lit, though we didn't need them, it being only a little past noon and sunlight streaming in the windows through the lacy white curtains. Enough polished silver at each plate to sink a rowboat—knife rests, bone dishes, those little things you set your cup on when you're sipping out of your saucer, I don't know what they're called. Only thing I didn't like was having to be so damn careful not to spill nothing on Mrs. Cole's nice Irish linen tablecloth.

"Why, yes mam, I will have a little more goose. Just don't load me up quite so heavy as you did them last two times, please. Mighty fine bird, a goose, this one specially. You don't get to eat one every day, not cooked this good you don't." I said a lot more like that, just trying to be polite. Every time I did, Sarah smiled into her napkin like she was both happy I was doing it and a little embarrassed I was doing it so much. After a while Billy caught on, and when he wasn't too busy swallowing even more of that roast goose, which *was* awful good—even if it wasn't quite so good as I kept saying—he joined in with his mamma at having some fun watching how big a fool I could make of myself. But, shoot, I didn't care, and Mrs. Cole sure didn't either. Like a lot of women who like to cook and feed people, she liked a man who liked to eat and then praised her for it.

And *she* didn't think I was making too much of her food at all, which she had cooked herself—but with Sarah's help, of course, Sarah being nearly as good a cook as she was, she said. Yes, she told me, she liked to prepare each dish herself on special occasions, like Christmas dinner was, and her cook appreciated having Christmas day to spend with her family, too.

She was awful sorry we didn't have no oysters this year, but we lived terrible far from the ocean here in Missouri for oysters, and sometimes they just didn't make it this far fit to eat. Since she'd grew up in Tidewater Virginia, it didn't really seem like Christmas to her without her oysters baked in cream and butter, she said with a big sigh, and just smothered with bread crumbs—*toasted* bread crumbs, mind you! She told me she was a Minor before she was married, which she said like *mine-uh*. I couldn't understand just what she meant at first, asked her to repeat it, she talked the South so much, and before I figgered out that's what her family name was before she was married, I thought she was telling me she was a *miner*, but I couldn't see her with no pick and shovel and also couldn't see her cooking in no mining camp either, the rowdy way men are there. But I went along with it saying *Oh, is that so?* like you do sometimes before you figger out what in the *hell* somebody is talking about.

What Mrs. Cole *really* enjoyed, though, was saying what was in each dish, how much of this and how much of that, telling me just how to go about making it, too, like I might just decide to cook a big dinner like this myself for a dozen people or so some Christmas Day. I looked interested and asked whatever fool questions I could think up whenever she give me a little room to talk. But no matter how big I praised her dinner, she just nodded her head like I was exactly right—and should go on. I think if I had said that one forkful of her mashed potatoes would get you into heaven direct, no questions asked no matter how many churches you'd burned down when you was alive, she would of just nodded some more for me to keep it up.

Sarah's daddy was another story. He didn't say nothing at all, except pass this, and pass that, please. Sarah had warned me how he was at the table, and I wasn't to take it wrong or personal if he didn't talk to me, because he never talked to nobody while he was eating. Afterward he might, but while he was eating, no sir. Oh, he'd answer a question if he was asked direct and if he could answer it with a yes or no, but beyond that, J. Richard Cole wouldn't go—not when he was feeding his face, he wouldn't.

That's how he signed his name, Sarah said, *J.* Richard Cole. And I was *not* to forget and call him *Jesse*, which *was* his name. But ever since his nephew, the one his sister Zerelda had went and named after Mr. Cole, ever since Mr. Jesse Woodson James made everbody in the country think you was an outlaw if your name was Jesse, J. Richard didn't go by his old name no more. And if that don't tell you what he thought of his nephew Jesse James, the robbing and such—even to changing how he signed his name—then nothing will.

"Would you care for a cigar, Mr. Goodwin?" J. Richard Cole asked me after we'd all stuffed ourselfs about as solid as it would go, finishing up with pumpkin pie, walnut cake, and coffee at the end. It was the biggest string of words I'd heard come out of him since I got there, and it about half surprised me to hear him say a whole question like that all at one time.

Sarah's momma had a look on her face like her husband had just farted in front of the company—instead of just asking me for a smoke, which I was about ready for by then anyway. "Richard! We agreed to open our *presents* after dinner! Joan and her husband will be here very soon!"

J. Richard didn't bat an eye. He stood up, got his cigar case out of his pocket, took my arm, and back we went toward his office sort of room, me looking back at Sarah, who didn't seem too surprised at all this, nodding to me to just go along with him. Sarah's mamma, though, looked like she was going to cry.

J. Richard Cole shut the door behind us. "Damn women and their noisy ways, anyhow!" he said, not so loud as to be heard back in the dining room, I noticed. He more or less pushed me into a big leather chair, handed me a cigar, sat himself down in a tall wing-back chair alongside, and went at his cigar like lightning, with a little pair of clippers, which he tossed me after he was done. We lit up. They was good cigars, all right. Stong and mellow as any I ever had. We sat there silent and smoking till the cigars was almost half gone.

"Sarah says you're from Texas," J. Richard said out of the blue, surprising me with his sudden talk again.

"Yes, sir, I am. Been up north here a little less than—"

"Don't sir me! I'm not that much older than you!"

I waited a minute. "All right, Mr. Cole. I'll not say sir to you if you don't want me to. I was just trying to be polite is all. But I'll ask you to talk a little more civil to me, if you please. It's true I'm in your house here, and I'm here mostly so you'll approve of me seeing your daughter some more, who I do truly care for, but I won't sit still for nobody barking at me. I won't." I tried not to fly off the handle so much like I tend to do sometimes, and for the most part I didn't.

Well, the look on his face said thunder, but after a minute the clouds broke up and the sun shined through when he smiled. I seen then we was going to get along just fine—well, at least all right. What he really wanted was for me to stand up to him a little—and be a *little* polite at the same time. We finished our cigars with a drop of brandy he poured, talking of crops and horses, then almost right away we got up and went down the hall to the front room.

J. Richard Cole's wife and daughter Sarah was sitting quiet—watching us come in and waiting for us to get there before they opened their presents. A broad stone fireplace blazing away on one short wall and down at the other, a big pine tree filling the room with its wonderful smell and all decorated up with candy canes and red and green satin bows tied on to gilded pine cones, a star on the top somebody'd made out of bright gold straw. Presents wrapped in different colors of paper and laid out neat on an ebony table right beside. Billy was laying with his head under the tree looking up through the branches. Sarah's ma didn't say nothing when we stepped into the room, J. Richard acting like nothing much out of the ordinary'd happened, Sarah smiling at me sweet as could be, so I just acted like people always had a little spat to go along with their Christmas dinners.

About that time Sarah's sister Joan and her husband and their five kids pulled up outside in a long wagon that somebody'd tied sleigh bells on from somewhere, and them coming sort of took the edge off things when they all come trooping in wishing everbody Merry Christmas, their arms full of more presents, running to kiss grandma and shake grandpa's hand, the boys who was old enough.

Billy played Indians outside with some of his cousins

after the children opened their presents and found a lot of them had got little bows and arrows with gum-rubber balls on the end—all the same. Sarah talked to her sister Joan a while and Joan's husband and me waded though some talk about how cold it'd been. Then Sarah took my hand and me and her went off into a sort of side room by ourselfs. Sarah give me my present then, a nice silver-backed hairbrush, and then I got her present out of my vest pocket.

"I didn't wrap this, Sarah, because I was hoping it'd go right on." I handed her the pin I'd got her, one with an even bigger emerald than the one I'd give her down at the Younger's. There wasn't no little pearls circling this one, but a pair of small diamonds to either side give it more sparkle than the other one had. "And this one ain't stole from no lady on a train, neither. I bought it new in a Kansas City jewelry store with money that wasn't stole from nobody neither. Money I got elsewheres. I can show you the receipt if you want to see it, it's right here in my pocket, alongside where your pin was. I'd prefer you not see it, you understand, because you ain't supposed to know what I paid for it is the way I learned it. But we can forget about that rule if you—"

She laughed and then kissed me. "It's beautiful, Willie! And no, I don't need to look at the receipt. If you say that's how you got it, I'm sure you did. Seems like you're turning over a new leaf these days, aren't you? I know you and Jesse had a falling out before you left the Youngers, too. June told me. I admire the way you're refraining from doing the terrible things my cousins Jesse and Frank do, as much temptation as that must be, all that money."

We talked a while, and I explained how things was with me—as best I could and still stay away from me and the Pinkertons. And then I told her what I hoped to do before long, get completely away from Frank and Jesse. "Of course, that'll mean I'll have to leave here," I said to her. "Only I don't want that to be the end of me and you, Sarah, but I won't be able to stay around Missouri once I get all the way out, you understand." I told her about Blackfoot Bill then. While she was a little took aback at first, maybe didn't even believe me all the way at first either, in the end she wasn't really surprised Jesse'd done what he must of done to Blackfoot Bill. I wanted to tell her about me and the Pinkertons then too, she seemed so forgiving right then, but damned if I could do it.

"We'll just have to see what happens, won't we, Willie?" she said. You could see the worry down deep in her mind, though she put a bright face on things.

"Yes we will," I told her. "But I hope you'll think about coming away with me when I go. Billy too, naturally. I really want you to, Sarah, and I'd want to marry you, too, of course, after we got—"

"Yes, I'll think some about all that," Sarah said, shaking her head and then standing sudden. She took my arm when I stood up too. Her face was smiles and shadows all at the same time right then, and, I don't know, I thought she'd be pleased to be proposed to, even if it was sort of a left-handed, side-door sort of way for me to do it. It was the first time *I* even done it, I'll tell you that, and it was the best I could do on such short notice, for I'd not planned on stepping into *those* deep waters that Christmas Day, I'll tell you.

She wasn't what you'd call entirely unhappy. A little confused and perplexed is the best way to say it, I suppose. "But today's Christmas, Willie," she said, looking at her new pin in her gloved hand, "and I'd rather not think about leaving home just yet. Can you see . . . ?"

"Of course I can, Sarah," I told her, though it seemed there was I lot there I wasn't really seeing. "There ain't no rush about things just now, just so you'll think on it."

"I promise I will," she said, leading me out of that little side room back into the confusion of all them kids who'd come back inside and was now opening the presents grandma and grandpa had got them and squealing like little piggies gone to market.

When that was done, Sarah's sister Joan played carols

on a little piano sort of thing Sarah's mamma said was a virginal and had been in her family a long time. All the children sang, them that was old enough. After three or four songs, Sarah sat down with her sister and they played some Christmas songs together, the last one being "O Come all Ye Faithful."

Joan's husband tried making a joke about these two sisters playing a *virginal* together and maybe it'd break before *they* was done playing it. I started to laugh a little, just to be polite, but nobody else thought it was very funny. That sort of broke up the singing part of the party.

After we sat around a while, and after Mr. Cole and Joan's husband and me went outside for another smoke, we sat down to the same meal again warmed up, there was still a lot left. I had more room for the pie that time, I remember. Oh, and there was a mincemeat pie this time, one we didn't get to before.

After that, Sarah walked me out to the barn and stayed inside there with me while I saddled my horse. It'd got cold all of a sudden and the sky gray with clouds, our breaths making little clouds inside the barn too. When I was ready to go I pulled her in close to me, we was still in the barn, not out where folks could see us, and kissed her good like I'd been wanting to all day.

She handed me the pin I'd got her for Christmas and for a minute I feared she was giving *this* one back too, though I couldn't guess why.

"Pin it on me, silly," Sarah said, a sweet look on her face, her eyes falling to her breast real bashful.

Well, of course I did what I was told. I was surprised I had such trouble pinning it to the velvet of her dress there, underneath her coat. I was breathing quick by the time I'd finished. You'd think it was hard work.

"I'll think about what you said, Willie. I don't know about leaving Missouri—leaving my family, you know. And I don't know what Billy..." She just let it trail off like that.

"Well, there's no hurry. They're not around here now,

Frank and Jesse. And I don't know when they'll be back this way. I'll just stay at Askew's till then. If you decide before then—"

"It'll probably be the end of January, then," Sarah said. "They always come back for their mamma's birthday, January 29th. They never miss that, they being such good boys to their mamma and all. You'd think they'd come for Christmas, wouldn't you? But they almost never do. Maybe because the marshalls and such might be looking for them then."

I just nodded.

"I never could understand those James boys," Sarah said as we was walking toward the barn door, me leading my horse. "Some of the things they do, stealing and killing and all, but then they're so good in other ways—to their mother, their families. It's odd, isn't it?"

"It is that," I said.

We stepped outside and a light sprinkle of tiny snowflakes floated in the cold air.

"Well I declare," Sarah said, looking up. A smile softening and smoothing the trouble from only a minute before. "Snow on Christmas!"

I pulled her close again. A tiny, perfect snowflake landed on her eyelashes and just when it started to melt, another one settled beside the first. "I love you, Sarah. Think on that, too."

"All right, Willie," she said, leaning up to be kissed, not caring who might see us from the house now.

I didn't either. I kissed her there in her daddy's yard bold as a bandit.

I looked back half a dozen times riding off and each time I looked, she was still there watching me going away. She waved each time.

It wasn't till I had got nearly back to Askew's that it hit me what she'd said. Jesse and Frank would be at Samuel's come the end of January—the 29th. They never missed their mamma's birthday, Sarah said.

24

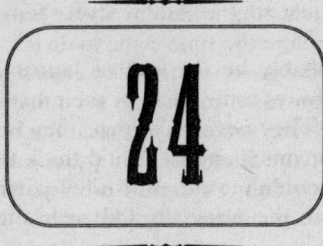

MORE GOLD COIN

And so I waited. Waited for New Year's to come, and it did, Sarah and me going to a big dancing sort of ball one of her girl cousins throwed over at their big house close to Excelsior Springs. Dressed up in funny costumes and false faces and everything, me in a patchwork suit that'd been Mr. Cole's—a harlequin suit is what Sarah said it was—but I couldn't get Frank and Jesse off my mind. They wasn't there at the party, thank goodness—I half thought they might be.

Sarah wanted to know what was wrong when we was twirling around the floor once, me in that awful patchwork suit smelling of moth crystals, and slippers with the toes turned up, looking dumb as a dunce. A red velvet hat with little silver bells that hung down all around and jingled every time I turned my head or took a step. Didn't I like the dancing, the punch, or something else? But of course I couldn't say—beyond that fool getup.

And then I waited for the ice storm to let up that come through right after New Year's. Then waited for it to melt, too, which Dan Askew said it would, and it did, just like he said, in the rainy spell that followed. It seemed a fearful long time, that month during the winter there after I'd decided to tell the Pinkertons about Jesse being at his mamma's and before the time come to do it.

I'd decided not to tell the Pinkertons right away, to leave me enough room to change my mind, if it seemed like I wanted to later on, or to just clear out of there all of a sudden without the Pinks knowing just *when* them boys would be at their family's farm. And also, the stupid way they did things sometimes, the Pinkertons, how they got things turned backwards mixed up and flummoxed, I didn't want to give them no extra time to come traipsing around here beforehand—tipping off the Jameses and getting me killed into the bargain. No, just tell them to be ready and let her go at that, I figgered. This here's the note I wrote them.

> Be ready to go on two days notice. Get yourselfs a locomotive and cars and about ten or fifteen men and guns and horses and all you will need on the train and be ready to go with two days notice. Tell your man who checks this place to check it twice a day from now on. I'll tell you when and how in the next note, it won't be long now. But if you go and do anything else, the birds will fly the coop before we can put up the net.

When I took my note down to the post hole safe that night, just when I was taking the post out, a man stepped out of the pines sudden right above me. I was going for my Colt's when I saw it was that fellow who was spooking around before, Moss his name was.

"Hold on there, Goodwin! Hold on!" he yelled, throwing his hands up. It was plain he thought I'd know him right off, but I didn't.

"What're you doing here?" I asked him after I was sure who it was, pushing the revolver Jesse had give me back into its holster.

It took him a minute catching his breath, which he

tried to hide he was doing. You wouldn't of guessed it from the look on his face, though, that I'd scared him. "Waiting for you, what's it look like? Just like the Pinkertons paid me to do, though it's goddamn cold waiting out here all day, day after day without a fire and no coffee, I'll tell you." He come the rest of the way down and stood facing me, kind of glaring at me. "And it'd be entirely unnecessary if you'd do your job right, reporting as often as you're supposed to." He turned his head about half sideways and looked at me out of the corner of his eye. "You know, I heard in town that 'Jack Ladd' was *really* one of the goddamn Jameses, that's what I heard."

"Yeah, and I heard you're a stupid asshole who'll believe any damn thing anybody tells him. I suppose that's why I'm leaving this note for the Pinks, telling them how to catch Frank and Jesse, because I'm working for the Jameses." I just stood and looked back at him, holding the folded note up a little for him to see it.

It was clear he didn't have nothing more to go on, or he'd of said it, he looked so cross. Oh, he'd prob'ly liked to've had something solider, but I had the note right there in my paw and he didn't have nothing but what some drunk said in a Liberty saloon. He looked madder'n a swarm of bees with a stoved-in hive, but he didn't say nothing more.

I held the note out to him, and when he reached for it, just before his hand got there, I dropped it in the dirt at his feet. He started to bend over for it, realized quick I done it apurpose, and stood back up with his chest stuck out, ready to fight me.

I tipped him my hat, went back to my horse, and mounted up. Oh, I suppose he picked it up by and by. He'd of almost had to, now, wouldn't he? After I got that damn Moss off my mind, I rode the rest of the way back to Askew's trying to figger out what in the hell to do about Sarah and Billy.

I'd been going over to Sarah's folk's place every couple of days there after Christmas, they let me know I was welcome to come back, her momma and her daddy both. Only every damn time I went over there I kept wanting to ask Sarah if she'd heard anything more about Jesse and Frank coming to visit their mamma on her birthday. You know what it's like having something on your mind like that all the time and not wanting to say it, *can't* say it. And I just didn't want to be like that, either, I felt bad enough already knowing I was going to get them boys caught and hung from what Sarah'd already told me on accident.

Sarah asked me a time or two if she'd did something to make me angry with her. I said, no, it wasn't that. Then she thought it was that fool costume she made me wear, and she apologized so often one night I *did* get sore and told her to just stop it, though I wasn't really mad at her, just rubbed raw, you know. The next time she thought it was us not sleeping together I was mad about, though I never said nothing at all about that to make her think so. I kept telling her I wasn't mad about *nothing*, but the funny way I acted whenever we was together, I admit, me wanting to ask about the Jameses all the time and fighting it down, I ain't surprised she didn't all the way believe me. She said more than once she was gonna come over to my place some night soon and we'd see about—

"No, *that* ain't it either, Sarah," I told her after she'd said that for about the third time one night.

"What is it, then?" she asked. "Tell the truth, Willie."

"Well, it's complicated," I told her. "Are you ready to leave with me? Leave Missouri? Just come over to my place some night and then go off somewheres, somewheres far, you and Billy and me, and not come back for a couple of years? Not write and tell your daddy and momma just where we are, either? You *said* you would think about it."

She looked at me like I had all of a sudden went crazy and growed horns. "Leave my family like that?! Why, what on earth *for*, Willie?"

Of course I couldn't tell her, and that made things even worse between us. So the spaces between me going over there got longer and longer as the time went along, and I'd pretty much decided to stop going over by the third week of the month. January, it was, 1875. I didn't stop loving her, mind you, or stop thinking about her every night and every day, wondering if she was all right and what she was doing just then—and the like. It was just this damn Jesse James business hanging fire so long is what it was, I told myself.

I worked outside a little every day from the middle of the month on, miserable and rainy as it was, just so's I could maybe see when Jesse and Frank showed up at the Samuel place. The way it turned out, I wouldn't of had to do no outside work at all to find out when they come to visit.

I was just getting into bed one night at my little shed house there at the Askews' when a horse pulled up outside my door. For a minute I thought for sure it was Sarah, come to do what she said she was going to do, sleep with me—or maybe even say she was ready for us to go off together, no questions asked. I remember saying to myself, if she has Billy with her and wants to go right now, that's just what we'll do—the hell with the Jameses and the Pinks both. Only it wasn't her.

When I sat up and looked out the window I saw it was a man. And then I thought maybe it was June in her man's clothes, but after a minute I seen whoever it was was too big for it to be June. I got my Colt's that Jesse had give me and looked through a crack between the boards. Because there was just a little slice of moon, I was still in the deep shadows, so whoever it was couldn't see me.

It was Frank James, and he kept sitting his horse and looking toward my shed. I put my revolver down and went out. I didn't know what to say when I walked up, so I didn't say nothing.

"Here," Frank said when I got close. He tossed me a leather pouch and when I caught it, from its weight and the way it clunked, I knowed it was gold coins.

"What's this?" I asked.

"It's what's left of the half eagles we took over in Kansas. You won't believe this, but Jesse gave the rest of them to some goddamn nigger preacher who was going to build a school. Imagine, a school for darkies." He shook his head.

"Yeah, I can see it, and I can also see Jesse doing it, too," I said. What I *didn't* say was that I could see him doing it so folks would think he was a big bug for being so generous—even to colored folk. "But I thought they was yours, that gold coin?"

"Yeah, well, so did I," Frank said, rubbing the back of his long skinny neck with his gloved hand. "But Jesse has his own ideas about who owns what, as well as what constitutes appropriate behavior—and loyalty." He adjusted his hat and even in the dim moonlight must of saw the look on my face. "As if I needed to tell you."

"No, you don't need to try and tell me the kind of odd ideas goes through Jesse's head sometimes, not me you don't," I said.

Frank nodded. "Keep a good watch the next few days. We're going to be over at mother's. I wouldn't advise you to come by paying your respects, though. Not in the mood Jesse's in now," Frank warned.

"Is he still that mad at me?" I asked him.

"I suppose he is," Frank said. "Though he never mentions it and I'm not sure he'd even remember why." He pulled up his coat collar. "Now someone's gone and told him the Pinkertons are around here again. And Jesse gets . . . "

Even when I didn't take the bait and finish it, he still figgered out what I was thinking. Nobody ever said Frank James wasn't smart. "Yes, you've seen it, a little of it, but— Aagh, it'll pass. It always does. But if I were you I'd ride the hell out of here before long. Just keep a good lookout during the day for anybody strange over the next week or so. We're pretty sure they won't try anything at night."

"What am I to do with these?" I asked, hefting the bag in my hand.

250 / CHARLES HACKENBERRY

"Up to you, I'm just Jesse's paymaster tonight. They're yours for keeping watch over here. Stick them up your ass for all I care." Frank James turned and rode out. No tip of the hat, no nothing.

I thought of John Whicher then, and after that, the Pinkerton man on the Iron Mountain train I'd heard stories of. They said after the conductor untied him, he got up, got dressed, took the nearest horse and rode straight out of there. And nobody'd heard from him since. Not even his wife and kids. My guess is he killed himself. Either that or he was drowning himself slow and ugly in the bottom of a cheap brown whiskey bottle in a string of dirty little towns, looking over his shoulder often when he rode on—and waking up sweaty every time anybody squeaked a floorboard in his hotel hallway late at night. Which is almost worse than looking down the barrel of your own pistol, come to think of it. I got out my bottle and drunk myself to sleep. Damn all that waiting, anyway.

The next day, a Thursday I think it was, about a week before Jesse's momma's birthday, I went into Excelsior Springs and wired William Pinkerton at the Northend Hotel in Kansas City that I was leaving a message in the usual place and he should be sure and get it. Then I sent the same message to him again in care of the Stationmaster in Kearney, just in case. Not with my own name on it, of course, but he'd know who it was from, the way I said it. Then I went down to the post hole safe again. This is the message I left there.

> Get your train with everbody aboard, horses and everthing else you'll need, to the siding in Kearney Monday afternoon, the 25th. Stay on the train till I get there, keep everbody on the train. That way the Jameses won't get tipped off. They don't expect no night attack, so our chance of taking them if we go out there at night is good unless you give the whole damn thing away. I'll be there about sundown and lead you out to the Jameses a back way I know.

25

PARTING AT NIGHT

Kearney, Missouri
January 25, 1875
Monday, 1:30 PM

A short train eased onto the single-track spur that formed the siding for the village of Kearney, Missouri. Behind the engine and tender rolled a single passenger car, followed by an old baggage car and then a car with perhaps a dozen horses in narrow stalls. A stack of saddles as high as a man's head leaned into one of the front corners of the car. A dark complexioned wrangler stuck his head out the door and looked nervously in the direction the slowing train was headed.

After they stopped he slid his narrow frame though the opening, dropped to the ground, and then pulled the heavy door shut after him. Hunkering down, he rolled a cigarette and lit it, looking the place over. There was still good grass here beside the tracks—well, good enough anyway, for January—and the horses could use it. He'd forgotten to load the hay and grain because one of those damned Pinkerton bosses had been badgering him to get the animals loaded in a hell of a hurry before he'd had his first cup of coffee that morning. And then that long wait at the main line anyhow. Wasn't his fault the hay and grain wasn't here. Wasn't his fault.

The wrangler walked up the tracks past the baggage car, flipped away his cigarette and swung up into the coach. Ten minutes later he stepped back down with another man following him, a shorter man in a dark suit and derby hat. Together they put the heavy ramp in place and unloaded the horses, tethering them along the tracks where they could browse on the withered grass. When they'd finished, the man in the dark suit ambled back to the passenger car assaying the weather, and the wrangler went looking for water. At least he'd remembered his buckets. When he went around the front of the still-hissing engine, he saw two men sneaking out of the passenger car on the other side. He dipped his four buckets into the trough by the tiny station. When he looked up again he saw the men duck into a saloon up the road. Not a bad idea once the horses were watered.

I had supper with Dan Askew and his wife so nothing would look differnt from usual if anybody was to ask later. It was ham cooked with green beans Mrs. Askew'd put up that summer. They had that about once a week there, and I'd got sort of used to it, boiled all day with potatoes the way she done it. They ate early, the Askews did, so I figgered I'd have plenty of time to get into Kearney before sundown. Old Dan teased me about not staying for pie, though. I must be seeing a mighty fine-looking gal in town to pass up his wife's custard pie, he laughed. She laughed too, at his compliment mostly, which he wasn't never too free with. Whatever happened that Cole girl he used to see me with, anyway? He liked ribbing me like that, and most times I would have jabbed him right back.

I was thinking more of what lay down the trail, though, mumbled and nodded my thanks when I left the table. Early that morning I'd put a waterproof canvas bag with my things in it behind a big rock up by the main road. I was sure they was coming, the Pinkertons, for my note was gone that morning and theirs said "Be ready and on time." That's all it said, "Be ready and on time." The thing was, I'd decided already to be ready—ready to get the hell out of there in a minute if I had to.

The way I figgered it, if the Pinks *caught* Jesse and Frank and the rest of whoever was there at Samuel's with them, then of course there wouldn't be no need for me to light out of there all of a sudden. But if they got away, those Jameses, and they just might, especially if the Pinkertons bitched this job up as bad as they did some of their other work I had already saw, then I'd best be all ready to go in a minute—and ride out of there quicker'n a Missouri whore leaves your bed. Yes, I was gonna be ready like they said, but ready in more ways than them damn Pinks'd thought of.

I saddled my horse and rode easy and natural as I could toward Kearney, burping that strong ham from time to time, especially when I got to thinking about what I was going to do instead of keeping my horse from trotting, like he wanted. It was a Monday, and I didn't have no regular reason for going into town, but I thought if I just went easy like everthing was normal, it'd look all right and nobody'd notice much. Just going to one of the bars again, maybe, they'd think.

A man coming toward me around a corner, about half a mile before the back-way cutoff, he didn't think going easy was the way to go, though, for he was spurring his horse to blazes. Flapping his elbows in time with the gallop, too, the awkward way some men will do, his floppy brimmed black hat pulled down hard and his eyes as wild as Satan chasing him when he went past, it looked like he barely saw me.

I stopped and watched him till he was out of sight back the way I'd just come, around a bend in the road. I had half a mind to turn and ride after to see where the hell he was going in such an all-fired hurry. What if he was maybe going to warn the Jameses? But then I figgered that was just me being screwed up tighter than a tin drum over doing what I was doing. Hell, it could be any number of things made a man ride like that. No, it was just worry making me think like that I told myself and headed toward town slow and easy again.

I cut off the road on the path I was going to use to lead the Pinkertons out to the Samuel place. The reason I picked this one, it angled over to hit the railway siding direct. I couldn't believe what I saw when I come out there. Horses all along the track, like the circus come to town, and a *passenger* car in the middle of the train stopped there on the siding, two or three men in derby hats standing guard with rifles.

"Why don't you just put up a goddamn sign saying 'Pinkerton Special?' on the side of the engine?" I yelled at William Pinkerton as soon as I stepped inside the car. He was sitting down at the far end sharing a seat with a shorter man. The car'd been noisy when I stepped inside, a dozen or more men in there all talking, but it got quiet as a cave at midnight when I said that, the smoke of their cigars thick as fog and laying in layers.

He looked up at me with a look on his face, William Pinkerton did, that froze me in the aisle, halfway down to where he sat. If he'd a been mad, or surprised even, it'd been what I expected, but the look on that man's face, which was white as paper when he stood up, was something I'll never forget. He walked up to me slow in the aisle clearing his throat.

And when he spoke to me it was almost a whisper, all those men watching and listening in that smoky, musty car, and all of them knowing already whatever it was that I didn't, you could just tell, their eyes. "Willie, for goodness sake. I'm sorry, very sorry." He held an envelope out towards me, one of them black-edged envelopes that warn you someone has died and you had best get ready for some awful bad news inside.

Then he took me back to where he'd sat, by the elbow, set me down and stood in the aisle, waiting for me

I RODE WITH JESSE JAMES / 255

to read it. I looked up at him first, and you will not believe this I know, but there was a big, bright tear making its slow way down that beefy-faced man's cheek. William Pinkerton, honest to God, was shedding a tear. It was that more'n anything made my heart drop. Two sheets inside, from Lottie Hudspeth it said on the envelope and at the bottom, so I knowed already who it was that must of died.

The farm of Dr. Reuben Samuel
and his wife Zerelda Cole James Samuel
January 25, 1875
Monday, 6:15 PM

Two women stood facing each other, holding one another by the arms on the porch of the low, log farm house, one young and lovely in her child-bearing years—the older woman built on a larger and ruder pattern, worn with work and worry, looking a decade older than her age, only a few days short of her fiftieth birthday. Each woman stood and gazed deeply into the face of the other. They shared a strong family resemblance, their images reflected in a pair of eerie mirrors that took little account of either time or turmoil.

"I'm sorry we must leave so suddenly like this, Mother Samuel," Zee Mimms James said and then quickly kissed her mother-in-law, the woman whom she had always called Aunt Zerelda before she had married the dear woman's son. Zee had, in fact, been named after this hickory-hard woman with the deeply lined face, which, in the last light of a glorious winter sunset, showed no trace of either softness or smile.

Mrs. Zerelda James Samuel's grown boys, Jesse and Frank, stood behind Jesse's wife, waiting their turn to say good-bye to Mother, whom everyone knew was the true head of this family, even Dr. Samuel, who sat on a chair without a back down the porch a distance and—chin on fist, elbow on knee—appeared to ponder something out in the darkening yard, something that appeared to toy with his ravaged, ruined brain. At his mother's side hung nine-year-old Archey Peyton Samuel sucking his thumb, his other hand in her apron pocket, as it often was, stubby fingers searching, groping—a child nobody knew what to make of. Small for his age, he sometimes seemed to have inherited his father's incapacity, though that was impossible. At other times his wit and keen observations startled even those strangers, few though they were, who found welcome and refuge at this tainted backwoods Eden.

As Zee stepped down into the yard, pulling her coat more tightly around her as she walked toward the wagon, Frank James stepped forward and took both his mother's hands in his long bony ones. "I'll be back soon, Mother, and I'll bring Annie then. Her family—" Frank swallowed visibly and then shook his head.

"It's all right, Frank," Mrs. Samuel said. "All right. They'll come around after they find out what a good husband you are to her. Annie's awfully young, you've got to remember, and it takes a family a while to get used to the idea after a daughter marries someone they don't approve of. It's a little like the way it is with us and our Susan's man. We'll wait and see. And so will they, Frank. Just be patient and bring her when the time's right." She patted his hand. He nodded, smiled wanly, and then stepped down to join Zee and help her into the wagon.

"I don't think I've missed your birthday since the War, Mother," Jesse said, taking his mother in his arms and kissing her lightly on the forehead. "I hate having to leave now like this, just hate it."

"I know, I know," Mrs. Samuel said quietly. "Next year, maybe things will be all worked out." She pulled away to arm's length, though she held onto her son's forearms tightly and cocked her head at him. "Now don't you go back on your promise to me, Jesse. You know you can't fight them, there are just too many. And you promised me you wouldn't." She watched his face closely, waiting for him to reply.

After a few seconds he nodded. "All right, Mother. All right. I'm just afraid—"

Mrs. Samuel shook her head sharply. "No, they'll not come out here. Not tonight they won't. They wouldn't dare risk that." She turned and addressed her family and the others standing in the yard, though still holding onto her son. "They're foolish, but they're not that foolish."

Everyone laughed quietly.

"And when they come out tomorrow and no one is here but Dr. Samuel and the children and me, why, we'll tell them we haven't seen you all in years. And what can they do then?"

Bob Younger crawled up in the wagon beside Zee and untied the reins. Frank mounted his beautiful horse and then checked the sky. Others stowed things in saddlebags and tightened cinches.

Jesse walked up to the man in the floppy brimmed black hat holding his horse. "Here you are," he said, offering him a thick wad of bills.

"I don't want that," the man said, astonishment looking out of place on his angular face.

"Take it anyway," Jesse said, stuffing the bills into the man's jacket pocket, taking the reins and then snap-mounting Stonewall.

"I'd rather ride with you than take this," the man in the floppy brimmed hat said, a quiver in his high-pitched voice.

Jesse called over to Frank, a thin smile on his face. "Did you hear that?"

"Yeah," Frank growled, scowling theatrically. "Tell him we'll talk about it next time we come back—and that he needs to get a better looking hat if he wants to ride with the James-Younger gang."

Bob Younger hooted and then gave the rebel yell and Zee threw her head back and laughed lustily, her breath forming white puffs in the winter-chilled air. Even the man in the ugly hat had to chuckle. Bob slapped the horses with the reins and the wagon moved forward with a lurch.

"Say hello to Uncle Hite for me when you get to Kentucky," Mrs. Samuel called from the porch.

Both Jesse and Frank nodded, almost in unison.

One rider shot ahead to scout the way. The rest of the horsemen, seven of them Dr. Samuel counted as they went by, followed in the wagon's wake. Zerelda Samuel stood on her porch and waved her handkerchief till they were out of sight, then touched her husband's elbow and, after he had stood and collected himself a bit, followed him inside and began to light the lamps. Little Archie leaned out from the porch, an arm cocked around one of its posts. He swung back and forth and listened to the retreating wagon and horses as long as he could hear them. At the end he wasn't sure whether he was really still hearing the distant rattle of the wagon or only imagining it.

26

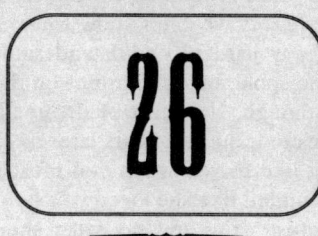

A MOUSE IN CHEESE

Dear Willie,—

I write to give you the sory news your momma died in her sleep last night. We were expecting it for some time now, she had some other little fits the doctor said was appleplexy, but the end came so sudden it took us a little by surprise, too. She didn't suffer hardly none at all. That's to be thankful for, now, isn't it?

The other week we asked her should we send for you and she was real strong about us not doing it. She said you had important work up there in Chicago, Illinois, and there was nothing you could do down here in Texas for an old woman who'd lived long enough already to suit her. She said every day after that we were not to send for you, so that's why we didn't. We had Doctor Moore from Dechman come over after she had her first one, and he said there was nothing he could do for her.

Len and me are awful sory for you Willie, and hope you won't think wrong of us for not writing how bad she was when she first got sick there, but honest she didn't want us to, honest to Pete she didn't. We're sory we don't know what her last words were, she was hard to understand sometimes after her fits. She spoke of you betimes on the day before she died, though, she must of dreamed of you, we said. You were in her thoughts later on that day, too, her talking like to you when you must have been a boy, she sounded like she loved you so.

You must write and say what should be done with the farm now, Willie. Len has been farming it on reglar fifty-fifty shares since you left, and we would be willing to keep on doing that if you wanted. I keep good acounts and will send you your share every year if you like. Or we could sell it for you, maybe buy it ourselfs if we could aford it, if it wasn't to much. Write and say what we're to do.

She's burried neat and peaceful in your family plot up there on the place, right between your pa and your little baby brother like she wanted, her name on the stone allready, all three of them just beneath the edge of that big old live oak up there, you remember? We're sory for you, Willie, please acept our being sory. I remain,

Your old Friend,

Lottie Hudspeth

"I'm sorry I opened it," William Pinkerton said, standing in the aisle. "I felt I had to. You—"

"It's all right," I said, feeling kind of not all there. "Hell, ma opened my mail half the time at home, anyway. It, uh . . ." I forgot what it was I was going to say right in the middle of saying it and just sat there a good while, the train car quiet, the few men that was talking was just a low rumble. I realized then it was me they was being mindful of, being quiet like that. I looked up at Pinkerton and nodded him my thanks.

He put his hand on my shoulder. "I'm sorry, Goodwin, I truly am. And don't worry about leading us out there, either. Sheriff Moss is on hand. He's rounded up some good men from around here, and he can do the job. You just stay here on the train if you want." He patted my shoulder a few times more, and much as I didn't like him sometimes, right then he seemed like the best friend I had in the world. I looked down the car the way he was looking and saw O. P. Moss standing down at the far end, his hat in his hands and looking back at us. He nodded at me about half friendly.

"No, it's all right. I can still do it," I said. "My ma didn't send for me so's I could do what I had to do up here, and it'd be a shame now if I didn't do it. She'd want me to."

Pinkerton looked surprised, but after a minute he nodded a couple of times. "Well, all right, if you're sure you're up to it."

"I'm sure *enough* that I can do it," I said standing up, "But I ain't none too sure it can be done." I put Lottie's letter in my pocket and set my hat on straight.

Pinkerton blinked half a dozen or so times and looked at me a little stern. "What?"

"Well, what I started yelling about when I come in here was that I wouldn't be surprised none if the Jameses has left their momma's place by now."

"But you said they'd be here for more than a week," Pinkerton said with some heat behind it.

"Yes, I did," I said. "And I also said to come right at sundown and to keep everone inside the train. Now there's men standin out there with rifles keeping guard, a blind man could see who was here and what for. A whole herd of horses out along the tracks so anybody in Kearney with fingers and toes enough can count how many's riding out there. I think you already give the Jameses all the warning they need. And they're long gone by now is how I see it." I don't know why, but I decided not to say nothing about that man I'd saw riding out there like a ghost was chasing him, but that entered into it too.

Moss had stepped down our way while I was talking

and he figgered this was as good a time as any to have his say. "And I think you're being paid by Jesse James to protect them." He poked his finger sharp toward me while he was talking. "And you're saying all this just to stop us, that's what I think."

"Here, here! That's a damn serious charge, mister!" Pinkerton said to him. "And there's no—"

"What you men can't seem to get through your damn thick heads—and it surprises me about you more'n anybody, Moss— is that folks around here *likes* the Jameses. People take them for one outfit from the South, at least, that ain't turned in their side arms and ain't rolled over and played dead yet—and ain't ever likely to." I shook my head and looked back at Pinkerton. "And even them that don't care no more about who won the War, the Jameses pay them damn good money to watch out for things just *like* this, an armed train parked for hours on the siding and horses enough for a company of cavalry. No, the Jameses ain't even *near* here no more, I'd bet money on it, and it's all because you didn't do like I said." I turned back to O. P. Moss and it was my turn now to poke a finger. "And *not* because I'm workin for Frank and Jesse James, either." Well, it was true enough, as far as it went. I didn't come right out and say I *wasn't* being paid by them, did I?

Moss cocked an eye at me and looked sour as vinegar.

Pinkerton scratched his head under his derby hat and shifted his weight back and forth from one hefty leg to the other for a minute before he spoke. "Well, we're going out there. I didn't spend all this money hiring men and trains and get this all together just to turn around and go back now. I can't imagine what I'd tell my father. If you want to lead us, Goodwin, it's still your job. It's obvious to me you've been risking your life out here to gather information, despite what this man seems to think. But if you don't want to—or can't—Moss knows the country too. He can get us there about as well as you could, I suspect." Pinkerton must of had second thoughts just then for he turned sharp to Moss. "Thats true, isn't it?"

Moss nodded big, his eyes narrow on me to see what I was going to say or do next.

"Well, all right," I said. "I don't think it'll do any good, but if you want to take this troop out there I'll show you the best way—though who we're fooling now by being secret about it is way beyond me."

So that's what we done. Sort of. You would not believe how long it took for everbody to get everthing ready. The horses all saddled, some of the saddles missing and somebody else gone to the livery to find replacements for them—and he didn't come back for so long everbody thought he had give it up and got drunk instead, which he almost was when he finally got back. That short man had something like a narrow Red River cart on the train with all sorts of gear that had to be loaded just so, a horse harnessed special to pull it.

Everbody was hungry in the meantime, they'd missed getting their supper somehow, and grumbled like so many crybabies over heading out with nothing at all in their bellies and all weak besides, they said. How could you expect a man to work and not eat, they said. So sandwiches and coffee was sent for up to the cafe in Kearney, two apiece, which was closed by then and the owner had to be found, rousted out of the whorehouse, and convinced it was worth his while to open the cafe back up—the cook found, and I don't know what-all-else besides. And of course it'd started to snow about the time it got really good and dark. To tell it short, it was a little after eleven till we got started, the sleety snow coming down light but steady, and it getting colder by the hour. Since Frank James'd said about them not expecting to be raided at night, I'd planned on doing this late—but not *this* late.

I was thinking some about my mamma on the way out there, leading both the little gang Moss'd got together as well as the Pinkerton crew, which looked a lot tougher than that sorry-assed bunch that had went down where Jesse'd honeymooned. Farnum was the only one from that crew along on this fandango, thank God.

It was quiet in the patches of woods we passed through, the icy snow almost ankle deep by now and still falling—making tappety, hissing sorts of noises on the dead leaves that still hung on a lot of the oak trees. It come to mind then how ma was always proud of me, even when I was in prison, for she knowed I didn't do what they'd said. I seen her face so clear there in the dark for a minute it surprised me. Only I wasn't sure she'd be proud of me now, jumping back and forth like I'd been doing between the Jameses and the Pinkertons. "Pick the right side and stick with that," is what I heard her saying in my head.

And damned if I didn't miss the cut-off up by the main road when we come out that way. I could say it was the dark and how different everthing looked in the snow, but the truth is I wasn't paying attention like I should of been.

Finally, I seen my mistake and just stopped and looked around. So did all the men behind me. Lucky for me, I knowed *about* where I was, anyway.

"I wondered where the hell you were going," Moss says. He was riding right behind Pinkerton and me, and in front of the fifteen or so men on horseback following along behind. "You're lost, aren't you?" And before I had a chance to answer he turned to William Pinkerton, wrapped up in a big fur coat now, a big tall fur hat too, and says to him, "I knew this man didn't know what the hell he was doing. I *knew* it."

"Willie?" Pinkerton asked.

"I just missed the cut-off trail is all," I said. "Come on, it's only a quarter mile or so back the way we come." I went towards the rear and Pinkerton and Moss turned their horses and come along, the rest of the men just sitting watching us as we went past, the looks on their faces asking what in the *hell* was wrong *now*.

"God damn it!" I heard Moss curse only about half under his breath back behind me. I wanted to punch that son of a bitch but I let it go.

Finally we come out on the Haynesville Road, cutting

through Dan Askew's big field and then hitting the property line of the Samuel place, just where I knowed we would, and we went back into the trees a piece from there like I'd planned. You couldn't see the Samuel house from where we stopped, even if it was daylight, which it sure as hell wan't. But we was close enough to the house to walk, between a quarter and a half mile off, I figgered, and over a little rise.

I dismounted and nodded at Pinkerton, who told the men to climb down too.

"You all keep your voices down and wait here till I come back," I told them. "There's a place up behind the house I want to check first to see if there's anybody's there." Where I meant was where some of the gang camped sometimes while Jesse and Frank stayed at the house. Up close by where Jesse'd gave me my shooting lessons from time to time. Though I didn't tell them *that*.

"I'm going along," Moss said.

"No you're not," I told him, handing him the reins of my horse.

"Like hell I'm—"

"You know, Moss, you're fast on your way to getting your nose busted."

He started to say something back but Pinkerton stepped in between us. "If he wants to go it alone, that's the way we'll do it," he told Moss, then turned to me and spoke a little quieter. "Only remember what happened down there at that cabin, Goodwin, will you? Down there close to the Territory where he got away from us." It struck me he was some differnt from back then, had maybe even learned a lesson or two himself.

"I'll remember," I told him, and started back towards where the gang camped. I took it slow and made as little noise as I could. The snow helped a lot, both quieting the leaves underfoot when you stepped and also making a little noise of its own falling on the dead leaves still on, you couldn't hardly hear me.

But like I thought, no one was there. Only someone

had been there not too long ago, though. Fresh horseshit melted the snow that'd fell on it, and underneath the ashes of the campfire, red coals still glowed when I stirred it. They had took off out of there in a hurry, I figgered. I found a shirt someone'd hung over a tree limb and forgot, and a pouch full of tobacco on one of the stones of the fire circle.

That man in the black floppy hat, I said to myself standing there in that little clearing up from the stream, that was who warned them. I *should* of followed him.

"There's no one back there," I told Pinkerton. "They was there until a few hours ago, but they ain't now," I told him.

"Could you see anyone at the house?" he asked, whispering to Moss and me, though there was no reason for it.

I shook my head. "I didn't look, there's no need to. I was back where the gang stays—when the boys sleep at their mamma's. And there was more'n Frank and Jesse here a couple days ago. If they're gone now, Frank and Jesse are too."

"That's bullshit!" Moss hissed. "You get a train and come all the way up here and he tells us to turn around without even checking the house. For Christsakes!"

Pinkerton nodded and looked at me. "He's right, you know."

I could see his point.

"Shall I lead the men, sir?" Moss asked him.

"No, Mr. Goodwin will do so, if he still wants," Pinkerton said, drawing his little revolver and checking the cartridges for about the third time since we'd left the train. Then he looked at me with the question in his eye.

"All right," I said. "We have enough men, we might as well surround the place, then." The short man unloaded his cart affair, and some of us carried his boxes and things. I got all the men in close to me and told them what we were gonna do, best as I could see it. We tied the horses and left the wrangler behind with them. Walking slow, we got up to where you could see the place, the snow making everthing brighter, despite there being no moon. The house was all dark, not a light showing nowhere—just like I knowed it'd be.

I put the men in place as we snuck around their house, making a raggedy sort of circle, some men with rifles, some with revolvers, and some with both. If some was as far as fifty feet from the house, others was as close as thirty in places they had something to hide behind. Moss hung on Pinkerton's hind pockets like a tail on a raccoon when we was making our circle, and they ended up together over by the icehouse. That short man and the two fellows carryin most of his gear, they stayed close to me. Them and me'd had to wade the stream coming up at the last, and their feet must of been as cold and wet as mine was. We ended up right beside Samuel's stable, me and the short man's little crew, the circle closed now. I ducked inside the stable and counted the horses. Only two. And neither of them the showy kind that Frank favored or Jesse's fine gray, Stonewall.

It was quiet now, the snow'd stopped and nothing happening for a minute or so. Off in the trees a distance, an old barn owl started making his shivery call. You could just barely see the men over there by the icehouse and couldn't see none at all over on the other side, the side I guess you'd call the front of the place, where the veranda was, over where they'd fed me my dinner once, I remembered then. After a while, I seen Pinkerton start towards where we was, I thought he wanted a word with me.

But it was the short man he spoke to. "Are you ready, Mr. Johnson?" he asked him.

"Yes, indeed," the small man said. "Shall we fire the place first or just throw the devices inside?"

"Well, what would you—"

"Wait a minute!" I said, a little louder than I should have, I suppose. "You mean you're going to set their house on fire not even knowing who's *in* there?"

"These people have brought this on themselves, Goodwin," Pinkerton said, "the lawless way they live."

I couldn't rightly believe what I was hearing. "Well, *maybe* you could say that about Jesse James, but he ain't even there. I checked the stable and his horse—"

"Inconclusive!" that little man said, madder'n a hornet all of a sudden. "Give 'em the works *now*, I say!" He punctuated this by smacking his fist into the palm of his other hand, then started fussing with his boxes and bags and cans and such, quick and jerky as a mouse in cheese.

"You can't do that!" I said in William Pinkerton's face.

"What the hell's the trouble over here?" Moss hissed, coming around the corner of the stable.

"Goodwin here doesn't think we should use the incendiary devices," Pinkerton told him, no more ashamed of himself than if he was telling you the time of day.

"Good God," I said. "You mean to say you got me to lead you out here so's you could throw a firebomb inside where women and little ones are sleeping? The James boys *momma* is in there and her children, one who ain't even completely right in the head! Their servant lady and her boy too—what did *they* do? And what you ain't even thinking of is that Jesse and Frank James sure as hell *ain't* in there. For Lord's sake, Jesse *James* don't even do things this bad, *this* wrong."

"What'd I tell you?" Moss says to Pinkerton.

27

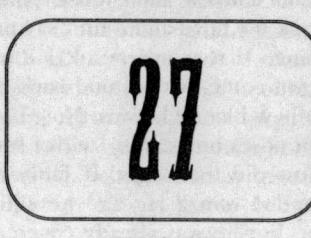

DEAD A HUNDRED YEARS

I stepped into Moss and give him a quick short poke and then throwed my best right-hand haymaker right behind it—the second falling flat on top of where the first one did, both of them square to the middle of his stupid face. They caught him entirely by surprise, that pair of punches did, and they caught him a little on the cheek but mostly on the nose, which give off the nicest, sweetest crunch you ever heard. Somewhere between cracking your knuckles and busting open a roasted peanut. He let out a grunt and fell back hard on his arse.

"And what'd I tell *you*?" I said, standing over him, my fists still balled up. It surprised me I done it, I never even thought about it—just done it.

About that time Pinkerton grabbed me, threw his arms around my middle, and pinned my elbows to my short ribs. "Here, here! For God's sake, get control of yourselves, you two!" He pulled me back and a couple men held me should I decide to go after Moss again. But I didn't give them no trouble, for I'd already give Moss just what he needed.

"Goodwin, for God's sakes, come to your senses," Pinkerton said. "We've got to see inside the house there, don't we? Find out who's there!? And we can't just knock on the damn door and ask, can't you see that?"

I just shook my head and didn't say nothing, for *nothing* would change that man's mind, I knowed, sure as I knowed my own name. Moss stood back up and that was the first I saw how bloody he was. Now I've saw plenty of men with their noses broke, but I never saw none of them bleed like Moss did that night. It fairly run out of him. Somebody handed him a rag and he squeezed his nose shut with that, but he was already covered with blood in front, his mustache and chin and his shirt dark with it, even the bandanna around his neck was already half soaked. He was a damn mess, Moss was, and he didn't look my way even once more that I saw.

"All right," Pinkerton said, taking a deep breath. "We won't use the Greek Fire, but we will use the coal oil alongside the door and then the turpentine flare if we have to, if we can't tell for certain whether the James boys are in there or not." He turned more to me then. "I can't just forfeit the element of surprise entirely, Goodwin. I just can't!" He turned and went over to where he could see the house a little better.

That short man poured out some coal oil in two pails and then handed Farnum a couple of things, including one of those flint striking affairs like miners use.

"You can let me go now," I told the fellows holding me. "I ain't going to do nothing more to him."

Pinkerton looked back and nodded, and they turned me loose. Moss started over toward the icehouse still pinching his nose shut with the rag. "God damb you, Goodwin!" he said when he'd got a couple steps off.

Farnum and the other fellow, a big man, sneaked up toward the house quiet. When they got there, the big fellow sloshed his bucket of coal oil up alongside the doorway—like you'd throw a bucket of water up against a wall once you was finished scrubbing it down, to rinse it off. Then Tom handed him the other bucket and he done the same with that, only on the other side of the door. You could smell the sickly smell of that coal oil hanging in the cold air then, even back where we stood watching.

I don't know which of them men flicked that striker thing, but the fire licked up that bare wood faster than you'd think it would, I doubted it was really all kerosene in them buckets. Fire on both sides of their door, leaping higher than the roof overhang after only a few seconds, the blaze as bright as day then, reflecting off the snow too, the light in the yard orange as sundown. My eyes was full used to the dark, so maybe it seemed brighter than it really was, but it like to blinded me at first.

That's when we heard a man yell from inside and then a woman scream.

One of our gang laughed, a man over on the other side of Pinkerton. "That'll bring the sons-of-bitches out!" he called to the men across the other way, who laughed even louder and yelled something back about flames and a woman's private parts I don't want to say.

I grabbed Pinkerton by the shoulder, and he pulled away half scared I was going to hit him. "Is this what you wanted?" I yelled at him. "Is this—"

A wild-haired old man run out in his nightshirt before I could finish or Pinkerton could answer—it was Doc Samuel, I saw almost right away—running like old men do, kind of shuffling his bare feet in the snow and throwing his arms around like he didn't know what to do, jumping around in a kind of a jaggedy jig that would of been comical if it wasn't for his place on fire. He stopped stone dead and then just stood staring for a minute at his house starting to catch good.

He yelled something to them inside I couldn't understand, and right away you knowed it was him that'd yelled there at first, not Jesse or Frank or no other man. Then he started to pull at the burning wood, door framing I think it was, tearing pieces off the building. It made you just sick, for you knowed he was burning his hands doing that, but it was like he didn't feel it.

About that time Jesse's mamma come running out carrying a quilt that was smouldering and smoking and throwed it into the yard, it landing over the handle of a pump there, catching into flames more than before. "Doctor, come back inside!" she yelled at him and he followed her in quick as that shuffle kind of run of his would take him, the framing or siding still smoking and glowing red in spots, though none of it was flaming up any more by then.

I didn't even notice at first when Tom and the big man moved down to the window just past me, not far off at all, one of them lighting something and then the other throwing a big burning ball inside. I couldn't believe it! A turpentine flare I heard someone say right after. Glass breaking and the wood splintering when that fire ball was flung inside, a heavy thump on the board floor in there.

It was bright as daylight inside that house with that thing rolling around, the two older ones sort of bent over it, trying to get it the hell out of there with brooms or something. If Frank or Jesse would of been anywheres around, they'd of been there doing it too—or more likely running out to kill us. You could of bet anything on that.

I looked over at Pinkerton. He was staring at the Samuels, them trying to save their house, just like I'd a been doing—or him too. "It look to you like Frank and Jesse James is in there?" I asked him.

He didn't answer me, just kept watching.

"How do you like your little party now, Mr. Pinkerton?" I asked him then.

He looked at me for just a second, and what was on his face was shame, pure and simple, though he tried to cover it up by looking back at the house quick. He knowed they weren't in there. It struck me then he probly knowed it all along.

I started running toward the house to help Jesse's mamma and stepdaddy put out their fires when I saw that big man with Farnum stand up sudden and toss another burning ball into the house, this one bigger than the first, which must of been dying out some by that time, for it wan't nearly so bright in the house by the time he throwed that second one inside with a crash of something knocked over into the bargain.

"No!" Pinkerton yelled behind me. I turned around and looked back at him, so much something in his voice—I couldn't tell what—it like to froze me fast to where I'd stopped in the snowy yard, halfway between the Pinks and the Jameses.

He was pointing towards the house, Pinkerton was, there towards where Farnum and the big man had started coming back from, the window there, the flames inside higher again and lighting up Pinkerton's face, too, making him look like the devil in hell shouting out orders to his demons. "No!" he yelled again. "For God's sake, that's— you can't—"

He started running toward the place just like I'd did a few seconds before, and I had just turned around again to run inside and help, I was closer than him, when a blast flashed inside the house like a keg of gunpowder going off, the bang so loud I felt the air from it hit my face the same time as the hard, flat sound, big as a mountain, staggering me back.

Right on top of that explosion, something smacked me in the back, something terrible hot and heavy, a big black fist the size of a coal bucket it felt like. It knocked me forward off my feet and the last thing I knowed, falling facedown, it was like I had dove down into a cold black well with no bottom, mile after mile of black water below me, the light getting dimmer up above, sinking slow, down and down, not able to swim, not able to stop myself sliding down, not able to move even a muscle—only watching myself go deeper and deeper down, where I knowed for certain sure I would drown.

The last sound I heard, the last one that I knowed for certain what it was, was a child screaming in pain, and it echoed in my brain, again and again, while I slid down and down.

A child screaming in pain, and if there's one sound you do not want echoing inside you while things are all bending and stretching so out of shape you don't know *how* long it is, it's a sound bouncing like a big gum-rubber ball, bouncing everywhere in a smooth water-worn cave—the scream of a child in pain.

I slid down into all that darkness and then further down into a nothing so thin it didn't even feel like I was in water no more, or in nothing no more, and on down into more nothing than that below—all still and dark and quiet as being dead a hundred years.

28

A TIRED ANGEL

It's strange to recall, but in all that empty space I sort of swum down through, all that quiet, it was like I'd dream from time to time. Only the dreams was more like sounds than things you'd see, like in regular dreams. A bouncing kind of a noise, a thunk or a thud that come close sometimes and went away from me others. I thought it was that second burning ball throwed inside again, over and over, is what I thought, though it never exploded like I was always sure it was going to when I heard it coming—or bumping away. Being afraid it was going to go off again, deathly afraid.

And a clackety kind of rattle too, mixed in with the thumping, a tapping I kept thinking was bugs of some kind clicking to one another, talking among themselves with their clackety-tap-tapping sounds, making plans to eat something or somebody, clicking like beetles would, I guess, but even when I was thinking that, that it was bugs talking, making their plans, I knowed that wasn't right, and sometimes I knowed it was even crazy to think that. A time or two there, I almost laughed to think that I thought that tapping noise was bugs *talking*, but then I kept asking myself—who's this *I* that feels like laughing, anyway? Who is *that*? And I couldn't get no answer to a question as simple as that, can you believe it? It sure didn't seem like nobody I ever knowed, and it sure as *hell* did not seem like me in that time there that was sort of like a dream, and seemed real enough and also like, sort of it didn't either—everthing all melted together, as crazy as *that* sounds.

And running though it all was that child screaming and screaming, I wanted it out of my head so, out of the place I was, *wherever* that was. That was the main thing, to get away from the sound of that child wailing in pain, suffering, and of course I couldn't do it. Couldn't move at all.

And that was just what I *heard*. Flashes of light sometimes, like the explosion, only the damndest colors you ever saw—purple like a sunset, and then like my ma's lilacs only paler, and then everbody's face, one after the other or all sort of the same face, purple and lilac color, made up out of pieces of faces of all the folks I ever knowed, or one after the other their faces going by so fast you couldn't tell them apart, one from the other, but at other times changing so slow it'd be one person you were looking at, them maybe saying something to you, and then you'd notice it was really somebody else, and it'd change from Dan Askew asking you about draining the field to your mamma talking about her sewing, and then to Sarah saying something I couldn't understand and then back to Askew and you not even noticing it was changing like that until one had went past and the next come in while you was still hearing Askew.

I know that sounds crazy, but that's the way it was, the best I'm able to *say* how it was, it was so strange.

Until one time the face just stayed pretty much the same, looking at me with such worry I pitied her, whoever she was. So much love, and she went from Sarah to being my ma and then both together and then back to Sarah. And then finally she stayed Sarah, holding a washrag, warm and soapy a little, and washing my face slow and careful—like you would a child's.

"Sarah?" I asked her, my voice sounding like a damn frog croaking, all rusty and rough. "Sarah?" I sputtered. What in the hell—

"Willie?" Sarah asked, like she wasn't really sure it was me. "Willie?!" A big smile breaking over her face, I was afraid for a second or so she was going to turn into someone else again.

Something hurt. I looked down and couldn't believe I was wearing a nightshirt, which I never owned one of in my life. "Well, yeah, it's me I think. Where the hell *am* I, anyway?" There was bandages wrapped around my head, too, a lot of them. I tried sitting up, but couldn't hardly do it.

She kissed me, right while I was trying to sit up. I looked around for the Pinkerton bunch, it seemed so odd they wasn't there no more, they was there a minute ago. But then I was glad they wasn't, Sarah being there and all. I'd a been damned ashamed if she was to see me with them and figger it out. But of course they wasn't really there, only in my mind a second or two.

She stood up, laughed, put the washcloth and a basin down, toweled off my face, and kissed me a little peck again, finally sliding down on top of me, smothering me with kisses this time, laughing, and something hurting like fire, like being branded there at my side. Lord!

I guess I cursed or squealed or something. And happy as I was to see her, I couldn't kiss her back, whatever it was that was wrong with me hurting like the blue be-damneds.

"Oh, I'm sorry!" she said getting up quick, which also hurt like hell. "Oh, Willie, I'm—I shouldn't have— Oh dear, I'm so sorry, Willie!" Sometime about then she called for her mamma, and that's how I finally figgered out for sure I was at their house, upstairs in a bedroom.

"I'll be right back," Sarah said at last, bending over me again, but being careful not to touch me this time, I saw. "Oh Willie, I'm so glad you're—"

Her mamma called something from what sounded like downstairs, only an awful long way off, too.

"I'll be back in a minute," she said. "Just lie still now, and I'll be right back." She ducked out the door, pulling it shut behind her, trying not to make much noise, like I was still asleep or something. Golden yeller sunlight streamed in the window, a happy sight, all over the bed I was in, and I laid there just trying to breath regular again, it seemed like I couldn't get a full breath, and also trying to figger out what the hell was going on here. She stuck her head back in. "Now don't you try getting out of bed," she said, shaking her finger at me. "Or even try and sit up, you hear me?"

I nodded a little, and my, was I ever tired and thirsty, just doing that and talking the little I had talked to her. I heard her go down the hall and down some steps, calling for her mamma a second time, but I didn't hear nothing more after that, and when I opened my eyes again it was dark, the middle of the night it looked like out the window.

On the stand to the left of the big brass bed I was in, an old oil lamp was burning low, so I could see around the room a little—a washstand with a pitcher and bowl along the wall, a tall chest of drawers down in the corner, a little fireplace off beyond the foot of the bed with a fire burned low but giving off good heat. And Good Lord, there sat Sarah in a rocking chair pulled up beside the bed on the other side—fast asleep. I was about to say something to her to wake her up, but she looked so nice sitting there sleeping, sort of like a tired angel, I just wanted to look at her pretty face a while first. After I'd looked at her for a minute or two, starting to notice what was really there instead of just seeing what warmed my heart so, I seen she was kind of pale and a little drained looking. Peaked, my mamma would of said. How the hell long'd I *been* here, anyways?

Her eyelids looked a little dark, and she slept with them open just the least little bit the way some people do that's a little scary, you can't tell if they're awake or asleep or maybe even dead—only with the way her breath rose her breasts and then they fell, I knowed she was just asleep. A big springy curl of her dark brown hair had come loose from on top and hung down over her cheek. She was the most welcome, beautiful sight of my entire life sitting there with a quilt pulled up to her neck, sleeping and snoring just the least little bit, it made me smile and then laugh to hear her, and then that made me cough, and that made me hurt like hell down in my side and back there somewheres.

She woke up with a start. "Willie, my word, are you all right?"

I nodded and pulled myself up a little, Sarah telling me not to, but then getting under my arms and helping me slide up some after it was plain I wasn't going to listen. I asked her for water and she give me a big drink. Though I was still weak, I felt stronger than when I'd talked to her—before! "You're . . . I talked to you before, didn't I? Since I been here in your house, I mean." I was confused as a hoot owl in a twister.

"Yes," she said, "day before yesterday. But by the time I got back with mamma, you were gone again."

"Damn, that was two days ago, huh? Well, how long have I been here all together, then? It seems nearly a week."

Sarah looked at her hands and then looked into my eyes again. "We thought for a while—before Doc Kimball figured out how to get some water into you—" She stopped whatever it was she was going to say and turned the lamp up. Then she smiled. "It'll be three weeks tomorrow they brought you, Willie. How do you f—"

"Three weeks!" I said. "How did— What happened to me?" I asked, reaching down to my middle and feeling the bandages there.

Sarah stood up, the quilt over her sliding to the floor. She went over and put a couple pieces of limb wood on the fire from a big basket thing, stood and looked back at me over her shoulder. "You were shot in the back, Willie. And then hit on the head with something heavy, the doctor said."

"Shot?! Why, I've never been shot before in my life. Wait a minute . . ." *Who shot me?* I almost asked her, but then right away decided against it, something warning me not to. I reached up and felt my head was all bandaged too.

"You don't know what happened, do you?" she asked. She took the globe off another lamp over there and lit a pine splinter from the fireplace.

"Know what?" I asked her.

She lit the lamp with the pine splinter and then set it up on the high mantel, the room a good deal brighter then. "Why, that you were hurt when those damn Pinkertons raided Aunt Zerelda's farm. What did you think I meant?"

I shook my head. "Nothing, nothing Sarah. I'm just kind of confused, and I don't remember . . . much . . ." I hated this dancing around, me not knowing what she knowed, what she thought—or what to say. But I knowed this wasn't the time to straighten all them things out, though I promised myself right then I'd tell her the whole thing just as soon as I could, as soon as it seemed right to. It just wasn't fair to her not to.

She come over and sat down on the edge of the bed, facing me straight again, taking my hands in hers and looking deep into my eyes. "It's all right, Willie. It's all right. What's important now is for you to get well, get all healed up. Take care of that first." After I thought about it a second, it was like she was saying there might be something *more* to take care of later, but the look on her face and the sound of her voice didn't say just what, though. Maybe I was only imagining things, but I didn't like it, I sure didn't like the feel of it.

My, she was pretty that night, though, for all the peaked she looked. Her face soft in the lamp light, but I didn't enjoy looking at her so much as I might have, wondering what was going on in her mind and thinking that I should have told her about the Pinkertons way before this. She did love me still, that much was clear, and she was glad I'd come out of whatever fog I was in, that was certain too. And that'd be enough for right now. It'd have to be.

Sarah patted my hands and stood up. "I'm going downstairs to get you some soup. You lost a lot of blood right after, Willie. And some weight too, since then—since you've been unconscious and couldn't eat."

"I don't think I—"

"No arguments, now," she said, smiling and going out the door.

I woke up when she come back in that time, though you'd a thought I'd of slept enough in three weeks, wouldn't you? She wouldn't hear of nothing but that she fed me, spooned that nice hot soup into me as quick and as long as I could swaller her down.

Sarah took care of me good over the next week or so, feeding me by hand just like you would a sick colt, until I said no and finally meant it.

Her mamma come in every day and talked and talked until I either fell asleep on her or pretended to. Sarah's daddy come in only once to show me some game he'd shot, but Sarah shoved him and his three bloody rabbits out of there quick. I wanted to get up soon after I started feeding myself but that wouldn't do, the doctor said.

He was a tall old drink-of-water, two dozen or more years older'n me, Doc Kimball I think his name was. "Later," he was fond of saying whether you asked him either what was done to me or when I could get out of there. "Later," was sort of his answer to nearly everthing you asked him. He give you orders like he was a general or something and expected you to follow them to the letter, no questions asked and right away. Sarah made me stick to his orders, too. Even when that meant getting me the bed pan, which I hated her doing that, but what could I do?

She said, shoot, she'd nursed her brother and her boy and her husband more than once, and why didn't I just forget about it and get it over with? It didn't bother her, so why should it bother me? Well, that helped some I admit, but still . . .

She'd let me sleep as late as I could every day, and then rubbed my back and neck and then put the ointment on my wounds twice a day, morning and night, like the doctor said to, and every day there I got a little stronger. About all I could learn about what was wrong with me was that somebody'd shot me in the back, off to the right of my spine some, and that I was luckier than hell, Doc Kimball said, because the bullet bounced off one of my ribs in back after smashing it, nicked my lung a little toward the bottom corner, which is why I coughed and spit blood once in a while, and then went out my side. Whoever'd shot me, he clubbed me on the head with something heavy too, after I was down on my face. More than once they hit me, was what I gathered, and'd probly used a rifle barrel doing it. Lucky I had such a damned hard head, too, Doc Kimball said just about every time he was there, which was twice a week at first, the best I could keep track of time, which wasn't all that good, I got to admit. He said my skull'd been cracked in two places that he knowed of and maybe more besides, and I was lucky to have left what few brains I was born with, that was the way he talked to you.

Some days I felt good and couldn't believe anything was wrong with me at all unless I turned a certain way or started coughing again. I had a pretty big hole there in my side, sort of toward the front, where the bullet had come out clean, and that started throbbing when I coughed too. The one in back I couldn't see, though I didn't have no trouble feeling it, I'll tell you. Other days there was a ringing in my head so loud it was like I had it shoved up the asshole of a church bell and my head ached so bad I like to screamed. Those days I took the laudanum Sarah spooned into me without no fuss at all, then sometimes drifting into dreams of floating in a bunch of puffy clouds striped like peppermint candy and rosy sunshine everwhere. But them times when I needed it got fewer and fewer.

After a while I was sitting up out of bed, in a padded chair they had moved in there, and Sarah and me'd make the time pass by playing checkers, which she always beat me at, or playing poker for matchsticks, which I begun to suspect she was letting me win just so's I'd feel better about something.

One afternoon we was sitting there playing poker, and I was about to draw one card into two pairs, the best hand I'd got all day, when I heard a noise I couldn't tell what it was, though I was sure I'd heard it before. All of a sudden I knowed it was that thump-thump from my dreams there while I was out for so long—along with that tappety-tap clicking noise right along with it.

"What *is* that noise?" I asked Sarah.

She listened a minute. "Oh, I'm sorry," she said, getting up. "I keep telling him not to play with Bobby in the hall, but when the weather's like this and they can't be outside long—"

"What?" I asked her. "I don't know what you mean."

She put her cards down. "It's Billy and his dog Bobby playing ball in the hallway. That little dog just *loves* to play ball."

"Oh, is that all it is?" I said. It made sense then. That thumping was a gum-rubber ball bouncing down the hallway and maybe into a wall, and the tap-clicking noise was the dog's toenails on the board floor.

Sarah went toward the door. "I'll tell him to stop now, but there's no guarantee he won't do it again tomorrow. I wish that boy—"

"You do no such a thing," I told her. "It don't bother me none at all, it was just like I kind of heard it when I was knocked out there, and then hearing it again now ... Tell him to come in here, I'd like to see him again. There ain't nothing wrong with the way you look, certainly, but I ain't seen no one else but your mamma for some time and—"

"Oh, shut up," she said, laughing at me underneath it. She went out and in a minute the door swung open and Sarah's boy Billy stood there with his one hand on the door knob and in his other arm the cutest little dog you ever saw, Sarah standing behind them smiling, making it a picture you could hang up, look at every morning for the rest of your life and never get tired of looking at it.

Billy's dog was a small terrier or some sort, mostly white, and he had about the biggest ears a dog that size could have and not tip over in front when he walked his perky, prancy little walk, which he did as soon as Billy put him down, right up to my chair, looking at me funny, trying to figger out who the devil I was, anyway, mister? I was surprised he didn't bark, that was his first time seeing me, but he didn't. Those ears stood straight up, his head cocked way crooked first to one side and then the other, those big brown eyes looking at me for all they was worth.

That little dog hopped his front paws up on my leg to look me over better, his face all smiling and a long thin pink tongue hanging out as he panted at me, and he licked my hand once, sort of to see if I tasted all right. I guess I passed muster.

He had two brown patches on his head, one covered an ear and the eye on one side and the other brown patch the eye and ear on the other. Only the two brown patches was sort of growed together in the middle, so the white that run up his nose didn't come all the way through, kind of lopsided, giving his face a sort of crookedy grin look to it. And each of his eyes was lined with black, so he looked sort of like a circus clown, too, or a stage actor maybe. He was one of them little dogs you liked right off, and wanted to pick him up and hold him—though you knowed he would lick your face if you did.

"What do you call this critter," I asked the boy, reaching over and petting that cute little dog on top of his head.

Billy sat down beside him and the dog turned quick and nipped at his fingers a little, just gentle and playful, you understand. "This here's Bobby."

"'This *is* Bobby,'" Sarah corrected him, putting a hand on her hip. "Or 'His *name's* Bobby,' but not—"

The boy looked at me, a little hint of ashamed on his face, like egg yolk after breakfast. I winked and he smiled. "Maybe this *here* ain't the time for teaching him how to sound like no schoolmaster," I said, Billy starting to giggle into the neck of that little dog, who was squirming and wiggling to beat anything with Billy tussling with him and tickling him now.

Sarah give me a look, putting the other hand on her other hip, but then she saw the fun of it. After I'd throwed his ball for him a time a two, she scooted both dog and boy out of there.

They come back often to see me, Billy and Bobby did, the dog always bringing his ball and dropping it either on the bed for me to throw or beside my leg if I was sitting up in the padded chair. Sarah was right, that little dog seemed like he would fetch his ball for as long as you'd have the gumption to throw it for him.

One day Billy and me decided we'd see just how long he'd go, chasing that ball, timing him with my pocket watch. And with Billy and me taking turns throwing, that feisty little dog chased that ball for one hour and fifty-two minutes with no stopping at all. He might of went longer than that if Sarah hadn't of come in the room at that point to chase them out, no matter we told her what we was doing and wasn't through, because Bobby wasn't even starting to slow down yet.

"I'm sorry, boys, but you'll have to start your game over some other time. Mr. Goodwin has another visitor who says he can't wait around for you two to finish." She throwed Bobby's ball out into the hallway and of course he went after it. Then she took Billy's shoulders and moved him out into the hall with her, turning around and giving me a look before she closed the door behind her, him complaining a little to her as they went down the stairs, I heard.

I sat there a minute trying to figger out what that look was all about. I guessed my visitor was probly old Doc Kimball, for he came every week or so after I started getting better, and I didn't see him yet that week. That's why I was so surprised when my door flew open with a rush and there stood Jesse James.

29

JESSE JAMES'S NEWSPAPER

*The farm of Dr. Reuben Samuel
and his wife Zerelda Cole James Samuel
January 26, 1875
Early Tuesday morning, 1:25 AM*

Charlotta Addams, who had been with the Samuels since long before emancipation, awoke with a start—with the ghost of a strange smell drifting around her in the chilly room.

She sat up and sniffed. At first she thought perhaps the fireplace was smoking a little into the room. Perhaps she had just imagined . . . She lay her head back down on her pillow and began a drowsy prayer. But before she could finish it, the dishes, all the crockery, everything in the room was suddenly and brilliantly illuminated, flickering with an unnaturally vivid orange light. The house was on fire!

She threw off her covers, flinging them in a heap against the log wall beside the doorway, and tried to wake her grandson who slept in the trundle bed below. "Ambrose, Ambrose!" she called harshly.

Sixteen-year-old Ambrose Addams pulled out of her clawing grasp and curled back into his visions of naked women dancing around a fire. He was still struggling to see them again as his grandmother dragged him into the adjoining room where Doctor and Mrs. Samuel slept. Charlotta had been fighting to keep from screaming ever since she first saw the flames on both sides of the doorway through the cracks, and the desire to call out in terror was still as strong as the urge to breathe. She shook Miz Samuel awake, proud that she had not called out like a frightened child.

Rueben Samuel broke the silence of the house. He shouted and flailed his arms like a drowning man when his wife shook him, convinced blue-coat cavalrymen had returned and were going to try and hang him again. He jumped out of bed and, still shouting, ran outside to get away from the Yankees, whom he imagined were lurking in the dark corners of his bedroom. The doctor's cries loosed the flood of fear in Charlotta's mind and finally spilled it into her throat, bitter as bile.

Zerelda Samuel's Victorian modesty made her find her heavy robe and pull it on before she did anything else— even though the room was rapidly filling with smoke that was beginning to choke her as she fastened the last button. Once decently covered, she ran to the other room to find Charlotta's quilt in flames against the wall. She snatched a tobacco drying stick from where it had been propped in a corner, got the quilt onto it, and carried it quickly though the back doorway the doctor had left open. When she flung the quilt through the air into the yard, it flamed up brilliantly before settling over the handle of the pump. She saw the doctor had the fire around the doorway nearly out. Thank heavens the overhang didn't catch.

With the last of the light from the fire she peered into the chilling January night and saw men crouching behind fences, saw men with eyes like wolves who licked their lips in hunger, watching her husband and herself fight the flames for their home.

When she was sure the fire could no longer consume the house, lick the light and warmth out of her family with its sharp orange tongue, she called to the doctor to come back in with her—as much to keep him from their vulpine stares as anything else. He ran past her at a doddering jog.

Zerelda went back in and, after barring the door behind her, began to look for her children, three of whom slept in a half-story loft and the youngest, Archie, who rested on a pallet bed upon the floor. The older children called down to her from their perch, so despite the lingering smoke she knew they were safe. But she could not find little Archie. He was not in his covers, and even when the smoke began to clear somewhat, Zerelda could not find him.

Frantically she looked under her bed and behind the other furniture. Then she heard him call "Mamma! Mamma!?" from out in the other room.

No sooner had she spotted him, standing by the fireplace anxiously sucking his thumb and crying at the same time, than a ball of fire the size of a large pumpkin burst through the back window, smashing glass and window framing and rolling on the bare wooden floor toward the center of the room. The doctor stood watching it, shuffling his bare feet, dumbfounded and amazed, pulling at his long white hair.

Zerelda thrust a tobacco stick into his hands. "The fireplace!" she shouted. The ball appeared to be covered with cotton soaked in some kind of flammable liquid, that dribbled in burning, oily globs onto the floor as they rolled it with their sticks toward the hearth. Ambrose beat out the little firelets that trailed after the diminutive sun with an old broom as the Samuels rolled it toward what they hoped would be its ashen grave.

Just as they got the fiery ball onto the bricks of the hearth and just as it had begun to sputter out and dim, they heard a second one come hurtling through the now-ruined window. Flaming hotter and more brightly than the first, it landed with a crash on the marble-topped stand and splayed its angled legs out in four directions, smashing the green-veined pale marble slab into hundreds of pieces when it hit the plank floor, shattering at the same instant a tall, ruby-glass coal oil lamp, now mercifully empty. The lamp globe became a sudden shower of purest pyral crystal, the ruby shade bursting out into a giant shattering rose for half a frozen instant, a wildly opening centifolia that sailed triangular, knife-sharp petals radiating in all directions across the floor, sliding under bare, trampling feet.

Larger than the first, this new fireball was much too heavy for Zerelda's tobacco stick. But the doctor leaped after it. With a square bladed shovel he managed to nudge it, bowling and rumbling, toward the fireplace. Ambrose beat out the fire puddles behind it with his smoking, unraveling broom. Past the now-dead hulk of the first incendiary device the iron leviathan tumbled, clanking and flaring brightly when it hit the bricks at the back, coming to rest at last, lodging soundly against the large oak log at the back, its embers glowing hotly now that its covering of white ash had been dashed off.

Doctor Samuel was just starting to step back and admire the results of his sooty, sweaty handiwork, when the burning sphere exploded.

Its roar shook neighboring farmers out of their sleep and rolled them out of their beds miles away. The echo of the explosion bounced across the hills and hollows of Clay County, a cannon blast rolling along through the darkened Western Missouri countryside, made shimmering bright when a slice of moon tore through the high clouds and sparkled the snow with pale flakes of mica.

The blast flowed out in ever-widening circles, gaining speed going down the windward slope of the Rockies toward the Pacific. Other waves hurtled backward through the prairie states where it spread like a grass fire. It raged through the populous East like a rumor of adultery in high places.

From the Shenandoah Valley to Dakota Territory, farmers and ranchers scratched their heads and wondered how it could be that a company paid to enforce the law, one hired in the past by President Lincoln himself, no less, could come to break the law with such abandon and impunity?

Fishermen and banker's daughters heard the far-off rumble from their country's heartland and from the distant thunder, people fashioned not only a clutch of skulking villains, Allen Pinkerton and his sons and dark-suited henchmen, but also they made for themselves a set of heroes from a pair of rude backwoods brothers. Their brash and daring deeds—at least that was how they were reported—made the readers of morning newspapers remember an English hero, but instead of the ash longbow, a Colt's six shooter this young one clenched in his iron-hard hand, and in place of the pointed, feathered cap of Robin Hood, there sat the dusty brown fedora pulled low over the hauntingly blue and glassy eyes of Jesse James.

He stood in the doorway looking right at me, a newspaper in one hand and a big revolver in the other. I was sure my time was up right then, that this here'd be the day I died, but I decided right then the one thing I was not going to do was beg for my life from the man who was going to murder me anyway, no matter what I said. I had thought about maybe Jesse showing up here at Sarah's, but I always thought I'd have more time than this and I'd maybe be out of there till he come back. Only he was here *now*, and the way he was looking at me—me sitting there in that padded chair right in front of him, not able to get up and walk more'n a short way by myself let alone go up against him— the way he eyed me, I figgered I was in for it then. Hell, my Colt's, the one he'd gave me, was way over in the drawer there, no use to me now at all—even if it was loaded, which I wasn't even sure it was.

I looked out the window instead. I can't tell you why it seems like a odd kind of thing to do now I look back on it, even to me. It was sunny that day, a few high clouds sailing by in a sky almost as blue as Jesse's eyes. The bud-on the tree out there was swelled and big, getting ready to bust open. Springtime again. Funny I didn't notice before, I remember thinking. Fact is, I didn't even know if it was still February or if it'd turned March yet. You'd think a man'd know *that* at least, wouldn't you? Horse chestnut, I was pretty sure it was, and then I remembered seeing that same kind of a tree up there in Chicago that was just leafing out then. A year ago, more or less. I'd lasted a year going after these Jameses. Or was it two? It was more than Whicher'd did, anyways.

I looked back at Jesse. "Well, it's a nice day for it, at least," I said to him.

He looked puzzled, and then he come over to me slow and kneeled down to look me right in the face. "You remember me, Willie?" he asked.

He surprised me there a minute saying that. One of the most famous men in the country them days, and him asking if I knowed who he was! But then you couldn't never quite tell about him, how he'd trick you and turn things around on you before you caught on. So I was careful as I could be. I guessed my taking a minute to try and figger things out there made him think I was different than the way I really was. So maybe if I didn't say nothing—

"It's Jesse," he said. "Jesse James! Don't you remember me at all, Willie?"

I seen then he thought I'd lost my memory. It was true I'd lost it some, a little bit anyways, right after coming out of that long sleep I'd had after being cracked on the head. I asked Sarah once, not too long after I'd come out of it, what'd happened to the folks over at the Samuel's place in the raid, was they all right, and she stared at me like she'd been hit over the head with a board. Then she said she'd already told me twice about what happened to them, didn't I remember that?

"Oh sure, sure," I said, letting on I did remember, finally, but the truth was I didn't. From the way she talked, you knowed they'd been hurt some, though. Maybe someone'd told Jesse about me forgetting like that. Sarah, probly.

But I was my old self by the time he paid his visit that day, mostly. By the time he come around there to see me. At least in the thinking department I was all right. True, I could walk only a little ways without feeling tired as a newborn calf, and I had headaches near every day, and I still coughed and spit blood once in a while, and the place in my side was only now scabbing up right, but there was nothing wrong with my head, at least not the way it worked on the inside there wasn't. I don't think. But I decided it might be better to act like maybe I didn't know much, or at least wasn't sure.

"Well, in a way I remember you, but in another way I don't, rightly," I told him. "Jesse James, you say?"

He pulled up a little stool there and sat in front of me, putting the newspaper on the floor beside him and the big revolver on top of it.

I guess he saw me looking at the shooting iron.

"Oh! It's all right, Willie," he said, picking up the revolver again. "Don't worry, it's all right." It was some kind I didn't know, not a Colt's or a Remington or a Smith's or nothing regular like that, an M and H maybe, and he held it up for me to see good, after a minute putting it into my hands. I turned it over and over, looking it over careful for his benefit, mostly, but at the same time checking to see if it was loaded. Maybe this'd be how I got out of that room alive, I thought to myself.

But of course it wasn't loaded. Maybe that was one of his tricks, to hand me an empty pistol and see if I'd try and turn it on him, like back when we was shooting nuts. I handed it back to him.

"No, no. Look here," he said, pointing at the side of the barrel and then giving it back to me. "Can you see what's engraved there? It's not very clear, but you can read it, can't you?"

I seen what he was pointing to then, the letters P. G. G. engraved into the metal, awful shallow though. I knowed what them letters stood for, too, Pinkerton Government Guard. That's what they put on all their equipment, pistols and everthing, back before they changed their name. But there was still a lot of their things around with P. G. G. on it. The big revolver wasn't mine, though, they'd never handed none out to me—with or without their initials on it. Was *that* what Jesse James was trying to say, that he thought this here big revolver was *mine*? Or that I ought to know about pistols like this one because I worked for the Pinks and now he knowed I did? Is that what he meant? Was he showing me this just to see the look on my face when he did it? And see what I'd have to say? I decided the best thing was just to play dumb, and lots of folks who know me good might say that'd be easy for me to do, but it wasn't. Not apurpose like that.

I handed it back to him with the blankest look I could muster.

"This was found in mother's side yard the morning after the attack, Willie" he explained to me like I was a child. "It proves that it was Pinkerton agents who attacked my family. Don't you see? Don't you see how important this is Willie? Why, it proves that they're *guilty*!" He looked at me there for the longest minute, looked right into my eyes as steady as could be, but I didn't say or do nothing at all.

Then he watched me watch him set that big revolver back on the floor on top of the newspaper again, and then he looked peculiar at me all of a sudden and then a little smile on top of that. "Good heavens no, Willie! Mother told me how they found you—after the Pinkertons shot you. Good Lord, how could you think—" He shook his head. "No, I came to *thank* you, Willie, for trying to save my family. Not to *shoot* you, Good Lord..." He leaned forward and patted my hands, where they rested in my lap, and then patted my shoulder when he stood up, bending over towards me there, his hands on his knees after that, his face less'n a foot from mine.

"I came to ask you to help us catch and punish the damn cowards who *did* this terrible thing to my family—

and to *you*!" He took a deep breath then and let it out slow. "But I see you're not well enough yet to..." He reached down and took my hand and I let him. He started shaking hands with me, sort of, only I didn't give him no help with it. "Thank you, Willie. I'll never forget what you tried to do. Never."

I never did find out what he had that newspaper for. Maybe he wrapped that Pinkerton revolver up in it for some reason, or maybe he was just reading it, I never knowed.

30

YOU JUST NEVER KNOW, DO YOU?

*The farm of Dr. Reuben Samuel
and his wife Zerelda Cole James Samuel
January 26, 1875
Early Tuesday morning, 1:32 AM*

The brilliant blast threw William Pinkerton backward into the shadows. He landed beside the fence where he'd been watching from earlier, before he had started running toward the house. Two of his men saw him on the ground and helped him to his feet. He looked at them like he wasn't sure who they were. And then he suddenly looked at the bombed-out house.

"The Greek fire," he said to the one man. He turned to the other. "The Greek fire!"

"Cracked like hell, didn't she!" the short munitions man said, running up to him. "Just like I told your daddy it would!" He was elated. He jabbered to whoever would listen to him while the rest of the men circling the house cheered and then cheered again. Over on the far side someone started shooting into the log dwelling, and within seconds they had all drawn their revolvers and started firing

at the now darkened building. With its windows blasted out and its doors blown open it looked like a giant jawless skull sitting in the snowy yard.

"Stop!" William Pinkerton yelled, moving from man to man. "Stop this!" He approached another group of men, most of whom were reloading their pistols. "Stop!" he told them, his hands in the air now. "They're not in there! Frank and Jesse James aren't there!"

"Who gives a shit," O. P. Moss said to him, getting some shells from the man beside him. Then he pulled up his twelve-gauge shotgun and fired into the smoldering building.

"You'd better do as you're told, Moss," William Pinkerton said, suddenly shoving his small 32 calibre revolver directly into Moss's ear, "or I'll shoot you right now."

The other men in that group saw him do it, and it brought an end to their firing as well. Within seconds the Samuel farm was as quiet as a country cemetery, a thin feather of smoke from the smoldering doorway lifting into the night sky.

"We're leaving now!" Pinkerton shouted. "Maybe we'll come back later. Get back to the horses the shortest way." Nobody seemed to notice that Goodwin no longer led them. Hours later, as false dawn began to stain the eastern sky a dusky, bloody hue, the Pinkerton train pulled slowly out of the siding at Kearney and made the switch for Kansas City.

You just never know how a thing will turn out, do you? If anyone'd ever told me Jesse James would come around wanting to shake my hand after I led the Pinkertons out there on that damn raid against his momma's farm, why, I'd a never believed him. But sometimes the things you are sure are going to go bad for you really do turn out in your favor, there's no denying it, and that's always welcome as finding a silver dollar in the mud of the street. But the ones you think are going to go your way and then blow up in your face, well, those're the ones that really take you off your gait and make you more or less disgusted with life.

Take for example me and Sarah. She was just as nice as pie to me there at her house, her folk's house, after I was banged up the way I was, after Moss'd shot me and cracked me on the head after I was already out cold. Oh, I knowed all along who it was who shot me, all right. All along, that is, after my memory come back to me good and I could begin to tell today from yesterday. It couldn't of been nobody else but O. P. Moss.

There wasn't no way for me to do nothing about it till I got well, I knowed that. Not till I could ride and fight and shoot again. But still, that time was coming, getting a little closer every day there, and I promised myself I would go find that son of a bitch no matter what corner he was hid in by then, no matter where he'd got to by that time, that was something I promised myself.

But getting back to Sarah there, like I'd started on, she was so sweet to me that I begun to see how nice being hitched to her permanent would be. And with Billy throwed into the bargain, that would make things even better so far as I was concerned. And just as well with him too, it seemed like, as good as we got along, as far as I could tell and not come right out and ask him, which of course you wouldn't want to do till you had got everthing else squared away with his mamma first.

Sarah, though, I *did* come right out and ask—ask her again, that is, if she was ready to go off with me as soon as I was able. And of course, when I said about going off together, she wanted to know what was wrong with staying around there? Her daddy was ready for someone to take over the farm, he talked about it often, she said. Or I could do whatever suited me there in that part of Missouri if I didn't like the idea of farming, she didn't really have her heart set on that. Anything except outlawing anymore with Frank and Jesse, I think she meant. We could even live in Kansas City, she'd go that far, she said. Of course it was real tempting to say all right, we'll do 'er that way, Sarah. Specially now that I seen Jesse didn't know I was with the Pinkertons, and I sure as hell knowed I was finished with *that* outfit after the way they done with the Samuels.

But just about every time I had myself convinced it'd be all right to stay in them parts, I'd remember Blackfoot Bill. And then I *knowed* it would only be a matter of time till Jesse or Frank or somebody figgered out what I done for the Pinkertons. And no matter which side I had finally come down on, even if it was the James's side I landed on permanent, even marrying in amongst them, the idea that I'd *once* helped the Pinkertons would be all it would take to get me killed, no matter what Jesse James'd said about not ever forgetting about what I tried to do for his family, which was true enough in its own way—there at the end, anyway—but there'd be no way he could ever look at it like that once he knowed I was the one who'd led that bunch out there. No, the only thing for me to do, if I wanted to stay alive for any time at all, was to get the hell out of there. Naturally, I didn't want to say none of that to Sarah.

That time I was talking about, when I asked her again about us going away together, that was one day when I was just getting up from one of the naps she made me take every afternoon. I was setting on the side of the bed when I asked her. She was in my room bringing me fresh towels or a pitcher of wash water or something like that.

She stopped what she was doing, put her hand on her hip like she was fond of, and just looked at me with them big green eyes a minute. "How can you be so sure, Mr. Goodwin, it would work out all right between us?" she asked me real sharp. "Sometimes I'm—"

"Well, I just *know* it would is all," I told her, butting right in and flapping my jawbone. "I never met a gal I liked half so good as you, and you're more of a—"

She had come over to the bed, where I was still sitting on the side of it, and she give me a sort of a push on the shoulder. I could have fought her back more than I did, but she was being playful with me and I just fell back and went along with it, my feet still on the floor.

"Hey, you watch that now," I said, holding my hand out for her to pull me back up. Truth to tell, I had about half a mind to pull her down on top of me if she'd allow it. "I hear tell I'm a very sick man, and it ain't fair to take advantage of a man when he cain't rightly defend hisse'f from y'all." I liked to tease her that way, the funny half-Southern way her and her family talked, because she couldn't *not* talk that way to save her soul and she knowed it.

She took my hand, all right, and taking the other one as well, she leaned over me and then straddled right down on top of me, just at my hips—her full, loose skirts and petticoats riding up. I could feel her warmth through my pants.

I was a mite surprised she'd do something like that.

"Now see here, Mr. Goodwin," she said, her face only a couple of inches above mine, "I have you in my power now, sir. So do not try and resist me!"

"I am your slave, mam," I told her, giving up entirely.

"Good," she said, crawling back up slow, rubbing against me more'n she'd of had to down there, I thought. And then untying her apron affair and letting it slide to the floor in front of her while she kept her eyes on me. "I think we ought to take care of both our problems at the same time, don't you, Willie?" she asked.

"Whatta you mean?"

She started undoing the tiny little buttons of her shirt-affair thing she had on, silky white it was, with buttons like little pearls, eyeing me the whole time she was doing it.

"Why Sarah Jane Cole, you shameless hussy, you!" I said, laughing and covering up my eyes like one of them monkeys that ain't supposed to see no evil.

She didn't say nothing, though I was sure she would, and I waited some time till I took my hands down and propped myself up with my elbows behind me. "Good heavens," I said.

She stood there with nothing on but a smile, a beautiful sight, her dark hair unpinned now too and falling over her shoulders in curls, her petticoats and such in a pile at her feet. Her one arm was sort of across her breasts, and the other arm was down in front so her hand could sort of cover up her female parts down there. Sort of. It struck me I'd saw a painting behind some bar somewheres where the lady stood just like that, but naturally I didn't say so to Sarah.

She blushed then, more than just her face too, looked down—at herself, maybe, or maybe just at the floor, I wasn't certain which—and then looked back up at me, bold as anything. "What I had in mind is, we get this li'l problem of making love straightened out, finally, and then you'll tell me the *real* reason why you want to leave here. Do we have an agreement, sir?"

I sat up and held my hand out towards her, and she come forward and took it, sitting across my lap, finally, and kissing me long and deep. Somewhere about then we fell back on the bed, or I guess I fell back and she come along for the ride would be more accurate, I suppose. And, my, I nearly drowned there with her over top of me, her sweet-scented hair wrapping around both our faces and sort of closing us in, away from everything else, you might say.

She straddled me again, only now she didn't have no clothes on at all, and looked down at me full when I wasn't kissing her. "Is this what you want, Sarah? Are you *sure* this is what you want?"

She smiled and nodded. "Yes it is, Willie. I do love you, and I've wanted to make love with you ever since you kissed me that day you came out to the dance at Dogtown, you remember? Yes, this is what I want. I hope it's—"

I told her I loved her too, and then I kissed her again, but she pulled back a little after a time and slid down beside me.

"And then I *do* want you to tell me why you don't want to live around here, Willie, I really do. Will you promise?"

I nodded I would. I figgered this was probly the best

chance I was ever going to get to come clean with her. "Just so long as you hear me out, hear all I got to say on the *whole* subject of why we should live elsewheres."

She nodded she would. "I know you must think it's silly, but my family is important to me, Willie. I don't want to leave them again, and they do love Billy, no matter if they don't always show it so well."

I sort of sat up a little. "I know staying around here's important to you, Sarah. I understand. I think I do, at any rate. But if we're going to get this all straightened out and settled now, I think I ought to go first and tell you why we can't stay here, why *I* can't stay here, and then, if you still want to, we'll . . ."

She smiled. "All right, sir. Gentlemen first this afternoon. Go ahead." It didn't seem to bother her at all she didn't have a stitch on.

Wellsir, I started back in Texas with the letter I got there and told her about going up to Chicago and then about coming over here to Missouri. I said about Hardwicke and Blackfoot Bill and about how her inviting me to Jesse's wedding let me find out more about the brothers. She looked for a minute like she didn't quite believe me. I told her then about warning Jesse down there in the Elk River country on his honeymoon, though I still didn't know why I done that, warning him at the last minute that way. And then I told her why I'd went down there in the first place.

I told her about the Youngers and how it come about that I went on the train robbery with Frank and Jesse and the boys. She looked awful surprised when I told about what'd happened over there at the Youngers after she'd left—and then deciding to turn Jesse in. I told her about Jesse shooting that banker, and about finding out Jesse'd killed Blackfoot Bill, getting things mixed up and out of order some, I'm not even sure I've got them all straightened out even now.

I told her about setting up the raid on the Samuel place, with the notes going back and forth. But it wasn't till

I got to me leading them Pinkerton fellows out there, out to the Samuel place, that she started to cry. I didn't say the word *Pinkerton* to her, not even once, but she knowed, of course. When I got to the part about the explosion she stood up, crying even harder than before, and throwed around her shoulders the robe of her father's I'd been using.

"Sarah, you got to let me finish," I said watching her gather up her clothes off the floor. "You *got* to hear me out on this."

She looked up at me and shook her head, the tears streaming down her face and her crying even harder than before. That was the saddest, sorriest face I ever seen—no matter it was also the dearest face in the world to me too. In her bare feet and wearing her daddy's big floppy robe, she gathered up her shoes and clothes in her arms, turned, and without a word went right out the door.

You just never know how a thing will turn out, do you?

31

ANOTHER STRANGE TELEGRAM

*The farm of Dr. Reuben Samuel
and his wife Zerelda Cole James Samuel
January 26, 1875
Early Tuesday morning, 1:32 AM*

The explosion was deafening. Dr. Samuel felt himself yanked violently off his feet and flung against the wooden ceiling as if a giant hound had shaken him and sent his rag-loose body flying. He landed in a corner and lay there in a crumpled, disheveled daze. A gentle winter breeze began to clear the smoke and fumes from the room; all the windows and doors had been blown out.

After Reuben Samuel eventually sat up and found, miraculously, that he was not bleeding anywhere very much and that no bones were broken, it occurred to him that the room had become black as night, for he could see nothing. How strange! For a moment he could hear nothing either, but gradually his hearing returned: from outside, men were firing into the house, for things were breaking in the cupboard, a lead slug clanged an iron pot; cheering outside, too, a crowd of men giving one hurrah after another; over behind the dry sink in the darkened room, Charlotta was whimpering now; something thumping, thumping; off somewhere, he couldn't tell just where it was, his wife saying "Oh no, Oh Dear Lord, no!"; and suddenly, right beside him, the saddest sound a father can know, his child crying in pain, deep pain.

"Mamma! Mamma!" Archie Samuel cried. "Mamma!"

"Can you help him, Doctor?" Zeralda called across the room. "I am too . . ."

Doctor Samuel nodded, then realized no one could see him. "Yes, my dear. He's right here. Right beside me." Doctor Samuel rose, his back aching painfully, and groping with both hands found a candle stub on the mantel and then a match. The shooting stopped suddenly.

Coming back with the lighted candle, he saw that a chair had fallen on the boy, and when he lifted it off, his heart froze at the sight of Archie's wound. Blood, oh all that blood lost! Low on the boy's side, starting just above his left hip, a deep slash curved around to nearly his navel. The gash fell open like a hungry canine mouth, spilling a fresh rush of bloody saliva onto the tatters of what had been the boy's white jersey shirt. Instead of fangs, the maw grinned with teeth of iron: a jagged shard of shrapnel, that which had cut the boy so cruelly, was still lodged in place. With both hands, kneeling, the aged father closed his son's wound without removing the object. Then he wept.

From where she lay Zeralda heard her husband crying. "Oh my God, is he alive, Reuben?" she called.

"But barely," the doctor whimpered. "But barely." With strips torn from his nightshirt, he bound the boy's wound as tightly as he dared. Ambrose had found his mother's mattress and spread it on the floor. Together the young man and the old lay the boy on it as gently as they could. Nevertheless, little Archie groaned and writhed in agony. Charlotta, quiet now after the shooting had stopped, brought another candle, and when she did Doctor Samuel turned and searched for his wife.

"My hand, my right hand!" she said when first he

found her. "I can't—Is it—bad?" she asked him. She knew her husband took no patients these days, but she had seen time and again that he had lost none of his wonderful store of knowledge about the human body and its ailments.

So when his face turned ashen as he examined her right hand and arm, even in the candlelight, she knew it was as bad as it could be.

A sharp intake of breath. "Is it a whole finger I'll lose, Reuben? More than one?" she asked, trying to sit up a little to see. Gently her husband tried to hold her back, but she would have none of that. She looked down at the bloody ruination. "Oh God, not the whole hand, is it!?"

"Would that it were mine instead," he said, his eyes brimming over again. It's odd, he thought, here I have not cried in years, and now—twice in one night.

Zerelda gave herself over to tears completely, something she almost never did. Reuben staunched the flow of blood and bandaged her arm temporarily. Would he have to be the one to finish it?

Ambrose and the doctor carried the mattress with Archie on it over beside his mother, and then the doctor went outside and screamed. After a minute of continuous wailing, even he knew his screaming was more than just a cry for help. It wasn't till after he abruptly stopped screaming and the silence lapped back up at his feet that he remembered there had been men out here—and then noticed that they were gone. Who were they, anyway, and why had they done this to his family? One of them, at least, had paid a price for this work of the Devil, for he still lay facedown in the yard. Good, Reuben said to himself. Good. Then he looked up to watch the moon, like the blade of an Arab's sword, slice through the quickly-moving clouds.

Very soon Doc Samuel's neighbors began arriving. One led the stooped, bare-chested doctor back inside to face the havoc and destruction that had visited itself upon his family. Daniel Askew's wife hurried up the lane carrying a basket on her arm. Another neighbor, James A. Hall, after seeing the gruesome scene inside the house, rode off hurriedly

> *to fetch Doctor Scruggs from Kearney. There was no way old Doc Samuel was going to be able to do the grisly work that remained to be done this night, and best done quickly at that, on both Mrs. Samuel and their poor, poor boy.*

About a week after Jesse'd come to see me, I started going outside on nice days. Doc Kimball's idea that was. I was to walk around the yard some and up the lane or down by the creek till I got tired out and then go sit in that padded chair from my room till I could go do it all over again. I wasn't to go too far, he said, but I was to get myself good and tired out a couple times before dinner, when it wasn't raining, and then a couple more times in the afternoon as well—after my nap.

Sarah'd get one of the hired men to bring my chair down in the morning, and it'd stay out there for me all day under the horse chestnut tree that was about half in leaf by then. Sarah was still sweet with me, more polite and helpful than anything else, you could say. But there wasn't no kissing no more, and no talk about what might happen later on—not since she'd left my room that day I told her what I'd did. I didn't know at first if she was going to tell anybody what I'd said or not, and there wasn't much I could do about it should she decide to, weak as I was. I also didn't know what she'd do if I was to try and kiss her or hold her either, so I didn't do nothing much in that way neither. Mostly, I just tried to get well again and, once I was better, I thought, I'd just take it from there—with both her and the Jameses.

I thought it was a pretty foolish idea of Kimball's when I first started doing it, all that walking around, but I got to admit I started getting stronger from that first day on. And, hell, maybe it even helped with my side and head too like he said it would, I don't know. I still got out of breath awful easy, though. That didn't change much.

Often times Sarah would bring a kitchen chair out and sit with me when she seen I was back resting under the horse chestnut after one of my "strolls" as she like to call them. Some times she'd bring a glass of milk or beer for me along out with her, some times an apple from the cold cellar. They had some servants, the Coles did, but they done a lot of the work on that farm theirselves. Often as not that week, Sarah'd make a sandwich or slice a piece of bread for me, hot and fresh out of the oven with lots of butter they'd churned earlier from their own cream, the butter melting down into the warm bread. This was Doc Kimball's idea too, me eating extra like that, and I thought that made a lot more sense than getting so tired out walking around all the time.

I was sitting there under the tree finishing a nice piece of bread with both butter and apple butter on it one day, a few puffy clouds sailing along up high, Sarah'd just went back in to do something with her mother, when two riders come down the road and then turned up the lane, one of them leading my horse. Of course I seen it was Frank and Jesse right away. Jesse was on that gray he favored, Stonewall he was called, a fine strong horse with more gaits than a picket fence all the way around Texas. Coming down the lane he was doing that side-to-side sort of trot some horses can be taught to do, pleasure horses and such mostly, where both legs on one side moves together and then both on the other. From the way Jesse rode him, it looked almost as comfortable as my padded chair. Jesse was a rider who used a lot of leg and stirrup, though, even if his horse was easy to sit, but Frank kind of moved his seat more front and back and side to side, going with whatever way his horse moved, very little leg in it. And his horse didn't know no fancy trots, neither. A couple hounds run out to greet them, but they didn't bark.

Jesse was just stepping down when Sarah come back out, she must of seen them from inside. "Good morning, Cousin," Jesse called to her, tying up my horse first and then his own.

Frank just sat up there and looked about as happy as a

hen somebody'd poured a bucket of water over, only he wasn't wet.

"Good morning, Willie," Jesse said, smiling a little and coming over to where I was. "I thought you might be needing your horse when we do that work I spoke to you of earlier. He came in to the stable over at mother's the day after you were shot."

"Thank you," I said. I thought about standing up, but didn't do it, just nodded instead. He didn't offer his hand, I noticed.

Sarah come over under the tree too and give him a kiss on the cheek. "We should run a hospital here all the time," she said. "Then we'd see you boys more often, I suppose. How come Zee isn't with you, a nice morning like this?"

"She's still in Kentucky," Jesse said. "She didn't come along back this time. We're just here to see Mother and take care of a few things."

Sarah nodded, and when it appeared Jesse didn't have nothing more to say she turned to his brother. "What's the matter, Frank?" she called down the yard to him. "Do you have somewhere better to be this morning? Wouldn't you like a piece of fresh bread and apple butter?"

"Thank you kindly, no," Frank said, touching his hat brim. "We must get back over to mother's soon. Annie's orders, you know." He spat tobacco juice into the yard.

Jesse sat down in the chair beside me, and Sarah laughed good. "Isn't married life the bed of roses you'd hoped it would be, Franklin?"

Frank put his hands out wide, shook his head, and then looked up in the air. "'Maids are May when they are maids, but the sky changes when they are wives.'"

Sarah laughed again.

Jesse smiled a little broader before he spoke. "Poor Frank, unlucky in love and mistrustful of people to boot." He turned and looked at me then, the smile still on his face but pinched a little, and he was still looking at me with them blue, blue eyes when he said to Sarah, "*I'll* have some of your nice fresh bread, Cousin, if I may. And a cup of your coffee too, if it's not too much trouble."

"No, it's no trouble," she said. "If you don't mind waiting for me to make some."

"No, I don't mind. Thank you, Cousin."

Sarah started in, but then stopped and looked back at us sharp. I think she saw through Jesse saying he wanted a cup of coffee right then—I seen it too. He just wanted to talk to me without her there. The good of it was that look on her face said she still cared enough for me to be worried about me. And it also meant she probly didn't say nothing to them about what I'd told her.

She smiled at me, but her lips was tight, fearful.

Jesse looked out across the fields just greening up till she was inside. "We heard you got a strange telegram," he said.

I nodded and thought fast. "Yes I did, but I'll be damned if I know what it says," I said.

"Really? I thought you could read?"

"Well, I can read all right, but I can't begin to read *that* thing."

Jesse turned and looked at me real curious and Frank sat out by the hitching rail and frowned at us both, though I doubt he could hear what was said. "Do you still have it?" he asked.

I said I did and I think I surprised him when I asked him right off if he'd like to see it. He hemmed and hawed some, not wanting to seem too eager, not wanting to say right out that he did, but he *was* curious about it and all, from what he'd been told about it, he said. I almost asked him who told him, but then I changed my mind. Maybe I didn't really want to know.

Sarah'd gave it to me the day before, this telegram I'm talking of here. No envelope or nothing like that on it. Because of the way things between me and her'd been, I didn't want to risk making them worse asking her how come she'd signed for a telegram addressed to me, though it did rub me the wrong way a little bit, I admit.

Of course it was one of them damn code things from Lawyer Hardwicke, and I didn't have that paper anymore he'd gave me to figger them damn things out, naturally. I'd lost that a long time ago. I was counting on Jesse not knowing how to figger it out either, otherwise I'd of never offered to let him see it. Counting on it *hard*, is what I mean. Because though I couldn't read it, I sure as hell knowed it'd have something to do with me and the Pinkertons, whatever it said, put me right in the nest beside them.

I started inside to get it. Billy was coming out with his little dog just then, so the way my breathing was and all, I asked him if he'd go upstairs to my room to fetch the telegram, telling him where it was up there.

"Sure," he said. He tossed me the ball and naturally that little dog followed *me* then instead of tearing upstairs along with Billy. I went back out under the horse chestnut with Bobby tagging right along, bumping into my ankle for me to throw his ball for him to fetch it the whole way out there.

"Well, it's Sir Bobby!" Jesse said, motioning for me to give him the ball and then making such a fuss over that long-nosed little dog you wouldn't of believed it. He tossed that ball far out a number of times, and that little fellow tore after it for all he was worth, bringing it right back and dropping it for more, his long pink tongue hanging out far and him panting to beat all.

Frank didn't even bother watching him go down and back like a bat out of Arkansas, but Jesse praised that little dog so each time, then petted him down hard, tussling him around the neck and legs, Bobby loving every minute of it and Jesse too, grunting like a small dog himself and even barking at the little fellow, Bobby down on his front legs after a while and barking back at Jesse every time Jesse barked at him. My, they was having a time, both of them, there in the sunny yard, springtime coming on like a freight train round the bend.

I sat there and had trouble believing what I was looking at with my own eyes. There was the man I had saw shoot another man right in the face, point blank, a little man who couldn't defend hisself at all, no gun on him at all. And Jesse'd shot him down like a dog. And now here this little *dog* had made him gentle—and playful as a pup. No matter how I tried, I couldn't fit them two pieces of the puzzle together right. It didn't seem like they could both be the same man.

After a time Billy come outside, and then he throwed the ball for his dog hisself—instead of the murderer who tussled the boy's hair throwing it anymore.

I give the telegram right over to Jesse.

He looked at it close and frowned. "I see what you mean now," he said. "You can't read it?"

"No, it's in some sort of damn code that man likes to use. He give me a paper on it, Hardwicke did, how to read it, but I lost it some time ago. I saw him when I first come up here about some property I inherited from my family, my mamma's side. Do you know the man?"

Jesse shook his head. "No, but I've heard about him. They say he'll do whatever the banks and railroads ask him to, the big money boys." He seemed satisfied then the telegram wasn't more than what I said.

"Well, I guess I'll have to go see him about whatever the hell it is," I said.

"I wouldn't advise you to do that, Willie," he said standing up. "The less they see of us right now, the better. They've all got some comeuppance coming, but not right now." He started going over toward his horse and I trailed along behind.

"No, I've got to get that property thing straightened out, so I'll have to go see him."

He turned and looked at me strange then, but didn't say nothing.

I acted just a little bit huffy with him. "That *was* just *advice* you was handing out there for free, wasn't it? Like you said it was? About going to see him? Because I should get this took care of as soon as I feel better." I shook the telegram paper. "God knows what this says. I might lose the place if I don't see the man, Jesse."

Billy and Bobby was still playing ball over in the side yard.

Frank glared down at me. He never liked me very much anyway, and now he didn't trust me neither. His face said that clear as if it'd been writ there on his forehead with a piece of charcoal.

Jesse was a good bit better at holding his cards close to his vest. "No, it was just advice, sir. Just advice. Though I'd appreciate your lending me that telegram so I can show it to a man I know." There was a flicker of something in his eyes just then.

I handed it right over to him. "Sure. Keep it. It don't do me no good anyways. Just be sure and tell me if he figgers it out, all right? Before I go in there?" I knowed right then that this was like a test back in school.

And the look on his face made it feel like I'd passed with flying colors. "Oh, I'll be sure to," he said shoving the telegram into his vest pocket. He untied his reins and more or less sprung up into the saddle. "You be careful what you say, though, you hear? There's all sorts of talk around. It's hard to know what's true and what isn't," he said, patting Stonewall's neck good and hard.

Frank clucked and backed his horse away from the rail and headed up the lane.

Jesse turned that big gray towards me. "You hurry up and get well, now, you hear?" he said. "I still want you to help me take care of that damn Allen Pinkerton."

If he was that close to not trusting me about the telegram, how come he wants me in on that? I asked myself standing there in front of him. It was then I had the clearest picture I ever had of how lonesome and unsure of things it must be being Jesse James. "I'll do the best I can," I said.

"No, you'll have to do a whole lot better than that, Willie," he said, a little chuckle in his voice. "By the way, I know who shot you now. He's bragging of it all over Liberty."

So do I, I wanted to say to him, but of course I couldn't. "Who was it?" I asked.

"All in good time," he said. "All in good time, Willie. You help me with the man who hurt my family and I'll help you get the man who hurt you. They're the same den of snakes, you know."

I just nodded.

"Thank you again for coming to the defense of my family, sir. I'll not forget it. That was a brave thing you did, against all them. I only wish I'd been there."

All I could think to do was nod again.

He winked at me, yes he did that, then turned the head of that fine looking horse and just touched him with his spurs. He yelled something I couldn't make out to Frank and then caught up with him in about ten big strides. They raced down that lane like two farm boys out on a lark.

Goddamn that Hardwicke.

*The farm of Dr. Reuben Samuel
and his wife Zerelda Cole James Samuel
January 26, 1875
Early Tuesday morning, 2:51 AM*

The first thing pudgy Doctor Scruggs noticed when he and James Hall turned the bend in the moonlit lane at the Samuel place was that somebody was lying facedown in the snowy yard. "I thought you said Samuel was all right?" Scruggs said gruffly, getting down off his gelding.

"Well he was when I left," Hall replied stepping down too.

The doctor held the reins with one hand and pointed with the other. "Then who the hell's that?"

Hall looked. "Damned if I know," he said. He tied up quickly and then went over to the unconscious man and rolled him gently onto his back. "Oh! This's the fellow that works for Dan Askew, Jack Ladd his name is. I don't know what the hell he's doing here, though. I didn't notice him before I left."

"Is he dead?" Scruggs asked walking over, crunching thin snow under his boot soles and then bending forward at the waist to get a closer look.

"Not unless dead men can breathe," Jim Hall answered. "Some blood on the snow here by his head."

Scruggs snorted and then got down heavily and looked the unconscious man over for broken bones. Yes, the head looked bad all right. But he must not have bled too much or the bastard'd be dead by now. "He's been shot here in his side too and I can't see what else," Scruggs told Hall. "C'mon, let's take him inside. The poor sonofabitch would have frozen to death out here before morning." Together they carried the limp man into the log house.

Ambrose had got the fire burning again with dry pine, and the room was now lit by the blazing fireplace and three short candles. After doing what they could for Mrs. Samuel and her little boy, Charlotta and Ambrose had tacked blankets over the blown out windows and set the furniture back up. Still, the room was a shambles—broken dishes, broken furniture, fifty pounds of flour spilled and dusted over all the surfaces, nearly everything they owned a jumble on the board floor. Surprisingly, the explosion had touched off no fires and the heavy masonry of the fireplace had not even cracked. They laid the unconscious man on the floor in front of the fire to warm him.

"Who's that you've brought into my house?" Zerelda Samuels demanded. "If it's one of those Yankees, you can—"

"No, no," Doctor Scruggs reassured her. "Lie back now. It's just Dan Askew's hired man, and you—"

Zerelda Samuel rose anyway, though it gave her great pain to do so, and brushing past Scruggs, she hobbled toward the man they had stretched out on her hearth, refusing the arm Jim Hall offered when she got there. "Oh, it's that friend of—that Ladd fellow," she said looking down at his face a moment and then turning to look for Rose Askew, who had gone home by then. Zerelda moved slowly back to the pallet she now shared with her unconscious little boy. "Must of tried to stop them. Take him over to Brother Jesse's. This man courts their daughter and she can look after him better than we can now. Like Zee did for my Jesse." She lay back down with difficulty, her husband helping her. She took the limp child to her breast carefully and held him there, arranging the covers around his face with her good hand while she adored him in the firelight. She looked up suddenly. "Now! I mean now! Get him out of here. I don't want anybody but my family here now, you hear me?!"

Doctor Scruggs was shocked at her vehemence and the raw anger behind her voice. He tended to forget how strong-willed she was, but every time he saw her he was uncomfortably reminded of it afresh. He checked the man Ladd thoroughly and bandaged his back and side. He'd been shot from behind, a broken a rib in back, but the bullet had gone clean through. If it had punctured a lung, it wasn't very much of it. Lucky sonofabitch. Even with the candle up close it was too dim to probe that mess on the head there as well as he'd have liked, and he couldn't tell how bad it really was. He bandaged the man's head thoroughly, padding the fractured area very heavily, since he'd probably bounce around some in the wagon. Get word to Doctor Kimball to go over there first thing in the morning, he reminded himself. The man's still being unconscious worried him, though. Indeed it did.

32

KEEP YOUR HAND ON THE TREE

I probly shouldn't of been on a horse so soon, Sarah said I shouldn't of anyway, not for as far as I went that first Sunday in March. Matter-of-fact my side was starting to throb pretty good shortly after sunrise when I rode past Samuel Hardwicke's place out beyond Liberty. My headache was back too, like somebody smacking it with a dinner-bell thwanger.

I had argued with myself over going in to Hardwicke's office. The way *he* was, careful as a rabbit in a hole, he might not even of talked to me in there where he done his regular business. Not after that business out at the Samuel place. I'd do a whole lot better going to his house, I figgered, and Sarah's daddy told me just where he lived. Too, I didn't want to be seen all that much in town, either. For one thing, I wanted to be ready for it and a whole lot stronger the next time I run into Moss.

Hardwicke's place was a big one all right, a tall stone house with white columns. They had added white frame wings onto both sides, a new barn in front of an old one there wasn't nothing wrong with in the first place. A cedar shingled horse stable that'd hold more'n a dozen head easy in separate stalls, I don't know where they found the cedar around there, I never saw any. A big summer kitchen, and half a dozen other outbuildings all big and new and as good as you could build them.

Samuel Hardwicke must of been hauling it in with a hay rake, and it looked like a whole lot more'n just the Pinkertons was helping to make him a rich man. Yes, the big money boys, that's what Jesse'd called them, they must of been paying his fat fees pretty regular—railroads and banks mostly, I'd bet, the same fellows the Pinkertons liked to work for. He sure didn't get the kind of money it took to buy that place, and then improve on it, by defending the Askews or the Halls or any of the rest of the folks living around there who made what living they could by scratching in the dirt. The country in hard times to boot.

I turned my horse off to the right after I was well past the house, a third of a mile or so, and went up about half a path that wandered through a patch of woods, and then I circled over toward behind the house by coaxing my horse through the bare scrub, the buds in there big and just showing green. I tied him where he could graze a little and I could just start to see clearing through the trees. I walked careful over to where the house and buildings stood, nobody moving around. I went behind a building close to the stable and heard someone inside it whistling a bright, cheery tune and then giving orders to what I guessed was horses or mules and then whistling again. I come around the front, a carriage house I seen then, and slid around the end of one of the double open doors. A black man was harnessing a matched pair of big white mares to a black open rig I think they call a trap, a gentleman's carriage if ever I saw one.

I drew my Colt's but didn't cock it. Then I cleared my throat.

When the tall, powerful looking Negro fellow turned around quick and got a look at me holding a revolver on him, he dropped the harness he'd been working on and raised his arms straight up—almost to the rafters his hands reached. He was scared, all right, but not so much he lost control of hisself, as many a man would of. "Don't shoot me, suh, please don't," he said. "Whatevuh it is, I din do it."

"It's not you I want," I told him. "And you can put your hands back down. I just need your help so I can get to talk to the man I believe you work for." He wasn't wearing no revolver.

"Mistah Hardwicke?" he asked.

"That's right," I told him. "You go ahead and finish what you was doing there."

He turned around and went right back to work, looking over his shoulder at me from time to time. It took him about five more minutes, and when he was done he come edging slow over to where I was standing by the open doors looking toward the front door of the big place. His cap was in his long hands then, twisting it up. "'Scuse me, suh, I wuz jest wonderin', suh, you ain't Mistah Jesse James by any chance, is yo'?" he asked me.

He set me back asking me that. I didn't think I looked like no outlaw. "Well, if I was Jesse James, and if I told you straight out I was, then I'd have to shoot you before I left, wouldn't I? So nobody'd know I was here."

He shook his head sharp, set his cap back on, and then showed me the white palms of his hands. "No suh, I doan need to know that bad, I doan. Tha's all right." He went back and sat down on an upturned bucket, watching me close after that. "I's s'pposed to go up to the house wid it when I'm through," he said after a couple of minutes, tilting his head toward the rig. "Is that still what I's to do?"

"No, just wait,"

"Yassuh," he said.

I kept watching out of a corner of a window and after a few more minutes Hardwicke come out dressed in a checkerboard waistcoat. He stepped down off the veranda and into the yard—all the while looking up toward the building where we were. "Jonathan?!" he called.

Jonathan stood up quick and looked at me.

"Answer him," I said.

"Yassuh?!" he shouted.

"We're going to be late for church!" Hardwicke hollered.

"Step out where he can see you and tell him you're having some trouble and he should come down here."

Jonathan shook his head and looked at the dirt floor like something pained him bad. "Doan make me call him down heah to get kilt, Mistah James, please doan make—"

"I'm not going to shoot him!" I told the black man under my breath. "I'm just doing this so he won't try and feed me none of his bullshit, so he'll tell me the damn truth instead of all the goddamn— Do like I tell you or someone *will* get shot!" I waved him toward the outside with the barrel of my Colt's.

He looked me good in the face a second, and then bobbed his head slow. A hint of a smile slid across his dark face. "Yass, suh. I see yo's had dealin's wid Mistah Harddick befo'." He stepped out into the sunlight and called up to the man he worked for. "Could yo' step down heah a minute, suh, if yo' please, suh? I's having a powerful amount of trouble heah and needs yo' avice *awful* bad." I motioned him back inside and then pointed to his bucket.

Hardwicke started down toward us at a stiff-legged, quick tromp, muttering something to himself. He was red-faced and about as happy as a badger in a trap.

". . . than an hour ago, too—" He stopped in his tracks seeing me, looked quick over at his stable man, and then back at me. "Oh my God!" he said, then turned around and started walking the same jerky way back toward the house—only faster.

I stepped outside and watched him go. "It'd be a shame to shoot you in the back when all I wanted was to get the answer to a question or two," I called after him. "But I'll do it, you know damn well I will if I have to." Riding with an outfit like the Pinkertons or Jameses, it don't make no diffrence, will change the way you act towards people, like I said before. But it'll also change the way people act towards you, too, once they know it. Of course I wouldn't of really shot him, but he didn't know that. I don't think I would've, anyway—least I wouldn't *now*. Didn't even have my pistol cocked, but he didn't know that either.

He stopped sudden again, picturing what it would be like to be shot in the back, I guess. Shoot, I could of told him if he'd asked. He turned around slow and faced me. After a second he started toward me like he was walking to his own hanging, his face all of a sudden white as his Sunday school shirt. Scared, but angry too. We stepped back inside his carriage house.

"What are you doing here!" he hissed at me, like I didn't already tell him.

"You said when I was there last never to come back to your office again, so this was all you left me."

"You shouldn't *ever* come out here, either! Especially not after last—" He turned and looked at the black man and then back at me.

"Whyn't you walk over to that tree there, that tall one?" I said to the man Jonathan. "You see the one I mean?"

He stood right up. "Yass, indeed I do!" he said starting out. "You gentlemans have yo' private talk, suits me fine. Fact, I could go all the way ovuh to my—"

"No, just over to there. Keep your hand on that tree, and stand where I can see you," I told him.

Jonathan seemed a little disappointed. "Yassuh." When he got there he put his hand on the trunk and looked back.

I turned to Hardwicke. "What was in that fool telegram you sent?"

He huffed and sputtered. "Why, you had the key, I'm certain I gave—"

"I lost it," I told him. "What did it—"

"Oh my God. Oh my God! If someone was to get hold of a key to my code, then all my—"

"I don't give a good goddamn!" I said to him louder than I'd meant to. That man bothered me, the way he worried about his own problems no matter what yours was. Everbody's like that some, I know, but Hardwicke was like that a lot. "Just tell me what was in it!" I told him.

I thought his eyes was going to pop out there for a second. "You irresponsible damn—!"

I double clicked that .45 calibre Colt's on back to full cock and aimed it right between his eyes from about six feet. Even I couldn't of missed from that range. You'd be surprised how something like that will sometimes quiet a man right down. "Now. What did it *say*?"

He swallowed hard. "It's very likely you're going to be indicted next week for the murder of Archie Samuel."

It felt like the trapdoor on the bottom of my stomach had dropped open. Little Archie Samuel was dead! My God, that sweet boy who played in the yard there, swung around on the porch posts. They'd gone and killed him with that damn bomb! And then I remembered that Sarah'd told me that very same thing before, more than once it felt like. But how could that of been? How could I have forgot something like that, something so terrible as that?

"You and Allen Pinkerton and perhaps someone locally, I'm not sure whom," Hardwicke said, blinking and turning his face away a little. "Perhaps it will be me. Please don't point that weapon at me anymore," he said. "It *is* loaded, isn't it?"

I shook my head slow, but it wasn't about my Colt's being loaded. I let it down and uncocked it. "It wasn't my fault, I'm sure it wasn't," I told him. "Who the hell said it was *me*, anyway?" As soon as I said it, I knowed the answer.

Hardwicke and me said his name at the same time. "Moss."

"It ain't bad enough he shoots me and then clubs me with his rifle once I'm down," I said, holstering my Colt's. "But when he finds out he didn't get the job done right, he tells them it was me killed that boy. And it wouldn't matter a bit if I was cleared, not with the Jameses it wouldn't . . ."

"I know," Hardwicke said. "That's why I was trying to warn you. The Pinkertons want you to leave Missouri right away, Mr. Goodwin. That was in the telegram too. They didn't say this, of course, but I have reason to believe they plan to use their influence to get Allen Pinkerton acquitted, but you . . . I'm surprised it hasn't occurred to them to throw you to the Clay County coyotes as a sop. Perhaps it has by now." He looked at me even. That was the first time I ever felt there was a real person there behind them bulging eyes and that fat beaver face. A real person looking out at me and seeing the fix I was in, maybe even a little sorry about it too. A little, anyways.

"Well, I'm ready to clear out all right, I've been trying— But they owe me for this, those damn Pinkertons do. Owe me for clearing out and for keeping my mouth shut about them, too," I told him. "I want five thousand for it. Five thousand dollars in Yankee greenbacks, tens and twenties." I didn't need it. I had more money right then than I'd ever had before in my life. For one, I still had most all of what the Pinkertons'd paid me, and on top of that I had a deal of the money I got from the Jameses, some from my share of the train robbery and some from what *they* paid me for keeping a look out for them against the Pinkertons. No, I think making them pay me that five thousand dollars was just a way for me to make sure them damn Pinkertons was out *something* for what they done to Archie Samuel—and to me.

He shook his head. "I'm not sure they'll be willing to pay it, Mr. Goodwin."

"Well they damn well *better*!" I yelled at him. Jonathan over there leaning against his tree looked up sharp, worried some about his boss I suspect. I waved to him that everything was all right.

"If they don't pay me, I'll tell everthing I know about it—and about *them*. I don't give a damn if I go down with them. I can testify what William Pinkerton done and about half a dozen others, including that goddamn little bomb man—and I'll do 'er, too, if I have to. If anyone's to blame for Archie Samuel getting killed, it's him and that big man that throwed it in more'n anyone else. And I can prove it on them, too. I still have the notes they sent me." Naturally, I didn't have them, but I wanted them to think I did. "If I'm gonna hang, I'll line as many of 'em up up there beside me as I can, ropes around *all* our necks, hoods over *all* our heads. Take them *all* along with me for the ride, you tell them *that!* You included if you don't talk them into it."

"Oh my goodness," Hardwicke said. "Oh my God!"

I made him walk along over toward where my horse was so I could get a clean start, even though I knowed he wasn't going to try and do nothing against me now, send for nobody to catch me or nothing like that. I was glad he wasn't going to, for my head was aching even worse and my side was starting to bleed through my shirt some. I asked Hardwicke a bunch of questions I needed answers to on the way over there, and I told him where to have the Pinkertons leave my money, up by that big rock along the road where I'd put my things before. I waved to Jonathan from over close to the trees. He still had one hand on his tree, but he waved back with the other. I couldn't see if he was smiling or not, but I'd of bet he was. Hardwicke wasn't, though.

The farm of Dr. Reuben Samuel
and his wife Zerelda Cole James Samuel
January 26, 1875
Early Tuesday morning, 3:14 AM

When Scruggs had done all he could for Askew's hired man, Jack Ladd, he got Hall to hitch up the Samuel's team and then take the man down to the Cole place outside of Dogtown, even though it would have been better not to move him yet. He wasn't going to try and convince Zerelda Samuel of that, though. Then he turned his attention to the others who needed him.

Ambrose would be all right. Just some ugly cuts and

bad contusions. His mother was fine. But the other woman's arm would have to come off, no question about it. From the feisty way she had acted toward him, he guessed she didn't realize yet she was facing an amputation. Maybe Samuel could tell her. Might as well wait for the sun to come up so he could see what the hell he was doing. Probably there at the elbow would be best. No use saving an inch or two of forearm, nothing useful she could ever do with that. Might as well make it clean and even and give her the best chance he could of avoiding gangrene—and losing her life.

Her boy, though. My, my. There was nothing he could see to do for him now. Scruggs was a little surprised the older doctor hadn't tried to pull that sharp fragment of the bomb out of there right away. He himself might've made that mistake if it had been his own boy, and he thanked God right then it wasn't. The Samuel boy would've bled to death on the spot with that thing pulled out of there. That was clearer thinking than he'd have given old Samuel credit for, in his mental condition—and considering what it must have been like in here after that goddamn thing went off. Still, the father had bought his son only a few hours at best. Scruggs'd be damned surprised if Archie Samuel ever saw another sunrise, even though it was only hours away now.

Slowly the sky brightened in the east, thin shreds of cloud turning dusky rose and then orange and then pink through the black forking branches of the leafless trees—like a luminous summer bouquet smeared out along the horizon.

Doctor Samuel sat like a statue slumped in a straight-backed wooden chair, a look on his face like an Old Testament prophet gone gently mad. His legs stretched out in front of him, his chin on his chest, he appeared to gaze endlessly at his wife and youngest child, still the baby of the family. Except for his rhythmic breathing, Samuel seemed not to have moved at all for the last hour, listening like a rapt lover to his young son's occasional groans and his breath growing fainter and fainter.

Just before dawn Archie Samuel blinked and opened his eyes, the lids purple and translucent now. "Momma?" he whispered.

"Yes, child?" she said, her eyes spilling tears onto his downy cheek.

He labored for air. "Momma? Where's my . . . "

His breath soughed out in a long, lingering sigh. He did not draw another. After a moment his mother closed his eyes and then pulled him to her heart.

The sun rose golden and pure, the thinnest sliver of orange light edging past the blanket tacked over the east window, an amber scalpel blade slicing through the dust-laden air of the still room.

33

THE ECHO OF THE THIRD SHOT

The next week or so there, first thing in the morning, I'd ride over and look up behind that big stone alongside the road, close to Dan Askew's. Often I'd stop in to see them then, Dan's wife would pour me coffee and make me eat something, she said I looked so thin, Rose her name was. And then Dan and me would sit in the kitchen and play a little cribbage, a penny a point to keep it interesting, he said. I almost never won.

One day he told me some men from the sheriff's office in town had come out the day before asking about me, but he didn't tell them nothing, he said. He didn't know nothing and didn't want to know nothing. I wasn't to tell him, either. They couldn't expect him to tell what he didn't know, could they? "The hell with them," he said after a time and then grinned an old man's grin at me. I don't think Dan's heart let him work any at all by then. He'd got a new hired fellow for the chores, living out in my old place. A dutchman I think he told me. "Works like hell," Dan said. "All I got to do now is keep him from getting all wrapped up in draining the fields, running all the damn water off the place." He grinned again at that and shuffled the cards.

Time was heavy on my hands them days, not knowing what was going to happen about them naming me for murder and what I ought to do next—except get the hell out of there. If only Sarah'd go too. That's all I was waiting around for.

I was surprised nobody with a badge come out to the Coles to ask me questions or nothing like that. Then it struck me they didn't know where the hell I was, the law and such. That's what they'd wanted over at the Askews, to find out where I was living. Why the hell didn't Dan *say* that right out? I guess only the Jameses and their family knowed where I was, then.

I still didn't feel strong enough to help with the work for very long at a stretch, either over at Askew's or there at the Cole's. I harrowed a little, but that was all. Billy and me went fishing a time or two when he come home from school, but he had his friends of course, like boys do. Me and that little dog played ball so much sitting under that horse chestnut even he got tired of it, I think, though he'd never stop fetching it as long as you'd throw it.

Often when I come back from the Askews, I'd go see what Sarah was doing. Sometimes we'd take a picnic down along the creek if it was nice, but most times she'd be too busy doing things, her and her momma.

One afternoon right after an early supper we walked into Dogtown to that Quaker place where we'd went when I first come over to see her, there where I'd kissed her that first time—it seemed an awful long time ago, a lot longer than it was. We sat there in that peaceful quiet a while, but when I tried to talk to her about going away together, she shushed me and looked upset. Walking back it was like she'd either forgot about it or decided she didn't have nothing more to say on the subject right then, so I just let 'er go. Sometimes she'd let me take her hand when we was walking along and sometimes it'd seem like she didn't want me to any more, like that day walking back from Dogtown. You couldn't never tell.

When we was about halfway up the lane at her place, I seen Jesse's big gray tied at the rail. Frank's horse wasn't there, but I was surprised to see mine right beside Jesse's—and all saddled, too. Jesse James stepped out from underneath the shade of the horse chestnut when we got close to the house, I didn't even see him before. Waiting and sitting in my chair, I guess he'd been.

His look made you think he'd brought the piece of the shade that'd laid on his face along out from under the tree with him. "Excuse us please, Sarah," he said, something of a catch in his voice.

She dropped her eyes to the ground and went on inside, not even breaking her stride, I noticed.

"What is it?" I asked him, afraid he'd heard about the law maybe going to name me for Archie.

"I know who helped them now, led those damn Pinkertons out to Mother's," he said, untying his reins. "Come on." From the way he moved you could tell his blood was up, but not from the sound of his voice you couldn't, flat and quieter than he usually talked.

Uh-oh, I says to myself.

There'd be no arguing with him, I could see that. I was going along whether I wanted to or not, so I didn't even try not to. And I had no idea where we was headed. He could've shot me right there in the yard if he'd wanted, so I didn't see the benefit of pushing him into doing it. Not and have her maybe see it on top of everthing else. Someplace else I might get a chance is how I reasoned it— if it *was* as bad as I feared, but something told me maybe it wasn't.

We rode mostly without talking. I'd comment on things as we went along once in a while, you know how that goes, but he never said nothing back. After a while I just shut up.

I was surprised when we turned up Dan Askew's lane.

Dan was out by the rail by the time we come up, probly he was outside already and just happened to see us. "How-do, gentlemen," Dan said, touching his hat brim and then folding his arms across his skinny chest. "Surprised to see you again today, Willie."

Jesse turned his head a bit and looked at me out of the tail of his eye. It was clear he didn't know I was there that morning. He didn't step down off his horse so of course I didn't either. Seemed funny not to, though.

"How are you, Dan?" I said.

"Oh, I'm fine, fine," he said, just sort of marking time till Jesse made it clear what we was doing there, what was going on. "About as good as a man can once he gets in his seventies," Dan said, leaning over the hitching rail.

Jesse nodded. "That's the three-score-and-ten the Bible says you're allowed, isn't it?" he said. "Seventy?"

It surprised me he'd say that. Usually about the last thing you want to say to someone getting up in years is how much time they've got left—or how little.

Dan nodded and chuckled just the same, even though he appeared to suspect, about that point, that whatever was going on here wasn't exactly what you'd call neighborly. "Yes, I guess that's so, Jesse. I guess it is."

Jesse'd drawn his Smith's before I even knowed it was coming out. The only thing that told me it *was* out was the look on Dan's face and him taking a staggery step or two backwards.

"Then I guess you're ready to die today," Jesse said. Holy hell.

Dan recovered himself a little and didn't say nothing back right away. I couldn't believe what I was seeing and hearing, and I had about half an idea Dan couldn't either. "Why, what do you mean?" He didn't sound exactly scared, I'll give him that.

Jesse stepped down keeping his pistol and his eyes on Dan, even though that old fellow didn't have no gun strapped on. It hit me then I never even seen Dan wear one, I ain't sure he even *owned* a six shooter. A loaded double-barrel leaned into the corner of the cubbyhole by the back door, yes, one with hammers I'd saw there, maybe percussion, but a revolver . . . I don't believe so.

Jesse still had his eyes glued on Dan, hadn't took them off him ever since we rode up. Then he held his reins out towards me. I stepped down and tied us both up, like I guess he expected me to—Jesse *still* watching that old man like he was a rattlesnake that might decide to bite him.

Jesse took a paper out of his vest pocket with his right hand, folded over twice it was, and held it up for Dan to see. Did I say before Jesse James was left-handed? Well, he was. That was another time I noticed he was missing a joint on one finger, the middle finger on his left hand, the one still pointing his Smith's at Dan's heart. "A friend of Frank's from the war came up here the day after those damn Pinkertons killed my little brother. His letter says he followed their tracks from the siding in Kearney all the way out to our place. It'd snowed, you might recall." His voice had a nasty, sharp edge to it, even saying that about the snow. Then he pointed down to the corner of Dan's big field—without looking that way. He's an awful cautious man, Jesse James is. "They came right up through there, that's what this letter says. Right through your place. And you didn't even warn my folks, did you?" Jesse slid the letter back into his vest pocket.

Dan looked confused. "Well, no, I didn't. We didn't even know nothing was going on over to your place till we heard that big bang go off, Jesse. Hell, it was the middle of the night! How the devil would I know who was riding through my place at that hour? A man of seventy goes to bed!" Dan had got hisself a little worked up saying this, and he stood and looked at us, one then the other, still with a question on his face, shaking a little.

I wanted to say something to end this, but I didn't see no way to do it that wouldn't turn Jesse's revolver on *me*.

After a while Dan calmed down some. "Willie there was the one supposed to look out for your folks, wasn't he?"

Jesse took a quick step toward him, and Dan stumbled back some before he caught himself and stood his ground.

Jesse nodded. "Yes, he *was* supposed to. And that's what he did, too. That's how he got shot, doing what he was supposed to. He was over there watching the whole time, you know, and saw what went on—and who was *there*." He tilted his head toward me without looking my way, his Smith's still pointed at Dan's middle. "Isn't that so, Willie?"

I seen then where this was heading. "Yes, but—"

"Willie was *there*, Askew!"

Dan nodded and swallowed hard. "I guess he was if you say he was, but he didn't see *me* over there, not that night."

Finally I seen what *I* was doing there, what Jesse'd come and got *me* for. Jesse didn't know it of course, but I was the best one in the whole world to say that Dan Askew *didn't* have nothing to do with that Pinkerton outfit, instead of saying he did. Trouble was, I didn't have the nerve to say nothing.

Dan appeared to take heart a little then, like he had just thought of something else. "You know, my wife came over after—"

"You led them out there, didn't you!" Jesse screamed at the old man, not letting him finish.

Dan appeared to shrivel up and shrink a couple sizes smaller, sort of folding into himself, holding one wrist with his other hand down in front there and looking down too. "No. I didn't do nothin' like that, Jesse." He shook his head from side to side. "I been your neighbor here since before you were born, and I never did anything against you folks, none of you. Now you know that's a fact, isn't it?" He looked up at Jesse an awful minute there, begging for his life is what he was doing. Without coming right out and saying so. His face showed he realized the straits he was in, about like I guess a drowning man'd look after he knows he's already bobbed up for the third time and then feels himself starting to sink and slip down slow toward the bottom.

It was then Dan looked straight at me. I never

knowed for sure if he was trying to get me to speak up for him or if he had figgered out right then who'd *really* led them Pinkertons right up to the Samuel's door. I never learned which it was.

"I know for a fact he didn't lead them out there," I said.

Jesse's sneer was as thick as the winter coat on a wolf. "You were out cold. How could you be sure he wasn't the one?"

I'd just opened my mouth to tell him when he spun on his heel and shot Dan in the stomach, the sound loud as an explosion, it seemed like. Dan doubled over forward, a terrible look on his face. Jesse shot him in the face, and Dan went down backwards in the dirt. Then Jesse shot him between his legs.

I knowed he was dead even before the echo of the third shot'd died away.

34

TEN POUNDS OF SHEEP LIVER

My Colt's was out and pointed at Jesse James's back. Shoot him, shoot the sonofabitch! Something deep down inside was yelling at me to do it, do it! But even when my finger was tightening on the trigger, I knowed I couldn't send her home. Not with his back turned, I thought. I couldn't shoot no man with his back turned, even him.

He put his forty-four back in his holster, turned, and looked at me like he'd forgot I was even there. He didn't seem to notice my Colt's right away, maybe he was used to somebody standing behind him with a revolver at the ready, backing him up, I don't know. But after a minute he noticed. He saw it was cocked, too, and then he saw it was aimed right at his belly button from about four feet. He looked me square in the eye then, them awful blue eyes.

Now a lot of men would of been scared seeing what he must of saw in my eyes just then, for in that second I hated him like a copperhead. But a lot of men ain't Jesse James. I don't claim to be no mind reader, but just that minute I *knowed* he was thinking of drawing on me, weighing his chances of clearing leather against me putting a bullet into his belly from a forty-five already out and aimed. He stopped thinking about it, smiled, and walked right up on me, yes he did. He knowed it couldn't be done. No fear of being killed kept him from pulling.

And he didn't really care if I shot him, killed him. He walked past me, a look on his face so much as to say—*Well, if you're going to shoot me go ahead and get it over with. I really don't give two good Goddamns.*

I went up to Dan instead, bent down, though I knowed he was dead already. Blood still flowed out of a big hole over his left eye and'd run down all over his face in webby streams, blood filling up his open mouth. "Jesse!" I yelled, standing back up. He was about to his horse by then. He stopped and looked back, not saying a word.

I walked over to him slow as I could make myself, trying to calm down, my revolver on him again, the one he'd gave me. When I got there I looked him flush in the face a second. "I don't want this no more," I said, uncocking the Colt's and handing it to him grip first.

He shook his head the slightest bit, the devil's own smirk on his face. "Don't you understand anything at all, Goodwin?" he asked, ignoring me handing him the revolver. "He led the *Pinkertons* out to—"

He was starting to point to Dan laying there when I butted in. "No he didn't," I said. "And for all your wanting it to be him, just so's you could take it out on somebody, that don't make it so. No, you killed him because you were too mad not to—over what someone *else* did to your momma and little Archie. No, that old man didn't do what you said."

He glared at me.

"You tried to buffalo him into thinking I said he was there, but he didn't go for it, did he? No, people are starting to see you for what you are. A crazy man."

It surprises me now I said that to his face, but I did. His eyes got narrow as piss slits in the snow. He whipped that Colt's out of my hand and throwed it as far out into the tall grass as he could—an awful long ways.

I'd just turned my head back from watching that revolver fly when his Smith's come out like lightning leapt up from the ground. Thinking back on it, I believe he waited apurpose for me to be looking at him. He brought his revolver up in a blue streak so fast I didn't have time to even start to move out of the way of it. The barrel caught me under the chin, smashing my lower teeth into the upper ones with such a crack I felt something break in there like a china cup dropped on stones. I went down backwards about half dazed.

"You'd be dead now if you hadn't helped my ma the way you did," I heard him say above me, breathing hard. "What I owed you for that is paid now—in full. If ever I see you again I'll kill you on sight."

After a minute I sat up, spitting out a piece of a tooth and some blood. He was a good ways off by then, going fast and spurring Stonewall even faster.

I was just standing up when I heard someone call my name from some distance off behind me. There come Dan's wife Rose hurrying though the fields. She must've started running when first she heard the shots, and now she was out of breath but still going as fast as her short, heavy legs and her age would let her. It looked like her hat'd been tied on with a scarf under her chin to keep the wind from taking it, but now hat and scarf both was down and back behind her neck, blowing out behind. She was dropping spring greens of some kind out of her basket as she come towards me as fast as she could go.

"Dan!" she shouted, running to where he laid, there in a heap where Jesse's slugs had sprawled him. "Oh God!" she said falling down on her knees beside him. "Oh dear God!"

I went over and after a minute she looked up, her face a nest of tears and tribulation. "What— Why did you—?"

"I didn't do this!"

She got mad, for there Dan was and there I was—and

nobody else but her around. I turned and looked the direction Jesse'd went, but of course you couldn't see nothing of him by that time. Her face looked like a storm when first it starts to pour.

Standing up, she swung her basket hard and caught me on the cheek with it before I could get my hand up. I held her back—as gentle as I could and still keep her off me, trying to tell her the while it wasn't me. "It was Jesse, Jesse James!" I yelled at her. But I was the only one there, how could she believe it? And how could you blame her? Who'd believe Jesse James would just up and shoot an old farmer who'd never done him no harm? I'd of probly been trying to scratch someone's eyes out too, just like she was trying to do to me right then.

After a minute she stopped, turned around, and run towards her house. Too late it come to me she was going after that shotgun inside the door there. And what was I to do when she stepped outside with it pointed at me, shoot her? Hell, I didn't even have that Colt's no more, even if I *could* of brung myself to do it. I jumped on my horse and was gouging his ribs good by the time I heard the first barrel boom behind me. If there's anything worse than facing someone shooting at you its being shot at from behind, where you can't see what's coming. I was a ways out and bent low over my horse's neck when the second barrel went off, a load of buckshot whizzing and screaming right past my ear.

Of course I did what I always do. I went into town looking for a drink. And I found a lot more than one, like I always do when everything starts to look like a pile of horse shit and I don't know what to do next. After a couple of hours I ended up at what must of been about the unfriendliest saloon in Liberty. Walking in I nodded at two men at the bar and they turned their heads away. On top of the smell from out back and the spittoons, it didn't look like nobody'd swept up the damn sawdust on the floor in weeks. I asked for a bottle of rye after I finally managed to find the rail with my foot, but the barman took one look at me and shook his head. I'd had about a dozen before I'd stumbled in there and I suppose I looked it. He waited till I got my silver out, then poured me one, and then took my coin and the bottle away with him.

Well, the hell with this, I said to myself after I'd tossed her back. *If I can't find a better bar than this to fall down in I should give up drinking.* Course I knowed I was safe, that'd never happen.

I walked outside, looking up and down the street for the next place even before the door to this one'd banged shut. It'd been getting dark on the way into town and by the time I stood there in that side street in Liberty, it'd got darker, only the moon was up now throwing a powdery kind of light on everthing. Nobody was around.

I'd just started up the street, towards the only place I seen a light in the window, when somebody threw an arm around my neck and yanked me back into a space between two buildings, black as ink. I was so drunk and took by surprise I guess I didn't do much of nothing right off. Whoever he was, he had a powerful arm on him, cutting off my wind. Caught me with no air in my lungs to boot, and I was twisting and punching just to breathe. When it seemed I might could get loose, something whacked me on the forehead, the barrel of a revolver I figgered out later, and I went down like about ten pounds of sheep liver in a paper sack.

35

ALL ONE BLOOD

*The farm of Dr. Reuben Samuel
and his wife Zerelda Cole James Samuel
January 26, 1875
Tuesday morning, 9:11 AM*

Reuben Samuel knelt by the rushing stream down from his home, washing the blood from his hands and arms. Some, he knew, was his own blood, and some his wife's. And some Archie's, of course, his son Archie's. He stared at his hands. Little Archie's blood, Zerelda's blood, his own blood. All one blood, he thought. "It's all one blood," he said out loud, straightening his back and looking up into the rising sun, the weak winter sun climbing so slowly above the leafless trees. "It's all one blood!"

"You all right, Dr. Reuben?" someone said behind him.

Still on his knees, he turned his head and saw Charlotta standing up the bank a ways, a bundle in her hands, a blood-stained towel with something wrapped inside. Behind her stood her son Ambrose holding a shovel. Worry was etched sharply into the servant woman's lined, brown face, but he couldn't for the life of him figure out what troubled her.

"You all right, suh?" she asked again.

"Yes, yes, I'm fine," he said, turning back to the stream, rubbing sand between his hands and then rinsing them again in the frigid flowing water. "I'm fine, I'm fine."

Ambrose walked past his mother, the shovel over his shoulder. Charlotta stood a moment longer looking at the doctor, shook her head, and then slowly followed her son into the woods carrying her sorry, bloody burden.

I come to slow and groggy in a stable or shed of some kind, propped up a little between a stall gate and a hay bale, my legs sprawled out in front of me. Behind, I could hear a horse shifting his weight on the dirt floor and chewing hay. Moonlight was falling on the floor through the cracks between the boards, and my head was pounding like a circus drum.

"I thought I'd killed you," O. P. Moss said out of the shadows across the way when he must of saw me lift my head and look around. "I heard the other day you were still alive, but I didn't believe a man could have a head that hard. Now it looks like I'll have to kill you all over again— or turn you in, I haven't decided."

I slid my hand slow down toward my holster, but of course it was empty.

Moss laughed at me, then come over and hunkered down where I could see him some—but not close enough that I could make a grab for him.

"You seem to have lost your revolver as well as your memory, Goodwin. I suppose a few good bangs on the head will do that, even if it didn't kill you." Moss held a lever action of some kind, pointed right at my face.

"Then that *was* you, then, out at the Samuels', that shot me when that bomb went off?"

He didn't bother to answer, only snorted. "I just wish

I'd had more shells for this back then. You wouldn't be sitting here now if I had."

I seen then it was a lever-action shotgun, not an old yeller boy like I first thought. "What'd you hit me with? That thing?" I asked, meaning the lever action.

He didn't answer.

I pushed myself up a little straighter, drawing my boots up closer to my sitter, bringing my knees up. "I don't see what you got against me, fellow," I said. "I never done nothing to you except that punch, and you deserved that, you know damn well you did."

He stood up over me, like a dark cliff towering over you at night. "I never liked you, you sonofabitch," he said, the words tight in his throat. "You and those other bastards coming in here telling us what to do. The Jameses are *ours*, not yours! We'll catch them with no help from the likes of you and the rest of the goddamn Pinkertons. And on top of that, you flopped over and worked for the Jameses too, and don't say you didn't. For the *money*."

I rubbed my knee, though it didn't hurt that much by then, though I acted like it did. "Well, you got me there," I said. "And as long as I'm as good as dead, I might as well say it. I done what you said, rode with the Jameses for a stretch. But it sure wasn't the money."

He turned his head a little and cocked his eye at me, suspicious as anything. "Not the money?"

I shook my head and chuckled. "*Hell* no," I said, letting it hang there a minute. "Don't you know?"

He thought it over. "What'n hell are you talking about?"

"Look at it this way," I said. "Don't be so quick answering, now, and tell the truth—if the top-dog outlaw outfit in the whole country, if they was to ask *you* . . . ?"

He was quiet a minute. "You sonofabitch," he said at last. He kept that lever-action shotgun right on me, and it was cocked, no doubt about it, so it'd have one in the chamber and ready to go. But it wasn't *right* at my face no more.

I storied him. While I was working my hand down my leg slow and smooth as a tree snake, I told him how we took that train out in Kansas. Only I dandied it up—how we marched in there big as sin, our revolvers in our fists, demanding all their damn money, and right away, mister!

After I seen I had him roped, I went for the hog-tie. "And the women, my god, you wouldn't believe it how wild they are with outlaws. There outside Muncie, at that one saloon right afterward? Why, hell, every whore for miles around was lined up to get at us, once they heard the *James* gang was stopped there, sometimes two and three at a time, like flies on rotten meat, and that's no lie, neither," though of course it was. I couldn't see much of his face under his hat brim, standing way above me in that dark stable, but I could see his eyes all right, burning hot as coals. "And they wasn't just whores neither, Moss. Town girls got in line at the bar right along with their soiled sisters in the trade, some so young and crazy for it they—"

My hand was in my boot by then, and still making up all kinds of wild things them women was supposed to've did, I yanked Blackfoot Bill's little thirty-two Smith's out already cocked. I fired one into his belly and right away another somewheres close. I was cocking it for a third when the shotgun exploded. He missed me, of course, or I wouldn't be telling this. But not by much, he didn't. I got that third shot off—as wild as I was then, I'm surprised I didn't fire the fourth as well.

Then it was quiet, the smell of burnt powder strong in the air.

He was down. It was so quiet you could hear dogs barking off somewheres, barking their questions at the shots fired. "What? What? What?!"

I went over to Moss and he was still breathing, but out colder'n a stone. In the dark I couldn't tell how many times I'd hit him with Bill's little hideout piece, and I didn't care that much, neither, so long as he stayed down.

I got up and went outside. It was out of town a ways, but not so far you couldn't see Liberty from there. A shed behind where Moss lived, I guessed. And houses too close for neighbors not to of heard the shooting. While I stood there someone lit a lantern inside the house across the way, and up on a hill a little farther off somebody come out carrying another—hollering Moss' name a couple of times and then someone else's name I didn't reconize. I ducked back inside and got that horse out of the stall fast as I could, stumbling over Moss in the bargain. I didn't take the time to find a bridle or saddle, neither. I took the rope off a halter hanging there and forced it into his mouth, tying an Apache sort of bit out of it. It wouldn't last, but it was quick.

Then I yanked him outside by it, jumped up across, kicked my knee over, and sat up. About then that man with the lantern started yelling behind me, a lot closer now. I lit the hell out of there bareback as fast as I could make that damn horse go.

36

DARLIN SARAH

Though nobody chased me I pushed that horse hard. And I found out along the way he was, like myself, no youngster—or maybe just not used to rough company, for he was winded and a little staggery before we was even half way there. Made him a mite easier to control, though, which was a blessing considering that damn rope bit. Whatever was left of being drunk got wore off me on that ride, I'll tell you. I got to Sarah's place just about the time the moon was going down.

I stood under her window and looked up at it for a minute, wondering what to do. I was still trying to find little stones to throw against the panes when Sarah slid the sash up and motioned me toward the front door before sliding it back down again.

"Sarah, I'm sorry I—"

She quick put her finger up to her lips to shush me, opened the front door wide, took my hands, and led me up the stairs and into her room—shutting the hall door quiet behind us.

It was odd being in their house late, in the dark. Though I'd as good as lived there the last couple months, it was differnt there in her room that night, the house full of people sleeping, maybe dreaming, resting from yesterday and getting ready to wake up to tomorrow, taking whatever it'd bring them, living their life there in that place day by day, likely to live it all out there in that same place, and me long since gone down the road—and none of them, other than Sarah, not even knowing a man wanted for murder was there among 'em the night he done it.

"How'd you know I was down there?" I asked her.

"I don't know, I just woke up," Sarah said yawning a little, hiding it behind her hand. "Maybe I heard you ride up." She lit the lamp beside her bed. "My goodness, Willie, your head is all bloody! What happened to you?" she asked, sitting me down on the side of her bed and getting a washcloth and soap from over on her washstand. It struck me then I'd never saw her before in her nightgown, one of them big white affairs with only a little less cloth to it than the sails of a ship.

"Oh, I got banged on the head again, it ain't too bad. In front this time instead of in back—so it sort of levels me out, I guess. Done by the same fellow as before, too. It don't make you feel like dancing no polka, though, I'll say th—Ouch!"

She wiped at it gentle, I guess, but still it ached and stung. "I can't see how—"

"Sarah," I said, butting in on her while she was wiping away something on my cheek. "Sarah, I've got to leave here tonight, I—"

"Tonight! Why, what on Earth—" I couldn't tell if she looked mad or worried or some of both.

"Yes, I've got to go tonight," I said standing up. "I'm in a mess of trouble and only come here to say good-bye to you. I couldn't leave without seeing you one last time, girl. You're the only thing from here I'll miss—except Billy too, of course, and his little dog, I guess."

She come into my arms sobbing, and it felt like holding the old Sarah again, the one that'd loved me no matter what I done—back when she didn't know what-all I done, of course.

Then she wiped her eyes, sat me back down on the edge of the bed, unfolded a little chair and pulled it up close. "Why do you have to go now, Willie? What's wrong?"

"It's pretty bad," I told her. "Are you sure you want to hear it?"

She nodded, a tear going down her cheek I wiped away with my hand.

"All right," I said. "First, Dan Askew's dead and his wife thinks it was me who killed him."

"But you and Dan—!"

"I know," I said. "It don't make no sense, but she saw me there right after he was shot and, well, if you'd of been there you'd of saw why she thought it was me. I'm the one she'll tell the law on, anyway—if she ain't already. And I can't prove I *didn't* do it, so . . ."

Sarah's voice was quiet. "It must make you feel terrible to have his wife think you shot—" She sat up straighter. "Who did it, Willie? Who really shot Mr. Askew?"

I didn't say nothing for a minute.

"It was Jesse, wasn't it?" she asked. "That's where he took you, wasn't it?"

I nodded. "But, hell, I should of saw it coming, Sarah, and I should of done more to—"

She shook her head. "You really think you could have kept Jesse from killing someone? Once he'd set his mind on it?"

I looked at her good. "I guess not. I suppose I couldn't of stopped him right out. But I could of told the truth, anyway. He killed Dan Askew because he thought Dan was the one led the Pinkertons—"

Sarah put her fingers on my lips. She shook her head. "No, don't think that," she said. "He killed Mr. Askew because Jesse's been crazy to find someone to blame for killing his baby brother and hurting his momma so bad. It wasn't your fault, Willie."

I thought it over a minute. "Well, that's awful good of you to say that, Sarah." I leaned over and kissed her, she looked so pretty sitting there, her heart bleeding so for my troubles. "Another reason I got to go is Jesse'll know who really led them out there soon, maybe tomorrow. When the grand jury sits, they're going to name me for little Archie's death, along with Pinkerton, and I don't know who else."

Sarah looked at me a little funny then. "If only that bomb hadn't been thrown in there . . ."

"Yes, I know," I said. "But once that grand jury names me, it won't cut no ice with Jesse James I tried to help his folks after it was," I said. "And that's another thing I should have saw into before it happened, them throwing that damn bomb in the—"

"You didn't *know* about the bomb!?" Sarah said, a terrible look on her face, and then she started crying something awful. I was afraid for a minute she'd wake her folks.

"Well hell no!" I said. "I never thought they would do nothing like *that*." I told her then how surprised I was when that little man said about it and that big man throwed it in, how I was running toward the house to help the Samuels when it exploded.

"Oh God!" Sarah said, getting up and going over to the window. The moon was down behind the trees along the fence row over there toward the west, but you could still see it a little through the new leaves.

I went over to her and turned her around. "What is it, Sarah? What's—"

"When you said about being with the Pinkertons, I thought you knew they were going out there on purpose to bomb that poor family. Oh Willie, I should have *known* you wouldn't do anything like that!"

I held her at arm's length. "How come you didn't *ask* me about it, Sarah?"

The tears rolled down her cheeks then. "I was too— I—!" She started crying hard again then, saying how sorry she was over and over.

"It's all right Sarah, it's all right." I held her close and told her I could see how she might think that about me, since I didn't explain nothing to her about what really went on out there that night. I'd meant to, but things was all kind of fuzzy in my mind for a time afterward, and I didn't rightly want to admit *that*. Maybe I was sort of ashamed of myself doing all I *did* do, too.

I kissed her then, and she kissed me back like she never done before.

"Oh Willie, I want to make love with you now," she said, her voice so soft and sweet. I'm a little ashamed, saying right out loud what she said that night, but that's just what she said to me, hard as it is to believe—and as easy as it's been to remember them words ever since. "I want to make love with you now." I picked her up there by the window, the moon just down, and carried her over to her bed. Now I've loved my share of women, more'n my share some might say, but it was never like it was with Sarah Jane Cole that night.

37

I COULD NOT DO IT

Mount Olivet Cemetery
Kearney, Missouri
February 1, 1875
Early Monday afternoon, 12:30 PM

By twos and threes they gathered to bury little Archie. High in a nearby church steeple an iron bell tolled and tolled. A gentle snowfall dusted the black umbrellas and the black coats of the crowd when they carried him from the black hearse drawn by two black horses in tandem, black plumes at their heads, black manes blowing in the gentle wind that swept the flakes along. When the box was set in place over the hole, the black-frocked minister began to read from an old black leather Bible, "Therefore be ready, for in such an hour as ye think not—" though for the bell's tolling, tolling, no one could really make out what he was saying.

Black shawls and thin black leather gloves beneath the stark white faces of rows of family, close and distant. Tiny white stars of snow on the soft black fur of a sister's collar, on the black scarves of a brother and an older cousin, white diamonds on the black felt hats of aunts and great aunts.

Six-pointed crystals of snow fell onto the black velvet cloak, trimmed in jet beads, worn by an older woman so distantly related to the Coles not even she could quite piece the tattered web back together. They welcomed her graciously into the fourth row, however, no matter. No matter.

Most of the townsfolk of Kearney turned out in their best black suits and dresses, and almost half the people from Liberty, wearing their finest black attire, had come over on the special train, draped in black crepe, for the graveside service, the James family plot enclosed by a low, black wrought-iron fence, spears, and arrows. Reporters from Kansas City, St. Louis, from as far away as Chicago, standing in the snow in their black boots, stepping back and forth to warm their freezing feet, watching the crowd, writing in their heads their page four stories for tomorrow's editions, to be printed inside their paper's thickest, most maudlin black border.

At one time or another during the service, each of the town mourners glanced at the faces up close to the small casket finished in black muslin, the impassive faces of the immediate family. Jesse and Frank, of course, were not there—even though they bore much of the black burden of this day. Their ways and theirs alone, some public mourners thought to themselves that snowy noon, had brought this white desolation down upon their clan. Everyone understood their absence, but everyone longed so to see them that all the mourners looked anyway, wanting as a momento mori a glimpse of guilt and rage smeared scarlet across the brothers' grieving, hollow faces. Not to be, not to be.

The child's mother stood there still and mute; that much at least they got for the trouble of coming. Still and stolid she stood, as far above the rest as the gray stone angel who looked down over everyone's shoulders from the adjoining fenced-in plot.

Zerelda Samuel appeared to be staring at the casket, but really she stared beneath it into the gaping black hole that waited to receive her baby boy, the hole that lay

350 / CHARLES HACKENBERRY

beneath the planks beneath the black box. The caninal maw of raw earth waiting for its meal of tender child flesh.

Yes, the boy's mother would do if they couldn't have the outlaw brothers, though they wished she would at least cry. Because she had lost half her right arm less than a week earlier, the doctors insisted she stay home today. Instead, she cradled what was left of her mutilated member in a black sling over her long black coat and went proudly to the ceremony, wanting everyone to see all of what those Yankee Pinkertons had done to them. Black clothes on all the family standing in rows, black on everyone, public and family, united at last in black. The dust of a February snow settling softly over the leafless trees, the dead grass, settling over them all, a powdery snow nearly as white as they all imagined little Archie Samuel's soul to be.

I woke up with a start, the sun in my eyes, and Sarah coming through the door carrying a tray towards my bed—her bed. "What—what time is it?" I asked her.

"Time for your breakfast, sir," she said with a pretty smile, putting a tray with little short legs across my middle and then bringing pillows to prop me up so's I could eat it right in bed, like when I was getting better there. Eggs fried like I liked them, sausage, toast, and a whole pot of coffee.

"Where's yours?" I asked her, smelling everything.

"Oh, I ate an hour ago, but I'll have coffee with you." Sarah sat on the edge of the bed while I poured some in the cup for her and some in the saucer for me.

She liked to watch me eat, and I could tell she'd made this all herself. We talked and joked around while I was eating, no mention at all of me leaving, I noticed. I made a fuss over everything—from the coffee I started on first to the linen napkin I wiped my mouth with when I'd finished.

She give me a little peck of a kiss when she lifted the tray off and set it on the dresser. "You must be careful, sir, or you'll spoil me so bad I'll expect compliments every morning when I make your breakfast."

I just looked at her when she sat back down. It was a wonderment to me she would say that. I knowed she didn't forget I was leaving. Did she think I could just up and stay because I wanted to?

"No, I'm going along, Willie," she said, reading my thoughts or my face or both. "I hate to leave my family, but if that's—if the invitation still stands, of course."

Naturally, I was supposed to say of course it was still good, my invite for her to go along. I was supposed to say I was happy as anything she'd changed her mind. But when I didn't say nothing, nothing at *all*, I had to watch her pretty smile fade and wither like the last rose of summer.

"Oh, I see..." she said, her eyes dropping to her hands.

"No, I don't believe you *do* see, Sarah," I said.

She looked up at me sharp then, the only time I ever seen any resemblance between her and her cousin Jesse, but it lasted only the least flicker of an eye-blink.

I took both her hands in mine. "Don't you see how it's all changed now?" I asked her.

Even her frown was pretty that morning, a wavy strand of dark hair hanging down in front.

"Sarah, I'm going to be on the run once I leave here, don't you understand what that means? No regular job, no place regular to live, moving on all the time?"

She just looked at me.

"The grand jury's going to name me for killing little Archie, and another one for Dan Askew, even though I didn't do that one neither. When I ain't here to stand trial, they'll likely name me a fugitive, and maybe even put a price on my head. What kind of a life you figger that'd be for you and the boy? You ain't forgot about him, I suspect. Is that how you want him growing up? Never knowing what's gonna happen to him, not even going to school because he's running from the law with his momma and her—well, whatever I'd be to you?"

A tear leaked from her eye. "Why don't you stay and

stand trial, then? Take your chances that a jury would see you didn't do anything wrong?" she asked.

"'Cause there's more to it than that," I told her. "It's bound to come out I rode with Jesse on that train robbery, and if they don't get me for the killings, they'll get me for that for sure. And even if they didn't, I'll look like a double dealing snake, for it'll also come out I led those Pinkertons out to the Samuel's, and what do you suppose Jesse will do then?"

Sarah looked down and shook her head. "I didn't see it in that light."

"No, I'm not surprised," I said. "It ain't a very pretty light to look at it in, but it's the truth." I put a finger under her chin and lifted her face up till her eyes was on mine again. "Sarah, I want you, want to marry you, I surely do. But not this way."

She seen I was telling the truth, thank goodness, and the tears come even faster then.

"Aw, don't do that, honey," I said to her. "Don't do that, please."

She smiled, wiped tears away, laughed a little, and cried some more all at the same time. "We're like Shakespeare's star-crossed lovers, aren't we Willie, like Romeo and Juliet?" she said, making a joke of it even though you could feel the crying underneath.

"I don't think I ever seen or read that one, but something is all crossed up, that's for sure."

Sarah stood up, took the tray from the dresser and walked to the door with it. She turned back, give a big sigh and then a sad smile, went out, and closed the door behind her.

I got dressed and went downstairs with what little gear I had, looking for her daddy, who didn't seem to know I'd spent the night with his daughter. Or didn't let on. In his little office room I thanked him and told him I was leaving and would like to buy a horse and saddle from him, the one I rode there on the night before would have to be returned. That's how I put it, but he knowed what I meant. He said to take his young bay gelding, and think nothing of it, he wouldn't take no money neither. I couldn't figger out whether he was being generous or was just happy as hell to see me go. I said I'd take the horse as a present if he'd take my stock in return, the one I'd left in the livery stable over in Liberty, my good packhorse, and the young mule over at Askew's.

Maybe believing right off that he was a generous man would of been more generous of me, because when he also seen my empty holster there on my pile of gear he took a cap and ball revolver out of a drawer, a .36 calibre, powder and balls too. He said he'd take it as a favor if I'd take that lot also. He'd feel better, he said, knowing I was traveling with some sort of protection, though it wasn't the latest model.

I thanked him and took the revolver along with the rest of my gear when I went out to saddle the bay. When I was done, I walked that nice gelding out to the rail and tied him. Then I went back inside and found Sarah's momma and thanked her for feeding me and taking care of me in her house, I'd of surely died without what she done for me, I said. She just nodded, a little distracted, I don't think anyone'd even told her I was leaving.

When I got out to my new horse, Sarah was standing there waiting for me, like I hoped she'd be. "I hate to see you go, Willie," she said right off.

"And I hate leaving you," I said, taking her in my arms and kissing her.

"Will you write to me?" she asked.

"Why of course I will, honey," I said. "I'll sign them Will Jones, though, just in case. All right?"

"All right," she answered. Her chin quivered when she spoke.

I stepped up into the new saddle, it fit me all right, and looked down at her pretty face—trying to burn it into my memory. The sun was bright that morning, I recall, and enough wind to blow the horse's dark mane a little. She handed me something then, wrapped in a little cloth.

"What's this?" I asked.

She brushed back a strand of hair and asked me not to open it till later. "Just something to remember me by," she said, looking off into the trees behind the house.

"How could I ever forget you, gal?" I asked her, and then put whatever it was in my shirt pocket. "If there's ever a time I can come back here, I will do it," I said.

She wiped her eyes and nodded, though none too happy a look on her face just then.

Something caught my eye at an upstairs window. There stood Billy with his little dog Bobby sitting up straight in his arms, both of them watching me. The boy had one of his dog's forelegs in his hand, and he made that little dog appear to be waving good-bye to me with his paw.

I waved back, though I felt about half silly doing it, waving good-bye to a dog.

Sarah looked up and saw it. "Billy'll miss you too," she said, laughing a little through her tears.

"No more'n I'll miss him," I told her. "I want to see the man he grows up to be some day."

"Then come back and help me raise him," Sarah said, tucking her handkerchief into her sleeve, done with crying now, you could tell.

"Jesse James won't live forever," I said. "Somebody'll hang or shoot that sonofabitch some day, and after they do, you'll see me again," I told her. "Though I don't expect you to wait for me—I'm not asking you to," I said. "If you find someone you'd—I'd understand you not waiting around for me. It might could be a long time."

She smiled at me. "All right, Mr. Goodwin."

"All right, Sarah Jane Cole," I said and leaned down to kiss her one last time. Then I turned that young gelding's head and trotted him up the lane. Out at the road I looked back. Sarah was standing there watching me ride off. We each waved. I did not look back a second time from farther out the road where you could still see the place. I could not do it.

38

THANKS, MISTER

I rode over close to the Askew place, there behind that big stone by the road and got the things I'd hid there before. A mouse or something had chewed one corner of the waterproof bag a little but other than that, everything was all right. Money from the Pinkertons was right alongside in a tarred canvas, fold-over affair. No note or nothing.

I thought of going up to the house and trying to explain things to Mrs. Askew, Rose her name was, but I figgered it wouldn't do no more good this time than the last and would only stir her up again. Then I rode up to where you can see the Samuel place through the trees, there where Moss had spied on them. Nobody was around down below, it looked like—not even the doctor or the old lady.

I sat there on a log a while, probly the same one that damn Moss had sat on, looking down at the house through the new leaves and wishing I'd never led them Pinkertons out there, but wishing even more I'd spoke out and saved Dan Askew. Everthing else I done I could sort of forgive myself for.

You know, I never knowed whether he lived or died

after I shot him, Moss I mean. Nothing in the papers about it, nothing I ever seen anyways. Nobody I ever talked to knowed either. And no paper out on me afterwards, a sheriff I was friendly with a while back checked for me. How do you figger that?

That grand jury did name me for the murder of little Archie. Not by my real name, though, thank goodness, but by the name of Jack Ladd. That's what was in the papers. That case, though, the bombing *or* the murder of that little boy, it never come to trial. I figger the reason it never did was because they also indicted Hardwicke and Allen Pinkerton at the same time. It's a shame to say it, but if you have enough money in this country, or know the right people, you really *can* get away with murder.

But, no, I couldn't rightly forgive myself for what'd happened at the Askew place. And me not even seeing on the way out there what might could happen, can you believe that? *What you can't forgive you got to sleep with*, my ma always said. Well, that's what I've been doing off and on ever since, sleeping with being ashamed of what I done there. Or didn't do, it amounts to the same thing.

And I guess I'll have to keep sleeping with it till the day comes I can forgive myself. I plan on doing that someday, only I just ain't got around to it yet.

Climbing back up on that bay after watching the Samuel place nearly an hour, I begun to wonder where the hell I was going to go. I thought of Texas right off, but Ma was dead now and the farm didn't interest me much. On top of that, I remembered Blackfoot Bill, how Jesse must of shot him after he'd left Kearney, after he'd been on the road a while. Maybe I was just running scared at that point, but I determined to go opposite the direction Jesse'd figger I'd go, opposite Texas that'd be.

So I went into Kansas City, had a couple drinks and thought it over—only a couple. A nice quiet bar does help you think sometimes, don't it?

I bought a few things for the trail and crossed the river there. And once I was on the other side and feeling not so jittery, I headed north, north by west really, for I determined I'd go see them Rocky Mountains again. That'd be one thing Jesse James wouldn't expect me to do, for I'd never talked to him about the mountains, the way I like them and all. In addition to clearing the hell out of there, I could have the pleasure of seeing them mountains again to boot. The grandest damn sight in the whole world, the Rocky Mountains, at least the grandest of all the parts I saw so far.

I thought I'd go by way of Dakota Territory, mostly because I'd never been up this way before. And because it *couldn't* be no damn flatter than Kansas or Nebraska.

It was the second night when I was bedding down by my campfire that I rolled over onto something that poked my chest kind of painful, it felt like a stone. It was that thing Sarah'd gave me, wrapped up in a little cloth, still there in my shirt pocket where I'd put it and forgot it, no matter I had thought of *her* a hundred times already. Well, this *here* was later, I says to myself, like she'd said to look at it at.

I unwrapped the cloth and there was a small stone sort of affair with her picture painted on it—in a little silver wire frame. A mostly flat oval, I guess you'd say, a little longer than a silver dollar and a little narrower. See?

A fine likeness of her. Even in the firelight that night you could see the shine on her dark wavy hair, that pretty skin of hers, her smile, and her big green eyes—showing a lot of breast at the top of her dress there, too, I'm about half ashamed for her. Another fellow I showed it to in a bar down in Yankton a few years back said it was called a miniature and that mine, the one Sarah'd gave me, was a good one. Hell, I already *knowed* it was a good one, for it looked like *her*.

So much like her I've started back more'n a dozen times after spending an hour or so looking at that little thing over a glass or two of rye—often the courtesy of some gentleman or another. Only I'd always stop before I got back there. Once, I was nearly to Kansas City before I turned around.

And you know something? That money didn't last. I

run through it in a couple of years. Drank that outlawing money up right away. Drank that Pinkerton money down too, right after it, and chased 'em both with liquor I bought with the money from Ma and Pa's farm. Lost some at cards, too, of course. Even I couldn't of drunk all *that* much up in a few years and live to tell about it. All I got left is what I put in the bank there in Liberty, and of course I can't get to that or it'd probly be gone too.

I read the papers pretty regular and if ever I see where Jesse James is been shot or hung, I'll go back there and just see if she'll have me again, Sarah. Ain't a day goes by I don't think about doing that—someday.

That's what it'd take to straighten out my drinking, I believe—Sarah. But until I read he's dead, I'm going to stay away from Clay County, Missouri. Out here it ain't likely I'll ever run into him. And for long stretches I can sort of forget all about him. With the right amount of rye, you understand.

Back there, though, I couldn't drink enough liquor not to see them clear blue eyes when I come to lay down at night to sleep, not enough rye anywhere to keep them awful blue eyes from staring me to death in my sleep, in my dreams.

Funny thing is, I ain't seen the Rockies again. Not yet, anyways.

And I never wrote her no letter, either, Sarah, like I said I would. What would be the sense of that? It would only make it worse—for me *and* for her, I figger. She must know this here old busted-down saddle tramp still loves her, though, don't you think? Well, thanks for the drinks, mister.

Now you might think an old busted-down saddle tramp like me probly never knowed nobody worth hearing about. But the truth is, I rode with Jesse James, yes I did.

HarperPaperbacks *By Mail*

SADDLE UP AND READ THESE NOVELS OF THE GREAT FRONTIER!

FIRE ALONG THE BIG MUDDY
by John Legg

A bad-tempered deserter, Miles Barclay wanders into the arms of the fierce, warring Arikaras tribe. Rescued by a friendly Sioux, Barclay is brought back to the tribe to recover. There the misfit soldier learns a great deal about the people he had come west to fight.

LONE SURVIVOR
by Will Camp

As the War Between the States ends, a man-eating blood feud between the Bartons and the Trimbles begins. When it is over, all that remains of their lives is the newly minted legend of the Palo Pinto Kid . . . and one lone survivor.

RIDE FOR RIMFIRE
by Hank Edwards

Only Rimfire's foreman, Shell Harper, can save the famous ranch, and pass its title to the true heir, Emmy Gunnison. To do so he must stand alone against the infamous Billy Bishop gang, the last hope for Rimfire.

AN ORDINARY MAN
by J. R. McFarland

A drifting lawman with a knack for killing, MacLane was a lonely man—until an odd twist changed his fate. Only then did he have the chance to change the course of his life and become an ordinary man with an extraordinary message to deliver.

GRAY WARRIOR
by Hank Edwards

Jack Dalton was a rebel who would never surrender—even if it killed him. But the love of a beautiful woman brings changes all the killing in the world could not. In a savage wilderness of bullets and blood, Dalton finds something bigger and better than himself, something worth living for.

MAIL TO: **HarperCollins*Publishers***
P.O. Box 588 Dunmore, PA 18512-0588

❑ **FIRE ALONG THE BIG MUDDY** 100867-2 . . . . $3.99 U.S./$4.99 CAN.
❑ **LONE SURVIVOR** 100888-5 . . . . $4.50 U.S./$5.50 CAN.
❑ **RIDE FOR RIMFIRE** 100748-X . . . . $3.99 U.S./$4.99 CAN.
❑ **AN ORDINARY MAN** 100821-4 . . . . $3.99 U.S./$4.99 CAN.
❑ **GRAY WARRIOR** 100885-0 . . . . $4.50 U.S./$5.50 CAN.

Subtotal. . . . . $_____
Postage & Handling . . . . $_____
Sales Tax (Add applicable sales tax) . . . . $_____
Total . . . . $_____

Name_____
Address_____
City_____ State_____ Zip Code_____

Order 4 or more titles and postage & handling is **FREE!** Orders of less than 4 books please include $2.00 postage & handling. Remit in U.S. funds. Do not send cash. Allow up to 6 weeks for delivery. Prices subject to change.
Valid only in U.S. and Canada.   H12411

Visa & MasterCard holders—call 1-800-331-3761